DON'T STAND OUT.

BLEND IN.

# REMAIN INVISIBLE.

OTHER BOOKS IN THE
# PROJECT W. A. R. TRILOGY

ULTRAXENOPIA

TYPE X

SUBJECT ZERO


**COMPANION NARRATIVE**

THE RICHTER FILES

# ULTRAXENOPIA

## PROJECT W. A. R. BOOK ONE

# M. A. PHIPPS

# ULTRAXENOPIA
## PROJECT W.A.R. BOOK ONE



Cover design by Nathalia Suellen
Interior design by We Got You Covered Book Design
WWW.WEGOTYOUCOVEREDBOOKDESIGN.COM

## SHIRE-HILL PUBLICATIONS
UNITED KINGDOM

ISBN: 978-0-9932177-8-4

For everyone who believed in me

# TRIGGER WARNING

*Contains dark themes and scenes of violence*

North
Gate
West
Gate
South
Gate
Zone7
Zone6
Zone5
Zone4
Zone3
Zone2
Zone1
3
2

THE HEART
Population - 8.788.000
1. W.P. Headquarters
2. Magistrates Building
3. The DSD
4. Wynter's House
5. The Vega
East Gate
STATE PROPERTY

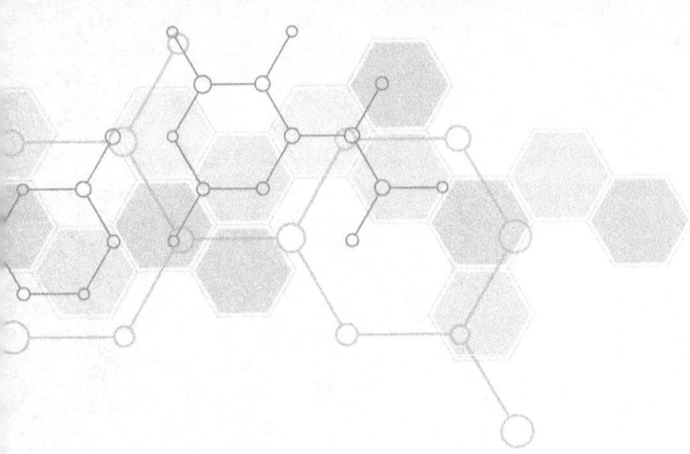

When the willfully blind finally open their eyes,
they see society for what it is:

Broken.

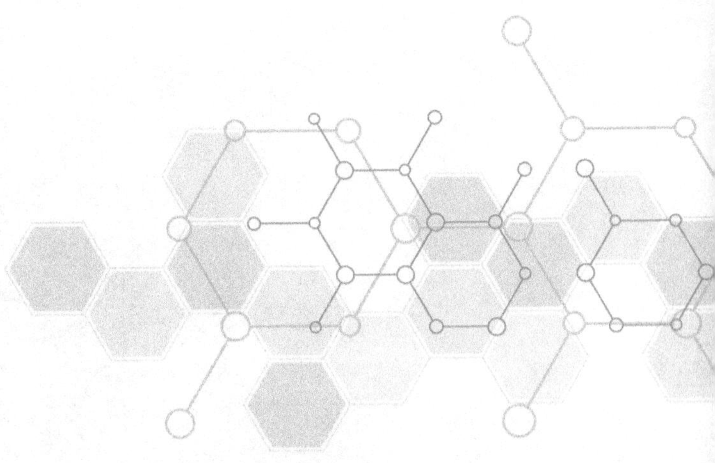

# ONE



*"THE TRAIN IS NOW APPROACHING Central Station. Disembark here for W. P. Headquarters and for access to the Department of Interzonal Affairs."*

I glance out the window. The darkness of the tunnel disappears in an instant, and before I can blink, the train is back above ground. The towering buildings of the capital rush past in a blur, blending into one confused mass of gray. Nothing stands out.

Everything is the same.

Grabbing my bag, I rise from my seat. The movement of the train is smooth and steady, but my fingers grip the nearest pole out of habit. Usually, I do this just to have something to keep my hands busy, so I don't accidentally fidget. This time, I do it to support my legs, which are in danger of giving out beneath me at any moment.

Taking slow steps, I make my way toward the door. A small group of passengers has already gathered in front of it, their faces blank and postures stiff, ready to start another monotonous day.

Sweat beads along my hairline and under my armpits as warm bodies close in on all sides, keeping their distance so as not to touch me but close enough I can feel the heat of someone's breath against the back of my neck, each pant keeping in time with my heartbeat. I should be used to this after thirteen years of education and countless weeks of preparation exams. By now, I'm no stranger to the crowds of Zone 1.

But today is different, and relief courses through me when the train decelerates and the doors spring open, flooding the car with a welcome swell of fresh air. An automated voice bellows over the loudspeaker, telling passengers to watch their step while disembarking. Other than that warning, the train and platform are silent. No one says anything. No one forces their way forward to get out of the car any quicker. Everyone is patient. Everyone waits their turn, just like always.

Including me.

Claustrophobia claws at my chest as I murmur the same words I repeat to myself every day. The same words I've been rehearsing on a loop since I was five years old. "Don't stand out. Blend in. Remain invisible."

Those are the rules I live by—that everyone lives by.

Those are the rules that ensure we all survive.

When I descend from the train, I'm immediately swallowed whole by an overpowering rush of noise. Footsteps intermingle with the jumbled beeps of turnstiles, combining in a cloud of sound, which echoes like thunder through the station lobby. Keeping my head down, I follow the silent herd shifting toward the station exit, each step nothing more than a sluggish crawl forward.

As I join the procession forming by the glass barriers up ahead, my fingers grope my coat, fumbling in the deep pockets for my government-issued rail card. Once I reach the front of the line, I scan my card across the machine just like I have every other day for as long as I can remember. Just like everyone else before me.

Another beep.

My feet carry me forward when the turnstile opens.

The warm glow of daylight reaches down to meet me as I trudge up the concrete staircase leading out into my birthplace, a massive walled-in city known as the Heart. Despite the cloudless day and hot sun overhead, the biting cold of autumn stings my cheeks.

A shiver races through me as I stand to one side of the exit to get my bearings and gather my nerves, my eyes flicking upwards to observe the detachment in each of the empty faces around me.

No one who passes says anything to me. No one asks how I am. No one looks at each other. Everyone minds their own business, just as they're supposed to. Just as *I'm* supposed to.

Bile rises in my throat, but I urge it back down.

"Don't stand out. Blend in. Remain invisible," I whisper under my breath.

Inhaling, I peer down at the silver watch on my wrist, and a mumbled curse escapes my lips when the numbers ignite across the mirrored face, telling me I'm running short on time. I can't afford to be late.

Not today.

Crossing my arms, I glance to the east in the general direction of my destination, careful to avoid eye contact with anyone passing. My skin tingles as if it's on fire, and my stomach twists into an uncomfortable, tight ball at the thought of what this day represents.

Ignoring the itch of anxiety crawling over my skin, I fall into formation with the crowd on the sidewalk.

The building I'm looking for isn't far—a few minutes' walk from the station at most. But with every step, the pounding of my heart grows more violent and my lungs tighten until I'm practically wheezing. I swallow, desperate to cast off the dread gripping me, but the sensation only continues to worsen.

Mere moments feel like hours before my feet skid to a stop. The carved stone of the familiar sign seems to sprout up from the ground like a petrified tree, looming over the spot where I stand with the same threat as the sky-scraping building behind it.

W. P. Headquarters. The workforce placement educational facilities where the rest of my future will be decided after the events of today. I suppose you could say this building is the foundation and epicenter of our society. Every person in this city—regardless of who they are—will intimately know this place. From our early days of education up until our eighteenth birthday, at which time a single exam at this very establishment determines the rest of our lives. Pass and move on to your designated career. Fail and receive a one-year sentence in Detention as punishment for lacking discipline, followed by a lifetime of the worst jobs imaginable—and not only in terms of pay.

I inhale around the rising lump in my throat.

*You can do this. You've studied. You know what you're doing.* With those reassuring words bouncing around in my skull, I breathe out and step forward through the revolving glass doors.

The interior of W. P. Headquarters is dreary and lifeless, just like everything else in the Heart. The furnishings are all gray, made of metal and glass, and security cameras mark every corner and wall. At least a dozen people stand in front of me, waiting in a line in the vestibule to gain entry to the building.

More beeps. More turnstiles.

As the minutes pass, a prickle of nerves forms an ache in my legs, coaxing me up onto the balls of my feet then back down onto my heels again. I know I shouldn't move around. Fidgeting is dangerous. Fidgeting makes me noticeable. And yet, every attempt to stay still is met with opposition from the very atoms making up the composition of my body, as if I can no longer control what it's doing.

To distract myself from my building unease, I bite the inside of my cheek and focus my narrowed gaze on a television embedded in a wall to my left. On the screen is footage showing the aftermath of a recent fire or bombing. I'm not sure which. I hadn't heard about an attack, which means it must've only just happened today. Some people are screaming. Others are covered in blood. Several corpses litter the ground.

I strain my ears to hear what the broadcaster is saying but try not to seem too interested. Curiosity is also dangerous and a sure-fire way to draw unwanted attention.

*"Thirty-two are reported dead in the devastating attack that occurred an hour ago on a hydroponic factory in Zone 4. Although investigators currently have no leads as to the motive behind the attack, it is believed to be the work of the insurgent group, PHOENIX. Anyone with information regarding the organization's whereabouts is urged to come forward and report to their local Enforcer unit. Any citizen found to be withholding information or aiding the terrorists will henceforth be branded an enemy of the State"*—the newscaster pauses for dramatic effect—*"and executed."*

A shiver ripples through me at the words "enemy of the State." That's what the government brands anyone who doesn't follow their rules. All it takes is a single mistake and boom, one-way trip to Termination.

A heavy weight returns to the pit of my stomach as I force myself to look away from the screen. From this point on, I keep my gaze fixed ahead of me.

After another ten minutes of waiting, the turnstile offering access to the building is finally within my reach. The only thing standing between us is a squat middle-aged woman sitting behind a sleek black counter, who signals with a crooked finger for me to step forward.

"Name?" she asks.

I balk under the intensity of her steely gaze, my voice choking out the words, "Wynter Reeves."

"Identification chip," she grumbles, holding up a handheld device.

I extend my left arm without hesitation, keeping as still as humanly possible as the gatekeeper moves the scanner over my wrist. A light at the top of the machine turns green. She then grabs my pointer finger and presses it against an upraised metal square on the counter where a needle juts out and pricks me for blood. I don't even have time to wince before a numbing agent steals away the pain.

"You're all clear," the woman grunts, looking around me and signaling to the next person in line.

The gate in front of me opens with a swish, the glass barriers sliding apart in welcome. My stomach turns as I press into the main lobby. The room is empty aside from the balding receptionist, who sits behind a marble counter stretching the full length of the two-story high wall. His head is down, his unblinking gaze glued to the computer in front of him.

"Name and purpose of visit?" he asks before I've even reached the counter.

"Wynter Reeves," I answer in a timid voice. "I'm here to take my placement exam."

His eyes dart to mine, and he holds out his hand.

"Identification chip."

Walking forward, I once again stretch out my arm, biting my tongue as the man repeats the process I just went through. My lungs hold in my breath the whole time as I wait for that little light to turn green. I only exhale when the machine beeps its approval.

I'm not new to any of this, and yet, my nerves are shredding my insides as if I'm five years old all over again and this is my very first time in this building. It probably only feels that way because so much is hanging on my exam.

If I screw this up, my life is over.

Silence is my companion as the man confirms my information on his computer—another check to ensure that I am who I say I am. Once he's satisfied with what he sees in the database, he hands me a laminated badge with my name and the word 'Examinee' typed in bold underneath it.

"The examination is on Floor 5. Reception up there will check you in."

I cast a nervous glance over my shoulder, following the man's outstretched wrinkled hand to the elevators at the far right side of the lobby as if I haven't used them a thousand times before. With a mumble of thanks, I turn from the counter, grateful no one else is around to notice how badly my legs and hands are shaking.

*You have to calm down,* I tell myself, running through the mental pep talk I've been practicing in front of the mirror at home every day the last week.

Dragging in a faltering breath through my nose, I head for the nearest elevator and swipe a finger across the silver call button. A glowing blue number appears above the steel doors, counting down to my location on the ground floor. The seconds tick by slowly, and while I wait, I use the time to fix the Examinee badge to the front of my shirt. My frazzled nerves make my fingers clumsy, and the badge nearly slips from my grasp several times. After four failed attempts, I manage to clip the pin shut.

I'm only on my own for about thirty seconds before several other students gather around the elevators. I recognize a few from my classes, and based on the Examinee badges clipped to their shirts, we're all convening for the same reason. Still, despite our mutual purpose for being here, no one says anything to each other. No words of greeting. No whispers of encouragement. Despite sharing this monumental milestone in our lives, every one of us is alone.

The elevator arrives with a ding, shaking me free from my morose thoughts. Since I was the first to arrive, I enter in front of the others, shrinking into the corner beside the control panel where I timidly press the call button for the fifth floor. The last person to step onto the elevator is an older man with deep brown skin and close-cropped black hair, who swipes a finger across the button for the fourth floor. As he positions himself in front of the closing doors, it occurs to me that I recognize him, although I can't work out where from.

After a moment, the elevator ascends, and my eyes drift to each separate floor number as they take turns lighting up above the stainless steel doors, the bright cobalt glow illuminating our metal surroundings. The only other movement comes from the red light blinking like an eye above the dark lens on the security camera in the corner to my right. Although I try to ignore it, I can't escape the feeling that the camera is watching me.

That the people behind it are watching me.

My heart jumps into my throat when the elevator pings and the doors slide open for the fourth floor. The older man who entered behind everyone else steps off without a backward glance, clearly in a hurry to get somewhere. I watch him storm away, once again wondering where it is I've seen him before.

When the doors close behind him, I risk another glance at the camera, the scrutiny of its gaze stronger than ever. Swallowing, I wipe a bead of sweat from my forehead.

A moment later, the doors open to the fifth floor. As I was the first one in, I'm the last one out, but I don't mind the wait. Those extra few seconds give me time to compose myself.

I take a much-needed moment alone then step out of the elevator into a busy reception area. I've never been on this floor—all my classes were always on the tenth level or higher—although, it looks just like any other part of the building: clinical and cold. Pressing my arms to my sides to keep them from trembling, I join the line forming in front of the counter at the opposite end of the room. Upon reaching the front, I find myself standing before a pretty short-haired woman who looks to be only a few years older than me.

"Name?" she asks.

"Wynter Reeves," I answer for what seems like the hundredth time today.

She holds out a delicate hand. "Identification chip."

Once again, I offer my arm and stand still as my wrist is scanned for the chip underneath my skin. The woman smiles when the light on the machine switches from red to green.

"The examination will be in Room Three," she says. "Follow this hall and you'll find it on your left."

With a nod, I turn away from the counter and continue down the corridor to my right. Room Three is situated at the end of the hallway. Five other students are lined up outside the door, waiting to pass through the final checkpoint and gain admittance into the exam room. Just like everyone before me, I wave my wrist across the screen affixed to the wall beside the door. Another beep. Another green light. Unlike the others, at this checkpoint, when the machine scans my chip, the screen lights up with a diagram of the exam room and indicates which desk I've been allocated. I study it for a moment then step through the doorway.

My heart hammers against my ribcage as I plop down into my designated seat and hang my coat and bag on the back of the hard metal chair. One by one, the seats around me fill up as the other Examinees file into the space, but, despite the number of students present, the room is eerily quiet. The silence only makes me more unsettled.

My lips twitch.

*It's going to be okay.*

Chewing on the inside of my lower lip, I glance down to assess my desktop. The computerized screen is deactivated, and in the top left corner, a red light burns under the glass, flickering in and out like a flame. Swallowing, I hold my wrist out over the sensor, spurring the computer to life. White floods my field of vision apart from where my name is emblazoned in large black letters across the top of the screen.

# WYNTER A. REEVES

Today's date appears underneath it: October 14th, 2061. A longer number is printed just below that, which reads 73956241. I'd know that number anywhere. Hell, I know it as well as I know my own name. It's my identification number. The number I was assigned at birth to designate my place in the State. In many ways, that number is all I am.

Other than that, the screen is blank.

A low buzzing draws my attention to the front of the room where a projector flashes a blue-tinted image across the full length of the bare wall. A stern-looking man manifests before us like an apparition, announcing himself to be the CEO of W. P. Headquarters.

As my eyes trail over his features, I see the older man in the elevator whose face I recognized but struggled to place.

Until now.

*I knew he looked familiar.*

The way he stares out across the room is unnerving, his expression cold and unwelcome, as if taking the time to speak to us is cutting into a thousand other things he'd rather be doing right now. His gruff, authoritative voice booms around me, sending a chill of fear down my spine.

*"The examination will begin momentarily. You will be given three hours to complete it. Anyone who finishes before this time may press the call button to submit their exam. Once you have submitted your exam, no revisions will be allowed. Good luck."* With those concluding words, the projector shuts off.

A breath catches in my lungs when the door to the room snaps closed, locking with a deafening click.

*There's no turning back now. You can do this,* I remind myself, although I don't quite believe it.

An automated female voice screeches overhead, echoing through the space and setting every hair on my body on end. *"The exam will now commence. You may begin."*

As silence returns, the screen below me flashes black and then white again, revealing the first part of the exam. My fingers wrap around the electronic stylus attached to the side of the desk, gently raising the pen from its holder, and with a quivering breath, I dive into the series of questions which will singlehandedly determine my future.

The automated voice returns every fifteen minutes to tell us the clock is ticking.

*"Two hours, forty-five minutes remaining."*

*"Two hours, thirty minutes remaining."*

*"Two hours, fifteen minutes remaining."*

The squawking reminders are grating, but I force myself to shut them out and concentrate only on the exam. For the most part, the answers come easily to me, although, there's the occasional question that seems out of place, as if it doesn't belong. Are these continuity errors, or are the test makers trying to throw me off—to confirm whether I belong in my projected sector or if I should be sacrificed to the lowest depths of society?

*"Two hours remaining,"* that annoying voice nags.

Sweat trickles down the sides of my face, and my stomach churns, threatening to bring up my breakfast. I try to swallow—to push down the sudden bout of nausea—but my throat is dry and my tongue is brittle, like old sandpaper, making it impossible. When I blink, my eyes lose focus until my surroundings are an indistinct spinning blur.

I shake my head to clear it, squinting hard at the screen, but the jerking movement only makes my vertigo worse.

*"One hour, forty-five minutes remaining."*

My lungs tighten as if to suffocate me, but I push through my discomfort, nudging my face a few inches closer to the screen, desperate to complete my exam.

Terrified of what will happen if I don't.

My gaze skims over the next hazy question, but only one part of the sentence is clear.

*"...end..."*

As I repeat that single word in my head, spasms erupt across my body and a strange pressure pushes at me from the inside, as if my organs are about to burst out of my skin. Control eludes me as I writhe in my seat, and I know without having to look that the other Examinees in the room are all staring at me.

I wish they wouldn't.

I wish this would stop.

I want to continue the test.

I don't want to fail.

I don't want them to see me.

*I don't want to stand out.*

A cry escapes my lips and echoes in my ears, ringing in my skull like a bell. Pain floods my head, and a tremor rolls over my hand, weakening my already limp hold on the stylus.

The world and all sound seem to move in slow motion as the pen slips from my fingers and clatters onto the tiled floor at my feet, the impact acting like a trigger as everything around me abruptly goes black.

# TWO

WHEN I OPEN MY EYES, the exam room is gone.

I turn around in my seat. The pain that consumed me before has diminished, but it's replaced by fear, confusion, and disbelief, which all attack me at once, overpowering the part of my brain that might actually be able to comprehend what's happening.

Is this a dream? A hallucination?

My legs quake as I push to my feet, my fingers clutching at the chair to hold me to the one real thing in this delusion. The air is thick with dust, but through the impairing fog, I recognize my surroundings. I glimpse the familiar sight of the Heart in the details crumbling around me. But there are no people crowding the streets. No lights. No sign of life at all. There's only me, standing here all alone, as the world I once knew succumbs to destruction.

Panic boils beneath my skin, squeezing my lungs in a vise grip. My eyes close on instinct, but some unseen power wrenches them open again, forcing me to watch every second of this nightmare. To see what I can only assume must be the end of the world.

In the blink of an eye, the destruction explodes in a torrent of flame, devouring everything. A blinding flash burns across my vision, but when it clears, the desolate landscape is nowhere to be seen.

Did I just imagine that?

Sweat suctions the thin fabric of my clothes to my body, and I wince away from the horrible screaming that it takes me a moment to realize is coming from me. I clamp my mouth shut to silence my building distress and tighten my grasp on the chair. Wisps of darkness dance in front of my eyes, and as they fade, I'm both relieved and terrified to find myself back in the exam room.

My chest constricts as I glance around at the other Examinees, every last one wearing the same wide-eyed expression. Despite the silence, I know what they're thinking. Those words from the news broadcast earlier vibrate through my head like the pitchy whine of a bad frequency.

*Enemy of the State*, their faces all say to me.

A sharp metallic stench fills my nose, and I stumble backward, suddenly light-headed and nauseous. I touch a shaking hand to my nostrils and pull it away, a strained whimper escaping my lips when I register the blood coating my fingers. Only one coherent thought rises from the depths of my panic.

*Something's wrong with me.*

My head snaps up at the click clack of footsteps, my attention narrowing on the moderator entering from the door in the back corner intended for staff. The harsh look she gives me slices through my terror.

*I can't stay here.* This realization slams into me, knocking the air from my lungs, and without another thought, I lunge forward and smack my hand against the button on my desk, submitting my unfinished exam. I don't have a plan, and I definitely haven't considered the consequences of what I'm doing. All I know is I need to get out of this building.

Grabbing my bag and coat off the back of my chair, I sprint for the exit, waving my wrist in front of the sensor controlling the lock for the door, which scans to check if I've turned in my exam. The response is immediate as the light turns green and the door springs open, granting me my much-needed freedom.

The lock bolts back into place behind me, separating me from the other students still in the exam room. Good. Fewer people to follow me, not that any of them would ever dare to get involved.

As I race down the hallway, I feel the ghostly weight of the other Examinees' stares on my skin, burnt into my back like an unwanted tattoo. I try to shake off the memory of the look they all gave me, but I find it again in every passing expression along my route to escape. Confused glances follow me in my panic.

I rush into the reception area for the fifth floor and come to a grinding halt in front of the elevator, keeping my eyes tilted downward. A stinging pain radiates across my palm as I slap it repeatedly against the call button. Why are elevators never on the floor where you need them?

"Excuse me, miss!" the woman with short hair calls after me.

The elevator arrives in the nick of time, and I bound inside to escape her just as she steps out from behind the counter. Letting out a breath, I slump against the back wall, taking in the mirrored surface of the steel doors, where my distorted reflection stares at me as if to ask me what the hell I'm doing. I shake my head, mortified by my appearance. My skin is ashen and glistens with sweat. My hair is plastered to my forehead and cheeks. My eyes are so bloodshot, the whites of them are barely even visible. Red smears stain the bottom half of my face.

I pull on my coat and press the cream-colored sleeve against my nose to staunch the bleeding. My gaze darts back up to my disfigured reflection and hangs there as my descent continues.

The seconds seem to drag as I consider what grim fate awaits me the moment these doors open again. I don't know what to expect. I wasn't even thinking when I ran out of the exam room. I should've composed myself and finished what I came here to do. Second chances aren't given in our society, and it's very likely, if not guaranteed, that my behavior before will come back to haunt me. Second chances don't exist.

This won't be forgiven.

The number signaling for the ground floor glows blue as the elevator slows to a stop and the doors slide open, offering me up to my fate like a sacrificial lamb to the slaughter. To my surprise, no one is waiting to apprehend me. The lobby is empty except for the balding receptionist, who doesn't spare me a glance. The exam moderator and short-haired woman upstairs must not have reported me. Yet.

The vestibule beyond the lobby beckons me onward, but I falter, unsure if I should go any farther. Maybe, if I turn myself in now, the State will be lenient and let me off with a warning. Maybe it will show me mercy.

A choked laugh rises up in my throat.

*No,* I tell myself. *It won't.*

Because the State doesn't know what mercy is.

Gritting my teeth, I focus on the one thing standing between me and the way out, and with one more backward glance at the man, I race toward the turnstiles up ahead. All I have to do is prick my finger so the computer can verify my identity.

A little blood, that's it, and then I can leave.

I press my finger to the small silver pad, offering the turnstile payment in blood and silently thanking whoever it was who thought to leave the exit turnstiles in this building unmanned. I don't even wait for the numbing agent, pressing onward the instant the partition slides open. A burning sensation radiates across my skin, my finger throbbing in protest, but I'm too set on getting out of here to care about pain.

I press on through the revolving glass doors into the welcoming chill of autumn. The breeze cools my flushing skin, but I'm too preoccupied with my fear to be able to enjoy the relief.

The people walking past me on the sidewalk all keep a wide berth, eyeing me uncertainly. I might as well have a sign over my head with the word 'danger' written across it in large red letters. Their reactions don't surprise me. Every last person in the Heart lives in fear, and I've given them cause to be afraid and wary of my erratic behavior.

As far as they're concerned, I'm a lost cause.

I pull up my coat collar and press my face deeper into my sleeve, shrinking into myself. My nose doesn't seem to be bleeding anymore, but I'm too scared to pull away the fabric in case someone recognizes me.

Better to keep my identity obscured.

I retrace my steps to Central Station, keeping my eyes on the ground as I try to walk at a normal pace and not run. My pulse quickens when I fumble, nearly dropping my rail card, and crash into a woman standing to my left. Muttering a half-hearted apology, I thrust myself through the nearest available turnstile.

I make it to the platform just as the next train arrives. Rushing on board, I head for a seat in the back, sinking against the wall of the car. I don't dare move a muscle the whole ride home.

In the twenty minutes the journey takes, my thoughts spiral out of control, bringing me to the brink of hysteria.

*Stop running,* my head tells me. *Turn around. Turn yourself in now before it's too late.*

My fear is strong, but my will to survive in this moment is stronger. When the train reaches my stop, I jump out of my seat, and for the first time in my life, I don't politely wait my turn to disembark. My hands wedge between the bodies in front of me, pushing forward through the crowd like small battering rams. Disgruntled complaints reverberate in my ears, but I ignore them, leaping onto the platform, and race through the station without looking back.

Once free of the confines of underground travel, I encounter fewer people. *Witnesses,* my brain has the nerve to remind me. At this time of day, the roads are mostly empty as everyone is at work or on the train, heading for one appointment or another. Regardless, I keep my head down as I walk and slow my pace to avoid further unwanted attention.

When I reach my street a few minutes later, I choke out a laugh at the welcome sight of my family's designated living quarters two blocks down. I'm almost there.

Sanctuary is almost in reach.

Our home is one in a row of terraced houses. Out of the seven zones in the Heart, we're fortunate enough to live in Zone 2. Zone 1 is reserved for high-ranking officials and other citizens of importance, and Zones 2 through 7 house everyone else. Residences are all allocated based on job placement, status, and wealth—the closer you live to the center of the city, the better off you are. When I was younger, we lived on the border to Zone 1, but our quarters were downsized a number of years ago due to the shrinking size of my family. I don't have any siblings and my father…well, he's not around anymore. For the last eleven years, it's just been Mother and me.

I run up the steps, skipping two at a time, and sweep my wrist across the security panel positioned above the handle on the door. The lock clicks open as soon as the scanner registers my chip, acknowledging me as a resident of this household.

Throwing a nervous glance over my shoulder, I race inside and slam the door shut behind me. My heart jackhammers in my chest, and I close my eyes, leaning back against the wall. Strangled breaths weave in and out of my lips.

It's strange. I know I'm in trouble—or if I'm not already, I will be soon. *Really* soon. Yet, now that I'm home, the events of today seem more like a bad dream than reality. Right now, in the refuge of my house, I can almost forget them and pretend that I'm safe.

Once my heart rate and breathing have returned to normal, I push away from the wall and head for the stairs. Mother won't be home for several hours yet, so I have some time to think of a lie to explain what happened with my exam. Assuming I'm not dragged away to Detention before then—

My feet pause beneath me at the muffled sound of voices coming from the other end of the hallway.

No one is supposed to be home.

"Mother?" I squeak, the word catching in my throat.

My footsteps echo off the white tiled floor as I shift away from the stairs and continue toward the reception room. Despite the sudden silence, I get the sense I'm not the only one here. The faint glimmer of light at the end of the corridor only confirms my suspicions. At this time of day, all the lights should be off.

"Mother?" I call again, my tone strained.

"I'm in the reception room," she answers.

Terror rushes through me as a thousand thoughts fly through my head. *Why is she home? She shouldn't be home. Does she know? What is she going to do?*

I scramble toward the sliding interior door, which is slightly ajar, first having the sense to take a look at myself in the mirror hanging on the wall at the end of the hallway. My coat absorbed most of the blood from my nose, but I still look ghostly pale.

Sick even.

*Something's wrong with me*, I think for the second time today. The realization twists my gut.

I scrub my sleeve across my face to erase the dried remnants of blood flaking on my pasty skin, hoping Mother won't notice how bedraggled I am. I then shrug off the coat and stroll into the room where she waits for me to break the news of my exam, keeping my expression neutral, as if today has been just another ordinary day.

The moment I cross the threshold, it becomes clear at once that my facade won't fool my mother. She glares at me from her seat on the sofa, flanked by two soldiers holding guns.

*Enforcers.* The thought is like a knife to my chest.

I would like to say I'm shocked by how quickly they've acted, but the State's policing units are always efficient, handling anyone who might pose a threat. But am I a threat? I had a panic attack, that's all. Sure, I didn't finish my exam, but is that such a big deal? Does what I did really warrant this kind of reaction?

The Enforcers rise to their feet, moving toward me in suits of black armor, their faces masked by opaque helmets, shielding their eyes. My mother stands alongside them, and when she meets my gaze, it's as if she's a different person than the woman I've known these past eighteen years. The distance in her face sets me on edge. The way she looks at me…

I've only ever seen that expression once before.

"There's nowhere to go, Wynter," she murmurs. "Submit."

My eyes spring wide, and the fear hits me all over again, shattering my brief illusion of safety. Submit? To what? My mind races with the possibilities, each one more dreadful than the last. Chances are I'll be sent to Detention for immediate Re-education. That's what the State always does to anyone who fails their exam. Not that I've ever seen or met anyone who's been re-integrated into society after that. Not that I would. The dregs stick to Zone 7.

I open my mouth to say something to plead my case, but my voice catches on a grunt when I take a defensive step away from the soldiers, my back slamming into something solid behind me.

Whipping around, I stare up into the expressionless face of a third man blocking my only escape. The white laboratory coat he's wearing confuses me. He isn't clothed in the Enforcers' regulation uniform, so who is he? And why is he here?

I barely have time to consider these questions before he plunges a needle into the side of my neck. My surroundings blur as the room goes hazy, and suddenly, my body is unbearably heavy, as if gravity is trying to crush me down to the ground. With what strength I can manage, I reach out to my mother.

*Help me,* I beg, but the words don't pass my lips.

My knees buckle beneath me, and as my eyes flutter closed, her voice floods my ears, unfeeling and cold.

"Do what you must," is the last thing I hear.

# THREE

A GROAN BREAKS THROUGH MY lips as my eyes struggle to open. The light beyond my lids is like a sun searing into my vision, and I wince, my body lurching back as if I've been burned by a flame. I try, time and again, to see past the glare, but my vision is bleary. All I can make out is white.

The plodding of shoes against tile pounds through my head like beats on a drum, dull and distant, as if I'm hearing every step from under water. Mumbling voices join the low tread of footsteps, making me aware of several people around me. But I don't know who they are. I don't know why I'm here.

I don't know where I am.

I try to make sense of the last thing I remember. In my mind, I see my mother again, accompanied by the two Enforcers as well as that third unknown man. I can also recall the pinch of a needle in my neck, but anything that occurred after that moment is lost to the black hole of unconsciousness. And now, I'm here.

Wherever here is.

Only one lucid train of thought takes hold in my brain. *Am I in Detention? Is this my Re-education?*

Over the next few moments, the grogginess in my head eases, bringing the room into focus. Grunting, I try to push up into a sitting position, but when I move, something solid constricts my body, pinning me flat to the surface beneath me.

I raise my head just enough to peer down at my chest, and it's only when I glimpse the steel band restraints across my legs and torso that I'm able to feel them. Panic washes over me as I fight to get free, thrashing and screaming until my voice is hoarse and I lack the energy to keep struggling. Ragged breaths scorch my lungs as my body goes limp.

I press my eyes shut for a minute then open them, risking a glance back down at my legs. I've been stripped of everything I was wearing before, right down to my watch. A skimpy white hospital gown has replaced my exam-approved clothes, and I'm strapped to a metal table in the middle of a bright room I don't recognize. A heart monitor beeps beside my head, mimicking every racing beat of my heart, while an IV stand is positioned on my other side, leading down into tubes protruding from the crook of my right elbow and hand. The second I glimpse them, that surge of panic returns. Suddenly, I no longer care why I'm here. I don't need to know what these people—whoever they are—intend to do to me. I just need to get out of this place.

"The subject is awake."

My gaze snaps in the direction of a woman's voice, locking on at least a dozen people standing a few feet to my right, all clothed in the same white coat the man who drugged me at my house was wearing.

Fear creeps across my skin like an itch as I glance between the curious faces observing me. One man scribbles down notes on a computerized tablet while another scratches his chin and looks me over like I'm bacteria in a Petri dish that he's viewing under a microscope. An older woman approaches me with a syringe clasped in her slender hand, her eyes dull and lacking even the slightest hint of concern. The others share her blank expression.

As I take in their faces, reality hits me. Laid out on this table, I'm helpless and weak. I can't move. I can't run away. I can't even find the strength to fight back when the woman pushes a needle into the vein at the crook of my elbow.

A hiss escapes me as she takes three vials worth of my blood, the deep red filling the glass tubes to the brim. Once finished, she removes the needle and sticks a small round bandage over the puncture mark in my skin. She then turns and walks away without saying a word.

As she crosses the room, I narrow my eyes, trying to sharpen her indistinct figure, but my head is still reeling from whatever I was injected with earlier. Through the smog clouding my head, I can make out her fingers tapping against a touchscreen keyboard embedded into the surface of a long countertop lining the white wall to my left. A hologram image projects above her head, displaying several rows of jumbled text, but my vision is too fuzzy to make out the words, my eyes swathed by dancing black cotton balls.

The woman swipes her fingers across the keyboard again then pivots to face a steel bowl set out on the gleaming countertop beside her. Part of me believes that bowl wasn't there before, but the drugs racing through my body are making it difficult to be sure of anything. Except the fear.

That much I'm certain of.

A sizzling sound floods the room as the woman pours the contents of the three vials into the bowl. Sparks of electricity jolt across the exterior, reacting to my blood, and wisps of smoke rise up from the metal, casting a slight haze over the counter.

Satisfied, the woman peers back at the hologram image, appraising it for a moment before tapping her nails against the keyboard again. At the press of a button, a lid snaps over the bowl and the metal container spins in place.

Each rotation is faster than the last, and as the bowl moves, a code manifests overhead—line after line of incomprehensible symbols scrawled across the glowing hologram image. I try to make sense of them, but there's nothing there to make sense of. I might as well be looking at a foreign language.

"Doctor," the woman gasps. "You need to see this."

Terror consumes me at her incredulous tone.

What is she seeing?

*What's wrong with me?*

Hysteria once again overpowers my senses, and I'm consumed by the need to escape this place. But I have no energy. My mouth is too dry to swallow, my head is spinning, and the fluorescent lights overhead are making me unbearably nauseous. Bile inches up my throat. I pull against my restraints one more time, my teeth clenching together to counter the strain.

The soft thud of footsteps draws my attention away from my struggle, and my body goes still as my eyes flick to the side, locking on the man now standing next to the woman, his hands tucked behind his waist as he examines the hologram image, his mouth set in a serious line. He's young—no older than his mid-twenties, if that—and he's tall, with auburn-brown hair parted neatly to one side and a clean-shaven jaw. Rectangular, thin-rimmed glasses frame perceptive gray eyes.

The woman leans toward him as he studies the hologram,

her voice just loud enough for me to hear over the hum of the spinning bowl. "Her blood type," she whispers, her husky tone dripping with awe. "It's...*changing*."

I may not know much about science, or anything medical having to do with the human body, but I know enough to be certain that what she's saying isn't possible. Not without unnatural intervention, at least.

The man straightens, adjusting his spotless white coat.

"Fascinating," he murmurs.

His eyes shift to mine, and the traitorous monitor beside me betrays me with a string of rapid beeps, the high-pitched computerized echo of my racing heart revealing my fear.

As the man approaches, his pale lips curl into a smile. "Hello, Wynter. My name is Dr. Richter. I'll be taking care of you."

*Taking care of me?*

"Why am I here?" I breathe, my voice raspy. "What are you going to do to me?"

"Shh, hush now," he croons, patting my shoulder. "I assure you, all your questions will be answered in time." He lowers his eyes, and I follow his gaze to his hand where a syringe is laid out on his palm. It takes me a moment to realize the glass vial is empty. "But for now"—a wave of vertigo hits me as the sharp features of his face melt into a blur—"you must sleep."

"How..." I trail off, my tongue too heavy to speak.

I lift my head as much as I'm able to, spotting the last of a blue liquid disappearing into my body through a thin tube in my arm. The drug acts quickly, stealing my words.

As the drowsiness returns to pull me under again, the doctor's smile is all I see.

# FOUR

WHEN I COME TO, I'M in another room I don't recognize. Unlike the room I woke up in before, this one is smaller and only has space for a table positioned at the base of a single bed and a toilet, shower, and sink, which are all crammed together against the wall opposite me, off to the left-hand side of the door. Everything is gray and metallic.

Cold.

Disoriented, and with a fair bit of effort, I push myself into a sitting position. My head is bleary and drug-addled, and my back is stiff, my muscles aching, no doubt from sleeping on the hard mattress beneath me. The springs creak when I shift my weight.

I swing my legs over the side of the bed and plant my feet on the floor, abruptly going still. A wave of nausea grips my stomach, making me wary of moving any more for the moment in case my body decides to throw up. Lifting my eyes, I study the confined space while I wait for the queasiness to pass, noting how there aren't any windows—just plain concrete walls boxing me in on all sides. A camera sits in the far corner to my left, hanging just below the ceiling, an ominous red light blinking on the side of the lens. Just like in the elevator at W. P. Headquarters, it's as if I can sense the people here watching me. I can feel their penetrating gazes without even seeing their faces, especially that of the doctor I met.

Richter, he called himself.

A second wave of vertigo slams into me, and I fly forward, stumbling to the sink, gripping the edges to catch myself. An eternity seems to pass before the nausea subsides.

Exhaling a shaking breath, I glance up into the mirror above the steel basin and let out a gasp. A deranged-looking girl stares back at me from the glass. Purple smudges stain the skin under her eyes, giving the appearance of bruises against the unhealthy pallor of her yellowish skin. She looks sick.

*Really* sick.

I look away, mortified by my appearance, haunted by the realization burning my thoughts like a hot iron brand searing into my flesh. The thought first occurred to me during my placement exam, and it's been chasing me since, begging me to face the truth.

And the truth is…something is wrong with me.

I choke back a sob as the walls around me seem to inch closer, pressing in on all sides. As my pulse thunders in my ears, my eyes snag on the corner of the mirror, catching on the reflection of a bundle of clothes folded in a pile on the mattress behind me.

Thankful for the distraction, I return to the bed and run my fingertips across the rough fabric. Also gray. Also cold. As my pulse evens out and my anxiety eases, I look down at the sweat-soaked gown chafing my skin and then back at the fresh clothes on the bed. Noting the difference makes me feel even filthier.

My gaze flits to the shower with longing. *Get clean. That's all I can do at the moment. Get clean now. Worry later.* But as my fingers graze the edges of the gown to remove it, I freeze, remembering the camera in the corner behind me. Just how much are the people here watching me? Are they observing everything I do?

I peer over my shoulder at the blinking red light and push a faltering breath out through my lips. A full minute passes before I come to the disheartening conclusion that privacy likely isn't something I'll be granted here. Goosebumps rise across my skin at that notion.

Pushing the thought away, I shrug out of the thin gown and immerse myself under the cascade of lukewarm water that rains down from the shower head when my shaking fingers turn the handle. My muscles tense as my fingernails move over my face, scraping away the dried blood and sweat—a reminder of what happened at W. P. Headquarters.

Behind the hum of the running water, my fear is stronger than ever, a constant deafening scream in my head. How long has it been since I was taken? It can't have been that long ago, can it? It scares me that I have no way of knowing for sure considering how many times I've been drugged by my captors. I settle on assuming it's only been a day or two since the fiasco with my placement exam. Maybe, if I'm lucky, my stay here won't be extended much longer.

I bite back a laugh and shake my head at my pitiful attempt to console myself. Deep down, I know the truth. However long these people plan to hold me, it will be for a while. I won't see the outside of these walls any time soon. Hell, if I'm in Detention, like I fear, I'm looking at a minimum sentence of a year. The thought makes my insides quiver. A year? For running out on my exam?

*It could be worse,* I remind myself. *They could've sent you to Termination.*

My fingers tremble as they grasp the handle and turn until the rush of water fades to a trickle. A white towel hangs within reach, and I grab it, wrapping the starchy fabric around my body. As I step out of the shower, I keep the towel draped around me while I change into the clean clothes provided on the bed in an effort to protect whatever modesty I have left. The pants are dark gray—almost black—and comfortably loose, although itchy against my skin. The top is a lighter gray and a few sizes too big for my body, hanging to the middle of my thighs. My feet slip easily into a pair of flat shoes I find tucked just under the foot of the bed.

As my hands work to towel-dry my hair, I risk another glance at my reflection. My complexion is brighter now, although those bruise-like bags remain under my eyes, making me look like I haven't slept in weeks. A knot forms in my chest as I comb my fingers through the damp strands of hair. The short brown ends drip onto my shoulders while my bangs lie slick against my forehead. I look awful, but this is the best I can do under the circumstances.

Once I'm dressed and dry, I plop down on the mattress, unsure what to do with myself. My hands clench and unclench, my fingers wringing the end of my shirt, as my eyes skirt over the room, taking in every detail no matter how small and unimportant it seems at first glance. On every pass, my focus catches on the white table at the end of the bed.

On a hunch, I tap the glossy surface with the tip of my finger, and as expected, a screen flashes to life under the glass, revealing a menu offering a multitude of options to the user.

They range from food and drink to other basic necessities, like toiletries and assistance—not that unlike the food delivery computers provided in every home in Zone 2. In this instance, the hospitality of the device is bewildering considering my prison-like surroundings.

I press the icon for food, opting for something bland in case my nausea decides to make a comeback. Almost as soon as I select my choice, a robotic arm descends from a sliding panel in the ceiling above me, holding a tray and presenting a meal that looks like a feast to my growling stomach. The arm sets the tray down on the table then retracts into the ceiling, leaving me alone with my food.

I'm reinvigorated after gorging on broth and bread, and for the first time since waking up in this place, my mind is clear and not bogged down with drugs. I stretch my legs and return to my feet, assessing my surroundings with renewed focus. There's only one route into this room, and I'd be willing to bet it's locked from the outside. I approach the door, scanning my eyes across the surface. No latch. No handle. No defining feature of any kind. Just a slab of steel blocking my only hope of getting out of this place.

As I flatten my palm against the cool metal, a shrill beeping seeps into the room from the other side of the threshold, as if in response to my touch. I rip my hand away and take a hurried step back at the same moment the door springs open.

A middle-aged man with sparse facial hair stands in the hallway beyond, his face devoid of emotion. He's wearing white clothes that are similar in style to mine, and he holds a large computerized tablet in the crook of his arm, the screen flat to his chest.

"Dr. Richter would like a word with you," he says, his pale eyes locking on mine. When I don't respond, he moves to one side of the doorway and extends his hand, gesturing for me to step into the corridor. "Follow me, please."

My racing heart climbs up into my throat and suffocates me as I inch out of the room. The hallway I step into seems to go on for miles in both directions, dotted with identical doors and at least ten other passages branching off on both sides.

Through the glare of the fluorescent lights overhead, I examine the labyrinth and consider my options. I could run, but it's unlikely I would find my way out before I get apprehended again. This place is a maze, and every turn looks the same. Any chance of escape is non-existent.

With a sigh of resignation, I give in to my lifelong habit of self-preservation, falling behind the man and matching the timing of his every step like a shadow. I don't like it, but I have to do as I'm told. Doing as I'm told is how I survive.

As we walk, I notice the man keeps his distance from me, and he only acknowledges my presence again when we reach our destination, stopping in front of a door that looks the same as every other one we've passed in this place. I wait to the side as he enters a sequence of numbers into the keypad above the handle. Each pressed number results in a beep, and with the last digit, a light on the console turns green and the door sweeps open, granting us entry.

The man steps back and signals with a rigid nod for me to enter the room. I have a bad feeling about this, but what other choice do I have except to obey? When I cross the threshold, the first thing I notice is a metal table, accompanied by two chairs facing each other. The room itself is plain and gray, apart from the wall on my left, which holds a large tinted mirror. A surveillance camera hangs in the far corner, watching me from its place by the ceiling.

"Take a seat," the man instructs. "Dr. Richter will be in momentarily."

As I look back over my shoulder, he sweeps his hand to the side of the table with the chair facing the mirror. The door then closes between us, locking me in.

My stomach clenches when I take a seat, my nerves writhing as the seconds tick by. Several minutes pass before the door slides open again. Dr. Richter strolls into the room, grinning as he sits down in the chair at the opposite side of the table.

"Hello, Wynter. How are you feeling?"

I gape at him, unsure what to say. Words suddenly spew from my lips like vomit. "I want to see my mother," I blurt out without thinking.

The smile slips from his face, and he looks down at his hands where they rest locked together on top of the table. "I'm... afraid that's not possible."

"Why?"

He smiles again, although more gently this time. "Since you had yet to be reassigned to a new sector at the time you were apprehended, you were still technically and lawfully under the guardianship of your mother. She has since relinquished her custodial rights, and you are now under the care and ownership of the State. Well..." He pauses. "The DSD, if we're being precise."

My eyes widen, and my blood runs cold. The DSD. The Department of Scientific Discoveries—a harmless enough name that ironically coincides with the last place in the world

I would ever want to be. The DSD makes Detention look like a playground and is where the State conducts human experimentation, poorly hidden behind the guise of research. It's also the home of Termination. The home of everyone's worst nightmare. Only criminals and those determined to be unredeemable are sent here, so what could they possibly want with me? Am I a criminal?

Am I unredeemable?

"This is your home for the foreseeable future."

Terror courses through me, rendering my tongue completely useless. I can't speak. I can't think.

I can't breathe.

"I understand what I'm telling you must come as a shock. But I assure you that you are perfectly safe and will be treated with civility during your stay here."

"And how long will that be?" I croak out in a whisper.

I glare at him as the truth strikes without mercy, the pain of it like sharpened claws slicing into my skin over and over again, stripping me down to the bone. My mother gave me up to these people. My own mother! Anger rockets through me, scorching everything in its path in a blistering wave of fire. All that's left in its wake is the betrayal tearing my heart into pieces.

My eyes clamp shut, but the darkness behind my lids only makes the spinning in my head worse.

"I'd like to discuss what you were doing prior to the incident."

My eyes snap open and lock on Dr. Richter, his right brow slightly cocked in a quizzical expression. As I process his words, it occurs to me that he never answered my question.

"What incident?" I ask.

He leans forward, fixing me with his metallic gray gaze. "At

W. P. Headquarters, during your exam."

I shrink back as a chill creeps up my spine. The memory of my hallucination is fresh, the destruction I witnessed still vivid in my mind.

"Is that why I'm here?" I gasp, breathless.

The smile returns to his lips, and he rests back in his seat, drumming a finger against the table. The seconds seem to drag as he considers my question.

"Yes," he says after a torturous moment.

My cheeks flush with heat as I scramble to find some excuse that will get me out of this mess. "W-What happened was a misunderstanding," I stammer. "I panicked, but I'm ready now. I'll retake my exam. It won't happen again—"

Amusement hooks into his features as he holds up a hand. "That won't be necessary."

Dr. Richter reaches under the table and produces a tablet, which he places between us. His fingers flit across the screen, and although there's a certain finesse to his movements, his mannerisms seem almost…forced. Insincere. As far as I can tell, the only natural thing about this conversation is my fear.

The fear I'm feeling is definitely real.

"Could you confirm the following, please?" he asks. "What is your full name?"

"Wynter Arabelle Reeves," I mutter, curious why he's asking when he already has this information.

"Identification number and date of birth?"

"73956241. October 14th, 2043."

He wavers for a moment to look down at the tablet. "Blood type?"

"O negative," I answer automatically. But as I grumble these words, a woman's voice fills my head.

*"Her blood type. It's…changing."*

Suddenly, I'm not so sure.

Dr. Richter nods, keeping his gaze on his tablet, then proceeds with his methodical line of questioning. "Mother's name?"

My teeth grit together as I think of my mother. Of what she did. Of how she didn't even defend me, her daughter. Her only child.

Her sole living family.

"Evandra Reeves," I hiss, blinking tears from my stinging eyes.

Dr. Richter ignores the sharp edge in my voice.

"Father's name and date of death?"

I startle, unsure why he's asking me this. Why does it matter what my father was named or when he died? He's not here anymore. To the State, you don't matter unless you contribute, and the dead can't do anything except haunt the living.

Swallowing, I try my best not to make it obvious the question has upset me. "Freston Reeves," I whisper. "September 9th… 2050."

"Address?" Dr. Richter continues without pause.

"A19, Unit 34, Zone 2."

"And what business did you have the other day at W. P. Headquarters?"

It takes every ounce of willpower I possess not to raise an eyebrow at him. He knows what I'm going to say, so what's the deal with this interrogation?

What exactly does he want with me?

"I was taking my placement exam," I say, drawing out each word in a slow careful breath.

He looks up. "What sector were you projected to enter?" There's a genuine curiosity in his tone.

"Financial." I knot my hands together under the table. "The banking branch."

An unsettling smirk upturns his lips. "You must be quite intelligent to have been designated to that particular career. Financial often leads to a stable and fulfilling life."

I blink, taken aback by his comment. He sounds just like the advertisements displayed in the classrooms throughout all my years of education, pitching one job or another to students. They were meant to target our interests, paving the way for the assessments that would determine what career would be ideal for each of us and play to our strengths.

At least, that's how the State wants the process portrayed, when in truth, our paths are already dictated from the day we're born based on our genetics. It's a widely known fact that our supposed strengths lie in our blood, which is why so many people end up with the same career selection their parents had. My mother works in the financial sector—hence why we live in Zone 2, Financial, among everyone else who works in banking, insurance, and in the departments that manage our State-allocated pensions. Generally, unless you screw up really badly—like, say, by running out on your exam—you'll just end up exactly where you started, following in your parents' footsteps.

Looks like I take after my father.

It's like that everywhere. Zone 1, Authority, is where our lawmakers and officials work and reside, superior in status to everyone else in the Heart. Zone 3, Commerce, is where the shopping departments and health centers, along with their employees, are located—with the exception of smaller emergency facilities, which are sprinkled throughout the other zones—while all the Heart's hydroponic farms and food production workers are based in Zone 4, Agriculture. Zone 5, Defense, is home to the city's Enforcers and their training grounds. Zone 6, Labor, is the base of all construction and engineering facilities and laborers. And then there's Zone 7, Detention…the zone home to those in the least desirable jobs and the location of the Heart's Detention facilities.

When it comes to work and residential status, everyone is kept separate, isolated to their delegated zones. There are exceptions, like when someone has an impressive IQ and qualifies for a job above their initial projection or when someone breaks the law and is sent to a Detention facility. That's why I've never seen anyone who's been sent for Re-education integrated back into society. The State makes it a point to keep us with others just like us, like pigs trapped in separate pens. No one residing in Zone 2 at this moment has ever been on the other side of the law.

*Unlike me.*

I shiver at the thought, clenching my jaw. I already know what my life would've been like. I don't need Dr. Richter to remind me, especially now that I have no idea what's going to happen moving forward. After all, I'm fairly certain that imprisonment at the DSD will leave a big black mark on my permanent record. My career and residential prospects will be tarnished by this. Assuming I make it out of here alive and get the chance to have a career. Or a life.

Dr. Richter knits his hands together again and stares at me over the rim of his glasses. Although I expect his question, it still catches me off guard.

"Could you please describe what happened during your exam?"

I pinch my lower lip between my teeth. Should I tell him the truth? What will happen if I do? Better yet, what will happen if I don't? I want to know what happened to me just as much, if not more so, than he does. If I tell him, maybe I'll get that answer.

"I...honestly don't know," I admit. "One minute, I was fine. The next, I had this splitting headache, my vision was blurring, and…" I trail off.

"And?" he presses, his gray eyes piercing.

"And…then, it was like I was someplace else. I was seeing things around me that weren't actually there, even though it really felt like they were. I was…hallucinating, I guess. Before I could make sense of what was happening, I was back in the exam room."

My pulse accelerates as I wait for Dr. Richter to speak. His stern expression tells me little.

"What *exactly* did you see?" he asks after a moment.

I hesitate, swallowing past the sudden lump in my throat. Why does he care what I saw? It was just a delusion.

It wasn't real.

*Was it?*

A one-word answer breaches my lips without thought.

"Destruction."

His eyes enlarge just enough for me to notice the change, but before I can properly assess his stunned expression, he clears his throat and looks down at the table, typing something into the tablet.

"I'd like you to examine the following documents." He turns the glowing screen around to face me before adjusting his glasses, pushing them farther up his nose. "Let me know if anything from this information seems familiar to you."

My fingers shake as they hover an inch above the glass

surface of the tablet. At Dr. Richter's encouraging nod, I scroll through what appear to be identification records, but I've never met or even heard of the people they belong to. I have no idea what I'm supposed to be looking for. The only similarity I notice between them is the cause of death listed at the bottom of each. They all suffered from one form or other of mental deterioration, and in the end, it killed them.

My stomach turns as my eyes trail over a sentence written in the record for a thirty-year-old woman named Leela.

**Suffered from vivid hallucinations.**

*Just like me,* I realize.

I flip through the other records, noting the same line inscribed at the bottom of every one. Panic induced or not, hallucinations aren't normal, which means I could be crazy, too. I could be like the people in these files, and I could just as easily end up the same way.

Dead.

"I'm sorry," I whimper, ignoring the sharp pain in my gut. "I don't recognize any of them—"

"Don't focus on the records, focus on their traits. Their physical appearance is key." Dr. Richter waves a dismissive hand, urging me to look again.

At his behest, I flick through the documents two more times, examining each picture with scrutiny. I'm not sure what he wants me to see. When I open my mouth to speak, he cuts me off, placing a mirror on the table in front of me.

"Look into it," he prompts.

Furrowing my brow, I peer into the mirror, fixing my gaze on my own mismatched eyes. One green. One blue. The same as they've always been since the day I was born.

"Have you ever heard of Ultraxenopia?"

I look up from my reflection and shake my head, my heart pounding as Dr. Richter reaches across the table, retrieving both the tablet and mirror.

"Like the people in these documents, you have a rare genetic defect known as Heterochromia. To put it in simple terms, your eyes are two different colors. Although the disorder itself is harmless, we are beginning to link it to a more serious condition. A phrenoextratic disease called Ultraxenopia."

He pauses, allowing a few seconds for this new information to sink in. Dread overtakes me, but I have no idea what any of it means.

A serious condition, he said.

But how serious?

"Ultraxenopia targets the occipital lobe of the brain, which affects our visual processing, along with the superior temporal gyrus, which helps us process sounds. As the condition takes root, it manifests by showing its victims things that aren't really there."

"Hallucinations," I breathe.

"Correct. But these aren't typical hallucinations by any measure. What you experienced during your exam…it wasn't a delusion, Wynter. What you saw might've been in your head, but it was *real*. It was a vision, and in that moment, I believe what you saw was a glimpse of the future."

I resist the urge to laugh, wondering if this is all some sick, twisted joke intended to torment me before sending me on my merry way to my death. A glimpse of the future? Now, who sounds crazy.

And yet, there's a part of me that wants to believe him. That needs something or someone to blame for the unexpected dissolution of my life. Besides, if what I saw wasn't a vision…

What was it?

"That's impossible," is all I can manage to say.

Dr. Richter doesn't seem surprised by my skepticism and responds by pulling out a handheld black device, which he sets on the table in front of me. With a swipe of his finger, a flickering hologram appears between us, revealing surveillance footage.

I instantly recognize the exam room at W. P. Headquarters. In the blue-tinted footage, I can hear the automated female voice droning on in the background, and I can see myself sitting at my allocated desk, my hand scribbling furiously across its surface.

My eyes follow my recorded movements, watching for the first signs of my breakdown. I glimpse them in the odd jerk of my head and in the way my back hunches over my desk. Finally, the hallucination takes hold, and I rise to my feet, staring blankly around me as if I'm seeing something beyond the walls of the room. The events that follow happen just as I remember them, from that bloodcurdling scream right up to the moment I chose to run away. The footage cuts out when I race out of the room.

Dr. Richter clicks off the device but says nothing. Shaking my head, I meet his gaze.

"That's impossible," I say again, louder this time.

"Perhaps," he says. "But, I must tell you, the tests we've already run show remarkable things. Things that, quite frankly, wouldn't be possible if you were normal. Nonetheless, we won't know for certain until we run more intensive tests. I'd like your permission to do that."

I scoff at his words. My permission? Like the DSD needs permission to do anything. "Won't you just do them anyway, regardless of what I say?"

"Yes." His lips peel back into a grin that I'm sure is meant to be reassuring but looks malicious, revealing predatory white teeth. "But I prefer my subjects to be cooperative. Besides," he adds, "you'd be providing a great service, not only to the advancement of science but to the State. What other reason could you need?"

Apprehension spreads through me like a poison, infecting every inch of my body. I can't trust this man, I know that. But what choice do I have except to cooperate? And if I *do* cooperate…what then?

Dr. Richter repeatedly taps one finger on the table, pressing me to speak. With a nervous twitch, I lick my cracked lips.

"If I cooperate…will you let me go?"

He averts his gaze and stands without saying a word, pushing the metal chair away from the table. The legs scratch against the floor, making me wince.

He then heads for the door, which swings open at his approach, and, pausing in the threshold, he turns and offers me a clipped smile. I know without having to ask that our conversation is over.

Inclining his head, he steps out into the corridor, leaving me alone again in the room.

As the door shuts behind him, I come to terms with the only answer I'm left with. He didn't say it out loud, but he didn't have to. His silence said it for him.

They will never let me go.

# FIVE

I DRAW IN A STRANGLED breath as two female attendants strap me down to the table. My eyes burn as I try to breathe past the assault of my heart as it attempts to punch a hole in my rib cage, driving my terror that much closer to the surface where I can no longer ignore it. I have to keep reminding myself that I agreed to this.

I agreed to let Dr. Richter run his tests.

Any sane person would ask me why—not that I had much say in the matter. Even if I hadn't relented, he would've proceeded and I would've wound up on this table. But, behind my fear, I'm curious to see what happens next. Regardless of what it takes, I want to know what's happening to me. I have nothing else. No home. No career prospects. No family.

I only have the need to understand what I saw.

Dr. Richter approaches the foot of the table and waves a hand, dismissing the two women beside me. With an obedient nod, they both slip away, stepping out of my line of vision.

"Are you ready?" he asks.

My lips press into a thin line. "That depends. What are you going to do to me?"

He smiles as if it'll reassure me. It doesn't.

"I want to recreate the experience you had the day of your placement exam. Hopefully, that will be enough to prove that I'm right about what you are. About your condition."

*And if it isn't?* I want to press, but I can't find the words. Instead, I mutter, "How do you plan to do that?"

"Well,"—he skirts around the table until he's standing next to my head—"we're going to inject you with an inhibitor that will slow down the normal functions of your brain. Once the inhibitor has set in, we'll send magnetic signals to a localized part of the occipital lobe, which is where the visions stem from. These signals should then follow a path to the superior temporal gyrus through a string of vibrations. If all goes according to plan, this will stimulate a response that should replicate what you experienced before."

*And if it doesn't go according to plan? What then?* But my fear of the answer prevents me from speaking.

My gaze drops away. I don't really understand what he said, but I grasp enough to come up with one final question. The only question that really matters.

"Will it hurt?" I whisper.

I peek up, and his smile deepens as he places a firm hand on my shoulder. "You'll feel a minor discomfort at most. Nothing to be concerned about. Rest easy. No harm will come to you here."

His fingers curl around my shoulder and squeeze, but his grip is too tight to be consoling. The straps securing me down keep me still and prevent me from wriggling away from his touch. I hold my breath until he lets go of my arm.

The seconds tick by in silence as he directs his attention to the equipment around me. To steady my nerves, I concentrate on the ceiling, counting the fluorescent lights and white tiles. None of my attempts to distract myself work, and my gaze snaps to the side at the clicking of footsteps. Another female attendant approaches the table, her face and eyes blank of any emotion—not that unlike everyone else in this city. Reaching for my arm, she wipes something wet across the skin at the crook of my elbow.

"You'll feel a slight pinch," she warns.

I grimace at the piercing sting of the needle, biting my tongue to keep from crying out as the attendant trails a line of tubing from the IV bag hanging from the stand beside the table down to my throbbing vein. Once everything is connected, she grabs a syringe of silver liquid off a nearby pushcart.

"Everything is ready."

At these words, Dr. Richter returns to my side, and a shudder of panic jolts through me when his fingers tug down the front of my gown, exposing the top of my chest. I struggle against the restraints as the same two thoughts strike me again and again.

*I've changed my mind. I don't want to do this.*

Tears curve down my cheeks as I bite back the protests pressing at the brink of my lips. I don't speak because I understand that what I want doesn't matter. I don't speak because fighting back will only draw this out and probably make it worse. Much worse. After all, the DSD owns me. I am their property to do whatever they want with.

At that thought, I go still and give in to what's coming. Thankfully, Dr. Richter's fingers move quickly, attaching three circular pads in a straight line just under my collarbone. Once he's finished, the sound of my heartbeat projects through the room.

I can hear my fear in the unsteady palpitations of my racing heart. The beeps grow more erratic when a metal halo drops down from the ceiling and encircles my head, at least a dozen bars extending from the inside of the ring and moving inward, pressing into my skull. Trapping me like an animal in a cage.

A buzzing sound fills my ears as a dew of sweat beads across my skin, a growl of frustration swelling in my throat as fear and anger go to war in my chest. Clenching my jaw, I peer sideways, watching Dr. Richter out of my peripheral vision. His back is turned toward me, his attention fixed on a glowing blue hologram screen above the white counter.

Beside him, a panel in the countertop opens, revealing a wide glass tube that looks to be at least a foot in diameter. It rises up, containing a handful of small silver objects, which float as if suspended in water. A purple aura pulsates around them as they orbit each other like tiny planets.

Dr. Richter nods. "Introduce the inhibitor."

I cast a terrified glance first at the woman then at the syringe in her hand. She pushes the needle into the tube hanging from the IV bag, injecting the silver liquid, which works its way through the plastic down into my vein. As it enters my arm, the drug feels strange—cold like ice, sending a chill through my body, followed by a wave of fire.

A convulsion tears through me, and I thrash against the table, a cry lodged in my throat.

"Thirty seconds until the inhibitor will enter the subject's brain," a deep male voice reports from across the room.

I try to look at whoever spoke, but I can't turn my head. The halo holds me still.

An automated female voice projects from the loudspeaker,

counting down to what I'm certain will be my demise. *"Twenty-five seconds remaining."*

As terror consumes me, I have to remind myself this would've happened either way. Even if I hadn't agreed to it, Dr. Richter would've run these experiments.

In the end, I never had a choice.

*"Twenty seconds remaining."*

My heart is pounding. I can feel it. I can hear it.

*"Ten seconds remaining."*

I don't want this. I'm scared.

*"Five seconds remaining."*

My eyes find Dr. Richter's as my mouth shapes the words needed to beg him to stop. But all that springs free from my dried lips is silence.

*"Four..."*

The floating objects cease mid-orbit, almost as if time has frozen around them.

*"Three..."*

The purple glow brightens as the silver balls move outward, shifting away from each other.

*"Two..."*

They draw together again with a flash and a bang, like an elastic band that's been pulled taut and then snapped. The entirety of the room goes white, blinding me.

*"One..."*

When the countdown hits zero, a scream explodes from my lungs. It's as if a thousand lightning bolts have all struck at once, hitting me in the same place in my head. I gasp for air, trying to breathe through the pain. But it's everywhere.

It's *everywhere.*

My vision clears just enough to make out the sharp planes of Dr. Richter's angular face. I follow his unblinking gaze to the silver objects, which have commenced their rotations. After a few orbits, they slow again, pulsing, and then—

"Again," Dr. Richter hisses.

This time, when the lightning strikes, my body goes limp.

"Her heart rate is dropping," a distant voice warns.

Dr. Richter doesn't even spare me a pitying look when he bites back, "Continue until there's a response."

*No more…* I try to plead, but I can't find my voice.

Over and over again, the lightning cuts into me, sawing my brain in half. I scream until I can't scream any longer and I lack the energy to do more than simply lie still, waiting for this torment to pass. The pain is too much.

I just want it to end.

When the lightning finally stops, the bursts of white surrounding me fade until my mind is lost to unending blackness. All that exists around me is pain, and I am floundering in a sea of it, drowning.

Surrendering to the waves determined to crush me, my eyelids droop closed, and my body gives in to the welcome embrace of unconsciousness.

# SIX

THE TORTURE CONTINUES FOR SEVERAL months. Every day, I'm dragged back into the blinding white laboratory and strapped to the metal table against my will. The events that come after always follow the same routine. The testing continues until I pass out, and when I come to, I'm back in this claustrophobic prison. There's nothing to do in this room except wait.

Wait for my torment to start all over again.

In the few moments of clarity I have where I can focus on something other than my constant agony, I think of Dr. Richter, obsessing over what he said in that strange mirrored room. How he promised no harm would come to me here.

I was stupid to believe that lie. What was even more foolish was allowing myself to believe my time here would ever actually end.

I'm not leaving this hellhole, I know that now. I'm just another dispensable tool to these people. My life means nothing to them, and when I eventually exhaust my usefulness, I'll be disposed of just like all the other victims before me. People don't leave the DSD. Not unless they're in a body bag.

My eyes trail over the puddles of liquefied mush scattered across the floor around me. Dr. Richter won't kill me, and he won't let me die. I've tried enough times to be sure of that. At first, I gave in to this madness, thinking there must be an end to it—that I could survive if I just held on and didn't allow myself to give up.

I know better now.

When I stopped eating altogether, they just forced that upon me in the same way they force everything else, even resorting to more invasive methods to provide sustenance when all other attempts to feed me had failed. They always find a way, no matter what.

There's nothing I can do to stop this.

I cringe at the memory of what these people have done to me, recalling one episode in particular, the brutal recollection still vivid even through the fog of near starvation. It was a typical day. Another failed experiment. Weak and worn down to my breaking point, I knew I wouldn't last much longer and I'd had enough.

I then dragged my withering body into the corner beside the toilet, hiding in the camera's one blind spot. I was cowering at death's door already and knew it wouldn't take much to push me the rest of the way.

At peace with the idea of ending my life, I jammed my fingers down my throat and regurgitated what little nourishment my body was still clinging to. But, somehow, Dr. Richter knew what I was doing, and as I retched, orderlies stormed into the room to stop me. One of them pinned me to the floor as another forced a tube down into my stomach. I gagged as they pumped me full of whatever it would take to keep me alive. To keep me in a physical state where they could continue to run their experiments.

I attempted to scream, but I couldn't. I tried to reject the feeding tube, but I couldn't. Their hands held me down as my body convulsed, and in the end, I couldn't fight them.

This method has now become a daily occurrence.

My eyes flicker open and closed, fighting sleep. The floor is cool against my clammy cheek, bringing a fleeting relief to my burning skin. There's an obscene smell perfuming the air that I'm well aware is coming from me, but I lack the energy to shower. I haven't washed in a long time now, apart from occasionally cleaning my teeth to spare myself from the constant rancid taste of bile and vomit. As for the rest of me, I guess I don't see the point.

I'm going to die anyway.

My eyes drift closed as fatigue overwhelms me. Through the haze of my wavering consciousness, a familiar beeping scratches at my eardrums, the sound so faint that, for a brief second, I think it's only in my head. But then the door springs open and footsteps beat against the floor and I realize it's real.

The torment is about to happen again.

*No!* I want to scream. Certainly, it hasn't been a whole day already?

The hands wrapping around me are rough as they peel my body off the sticky cement floor. Since I'm no longer able to support my own weight, they haul me to my feet and hold me upright, keeping a strong arm snaked around my back to brace me. In the beginning, they had to restrain me when they did this, but they don't bother anymore. They don't have to. Any fight I had has long since diminished.

I narrow my eyes at the man looming over me, who pushes

my head to one side and plunges a needle into the skin of my neck, his face devoid of any emotion. I know with that single vacant look that he doesn't care what happens to me here. No one does. Once claimed by the DSD, you're on your own.

The injection works its way through my system, but whatever the drug is, it doesn't quite knock me out. I'm still conscious, albeit just barely. My body, on the other hand, is paralyzed from the neck down. I can't fight, run, or do anything other than feel the lingering caress of pain.

The orderlies drag me out of the room and through the halls, leading me back to my place of torture. My feet burn from the chafing of my bare skin against the smooth tiled floor, making me wonder where my shoes went. I can't recall when I last saw them. The man supporting the bulk of my weight doesn't bother to lift me and spare me this one discomfort, even though he could do so with ease. Just goes to show what they think of me here.

Once again, I'm reminded of Dr. Richter's promise. No harm will come to me?

If I had the strength, I'd laugh.

At first, I don't notice when we enter the testing room, my head groggy from lack of sleep and mind delirious from the endless pain engulfing my body. My senses only sharpen when the cold metal surface of the table grazes my aching skin, snapping my brain to attention.

The fear buried inside me crawls back to the surface as what follows happens just as it did the first time. The IVs. The monitors. The group of doctors in white coats. The metal halo around my head.

A whimper rolls over my lips, but I can't find the will or

the energy to cry, even though that's all I want to do. Maybe because, despite how desperately I crave death, I don't want the people here to have the satisfaction of knowing they've broken me.

I don't want *him* to have that satisfaction.

"Proceed," Dr. Richter says with a smile.

A scream rips from my lungs as the lightning bolt cuts through my head, strike after strike exploding inside my brain and setting my vision on fire. I grind my teeth, searching for the strength to fight through the pain, but the ceaseless assault is unbearable. There's no escaping the agony, just like there's no escaping the fact that this will eventually kill me. But when?

When will this torment finally stop?

*Please,* I beg my body. *I don't care what you do. Just make it stop.*

For a moment, the strikes come to an end. I sag as much as the halo around my head and the steel bands retraining my torso and legs allow, gasping and gagging up the minimal contents of my stomach. Sweat drenches my skin, plastering the paper-thin gown against my emaciated limbs. I blink several times to clear my blurred vision, but the room and everything in it is obscured. All I can make out are indistinct figures.

A male voice enters my ears from somewhere on my right. "There's been a neural oscillation of her central nervous system."

I don't know what that means. I don't even care.

Until—

"Again," Dr. Richter commands.

*No!* I try to scream, but the word is cut off in my throat by the electric current passing through the halo straight into my head. It shoots through me in repetitive jolts, disabling every part of my body and rendering my thoughts incoherent. Tears stream down my face, and I cry out with each stab.

*End this!* I plead with myself. *End this!*

Another stab.

*End this!*

I release a strangled scream, but the sound is swallowed by the inky darkness stretching across the laboratory, drowning the sterile white of the room until all I can see is black. When my surroundings come back into focus, I'm standing in what I think is the middle of Zone 1, looking out upon a vast scene of destruction. It's just like it was the first time I saw it this way. Every last detail is exactly the same, from the murky air right down to the debris by my feet.

I turn in place—equal parts astounded and horrified by the crumbling city around me—and realize, although begrudgingly, that Dr. Richter's experiments seem to have worked. He's encouraged my brain to recreate what I saw during my exam, but what comes now that he's succeeded? What can he possibly garner from having me relive this frightening hallucination?

*Vision,* I correct myself. It's strange to admit, but I can feel in my bones that it's true. What I'm seeing…

It's the future that awaits us.

A shiver passes over my skin at the crunching of footsteps in dirt, and the hairs on the back of my neck all raise, like the hackles on a growling dog. Stance rigid, I crane my head, peeking over my shoulder.

A breath catches somewhere between my lungs and my throat as I meet the piercing gaze of the man standing behind me. He looks to be a few years older than me—his early twenties if I had to venture a guess. Disheveled blond hair lay matted against his forehead, slick with dirt and sweat, and his hazel eyes are bursting with warmth but also tinged with the unmistakable coldness of grief. Gray smudges from the ash in the air stain both his cheeks.

I glance between his face and the gun in his hand, then back again, rooted to the spot by fear. Tears flood his eyes, and one breaks loose, cutting a clean line through the filth on his skin. As another tear follows, his lips move, shaping words, but the silence swallows each one. Even when I strain my ears, his voice still doesn't reach me.

Although my eyes and mind are entrenched in this vision, it's as if my body and hearing are stuck back in the laboratory at the DSD. They anchor me to my horrific reality.

"We can't get a clear picture, Doctor," a female voice announces from somewhere on my right.

"You have my authorization to proceed with the intravenous method we discussed earlier. Do whatever you feel is necessary. I *want* that picture."

A hand runs over my face, but I can't see it. I can only feel the fingers prying my eyelids apart and the burning sensation sinking into my pupils. Screams rip from my chest, but the restraints hold me still.

Bursts of static distort the stranger's face as a searing heat radiates over my eyeballs. It's as if two knife-points are piercing my pupils, and no amount of begging will make my suffering end. I am at Dr. Richter's mercy, and he doesn't seem to know what that word means.

More screams escape as the burning continues. A jostling movement knocks my head, and then everything jumps into sharp focus.

"There! Stop! We have a clear picture now!"

The pain ceases at once, and everything around me goes still. At a glance, my surroundings seem unchanged apart from the sudden deafening hiss of wind, which whips back and forth around me, kicking up a fog of dust.

I peer at the man through the haze, wondering if I'll be able to hear him now, but his face is a blur. Tears obscure my vision, hiding his face.

"I'm sorry, Wynter," he breathes, giving his head a slight shake. I blink the moisture from my eyes as his fingers slacken, and the gun in his hand drops to the dirt with a resounding thud.

"End the session," Dr. Richter commands.

The pain in my eyes returns as the vision dissolves and I fall back into welcoming darkness. Unconsciousness envelops me, but I'm shaken awake by a hand forcefully slapping my cheek.

"How do you know him?"

A weary breath passes through my cracked lips. "What?"

My eyes inch open. Dr. Richter stands over me, his leering gaze pressing me for answers I don't have.

In my peripheral vision, I take note of the silver cart positioned next to the table. Two bloody needles lay on the tray, attached to thin tubes.

*"No harm will come to you,"* he had said.

I blink, and tears stream down the sides of my face.

"The facial recognition server has brought up a match," a woman says from the other side of the room. "The man in question is Ezra Laramie, age twenty-two. Suspected member of PHOENIX."

*PHOENIX?*

Dr. Richter lunges forward and grabs me roughly by the neck. "How do you know him?" he asks again, yelling this time.

"I don't!" I cry, my voice feeble and raspy.

He glares at me, searching my eyes for a lie, then straightens and releases his deadly grip on my throat. Exhaling through his nose, he takes a step back.

"You will," he promises, his tone lethal.

When he snaps his fingers, orderlies appear at my side as if popping out of thin air.

"Take the subject back to her quarters," Dr. Richter instructs them.

The orderlies unclip the restraints and raise the halo, then lower my trembling body from the sweat-drenched table. As they drag me toward the door—showing no compassion or mercy in how they handle me—my unfocused gaze creeps back toward Dr. Richter.

"Contact the authorities," he barks at a pink-faced older man, who jumps and runs from the room. "I want a red alert sent out on the fugitive."

I don't understand why he's so angry. What's caused this reaction in him? Why does he want the man I saw arrested? Is it because they think he's in PHOENIX?

Or is there another reason?

I raise my head, releasing a single strained word. "Why?" But he doesn't hear me, and within seconds, I'm once again surrounded by darkness.

# SEVEN

**I GRUNT WHEN MY BODY** hits the hard concrete floor, the impact jerking me awake. Black spots dance in front of my eyes as the orderlies retreat for the hallway, the echo of their footsteps rattling around in my brain like loose screws shaken free of their bearings. My fingers dig into my aching skull as the locking mechanism of the door clicks into place, trapping me once again in my prison.

My arms shudder beneath me when I push myself up, my elbows giving out under my weight when a stabbing in my temples drags me down to the floor. With each stab, I'm assaulted by what I saw in the laboratory, the images burnt into the backs of my eyelids, ensuring I can never escape them.

My eyes squeeze shut as my body convulses, and in my head, I see the man from my vision again. The silence between us is filled with those same three bewildering words he muttered before.

*"I'm sorry, Wynter."*

I press my cheek against the cold concrete and draw in one deep breath, then another. Gradually, the stabbing in my temples recedes. As the pain fades away, the stranger's face dissolves into darkness.

My eyes flutter open, my blurred vision slowly adjusting to the familiar surroundings of my room. My cell. As it all shifts back into focus, I glance at the table at the end of the bed. My mouth and throat are so dry the muscles are spasming, tightening like a hand around my neck. I can barely breathe past the sensation.

Desperate for water, I claw my way toward the table, dragging my limp legs behind me. The drugs Dr. Richter's underlings sedated me with have worn off a little, leaving my body paralyzed only from the waist down—a slight improvement but still crippling enough that relief eludes me. Between my unbearable thirst and the worrying, periodic pain eating away at my brain, Dr. Richter seems surprisingly determined to let me suffer for someone who claims to want me alive.

Fresh beads of sweat rise across my flaming skin, and my head is spinning by the time I cross the room to the glossy white table. With the last of my strength, I fling my hand onto the computerized surface, blindly pressing the touchscreen. As my fingers slip away, a robotic arm descends from the ceiling with what I hope will be my salvation.

To my relief, the arm places a transparent cup on the table, which I can see is filled almost to the brim with water. I reach for it hungrily and slump against the side of the bed, downing the cure for my thirst within seconds and without once stopping to take a breath. The instant I'm finished, my fingers slacken, and I drop the plastic cup to the floor.

Exhausted, I lean my head against the stiff mattress and close my eyes, eager to sleep off the events of today before the orderlies return tomorrow and I have to go through it all over again. Despite my fatigue, the memory of what I saw replays in my head on a loop, nagging at me. I can't shut it out anymore than I could shut out a screeching alarm drilling into my ears.

Who was that man I saw? Why was he sorry? How does he know me? Or, if what I saw was the future like Dr. Richter claims…

How *will* he know me?

The part I struggle to wrap my head around most is the idea of the man being a member of PHOENIX. If that's true, that means he's a terrorist. An insurgent. An enemy of the State. And if what I saw in my vision is real, then I have to assume this means I will eventually have ties to PHOENIX as well.

But how? I'll never leave this place alive, and no one is coming to save me. There's no way our paths would ever cross. Besides, I've always played by the rules. I'm not a rebel. I don't want to stand out. I don't want to fight back against the State or join a renegade organization, despite what I've been through here.

All I want is to survive.

In the midst of my frantic thoughts, it occurs to me that this is the first time I've actually been able to put a face to someone in PHOENIX. Their arrests and executions are never broadcast on the news—"So we don't give them the infamy they yearn for," my mother explained when I once asked her why. All we, the law-abiding citizens of the State, know is that the organization is comprised of criminals who would do anything and go to any lengths to ensure the collapse of society. I guess I've always figured its members would look the part they've been typecast to play.

The role of the monster.

But that man, Ezra Laramie, he seemed…normal, for lack of a better word. Grief-stricken, panicked, even, but normal.

The way he stared at me with that pleading expression, tears sliding down his cheeks…

Is that what a monster would look like?

Doubt spreads over my skin. Throughout my eighteen years in this world, I've been guided and shaped by the information supplied by the State and by the adults who know better than me. But now, I can't help wondering how much of what I've been force-fed my whole life is true. Even worse, how much of it was a lie? I've never questioned the State's teachings before. I never had cause to.

Until now.

Suddenly, I'm overwhelmed by the desire to find out the truth of this world for myself. To discover what's happening to me. To unbury the facts concerning the society we live in. To learn the truth about PHOENIX. I need to separate fact from fiction…

And I think I know where to look for those answers.

The only path forward is to track down Ezra Laramie, if not to get the answers I seek then to find out why he appeared in my vision. There has to be a reason. Besides, searching for PHOENIX—fearsome terrorist group or not—seems like a better alternative than staying here and suffering through another one of Dr. Richter's experiments.

I can't go back in that laboratory. Not after what I've just seen or what Dr. Richter and his lackeys put me through today. Regardless of whether they plan to kill me or simply run more tests, I can't take any more.

So, I need to escape. But how? No one leaves the DSD alive, and I can't exactly fight my way out. Plus, there's the other glaring issue. Even if I do manage to escape, how will I find Ezra Laramie?

The answer strikes me with the same intensity as before, and on reflex, my body doubles over as a sensation unlike anything I've ever felt before explodes inside my brain.

I'm too tired to scream, so I bite down on my tongue to distract myself from what feels like my skull splitting open. Blood pools in my mouth, and the metallic taste is almost pleasant compared to the pain.

As the stabbing in my head eases, the square gray room fades into the inky blackness of what looks to be a narrow street. The shine of halogen lights reflects off the broken asphalt from a dingy bar in the distance, pushing back the gloom. Even from the opposite end of the street, I can read the sign over the door with ease.

# THE VEGA

Each glowing letter flickers in turn as the bulbs buzz with a sinister hum.

I glance at a signpost behind my left shoulder, printed with the location name B42. The rusting metal also bears the circular symbol representing Zone 7.

A cry swells in my throat as the pressure inside my brain re-emerges and expands outward, beating against the walls of my skull as if searching for an escape. Or maybe it's just determined to cause me as much pain as possible. In my ears, I hear the unmistakable sound of glass shattering, and as a scream rips from my lungs, I lurch backward, a ringing vibration filling my head when it slams into something hard behind me. My chest heaves as my gaze moves across my fuzzy surroundings, noting the cold gray walls of my cell.

Bed. My head hit the bed.

My eyes flick up to what remains of the mirror above the sink then down to the floor where the rest of the glass lies scattered around my feet in large fragments. How did it break? Confusion barrels through me as I reach out a shaking hand and carefully pick up a shard. A shallow network of cracks spreads over the glass like a spiderweb, distorting what I can see of my face. The whites of my eyes are blood red again, and my pupils are blown wide, reducing the green and blue irises to a thin, barely visible rim.

I gape at my reflection in horror. How long have I looked like this? Days? Weeks? Or is my appearance a result of today's "successful" experiment? Either way, what's happening to me?

What has Dr. Richter done?

Clutching the jagged shard in my hand, I allow my head to flop back against the mattress and snap my eyes shut, lacking the energy to face all these questions right now. Time passes in a fitful daze as I drift in and out of consciousness. I'm not sure how long I stay this way, but eventually, the feeling returns to my numb legs, rousing me a little.

It's the shrill staccato of beeps outside the door that shakes me fully awake. My body tenses as my gaze moves from the closed door to the security camera in the corner to my left. The red light is still blinking, watching me, but if I'm going to escape, it's now or never. I might not survive the next experiment.

I turn, squaring my back to the camera, and wedge the glass shard in my hand beneath the mattress while resting my cheek on the blanket. To the unsuspecting eye, it will look like I've just moved into a more comfortable position to sleep. Hopefully.

The door springs open at the same moment my hand drops

to my side. Forcing a yawn, I make a show of opening my eyes, blinking sleepily at the tall female attendant in the doorway. To my complete lack of surprise, her blank expression matches the emotionless demeanor displayed by everyone else I've encountered here. Hell, it's the same look I've noticed on almost everyone throughout my life.

Everyone except my father.

The woman spares a quick glance at the shards on the floor, a hint of curiosity raising one thin brow before she looks back up at me. "Dr. Richter would like to speak with you. Once you're dressed, I will escort you to meet him."

She watches my every move with predatory focus as I push up from the floor, trying to find my balance on shaking legs that seem hell-bent on not supporting my weight. Trembling, I reach for the pants folded on the bedspread behind me, taking my time to slide them on underneath the sweat-soaked gown as I try to figure out my next plan of action. When I raise my arms to change into the starchy gray shirt, my body spasms, and I have to bite my lip to keep from crying out. A fresh pair of shoes sit beside my bed—the first I've noticed in weeks— which I slip my feet into, suppressing a whimper.

"Follow me," the woman says, her tone clipped.

As she turns into the hallway, my gaze falls to the mattress. *Now or never*, I remind myself.

I let out a breath and drop to one knee, yanking the shard out from its hiding place and tucking it inside the left sleeve of my shirt. The woman reappears in the doorway, annoyance creasing her brow, just as I press the glass flat to my wrist. I quickly look down at the floor and pretend to adjust the heel of my shoes.

After a convincing delay, I rise and follow her out into the otherwise empty corridor. The path we tread is familiar, even though I've only walked it once before. Eventually, we stop beside the closed door of our destination—one of many in an identical sea of doors but only one out of a few that I fear.

The woman enters the unlocking code into the keypad, each piercing beep like the smash of a hammer driving into my skull. When the door slides open, my eyes fall on Dr. Richter, who is already inside the room waiting for me.

"Take a seat," he orders.

I look back over my shoulder at the woman, but I only catch a glimpse of her face before the door slides shut between us.

Curling my fingers over the shard in my sleeve, I shuffle over to the chair opposite Dr. Richter.

He gives me a quick once-over. "You look like hell."

I clench my jaw. "What have you done to me?"

He removes his glasses and wipes the lenses clean on the lapel of his white coat. "I haven't done anything that your body wouldn't have naturally embraced on its own. I merely sped up the process."

My mouth goes dry. "What do you mean?"

Dr. Richter meets my gaze with a smirk, returning his glasses to their perch on his nose. "You are evolving. Developing abilities those unlike you can only dream of possessing. Although I was uncertain of it before, this last trial has confirmed my suspicions. You are precisely what I thought you would be."

*What. Not who,* I note.

"You said I wouldn't be harmed. You said I would be treated with civility—"

"Yes," he admits, interrupting me with a shrug. "But sacrifices must always be made for the advancement of science."

*Sacrifices?* I nearly scream.

How can he act so apathetic about what they've done to me? What *he's* done to me? What I went through was torture, plain and simple. Not that I shouldn't have seen it coming considering that's what the DSD is known for.

I chew on my lower lip for a moment, mulling over the questions piling up in my head. Is what he said true? Would the changes happening in my body have occurred anyway, even without his experiments? Was this pain, this agony, always inevitable?

Dr. Richter's voice is like a slap to the face, pulling me from the abyss of my thoughts. "I brought you here today to discuss what you saw." When I don't speak, he lets out a sharp exhalation, pinching the bridge of his nose between his thumb and forefinger. "Your vision." He sneers, clearly losing his patience. "Was it a continuation of what you saw during your placement exam?"

I shake my head. "More like...a missing piece out of the middle."

His eyes flash behind his glasses as he leans toward me, folding his hands on the table. "How does it end?"

His tone unnerves me, sending a jarring chill over my skin. I hesitate, and in this moment, I'm more certain than ever that my life is in danger. That certainty reaffirms my need to escape.

Dr. Richter pushes back his chair and jumps to his feet. Slamming his fists down on the table in front of me, he raises his voice, shouting, "How does it end?"

I notice the subtle twitch of his cheeks and the way sweat

beads along his neatly combed hairline. His fingers curl inward until his hands are in fists, the knuckles straining white against the metal surface of the table.

As his composure crumbles, I feel something that could almost be mistaken for happiness. For the first time since waking up in this horrible place, it's almost as if the roles are reversed. Now, he's the one showing weakness.

Now, I'm the one with the power.

"We all die," I say with a smile.

# EIGHT

AVERTING HIS GAZE, DR. RICHTER looks down at his tablet and swipes a finger across the top of the screen. In a calm voice, he says, "Could you please come back in?"

The woman from before re-enters the room, her expression hollow as she stands in the doorway like an obedient soldier, awaiting her orders.

"Take the subject back to the laboratory and prep the team for another session," Dr. Richter instructs.

"What?" My fingers grasp the edge of the table as panic weighs me down in my seat.

"So soon?" the woman asks, looking genuinely taken aback as she furrows her dark manicured brow.

Dr. Richter ignores the woman's question and approaches the door, brushing past her and stepping one foot out into the corridor. He then pauses to look back at me, his body straddling the threshold.

"We will retrieve the vision in its entirety, no matter what it takes."

I blink, my jaw dropping at the lack of remorse present in

both his gaze and tone. *Doesn't he realize that his last test could've killed me? Does he even care?*

I shake my head. "You know I can't control it—"

"You will learn to!" he growls. The anger behind his words spreads into his skin, flushing his cheeks until his whole face is ruddy. "You *will* lead me to him!"

*To him?* I muse, thinking of the blond stranger's face. *Or to PHOENIX?*

What is Dr. Richter actually after?

As this question takes shape in my head, a scream rips from my lungs, ravaging the inside of my throat. A sharp pain slices into every inch of my skull, and as the pain spreads, a violent spasm tears through my body, rattling me down to my bones. In what little awareness I manage to cling to, I wonder if I'm going to die. *Finally,* part of me thinks with relief while the rest of me screams, *No! I'm not ready!* Wrenching to the side, I fall out of my seat.

As my body seizes against the cold floor, a crystal clear image ignites in my brain. I see that bar again. *The Vega,* I recall from the glowing halogen sign. Except, this time, I'm inside the establishment rather than seeing it from the outside. An older man with a bushy beard and a shining bald head stands behind the wrap-around bar, drying a wet glass with a questionable looking gray and brown rag that's definitely seen better days. Before him, three people sit at the high counter, one of whom I recognize.

*It's him,* my brain registers as the image quickly fades before thrusting me into a fresh hell of pain. My hand shoots out and clutches the nearest table leg as I ride out the stabs in my head. Sweat and tears drip from my face to the floor.

"What have you just seen?" The rich timbre of Dr. Richter's lilting voice is a faint thrum on the edge of consciousness. The deafening ringing in my ears is almost enough to drown him out.

The soles of his shiny black shoes squeak against the floor as he closes the distance between us. Crouching beside me, he grabs hold of my shirt, his knuckles roughly grazing my collarbone.

"Answer me!"

His outburst ejects spittle onto my cheeks, but I don't raise a hand to wipe it away. I don't move at all. I don't even speak. I just glare into those soulless gray eyes in silence, determined not to cave.

Sneering, Dr. Richter loosens his claw-like grip on my shirt and shoves me away as he rises. My body careens to the side, and as I collide with the ground, my head slams into the tiles. Black spots stain my vision, and a moan rumbles low in my throat.

Biting back a sob, I reach up a trembling hand and grab the edge of the table. Slowly, I pull myself up to my feet, keeping one hand on the metal surface for support until my legs are steady.

Once I'm certain I won't tip over, I risk a wary glance at Dr. Richter. His focus has turned from me and is now fixed in the direction of the open doorway, his eyes locked with the female attendant's, who stands with a hand in her pocket, as if waiting for him to give her an order. My pulse skyrockets when he nods and she pulls a syringe free from her sterile white coat.

Tensing, I stumble back into the corner. I won't let them do this to me. Not anymore.

*Never again,* I silently vow.

Remembering the shard of mirror pressed close to my wrist, I shake the glass piece loose from my sleeve. The jagged edges dig into my palm. "Stay away from me," I whisper.

The woman inches toward me, disregarding my warnings, her hand clutching the syringe. My fingers tighten around the glass.

"I said stay away from me!" My arm shoots upward as I brandish the broken piece of mirror like a knife.

The woman hesitates, pausing mid-step, assessing the threat with a curious tilt of her head. I blink a few times to bring her face into focus, but her features are a blur, the sweat dripping into my eyes blinding me as I scramble for a way to escape this. But there is no escape, is there? The only way this ends is with me back on that table.

The only way this ends is with me dead.

Pressure pushes against the walls of my head, coaxing a strangled hiss from my lips. As the room spins, I wrap my free hand around the top of my skull, as if that will somehow keep my brain from exploding. My nails dig into my scalp as the pressure worsens, sinking into the skin, drawing blood. The warm sticky wetness seeps into my hair and runs in a single thin line down my cheek.

A shriek surges up from my lungs, and as the cry breaks loose, all the pain flows out of my body. The pressure shoots out of my head like a cannonball, targeting the mirror behind Dr. Richter, which shatters into hundreds of pieces, the shards falling away from the frame to reveal a hidden observation room on the other side of the wall. At least ten doctors stare back at me with shell-shocked expressions, every last one of them unmoving and exposed.

Chest heaving, I shift my sights back toward the woman. She hasn't moved from her previous spot, her body frozen and face contorted in terror. A tingle of energy buzzes over my skin, a wave of power rising up from within, pulsating like a beating heart as if it's a separate entity living inside me. As if it has a mind of its own. It reaches out for her, fed by my fear.

When my eyes narrow, her fingers slacken, dropping the syringe to the floor. My lips twitch. She reaches for her head, her fingers sliding over her scalp as she gasps. Blue streaks materialize, starting about an inch from her hairline, and creep across her face, displaying a swelling network of veins, which disappears down her neck and under her shirt.

Her eyes roll back, and she falls to her knees. Foam bubbles at the corners of her mouth as she writhes, the saliva mixing with the red tinge of blood. A panicked voice in the back of my head tells me she must've bitten her tongue, but I lack the ability to care. If anything, I only want to cause her more pain.

Dr. Richter drops to his knees and flips the woman onto her side, holding her firm against him throughout the convulsions. His eyes find mine as his lips shape hurried words, shouting at me, but I can't hear him.

My eyes squeeze shut as the pressure returns to my head, crushing my brain like a grape in a fist. My legs buckle, threatening to drag me back down to the floor, and every intake of air is a struggle as the chaos around me seems to slow to a standstill.

But then, the universe springs back into motion, forcing time into a forward lurch and popping the soundproof bubble around me. My eyelids pry apart at the inhuman wail that suddenly pierces my ears, and I glance down to find the attendant thrashing in Dr. Richter's arms, her skin so white it's almost translucent. Blood trickles in a steady, constant stream from her nose and ears as if her insides are melting.

With one last heaving cry, the woman goes limp. Dr. Richter stares at her unmoving body for a long moment before daring to meet my gaze. "What have you done to her?" he asks, his voice breathless.

A wave of dizziness knocks me off balance, and a surge of bile rushes into my mouth as whatever power possessed me releases its unwanted hold on my mind. It's as if a fog has been lifted off my senses, returning me to myself. I shake my head a few times to clear it.

The woman's still body catches my eye, and I know without having to ask that she's dead. Did I really do that to her? I couldn't have...could I?

I peer down at my hands. Although I didn't physically touch her, they might as well be covered with her blood. A tear streaks down my cheek.

I did this. I killed her.

Swallowing the urge to vomit, I stagger forward one unsteady step then force myself to take another. This place is destroying me, and if I don't jump at the chance to leave now, it'll consume not only what remains of my sanity but my humanity. I can't let that happen.

My entire arm trembles as I inch toward Dr. Richter and lift the shard of glass to his throat. "Take off your coat." When he doesn't move, I push the sharp tip of the mirror into his jugular until it draws blood. Only a pinprick but enough to show him I'm serious.

"All right," he says quickly. "Let's just remain calm. You're in shock, I can see that. Let me help you."

"Help?" A barking laugh rocks my body. "I don't want any more of your *help*." I spit the word like it's acid on my tongue. "I just want to leave. Now, I won't say it again. Take off your coat."

His lips press together as he shrugs out of the pristine white garment, and when he hands it to me, I pull it on, even though he's several inches taller than me and the fabric swamps my body. I look like a child dressed up in her father's clothing, but I only need it to disguise me enough that no one here will spare me a second glance. That's all it is. A disguise.

Well, the closest thing I'll find to one, anyway.

Peering at the empty doorway, I back away slowly from Dr. Richter, keeping my weapon raised in warning. My steps are calculated and cautious, spurred on by the tenuous belief that I might get out of here and actually achieve what no one before me has managed.

*I might leave the DSD alive.*

That thought gives me the courage to step out of the room, and yet...once I'm in the hallway, a burning question I can't find the strength to ignore any longer holds me back against my will. Pausing, I clench my hands into fists and peek over my shoulder at Dr. Richter. He hasn't moved from where he still sits on the floor, his gray eyes cast down at the small puddle of blood under the attendant's head stretching out across the white tile.

"That man I saw... Why do you want me to find him?" I ask.

His mouth hitches up into a tiny smile. "He's a criminal. And all enemies of the State must be brought to justice."

*Enemy of the State...*

"Is that really the reason?"

"Why?" He looks up at me through his glasses, cocking an eyebrow. "Is that who you're planning on running off to for help?"

I strain my jaw, afraid to say anything that might give even the slightest indication where I'm going after I leave this prison.

Dr. Richter seems to see right through my silence.

"If you think you can trust him, you're wrong. If you think he'll protect you, he won't."

Keeping my face blank, I glance down at the body beside him. "I don't think I need protection. Do you?"

As these words leave my lips, I turn away and press on down the corridor, desperate to put as much distance between myself and Dr. Richter as possible. I don't want him to see the tears in my eyes or the mask of false strength as it slips from my face. I just need to get away from him. Far, far away. Even if that means I have to join PHOENIX.

Trust doesn't come into the equation for me.

Still, his warning follows my every step as I move through the building, keeping my pace slow and controlled to avoid the attention of the watching cameras. At any moment, an influx of Enforcers will probably arrive to detain me. But no one comes.

No one tries to stop me.

My heart pounds in my ears, muting my footsteps, as I progress through the labyrinthine facility, taking blind turn after blind turn with no idea which direction I should head in. After countless corridors and what feels like several hours of searching, the main lobby slides into view.

Dread tickles my skin as I assess my surroundings. The space is large—spanning at least two stories—and open with minimal furnishings, which are all in varying shades of white and gray. Everything is clinical and clean. There's also nowhere to hide. The path to the doors is wide open, but to get there, I'd be in plain sight of the enemy.

A grimace warps my lips as I consider my options. Getting here was easy enough, but escaping from W. P. Headquarters was easy, too, and look how that fiasco turned out. Getting out of the DSD is a whole other story. I also can't figure out why Dr. Richter hasn't raised the alarm. He's had plenty of time to do so, and—tracking chip aside—it's not like I have a home to run to this time that he can track me down to and corner me at. I could go anywhere in the city, so why hasn't anyone come after me?

What is he waiting for?

I press my back to the wall beside me and glance around the corner, eyeing the row of revolving glass doors standing like sentries at the opposite side of the lobby. My way out. The *only* way out. Four guards keep watch by the long line of turnstiles separating me from liberation.

I draw in a wheezing breath, shrinking back out of sight, as panic claws at my throat. This won't be possible. It won't. There's no such thing as escape from this place.

My teeth grit together as I force myself to think of the man I saw in my vision. Possible or not, I've come this far. I can't give up now. I at least have to try.

I have to find out who he is.

Exhaling through my nose, I thrust the shard of glass into the right pocket of Dr. Richter's white coat. Then, before I can talk myself out of this half-baked, possibly—*most definitely*, I correct myself—suicidal plan, I turn the corner and trudge toward the doors with confidence, like I belong. Like I'm just another one of the monsters.

My footsteps merge with the others echoing through the lobby, adding to the quiet whir of movement. No one takes any notice of me, igniting a brief flicker of hope, which fades the closer I get to the turnstiles, my eyes landing on the small raised box connected to the closed partitions. Horror and realization both dawn on me at the same moment. If I prick my finger, the alarm will go off. I don't have the security clearance to leave, which means I'll just be handed back over to Dr. Richter and his team of minions. I've been dealing with these security checkpoints for eighteen years and I only just think of this now? What is wrong with me?

Well, aside from the obvious.

My stomach turns when it occurs to me that maybe this is why Dr. Richter hasn't raised the alarm. Why would he if he knows I have no way to escape?

Heart racing, I shift my eyes from side to side, frantically searching for a solution. To my right, eight doctors or maybe attendants—I'm not quite sure which—are walking in a tight-knit group, also on their way out of the building. Out of options, I make the split-second decision to fall into the line they're forming in front of the checkpoint. With my stolen disguise, I easily blend into the mass of white coats.

The weight on my chest eases just a little. "Thanks, Doc," I mutter under my breath.

The shrill beeping of the turnstile computers grows louder as we approach, screaming their approval. Beep, after beep, after beep as each person waiting proceeds forward through the glass barriers. When the man in front of me pricks his finger and the partition before us slides open with a hiss, I take advantage of the opportunity presenting itself.

This is the only chance I'll get.

Holding my breath, I press my chest flat against the man's back and push through the barrier just one step behind him before the gate can close. To my relief, the sensor doesn't pick up my intrusion.

As we come out on the other side, the man throws an odd look at me over his shoulder, no doubt startled by my unexpected proximity. I turn my head to hide my face, grumbling an apology. Before he can say anything in response, I hurry away toward the revolving glass doors.

When I step outside, the frigid winter breeze hits me like a slap in the face—cold but fresh in comparison to the stale, odorous air I've been breathing for months. Relishing the burn of every inhalation, I choke out a laugh and sprint away from this nightmare as fast as my legs can carry me.

As I race into the night, a worrying thought gnaws at me. What if I was only able to leave because the DSD allowed me to leave? Because Dr. Richter let me leave? What if, the entire time, he was watching me but chose not to intervene?

If that's the case, there's only one reason I can think of as to why he would do that. Why he would risk losing his precious experiment.

He thinks I'll lead him to the man from my vision.

He thinks I'll lead him to Ezra Laramie.

# NINE

MY GAZE LINGERS ON THE metal sign towering over me where the insignia for Zone 7 looms over the road. I have to keep moving. I can't go home, and there's no one else I can turn to for help. There's nowhere left for me to go.

Not if I want to survive.

Clenching my jaw, I peer down at my arm and tug up the white coat's oversized sleeve until my left wrist is exposed. Even though it isn't visible, I know the chip is there, buried under my skin—a homing beacon to Dr. Richter, telling him exactly where I am.

A stuttering breath trickles out from between my trembling lips. I can't put this off any longer. I escaped from the DSD hours ago, and at every point I stopped to remove the chip, one excuse or another held me back from doing what has to be done to be free of my captors for good. I told myself that if I left it in place, Dr. Richter would be more inclined to keep his distance because it would seem like I was leading him to PHOENIX, just like he wants. That if I removed it before the opportune moment, he would realize what I was planning and send his subordinates to haul me back to his lair. That's what I said to myself as a way of shifting the blame away from my fear.

But the excuses end now.

Tremors run over my fingers as I thrust them inside Dr. Richter's coat pocket, a gasp catching in my throat when the jagged edges of the broken mirror graze my skin. My nerves waver, but I tighten my grip, resolved.

"I can do this," I whisper.

With a hurried glance at my seemingly deserted surroundings, I slink into a nearby alley, stepping out of sight of any hidden prying eyes into a shroud of darkness. The cover of shadow obscures my vision, but that might be for the best. I don't want to see what I'm about to do anyway.

My hand twitches as I drag the sharp edge of the glass in a horizontal line a few inches above the hem of the coat, cutting back and forth through the fabric with rough jabs until a mangled strip comes loose from the stitching. I then roll the torn fabric into a ball and jam it inside my mouth, biting down.

Exhaling through my nose, I angle the pointed tip of the mirror against my naked wrist. Fear pulses through my body, and for a moment, I don't move any more than that, daunted by the potential consequences of what I'm about to do. One single slip is all it would take. One mistake and I'll die here in this alley.

*At least then I would be free of Dr. Richter.*

I shake my head to rid myself of that thought, pushing away the horrific mental image of my possible death. The chips are located in this spot for a reason—so people won't attempt what I'm so foolishly about to do. But it has to be done.

There's no other way.

Clamping my teeth down, I push the shard into my wrist,

piercing the flesh before I can talk myself out of it. A grunt swells in my chest, but my cries are muffled, muted by the ball of cloth in my mouth. Blood pools from the wound and drips from my arm onto the pavement below.

My fingers work the glass, turning the tip around inside my arm, as my nerve endings scream, making me light-headed and nauseous and a million other things in-between. Still, I jiggle the mirror, searching, even as drowsiness overwhelms me.

I squeeze my eyes shut so I don't have to look at the blood, the red somehow startlingly clear in the gloom. I bite down harder, straining my jaw.

*I have to stay awake. I have to find it.* I repeat these words to myself like a chant, clinging to consciousness, until, finally, after what seems like hours of agony, the glass tip scrapes something hard.

The chip.

Gasping, I fall back against the brick wall behind me and peek one eye open, trying not to jostle my arm. Through my blurring vision, I can just make out the glint of gold protruding from my wrist like a splinter.

I tilt the glass shard flat against my palm to free my pointer finger and thumb, which I use to pinch the small piece of metal, tugging it all the way free from my wrist. Wincing, I let out a shaking breath and carefully hold it up to eye level.

Fortunately, the chips, which are implanted right after we're born, are only good for identification and tracking purposes—and for making payments, since they're directly linked to our personal bank and pension accounts. They don't keep any record of vital signs, though, which means, if I leave the chip here in one piece, it'll look like I've just stopped to rest for the night. Dr. Richter and his team won't have any way of knowing I cut the damn thing out until tomorrow morning when they realize I haven't moved for a while and consider the option that I might be dead. By the time they come to investigate, I'll be long gone from here. Hopefully.

The vertigo swarming my head makes me think otherwise, threatening to topple me over. If I allow this exhaustion to consume me, I know I won't get up again. If I let it take hold, I'm as good as dead.

*Fight. Stay awake. You have to keep moving.*

At this thought, a burst of adrenaline rushes through my veins, and I find my balance, managing to stay on my feet. Before this energy can fade, I flick the chip into the densest patch of darkness at the other end of the alley where a large brick wall forms a clear dead end. The shadows swallow that small discarded piece of my identity whole.

I hiss as a burning pain expands over my wrist—the freezing night air grazing across my torn skin only making my discomfort worse—and with a low growl, I glance at the open wound and the blood, which is showing no signs of stopping or even slowing down any time soon. My jaw slackens, and the balled up fabric falls from my mouth, unraveling across my outstretched arm as a cloud of steam billows in the air in front of my face from where my hot breath reacts to the icy cold. Aware I need to get the bleeding under control if I'm going to last beyond the next ten minutes, I bite at the cloth, my teeth working in an awkward partnership with my fingers, wrapping it around my wrist and pulling the fabric as tight as I can bear. This makeshift bandage won't be enough to staunch the bleeding, but it'll have to do until I can close up the wound.

Or before I bleed to death.

Whichever comes first.

I blink a few times to clear the fuzzy haze from my eyes and pull Dr. Richter's coat sleeve back into position, the cuff hiding the bulk of the bandage. My fingers loosen to drop the shard but tighten at the last possible moment when I consider that I might need it again. Any weapon is better than no weapon at all, especially considering where I'm going.

Resolved, I drop the bloodied glass back inside the deep pocket.

When I push away from the wall, my legs buckle without the support, and the world spins on its axis as a sudden dizziness turns my stomach. Lurching forward, I retch several times, spewing stomach acid and bile onto the pavement.

Once the nausea stops triggering my gag reflex, I stumble out of the alley toward freedom. My feet drag, and I trip every few steps as I walk, searching for the sign from my vision, shivering against the cold. The night is thick, and the fog clouding my eyes only makes my task that much harder.

The streets are empty. I've never been this far from home before, and I can barely even believe I'm in the same city considering the significant differences between this zone and the one I grew up in. The buildings are derelict, the roads cracked and filthy, and the narrow homes are stacked so closely together they resemble shacks more than actual houses. The State must not bother with upkeep this far out from the central zones. There aren't even any security cameras hidden among the eaves of the buildings or attached to the street lamps that I can see—although, that's a good thing for me given the fact that I'm trying to stay off the DSD's radar.

Still, despite my need for invisibility, a shudder of fear

ricochets up my spine. Crime in this zone must run rampant without the constant watchful eye of the State. For all I know, I could be walking through these streets with a target on my back.

As I trudge forward, frantically searching the shadows for danger where it might not even exist, I find myself feeling sorry for those unfortunate enough to live out here, regardless of whether they're lawbreakers. Those born here are innocents, subjected to the horrors of residing in an outer zone. In Zone 2, I never had these concerns.

Unlike where I'm from, Zone 7 marks the edge of the city— the final zone before reaching the wall separating us from the unknown dangers outside. Other cities lie beyond the Heart's borders, but travel to them is prohibited without special clearance from the Board of Travel, which is typically only granted to those individuals working in the highest sectors of society. Or to Enforcers, for the rare occasion when their particular skill set is required somewhere else.

This zone is also the home of Detention, the group of facilities I initially thought I was imprisoned at when I first woke up in the DSD. Looking back at everything I've been through, I think Re-education would've been preferable to Dr. Richter's experiments, even if that meant undergoing brainwashing or whatever it is they do to keep people in line once they're released after their sentence. Even if it meant I would've spent the rest of my life in a terrible, low-income job and living in a slum just like this one.

Anything would've been better than torture.

The toe of my shoe catches on a dip in the pavement, and a gasp rips from my lungs when I trip. My arms thrust out to break my fall, my fingers clasping around the nearest object they can find to save my face from the tarmac.

When the ground is no longer rushing upward to meet me, I drag in a few shaking breaths to steady myself. Cold metal digs into my hips, pulling my gaze to the street sign supporting my weight. The emblem for Zone 7 fills my limited field of vision, along with the name of the road.

# B42

I blink, struggling to believe what I'm seeing. Up until now, part of me was still convinced the visions were nothing more than hallucinations concocted by my unhinged brain as a way of processing the stress from, first, my placement exam, and then from my time at the DSD. But seeing this sign in front of me, *really* seeing it, surrounded by a dreary street I've never been to and yet recognize… It's enough to tell me this is actually happening.

It's enough to tell me the visions are real.

My eyes skirt along the empty road, following the path as I see it again in my head. There's no one around, but it's late, and, if I had to guess, past curfew. I can't imagine anyone takes that risk, not even in the outer zones since Enforcers could be on patrol and are probably less lenient with the citizens here, considering their inferior status. Despite not having any cameras to watch them, it seems even the people living in the slums of Zone 7 abide by this one law of the State.

Everyone except for me.

At the far end of the road, I glimpse the bar from my vision. The exterior of the run-down building is just as I remember it, right down to the halogen sign hanging above the wide metal door. The lights seem to flicker at my approach, the bulbs buzzing with a hum of warning.

My feet maneuver around the rain-filled potholes, my steps slow and breathing labored. By the time I reach the door, my heart is beating so hard and fast I can barely think straight.

Swallowing, I raise my hand only to hesitate with my fingers an inch from the rusty handle. Whatever—*whoever*—I find on the other side of this door will change my life, I know it. The actions I take here will set me on a path I won't be able to turn from. If I step through this door, all hope of my old life is gone. Am I ready for that?

Nodding, I brace myself and pull.

As the door swings open, I'm greeted by low amber lighting and the musty, stale smell of old smoke. The stench leaves a strange taste on my tongue, and I grimace, snapping my mouth shut when the odor hits me. Breathing through my nose, I straighten my face into a neutral expression and step into The Vega.

As soon as I pass over the threshold, every eye in the room turns to look at me as if my presence has set off an alarm, stopping me short. I loiter by the doorway, unsure what to do.

Driven by my natural inclination to blend in, I inch forward and plop down on a stool at the bar. The bald bartender watches me with one eyebrow cocked as he dries the glass in his hand with the same dirty rag I saw in my vision. A toothpick sticks out of the left corner of his mouth.

"What can I get ya?" he asks in a gruff voice.

I lick my dried lips, suddenly parched and desperate for a drink. How did I not realize how thirsty I am until now?

"Water," I croak.

With a laugh, he shakes his head and picks up another glass to dry it. "Yer in a bar, sweet cheeks. Water ain't exactly on the menu. You'll have to order somethin' a bit more toxic."

I bite my lip. Alcoholic beverages aren't common in Zone 2. In the higher echelons of society, drinking is seen as a degrading habit, and because of that, it's no longer legal in many places across the Heart. The only reason it hasn't been banned in the outer zones is because consumption still provides a steady income stream—and escape from reality—for the poor. With little else to rely on, they need the support. Either that or the State is hoping it will eventually kill them.

Although I've never consumed alcohol before, I know from my schooling that it won't ease my thirst. Besides, I have no way to pay for a drink now that I don't have my chip. But, from the way the bartender glares at me, I know that if I don't order something soon, there's a good chance I'll be asked to leave. Or be forcibly removed. Then everything I did to get here, like murdering that attendant and nearly killing myself by cutting the tracking chip from my wrist...

All of it will have been for nothing.

As I consider what to do, my eyes trail over the dark, stuffy room, taking in the familiar but unfamiliar surroundings. They almost complete one full rotation of the space before catching on the occupied stool two seats down from mine.

As I take in the shadowed profile of the man sitting there, I forget all about the bartender, who still stands in front of me, waiting for my answer. The sole focus of my attention is the man perched on that seat.

"Well?"

The bartender's deep voice shakes me free of my thoughts, and I force my gaze back to him, clearing my throat. "I'll have what he's having."

I look left, risking another glance at the stranger from my vision. The reason why I'm here.

The bartender follows my gaze. "Sure thing."

He buzzes around behind the counter, returning a moment later with a large glass of amber liquid, which he places in front of me with a disgruntled frown, observing me with narrowed eyes. I wait for him to ask for payment, but he says nothing, instead moving on to serve another customer. I let out a breath, confused but relieved. I've dodged a bullet. For now.

I stare at the tall, chipped glass with uncertainty. I have no idea what to say or do from this point—I didn't plan anything beyond getting here. Maybe because I didn't think I would actually make it this far.

Or maybe because I know how crazy this all is.

I let my gaze drift back to Ezra Laramie, watching him out of my peripheral vision. Pushing aside my shock that he even exists, I ask myself what I should do. Should I tell him I was kidnapped by the DSD after seeing the end of the world during my placement exam? After having a vision that, following months of torture, he just so happened to appear in? I wouldn't blame him if he didn't believe me. Hell, I wouldn't blame him if he were to try to kill me at the mere mention of the DSD.

My fingers wrap around the glass, gripping tightly, and I lift the brim to my lips, hoping the drink will help clear my head. The taste washing over my tongue is unpleasant, and I sputter and choke as the bitter liquid slips down my throat. Coughing, I shove the glass away from me.

"It's an acquired taste."

My body tenses at the enchanting cadence of his voice. Although I've only heard him speak once, I know I would recognize that sound anywhere.

My heart slams into my ribs as I pivot on my stool. When our eyes meet, he jerks his chin toward my glass, his gaze flashing briefly down and then back up again, locking on mine. I glance at the barely touched liquid, embarrassed.

He swings around on his own stool to face me. "You're not from around here." It's not a question.

"I'm here on business," I answer quickly.

"Business?" Skepticism creases his brow, a slight smile tugging up one corner of his mouth as he throws back the rest of his drink. "There isn't much business going down in Zone 7."

My throat tightens. "Not even with PHOENIX?"

The stool legs creak as he shifts over onto the seat between us, bringing himself closer to me. Leaning in so his lips are practically touching my ear, he growls, "I don't know who you are, but you won't find anything involved with PHOENIX here. I'd stop looking if I were you."

He pulls away, his hazel eyes returning to mine, as Dr. Richter's warning purrs in my head.

*"If you think you can trust him, you're wrong. If you think he'll protect you, he won't."*

A shiver coaxes goosebumps to rise on my arms. I push away my unease, focusing on why I came here. It doesn't matter who I do or don't trust, and like I told Dr. Richter, I don't need anyone's protection nor do I expect it. The people of the Heart have always only cared about themselves and their own individual survival. Why would PHOENIX be any different?

No, all I want are answers.

And, like everyone else, I just want to survive.

"Then why else would you be here?" I ask before muttering the one thing I know will definitely get his attention. "Ezra Laramie."

His eyes spring wide as his name breaches my lips in a hiss, and in response, he jumps to his feet, stumbling back a few steps. The stool he was sitting on tips and clatters to the floor with a bang.

As he backs away from me, his gaze drops to the coat tucked around my frail body, his attention fixing on the insignia embroidered over my breast.

His eyes dart back up to mine. "Who are you?"

Before I can answer, he pulls something free from his belt and throws his arm up, pointing a gun at me.

My heart pounds in my ears as I slide off the stool, my balance unsteady as I stare down the polished black barrel.

"Who are you?" he asks again, shouting this time.

The other dozen or so people in the bar are all standing as well now, watching our altercation with interest. Every last one is also holding a weapon, including the bartender, who fixes me with a glare that could melt steel as he pulls a shotgun out from under the counter.

As panic twists my insides, it occurs to me this bar must be a safe house for PHOENIX members. The people in this room are all likely part of the group or support it in one way or another, explaining why my vision led me here.

Gulping, I turn my attention back to Ezra.

"This isn't how it looks."

"Is that so?" He sneers. "Because, from where I'm standing, it looks like you're one of *them*."

"I'm not." My protest is weak and unconvincing, even to my own ears.

He pushes the cold muzzle of the gun against my right temple, sending a shudder through my body, which rocks me right down to my marrow. He takes a step closer, lowering his voice to a venomous snarl. "And why should I believe you?"

I tense my jaw, spitting my response through clenched teeth. "If I was one of them, reinforcements would already be here."

The State doesn't play games. As a member of PHOENIX, he must know that better than anyone. The State wouldn't waste time sending in a single person to clear out this bar when it could more efficiently get the job done by sending a whole team to exterminate the lot. If I was one of them, the Enforcers would already be here.

If I was one of them, he would already be dead.

A flicker of doubt crosses his face, and he wavers. The point of his gun moves away from my skin, coaxing an unbidden whimper from my throat. His eyes cling to mine, making my heart beat even faster.

"We can't take any chances," an older man grumbles behind him. "We should kill her to be sure."

Terror shreds my composure to pieces as Ezra pushes the gun against my forehead. "How do you know my name?" he presses.

I stare at him, unsure how to answer that question. He won't believe the truth—not yet, anyway. And if I lie, that'll only give him cause to shoot me.

I swallow again, trying to push down the rising lump in my throat intent on choking me. My tongue feels too big for my mouth, and I can't seem to remember how to breathe properly let alone speak.

A shadow spreads across Ezra's face, seeping into the details of the bar and casting the world around me in a muted gray darkness. My fingers reach for the counter to steady myself, but my hand doesn't find the edge.

As I sway, Ezra takes a reflexive step back, his expression switching from anger to horror. My vision doubles as I follow his line of sight to the growing puddle of red on the floor by my feet.

My eyes drift down to my wrist, noting the red staining the sleeve of Dr. Richter's white coat. *I've bled through the bandage,* I realize, my thoughts hazy. *Looks like blood loss will be what kills me.*

I should've known what I did would catch up with me. I was stupid to think this would end any other way but with me dead.

My knees buckle, and I stagger forward a step. As I search for something to focus on, I see Ezra…just like he was in my vision. Everything about him is exactly the same. His face. His hair. Those hazel eyes. But unlike the vision, there are no tears. And why would there be? We don't know each other.

He won't cry for me when I die.

I stumble again and collapse to the floor, the bar vanishing into the dark void of blood loss. Arms snake around me, breaking my fall, warm against my shivering body. A sob escapes my throat at their touch.

Unconsciousness creeps in at the edges of my vision, but flickers of Ezra's face—present and future—help to keep me awake. He must've been the one who caught me. He shouts over his shoulder at someone behind him, but I can't make out what he says. His hands are covered with blood. My blood. A pressure pushing down on my wrist makes me moan.

All at once, the pain and fear are both gone, and when Ezra

looks down at me, doubt flooding those haunted eyes, I can't help it. I smile. Maybe I do it because I'm delirious, or maybe I'm just relieved I won't have to face death alone. I don't really know. And it doesn't really matter.

Not anymore.

"I saw you," I breathe, pressing a bloodied hand to his cheek as the world goes black.

# TEN

AFTER A WHILE, THE DARKNESS recedes, but the light doesn't seem ready to welcome me yet. The few sounds around me are faint, as if there's a glass box separating me from my surroundings, and everything is blurred, like my senses are dulled. Like I've been drugged. I fight to open and close my eyes, determined to climb my way out of unconsciousness.

A white hot pain overwhelms my left wrist, and my body shudders against what feels like a rickety bed, my skin ice-cold and slimy with sweat. My face and head burn as if they're on fire.

Through my muddled vision, I can just make out the silhouette of a person beside me. Their face isn't clear against the bright light behind them, but something about their posture reminds me of my mother. I try to reach out to them, but my arm is too heavy to lift it. I can't even find the strength to raise a finger.

"Where am I?" I rasp. My voice is distant, as if it's coming from someone else and not me.

A gentle hand brushes a strand of damp hair from my forehead. "Shh…you're safe." A woman's voice.

Mother's voice?

"Mother," I breathe. "Mother, is that you?"

A stray tear escapes from one eye and slides down my cheek, tracking over my skin. Although my mother betrayed me, although she gave me up, right now, I want nothing more than to be in her arms. To wrap myself in her reassuring embrace. To feel protected.

To feel safe.

Safe… This woman, whoever she is, claims that I'm safe. But how can I be? The State is after me, their hunt spearheaded by the DSD, and now, there's the added problem of PHOENIX thinking I'm their enemy.

How can I ever possibly be safe?

My eyes squeeze shut, but more tears break through.

"Mother," I gasp again. "Mother…"

The stranger's hand once again touches my cheek, and I take comfort in the feel of their soft skin against mine. I don't need to know why she's doing this, who she is, or even where I am. I just need to not feel so alone anymore.

"What are you doing in here?" a familiar voice asks.

I recognize it at once.

*Ezra.*

The woman retracts her hand. "She needed medical attention, you know that. I figured it was best to keep an eye on her until she's out of the woods."

Quick footsteps fall against a hard surface.

*Concrete. It sounds like shoes on concrete.*

"What she *needs* is to wake up and answer our questions."

"She's not the enemy, Ezra," the woman mutters under her breath.

Silence for a moment.

"How can you be so sure?"

She scoffs. "She cut the tracking chip out of her wrist. Why would she do that? Why would she risk her life if she was one of them?"

*I'm not one of them,* I try to say. My voice fails me.

"Maybe that's what they want us to think. Some elaborate ploy to gain our trust. To infiltrate our ranks." He lets out a humorless laugh.

"Believe what you want. But I think she came to us because she needs our help. Only desperation would make her do something so stupid."

*Help.* That single word claws through the space in my head, probing until Dr. Richter's voice resurfaces from the depths of my memory. *"Is that who you're planning on running off to for help?"*

I picture Ezra's face. The grim way he looked at me in my vision. The tears on his cheeks as he said he was sorry. Those images are slowly overlapped by reality until all I see is the anger in his eyes. The distrust in his expression. The way he held a gun to my face.

*No. No one will help me.*

"Always the optimist." Ezra snorts. "What makes you think she *wants* our help?" It's impossible to miss the doubt edging his voice.

"Look at her," the woman pleads. "I know I'm not a doctor, but I know enough to tell you something's not right. Someone's done something to her. Something bad. I just… I can't put my finger on what."

Ezra grunts. I imagine him sulking, crossing his arms and glaring down at the floor. He seems the type.

"When will she wake up?"

"I honestly don't know. She's running a high fever and severely dehydrated, not to mention extremely malnourished. Plus, there's the risk of infection, the chance of sepsis being the biggest concern." She pauses, and then there's a rustle of movement as her hand returns to its previous place on my cheek. "I'm doing everything I can, but I'll make sure you're the first to know when she does."

There's an unease in her tone I didn't notice before. Well, I notice it now, and I know what it means.

She doesn't think I'll wake up.

She doesn't think I'll survive.

*Maybe it would be better for everyone if I don't.*

A door slams shut, and my eyelids flutter open for a second, but they're too heavy to hold up. When they slide closed again, the darkness returns, drawing me into unconsciousness like an ocean wave determined to drown me. I succumb to its pull, too tired and weak to fight against my fatigue any longer.

I fall back into the black depths of sleep, knowing full well the woman's hand is the only thing holding me to this world.

# ELEVEN

"HELLO?"

A voice calls out from somewhere in the distance, seducing me away from the clutches of death. My eyelids twitch open, but everything in my range of vision is fuzzy, and the light hanging over my face is too bright, making it impossible to see anything.

"Can you hear me?"

My eyes squeeze shut as a surge of panic courses through my body, weighing down my limbs. This is all too similar, too reminiscent, of my first conscious moments at the DSD. Even the fear gripping me is exactly the same.

A cry sticks in the back of my throat. I don't want this. I just want to go home.

*Do I, though?*

My mother's face drifts to the forefront of my thoughts, her gaze cold and unfeeling, reminding me of her betrayal and of how easily she gave me up, as if I meant nothing to her.

No. Home is no longer an option.

"She's awake."

I peek open my eyes again, drawn to the voice filtering into my ears. A woman's voice.

*It's familiar*, I realize.

I anticipate the searing blindness of the light, recoiling a little, but the harsh glare doesn't burn as badly this time. My eyelids flick open and closed several times until the bleary fog hindering my vision clears enough for me to glimpse the young woman leaning over me. She looks to be in her early twenties and is tall and lean with light brown skin and shining brunette hair that hangs down her back in a perfectly straight glossy curtain. Large dark eyes gaze back into mine, beaming with a kindness that's alien to me.

Relief smooths out her worried expression, her lips curving into a smile as she exhales a strained breath. My stomach turns when the sound of her sigh is overshadowed by the low tramp of footsteps. I blink again against the blinding light as another figure steps into view, but all I can make out is a black silhouette.

As the room around me fully comes into focus, I'm able to see the face of the person staring down at me with disdain and distrust.

I'm able to see Ezra Laramie.

"It's time to talk," he says, his tone curt.

I wedge my elbows behind me to push myself up into a less vulnerable position, but everything hurts, and my attempts to sit up end in failure. Grimacing, I collapse back against the mattress beneath me, which smells strongly of mildew and sweat.

The woman lurches forward and takes hold of my shoulders, earning a sidelong glare from Ezra. "Careful. You're still weak," she murmurs.

The room spins as she helps me upright and props me into a sitting position against the cool concrete wall. The cot I'm sitting on is wedged into one corner of what looks to be a small storage space.

A sharp pain stabs behind my right eye and spreads across the side of my face, traveling up into my hairline where it fades to an irritating prickle. I press the heel of my hand against my temple, but this does little to ease my dizziness or the lingering ache in my head.

I wince. "What happened? Where am I?"

Ezra lets out a laugh that sounds more like a growl. "Someplace where no one will find you."

My trembling fingers comb through my hair as I try to recount the events from before I woke up here.

"What zone am I in?" I press, glancing around the small space. "How...how did I get here?"

The woman takes hold of my hand and brushes over my skin in soothing strokes with her thumb. "You blacked out from blood loss in a bar in Zone 7. If it wasn't for Ezra, you would be dead." She speaks slowly, keeping her tone calm and every word level. "That was seven days ago. You got pretty sick and were in and out of consciousness for a while. Do you remember any of that?"

My wrist throbs as if in response to her words, and I peer down at my arm, trying to piece together memories that seem reluctant to surface. I remember finding Ezra at The Vega, but our conversation after is a bit of a blur. All I can recall with clarity is his face in the middle of so much darkness.

I swallow. Could what she said be true?

Did Ezra really save my life?

My lips part to speak when a bang makes me jump, sending my racing heart up into my throat. Ezra and the woman both turn toward the door, which swings open, creaking on rusty hinges.

A tall man with messy black hair and shining blue eyes, who looks to be more or less my age, stands in the doorway, watching me with interest. His lips twist with the slightest trace of a grin. "Is that her?" he asks, cocking a mischievous eyebrow.

Scowling, Ezra crosses his arms. "Hey, I thought I told you to stay out of this."

"And miss all the excitement?" Rolling his eyes, the newcomer steps into the cramped room and kicks the metal door shut behind him with his boot.

Shoving his hands into his pockets, he ambles closer, stopping a foot away from the cot. Up close, I can see just how blue his eyes are.

"Hmm…she's pretty cute for a spy." He tilts his head, giving me a once-over.

"I'm not a spy," I grumble, frowning.

A slight movement draws my gaze over to Ezra, who holds up Dr. Richter's white coat. "Then why did you have this?" he asks. "They don't just hand these coats out to anyone."

My mouth is a desert as I force out the words, "It's complicated." They escape in a whisper.

Ezra drops the coat onto the mattress beside me. "Okay, then how do you know my name? When I asked you this question before, all you said was 'I saw you.' What did you mean by that?"

*I said that?*

I can practically feel the color drain from my face, and I hesitate, unsure what to say. I can't tell him the truth. The skeptical look in his eyes is the only indicator I need to know he'll never believe me. None of them will. Not without seeing what I can do for themselves.

"That's…also complicated."

His upper lip curls back into a sneer as he takes a step toward me, reaching for the gun on his belt. The woman steps between us to defuse the situation, throwing up her hands.

"Look," she says to me over her shoulder, keeping the bulk of her attention on Ezra, "we want to believe you, but you need to help us out a little. Just tell us something. *Please.*"

Her eyes dart to mine again, their chocolate depths pleading. She wants to help—I can tell as much by the subtle nod she gives me—but I'm so used to not trusting anyone that I'm reluctant to try doing so now. Trust is a luxury no one in the State can afford. Plus, the last person I placed my trust in handed me over to a sadistic monster to be tortured.

*She's not Mother*, I remind myself. Besides, it's not like I have much choice in the matter. If I don't tell them what they want to know, they might kill me. And if I do…well, they may still kill me. Both options are equally risky. I suppose I could try to escape, but all that's waiting for me is the DSD, and no way in hell am I ever going back there.

I risk another glance at Ezra before looking down at my hands. What was the point of escaping Dr. Richter, of cutting the chip from my arm, of any of this, if I don't get the answers I came for? I've found Ezra, like I set out to do, but I should've known that wouldn't be enough. He doesn't trust me. To him, I'm the enemy. That won't change, and he won't give me anything unless I give him something first.

"My name is Wynter Reeves. A couple of—" I falter when the realization strikes me. "I…I don't know how long it's been…"

How much time has passed since the day of my placement exam? It feels like years since I walked into W. P. Headquarters for the final time.

"Since what?" the woman asks, her warm hand still wrapped around mine.

I meet her expectant gaze and let out a breath. "Since I was taken by the DSD."

"Come again?"

The black-haired man gapes at me, and Ezra shoots him a death glare, snapping his name like a curse word. "Jenner."

The other man, Jenner, pulls a face behind Ezra's back, mocking his stern expression. If Ezra notices, he doesn't bother to comment.

I glance between them then look up at the ceiling, fixating my attention on the fluorescent strip lighting, even as it burns into my retinas. "I was taken following my placement exam. By the time I got home, the Enforcers were already there waiting for me."

"What did they want with you?" Ezra presses.

My cheeks flush. "I...I didn't complete the exam," I admit, hanging my head in shame. "I panicked and submitted it only half-finished."

"That doesn't make sense," the woman says. "The DSD doesn't deal with minor crimes. That would be a Detention sentence at worst."

"Is blowing off your exam even considered a punishable offense?" Jenner questions. "I thought you only get sent for Re-education if you fail."

"That's not why I was apprehended," I interrupt, my patience with this topic wearing thin. How many times have I been forced to think about that day? To relive exactly why I was taken?

All three sets of eyes looking at me narrow in confusion, but no one says a word. The shadow of curiosity crossing Ezra's face urges me to continue.

Sweat breaks out across the back of my neck.

"Something happened during my exam having to do with this rare condition I have. I didn't even know about it until someone at the DSD told me I have it. This guy named Richter. He's a…a doctor, of sorts."

Ezra and the woman exchange stunned glances.

"Richter?" she gasps. "Are you sure?"

When I nod, Ezra asks, "Did you happen to catch his first name?"

"No." My hand reaches for the white coat beside me, my thumb grazing over the blood-stained left sleeve. "But this belonged to him. I took it to disguise myself just before I escaped."

"You escaped?" Jenner scoffs, giving me a dubious look. "That's impossible. No one escapes the DSD."

An unsettled feeling weighs like lead in my bones. Because he's right. It *is* impossible.

No one escapes.

"Dr. Richter thinks I can find something the DSD is looking for. They could've stopped me at any time, but they didn't. All that security and they just let me walk out the front door? Trust me, this isn't the first time I've questioned what happened, which makes me think they had an ulterior motive. They probably figured, if they let me go, I'd eventually lead them to what they want."

"You mean us," the woman guesses.

Ezra reaches for the gun at his hip again, but then, at the

last second, seems to change his mind. Crossing his arms, he examines my face with a level of scrutiny that tells me he's searching for any holes in my story.

He's looking for a lie.

If only I was lying…then that would mean the horrors I went through at the DSD weren't real. It would mean this is all just a terrible nightmare.

"Is that why you cut out your tracking chip?" Ezra asks after a moment.

My eyes burn, and I can't find the strength to hold back the tears that now begin to stream down my cheeks.

"I can't go back there. I can't let them find me again. I did what I had to do to escape him."

A strange expression twists Ezra's face at these words. It could almost be pity. Or even regret. But, just as quickly as it appears, it dissolves, and all I find in its place is a mask of stone.

"Is that why you came to us? What about your family?" the woman asks, her tone soothing.

If only I had family to go to. Someone who would protect me from everything that's happened, or, at the very least, attempt to. Assuming protection from the State is possible.

Too bad I don't have anyone like that. I thought I did, but…

"My mother was the one who gave me up to the DSD. As far as I'm concerned, I don't have a family anymore."

"Wait a minute," Jenner says. "Am I the only one who feels like I'm missing something? I get why you would come to us for help, what with us being awesome outcasts of society and all, but—and I mean this with the utmost respect—how the *hell* did you even find us?"

Another question rings loud in the silence that follows. One none of them are daring to ask, probably out of fear of what it would mean.

How did the DSD know I could find them?

Images of The Vega manifest in my head, memories from the first time I saw it—in a vision in my cell at the DSD. How do I explain that to them? I had never heard of my condition until Dr. Richter made me aware of it, and even then, I didn't believe him at first. Chances are, no one in PHOENIX would have heard of it either. To them, the truth will just seem like a lie—a crazy story to get around telling them exactly how I found The Vega. How I found Ezra.

The seconds tick by, the silence pressuring me for an answer I have no way to give.

"That's difficult to explain," I mutter weakly when nothing else comes to me.

"Try," Ezra warns, his voice a threatening rumble.

My eyes cut to his. "You wouldn't believe me if I did."

"Oh, yeah? Why's that?"

I curl my fingers into tight fists as a ringing sound vibrates through my skull, making me dizzy. My fingernails dig half moons into my palms. "I didn't find you using…conventional methods."

Jenner's eyes flick between me and Ezra, his dark brows dragging down into a vee. "What does that mean? Like, you used a sniffer dog to find us or something? Wait…maybe you *are* the sniffer dog?"

The woman shakes her head, frowning at Jenner, before shifting her focus to me. "Most people don't know about PHOENIX's affiliation with The Vega. We're just trying to figure out how you did so we can make sure our people are safe. You said yourself that the DSD is somehow using you to find out our location. I'm sure you can understand how this might look from our point of view."

"I do," I breathe, my voice hitching. "And I promise, I didn't come here to cause problems for any of you. It's just...how I found you... Well, it's the sort of thing you'd have to see to believe."

"Then show us." The demand escaping Ezra's lips is ice-cold, yet I can sense a tremble of fear in his tone. On the surface, it reminds me of my mother's final words the last time I saw her before I woke up at the DSD. Before she handed me over to Dr. Richter. Before my life turned into a nightmare. But, beyond that, the fear in his voice reminds me of how I've felt every single day the last eleven years.

The fear in his voice reminds me of loss.

"I can't—" I begin to say, but I barely get the words out before Ezra unholsters his gun.

"Show us!"

He steps forward and jabs the metal barrel into my temple, but I don't recoil, unfazed by his threat. Something about what I've said has upset him, that much is clear, although I struggle to understand what. Regardless, I suspect he won't pull the trigger. Despite the crazed look in his eyes, I've witnessed another side of him that surpasses his distrust and anger—the side portrayed by the man in my vision. The memory of that man, of his words and his tears, is the one reason I have to believe he won't hurt me. If that side of him didn't already exist, he wouldn't have bothered saving my life at The Vega. I would be dead, the future I saw would be changed, and Dr. Richter would've been right to warn me about him.

But he wasn't. I know in my gut that he wasn't.

I stare up at Ezra, unwavering, as the room around us explodes into chaos.

"Ezra!" the woman shrieks, grabbing his arm.

"Hey, man, put the gun down!" Jenner pleads.

Ezra's upper lip peels back into a snarl, but he relents after a moment, clipping his gun back onto his belt. Scowling, he turns and storms from the room, the door slamming into the wall as he throws it open with way more force than necessary.

Just before stepping into the corridor, he pauses long enough to say, "She doesn't leave this room." He then trudges off without looking back.

The woman exchanges a long look with Jenner as the echo of Ezra's tromping footsteps gradually fades, leaving the three of us in an uneasy silence. He glances between us then lets out a loud groan.

"I'll go talk him down," he grumbles.

The woman nods, and we both watch as Jenner slumps his shoulders and heads for the open door, muttering something under his breath that involves a few choice curse words and something about being on babysitter duty. Once we're alone, she sits down beside me, unsettling the springy mattress.

"I'm sorry about Ezra. He…" She trails off, biting down on her lip. "He has a lot on his mind," she finishes lamely, following the words with a sigh. She clamps her hands together, her posture rigid, as if there's something on her mind and she's reluctant to say it. Finally, she asks, "That doctor you mentioned…what did you think of him? Was he a good man?"

I blink up at her, bemused by her question.

*A good man?* I suppress a laugh at the thought. Good is the last word I would use to describe him.

"No," I answer, my tone as sharp and cutting as the glass shard that sliced through my wrist. "But I don't think anyone in that place is good."

Her face drops, and a wave of guilt washes over me. I don't understand her reaction. Why does she seem so sad? What does she have to do with Dr. Richter?

She smiles at me, but, behind her kind facade, I sense her disappointment. It burns in her eyes like twin flickering flames.

Seeing it only makes my guilt worse.

As she clears her throat, tears pricking at the corners of her eyes, a realization stirs in my chest. The words to voice it spill from my lips in a rush. "You're so different from what I imagined. PHOENIX, I mean. You're nothing like how the State portrays you."

*You don't seem like monsters.*

She smiles again, although, this time, her expression is coy, as if she's in on a secret the rest of the world doesn't know. Arching an eyebrow, she lets out a soft tinkling laugh.

"That's because we're the good guys."

# TWELVE

**BLOOD SPATTERS ACROSS THE FLOOR,** staining large patches of the white carpet red. Grunts followed by whimpering sobs flood the house, but no one seems to care except me.

No one else steps forward to help.

My father drops to his knees in the middle of the reception room of my first home—the house I grew up in near the border to Zone 1 before Mother and I were relocated. Dribbles of blood seep from between his cracked lips, and I hardly recognize him past his facial injuries, his left eye swollen shut, the other tinged red where burst blood vessels have all but overtaken the white. His cheeks are marred with black and purple bruises, disfiguring his alabaster complexion.

My feet stumble backward as a cry lodges deep in my throat. Why is this happening?

And why is no one else trying to stop it?

My mother snatches my arm and jerks me away from him, dragging me back toward the hallway.

*Mother's here now,* I tell myself with relief. *Surely, she'll try to help.*

"Take her out of here. She doesn't need to see this," my mother hisses over her shoulder as a strong pair of hands lift me clean off the ground and haul me out of the reception room. Through my panic, I notice the man's black helmet, a standard element of the Enforcers' regulation uniform. The tears streaming down my splotchy red cheeks are reflected in the opaque shield hiding his face.

I stretch my hand out in desperation, screaming at the top of my lungs. My father looks up, his remaining good eye glassy, when I cry for them to leave him alone.

When I beg them not to take him away.

My cries cease as he mutters the last words he would ever say to me. "I'm sorry, Wynter."

Time seems to slow as I fight against the hands restraining me, but I'm not strong enough to escape them. As I struggle, my father's voice replays in my thoughts like an echo.

*"I'm sorry, Wynter."*

Static skews his face, and then he's just gone, taken from me as quickly as he was when I was a child.

I blink, heavy sobs wracking my lungs, as the memory of the worst day of my life falls away, piece by piece disintegrating into ash until all that's left before me is an endless wasteland of destruction.

I turn in place, taking in what remains of the Heart, my gaze catching on a familiar face—the only one among the apocalyptic nothingness. Ezra's here, just like the last time I saw this. Tears leave lines on his cinder-smeared cheeks as his lips shape the same words my father once said to me. Words that are now like a bullet ripping straight through my heart.

"I'm sorry, Wynter," he whispers.

Static again as their voices surround me, blending together and ringing in a torturous loop with the sole intent of driving me mad.

*"I'm sorry—"*

I clutch my head, dragging my fingernails over my scalp, as if that will somehow pull the voices out of my skull.

*"I'm sorry…"*

My eyes burn as the black hole of my shattered heart consumes me, and I drop to my knees, praying for the vision to end. I can't take it anymore.

*"Wynter…"*

*I can't take it.*

"Wynter?"

My eyes spring open, thrusting me back into consciousness. My chest heaves as I take in the details of the small storage room, the cramped space empty aside from a few shelving units and the uncomfortable folding cot underneath me. Warm tears wet my cheeks and leave a salty residue on my lips. I brush them away when the door creaks open.

"Wynter? I'm coming in."

I sit up just as the woman I met before walks into the room holding a thin metal tray. The sight of solid food makes me realize just how hungry I am, and my stomach growls at the delicious scent wafting into the space alongside her, coaxing a knowing grin onto her lips. I can only imagine how they fed me when I was unconscious, but I'm sure this method is preferable for both of us.

Her smile deepens when our eyes meet, as if she's genuinely happy to see me again, although I can't understand why she would be. If my nightmare just now has reminded me of anything, it's that standing against the State gets you killed. Harboring a fugitive is worse, *much* worse, and if you're caught, you'll wish for death before the DSD is even finished with you.

Her smile falters when fresh tears slip down my cheeks, and she sets the tray on the floor before taking a seat on the squeaky cot beside me.

"Are you all right?" Her fingers are warm as she places a gentle hand on my arm.

I flinch away from her touch, giving a quick jerky nod, but my unsteady breaths reveal the truth I'm too much of a coward to voice. My lips quiver with the threat of a sob as I wipe the moisture from my face.

"I had a dream about my father. About the last time I saw him alive."

"I'm sorry," she whispers, her voice consoling.

I don't know how to react to her sentiment. In the Heart, we're encouraged not to show our grief, and above all, never to express it to others, especially if the person our grief is aimed at was found guilty of breaking the law. *"Enemies of the State don't deserve to be mourned."* That's what the State has always taught us. And yet, even now, years later, I still can't help mourning my father.

I look down at the floor, unaccustomed to showing such weakness—to showing any emotion at all. *"To suppress is to survive,"* my mother's voice says in my head, surfacing from the depths of my memory, like a hand reaching out to catch me from falling. *"Don't let anyone see what you feel."*

So, that's how I lived until my time at the DSD. I followed three rules to ensure what I felt would always stay hidden from watchful eyes, just like everyone else in the Heart. Together, we feel nothing, and in feeling nothing, we are kept apart.

But the people here—this woman, Jenner, even Ezra—they all wear their emotions plainly, putting what they feel on full display for anyone around to witness. They don't bother to hide what's in their hearts. They don't try to mask who they are.

As I stare at the floor, my unblinking eyes boring imaginary holes into the concrete, I realize that I envy them. How they live here is in direct opposition to the forced emotional seclusion the State has manufactured in our society. I can only imagine how freeing it must be to allow yourself to be who you are, to let yourself feel what you truly feel, without fear of punishment.

"Do you mind if I ask what happened to him?" she says after a moment of silence has passed.

I glance at her out of the corner of my eye as the lump lodged in my throat seems to double in size.

"He was executed for treason," I breathe, every word a burden I can't seem to shake. "My last memory of him is of when he was taken. I never saw him again after that."

I don't know what I expect from her. Shock, maybe? Horror? Disgust? After all, it's not uncommon for people to distance themselves from someone who's been touched by death the way I have. Distance is safer. Distance ensures we remain unnoticed, that we're invisible to the State.

And to be invisible is to stay alive.

But she doesn't look at me that way. Instead, I see something in her gaze no one would ever dare publicly reveal. Pity. It shines in her eyes, along with an understanding of sorts, as if she can empathize with my pain.

As if she's felt that sort of grief, too.

"You know, everyone here has lost someone or something to

the State. But that's why we fight. So our losses don't have to be for nothing." She folds her fingers around mine and shifts closer, bumping my shoulder with her upper arm. The warmth I sensed from her before is only intensified by her touch. "We aren't that different, you know. I don't know why you were looking for Ezra, but maybe...you belong with us. Maybe you're here for a reason."

A frown tugs down the corners of my lips, and I resist the urge to snort. "I'm not so sure about that."

*You don't know what I am.*

*You don't know what I've done.*

The memory of that female attendant at the DSD comes rushing back, triggering a surge of bile to climb up my throat. Even now, I can see her seizing body so clearly.

Swallowing, I shake the recollection away.

I wish I could find the words to explain that I didn't search for PHOENIX because I desired acceptance. I only wanted to find Ezra to help me grasp what's happening to me. So I can get answers about this world I don't fully understand. So I can figure out what role he will eventually come to play in my life and in that terrible future I saw.

The woman chuckles under her breath. "I am. You and me... We're more alike than you know."

I lean away from her, gaping a little, unsure what to make of her bold but blind sense of trust. She grew up in the State, didn't she? She must know how dangerous trust can be.

"How can you say that when you don't even know me?" I ask, my voice failing to hide my amazement.

She squints at the ceiling as if considering her answer. "Call it a gut feeling. I just... I see the same fear in you I once saw in myself. That I *still* see in myself."

"What are you afraid of?" The words leave my lips before the thought has even fully registered.

I should know better than to pry—in the State, such an act is forbidden—but I can't help myself. Ever since the day of my placement exam, it's as if the rules of my old world are slipping away a little bit more every day. At what point will those rules no longer matter to me? At what point will I be free of their tether?

A kind smile unfurls across the woman's face when she meets my gaze again. "Everything."

I know what that feels like. To always be scared. To worry I'm only one breath away from doing something that would see me following in my father's footsteps far sooner than I would like. Hell, I know that feeling better than most.

Her unabashed honesty resonates with me in a way I wouldn't have ever expected. Maybe because this isn't how our world works. We don't make eye contact. We don't develop close relationships or talk to each other on a personal level. We don't show warmth or compassion to others, like she's displaying to me now.

In my world, fear is used to keep us apart, whereas she's using it to bring us together.

"I meant what I said before. I'm not here to cause any problems for you."

"I know," she says. "I can tell just by looking at you. You're one of the good guys, too."

I scoff. "Well, I'm definitely not a spy for the State."

Her eyes light up at my words, and she taps a finger against her lips, as if deep in thought. "So, maybe it's time we prove that to everyone."

*Everyone?*

My brow furrows when she jumps to her feet and tugs me off the bed, still clutching my hand. "Come on. I bet you're dying to stretch your legs and get out of this stuffy room for a while."

I hesitate, digging my heels into the floor as she tries to pull me toward the door. When she looks back at me, I stammer, "I-I don't know. Ezra said I wasn't allowed to leave this room." I don't want to make him any angrier or distrusting of me than he already is.

She rolls her eyes, waving a dismissive hand at me. "Despite what he thinks, Ezra is not in charge around here. I have just as much authority as he does, and I say we're going for a walk. If he has a problem with it, well, that's on him."

My heart hammers against my ribcage as she drags me along behind her, ignoring my protests.

"Oh, by the way," she adds as she throws open the door. "My name is Rai. Rai Dorne."

When she smiles once more, I'm disarmed by what I glimpse in her gaze—not just kindness but an offer of friendship. Such a concept is foreign to me. After all, friendship doesn't exist in the State. Maybe it's because of that deprivation I find myself wanting to know what it's like. Is someone like me even capable of it?

I trail Rai through a series of hallways, the footpath just wide enough for us to walk side by side. Fluorescent lights hang at even intervals overhead, placed between a maze-like network of pipes, which follow along the full length of the low ceiling. The damp, musty air has a mossy taste to it, and as we walk, I notice there aren't any windows. If the lights were to fail, we'd be swallowed by darkness.

The realization that follows this observation doesn't bring me any comfort. After so long trapped in the stifling confines of the DSD, breathing recycled air, the thought that I might be underground makes me anxious. It triggers memories I'd rather forget.

"Are you okay?" Rai asks.

I force a smile onto my face but say nothing.

For the first ten minutes or so since leaving the cramped storage room, Rai and I are alone. I follow her steps through the compound, wondering how such a place could exist without the State knowing about it, which in turn only reminds me of all the secrets I'm hiding. Why I'm here. What's wrong with me.

The fact that I've murdered someone.

*"We're more alike than you know,"* Rai had said.

*Are we, though?* I wonder.

The longer we walk, the more often we cross paths with the other residents here. They all stare at me with the same expression: confusion at first, followed by distrust. I don't blame them for viewing me as a threat—I'm sure they all know what happened at The Vega by now—but after the first dozen or so glances, I lower my eyes to escape the judgmental scrutiny of their gazes.

I only look up again when we enter a large cavernous space, the warehouse-like room empty apart from a border of benches and some crates, a handful upturned to double as seats. At the opposite end of the room, Jenner waves at us.

"Hey!" he shouts, his voice carrying in an echo.

Ezra stands beside him, staring me down with a look that says he does not share his companion's enthusiasm to see me. Even from a distance, I can sense his suspicion and something else all too reminiscent of loathing. Those emotions emanate from him like heat from a fire.

If I get too close, I might get burned.

Jenner runs toward us, skipping every third step. He stops next to me, flashing a broad grin as he bites into an apple. "How's it going?" he asks, spitting a little.

Before either of us can answer, Ezra skulks across the room, his furious gaze fixated on Rai. "Why did you let her out?" he barks.

Huffing, she plants her hands on her hips and tosses her long hair over her shoulder with a graceful sway of her head. "I already told you, she isn't our enemy. We should stop treating her like one," she snaps back.

I glance between them, taken aback by their annoyance with each other and afraid of being caught in the line of fire. I can feel their impending argument like the first drops of rain in the air.

Beside me, Jenner lets out a sigh. When I look over at him, he winks and then slings an arm around my shoulders, pulling me close to his side. "Hey, why don't we go sit down and have a chat? Sound good?"

I look back at Ezra and Rai. The fight I predicted is now erupting between them, an explosion of anger volleyed back and forth, like they're playing a verbal sport. It's amazing they can understand anything they're saying with the way they're screaming over each other. I can hardly make out a single word. It makes me wonder what they are to each other that gives them the right to speak so openly. Confrontation is frowned upon in our society. Confrontation means disobedience, and disobedience makes you an enemy of the State. Like most things, disobedience is dangerous.

Then again, I suppose they're free of those rules here.

I allow Jenner to steer me away to an unoccupied seating area in one corner of the large room—far away from Rai and Ezra but not so far we can't still hear the distant drone of their bickering. Once we settle on one of the benches, he reaches into a nearby crate and offers me a bottle of water.

"Thanks," I mutter.

He leans back, looking at me for a moment, then stretches his right arm out in front of me.

I peer down at his empty hand.

"I don't think I've properly introduced myself yet. The name's Jenner Rhodes."

Unsure what else to do, I extend my fingers, shivering a little when his skin grazes mine. As we shake hands, a memory hits the front of my thoughts.

My father once told me this is how people used to greet one other, but, like most things, the gesture died away along with everything else that existed before the State came into power. I can't help wondering why. Did the State outlaw this simple greeting, or did people just stop wanting to know one another because of their fear of betrayal? When did we stop caring about anything but our own survival?

We sit in silence for a while, staring out across the vast, empty space. Ezra and Rai have given up on their fight and subsequently stormed off in different directions. Part of me worries I should've followed Rai when she left, but I find Jenner's company too comforting to move. If I wasn't in good hands, she wouldn't have left me here.

"I agree with Rai, you know," he says. "I don't think you're one of *them*." It doesn't escape my notice how he spits that last word.

"You seem to be the only ones," I point out.

A crooked smile hooks up the left side of his mouth. "Nah, you're an innocent, I can tell. I've seen those bastards up close enough times to know the difference." He leans in, his breath warm against my ear. "Don't worry. Everyone else will see that soon enough."

*Even Ezra?* I'm tempted to ask.

I watch Jenner out of the corner of my eye, intrigued by his carefree manner and easygoing personality. Like Rai, he's choosing to trust me when I haven't given him any logical reason to. Why? Aren't these people supposed to be wanted criminals? Monsters, the State always called them. They don't seem like that to me, but, aside from a surface portrayal of kindness, what do I really know about them?

My thoughts turn back to Ezra. It's hard to believe the man who pointed a gun at my head twice now is the same man from my vision, and yet, even though he's keeping his distance from me, I can sense a connection between us—something that tells me what I saw in my vision was real. And the man I saw in that future wasn't a monster.

None of these people are.

"This place…" My eyes skirt across the dome-shaped ceiling. "None of it is like what I imagined."

Jenner laughs. "I know what you mean. I thought the same thing when I first arrived here. Maybe that's why I find it so easy to accept you considering I *was* you once. Everyone here was, they just don't want to admit it. Change can be hard for some to embrace." He grins at my confused expression.

"Ezra's not always such an ass, I promise. He's just trying to keep everyone safe, and responsibility sometimes comes with trust issues."

*"If you think you can trust him, you're wrong."*

As Dr. Richter's warning once again reverberates in my ears, it occurs to me that Ezra isn't the one who needs to be trusted in this scenario. He isn't the one in question. I am. I'm the one who needs to earn *his* trust, not the other way around.

"It's all lies, you know. Everything they say about us." Jenner hunches forward, resting his forearms on his knees and lacing his fingers together, joining his hands. There's a sadness in his eyes when he stares down at them. "All that violence in the Heart is attributed to PHOENIX, but, in reality, we don't cause any of it. Our goal isn't to hurt anyone. No one here wants blood on their hands."

"You mean the State?" I ask, raising my eyebrows.

He nods but doesn't meet my gaze. "Do you have any idea how it feels to be called a terrorist when you're just trying to survive?"

I sink my teeth into my lower lip, fighting back the burning sensation building along the edges of my vision. I can imagine all too well what Jenner must be feeling. Isn't that how I was treated just because I didn't finish my placement exam? Just because there's something wrong with me that I have no control over? Hell, the people at the DSD acted as if I wasn't even a human being.

But none of that, no matter how much sense it makes to me, explains why the State would lie about PHOENIX. What would it get out of frightening the masses with the constant threat of terrorism?

"If you aren't responsible for the attacks…"

"Fear leads to control, and control guarantees the government's longevity. I suppose that's all the incentive they need. I just wish people knew the truth about us. Mindless violence won't bring about change."

I stare at him for a long moment, haunted by that sentiment. Mindless violence…

Like what Dr. Richter did to me.

"What will?" I whisper.

"Honestly?" He peeks up at me through thick lashes, his expression youthful and uncertain. "I'm still trying to figure that one out."

For as long as I can remember, the State has always portrayed PHOENIX as a force to be reckoned with. To be feared. But, as I listen to Jenner, I can't help questioning who the victims really are in all this.

My exposure to the people here has been limited, but I've seen enough to know they aren't terrorists or murderers. They're no different than the people I've walked past on the street every single day of my life. They're just a group of scared individuals doing whatever it takes to survive.

The solemn look on Jenner's face makes me eager to change the subject. My thoughts shift back to Ezra and Rai, and a spark of curiosity forms my next question for me. "They're your friends, right? Ezra and Rai? How did they get involved with PHOENIX?"

He scratches his chin. "Well, Ez and Rai have known each other since they were kids. They've gone through all this together, every step of the way."

Together. On a personal level, I don't even know what that

word means.

"How about you?" I ask. "How did you end up joining?"

"I...uh..." He runs a hand through his disheveled obsidian hair as his cheeks turn a subtle shade of red. "I had a run-in with the authorities when I was seventeen. It was a misunderstanding more than anything else. A case of wrong place, wrong time. Anyway, Ezra and Rai got me out of that bind. That was three years ago, and they've been stuck with me ever since."

His tone gives off the distinct impression the life of a rebel wasn't something he wanted.

Looks like we have that in common.

"You don't seem too happy about that," I note.

He averts his gaze, wringing his hands in his lap. "It's not that I don't feel grateful toward them for saving my life. It's just that...from the moment they intervened, everything changed. I had to leave my entire life behind, and my family suffered as a result of my idiocy. I couldn't risk going to see them again, not even to say goodbye."

I grimace at the string of thoughts that forms. *Would they have wanted to say goodbye, or would they have been as callous as my mother? Would they have handed you over?*

"When the Enforcers couldn't find me, my parents and sister were brought in for questioning." He pauses, casting a meaningful glance at me. "You know what the DSD is like. My family didn't know anything about where I was or what I did, and yet, they were branded as enemies of the State just because we were related. They were sent to Termination shortly after."

I don't know what to say. What is there to say?

He's right. I do know what the DSD is like. I can imagine all too well the horrors his family would've gone through.

Jenner shakes his head then says, "I know I'm responsible for what happened to them. If I had died or just let the Enforcers apprehend me, the State wouldn't have had any reason to hurt them. It would've left them alone."

*You don't know that.*

My father's face fills up the space in my mind. Looking back, how close did Mother and I come to receiving the same punishment as Jenner's family?

Were we only spared because he got caught?

"At the same time…their deaths are my reason for fighting, you know?" His eyes lock on me, holding my attention rapt. "I want to prevent these kinds of needless tragedies from happening to anyone else."

A sharp pain clenches my heart, and the sympathy arising within me seems powerful enough to drown an entire city. I can't even comprehend Jenner's pain. Well, I can, but I was young when my father was taken, and with time, those memories will fade. But Jenner…he might not be so lucky.

That pain could live with him forever.

I startle when he pokes me in the cheek with his finger. "That right there," he says through a smile. "That's how I know you aren't one of them."

I reel back as goosebumps rise across my arms, my eyes narrowing in confusion. The way he's staring at me is unnerving. No one's ever looked at me this way before.

"What do you mean?" I ask.

The seconds roll by, but he doesn't answer.

Before I can press him, he looks away, turning his attention to the opposite side of the room. I follow his gaze to see Rai walking toward us.

"How'd it go?" he asks once she's closer.

She pushes a tired breath out through her nose. "He's being difficult, but he just needs some time to mull things over. He'll come around eventually."

I recall the sour expression on Ezra's face when he saw me and the rage in his eyes during his altercation with Rai. Why was he so angry? And what exactly were they fighting about?

*Me, probably.*

My heart sinks as Rai and Jenner launch into a conversation about one important thing or another, their voices growing faint as I rest back against the wooden slats of the bench and allow my troubled thoughts to devour me. The images in my head replay my nightmare from earlier…except, it isn't my father who I'm seeing this time.

It's Ezra.

My lungs constrict when he speaks.

*"I'm sorry, Wynter."*

He says those same words again, over and over, always the same words flooding my ears, but they never offer any explanation or give any hint about what will happen between us.

Or why he'll apologize for it.

He says them until I hear nothing else and the other sounds of the world die away.

# THIRTEEN

**THE NEXT HANDFUL OF DAYS** are spent touring the compound in the few hours when I'm allowed out of the storage room—a compromise Rai made with Ezra until we convince him that I'm not a threat. That's what she claims, anyway. But I have a feeling the order to keep me locked up came from someone above them in the PHOENIX hierarchy.

Someone I have yet to meet.

The structure is an underground facility from the pre-State days, but that's as much as anyone is willing to tell me, other than to say that we're safe from the State here. As if there could possibly be such a place.

Rai and Jenner are hospitable, and their friendly manner is almost enough to make me believe I'm not their prisoner…until we pass one of the other residents, and that person's wariness when they look at me triggers the reminder of where I am and why everyone views me as a threat. That single look forces me to remember that I'm not truly welcome here.

It also doesn't escape my notice there are things they make it a point not to show me. Specifically, the exits. Regardless of the kindness they're bestowing upon me, regardless of their words of acceptance, it's evident they don't trust me enough to risk letting me leave. I don't blame them. For all they know, I could be leading Dr. Richter right to them.

"Make yourself at home."

I scowl at Rai, unable to hold back a grimace.

"Really," she insists, pursing her lips and giving me a look that tells me I shouldn't doubt her.

I can't help it. Surely, making myself at home will only cause more problems for me in the long run. She and Jenner might like me enough to want me to stay, but I have a feeling that sentiment isn't shared by the others here. Especially Ezra.

Even now, nearly a week after waking up in this place, I struggle to see how he fits into my life or how we'll get to where we are in my vision. Maybe that's for the best considering the terrible future awaiting us. That destruction should be avoided at all costs, and maybe the way to do that is to avoid him.

Still, at this rate, I'll never understand who he is or the connection he holds to my condition, and the not knowing is what's driving me crazy.

"The first step to acceptance is exposure," Rai says, her musical trill snapping me back to attention. "The people here need to see you if they're expected to trust you, and that'll never happen if you're locked away all the time."

I cock a dubious eyebrow at her. *Last I checked, being locked up wasn't exactly my choice.*

Despite that thought, I say nothing, even though there's an obvious flaw in her logic. In the Heart, people often go their entire lives without trusting anyone, even those closest to them. So, how can she expect a group of strangers to trust me after such a short time together and only the odd interaction in passing? I haven't earned their trust, and frankly, I don't need it. I'm only here to discern the link between Ezra and my vision.

I came here for answers, nothing else.

Rai pauses beside the doorway leading into one of two galley kitchens and turns toward me, taking hold of my hands. "Anyway, this is where I leave you. I have some things I need to see to, and I think Jenner can take it from here. I hope you don't find this too forward, but I've arranged for you to have a shower. I would've taken you sooner, but everything we let you do has to be approved, and unfortunately, there was some…kickback."

"Kickback?" I ask, furrowing my brow.

She rolls her lower lip between perfect white teeth. "The showers are communal, and some of our residents here are… vulnerable. They weren't comfortable with the idea of you, a stranger, being in there with them unsupervised. But, at this time of day, the facility should be empty. Everyone is off doing their chores. Problem solved."

Her eyes flit to Jenner, who looks down at me and winks. "I'll make sure no one bothers you."

Rai says her goodbyes then disappears into the sweltering heat of the kitchen. Once we're alone, Jenner returns to our leisurely stroll, and I follow him through the endless corridors, trailing his every step like a shadow. We walk without speaking for so long I lose track of the time, but I don't mind the silence. His company is soothing and eases my growing distress about being underground surrounded by people who think I'm only here to harm them. It's strange when I put my feelings toward Jenner in perspective to the other relationships in my life. Thinking about it, I wasn't even this comfortable around my own mother.

"How many people live here?" I ask after a while.

"Twenty-six. But with you, we have twenty-seven," he answers.

My feet falter, and I stumble to a standstill.

*Twenty-six people?*

The fearsome terrorist organization PHOENIX only has twenty-six people?

"Is that it?" The question escapes me in a strangled whisper.

Jenner's lips crack into a lopsided smile. "We're just one branch in a much larger tree. PHOENIX has hundreds of sects in the Heart alone, some of which greatly outnumber ours."

"Oh." A sigh of relief crawls up my throat, but I catch myself mid-breath. I barely know these people, so why should I care if they have the support and numbers needed to stand up to the State? That's their problem. It has nothing to do with me.

Except, with every day that passes, I realize a bit more how untrue that is. I'm no insurgent—I didn't come here to join PHOENIX as some act of rebellion against the society I was raised in. I came here because I was scared and I didn't know what else to do. I'm nothing but a homeless runaway, who found kindness where I didn't expect it. And now, I'm terrified I might lose it. What else do I have without this?

Where else could I go?

"Here we are," Jenner announces, stopping beside an open door leading through to a narrow hallway. There's a bathroom not far from the storage room, which Rai accompanies me to a few times a day, but that facility doesn't have a shower.

As I stare through the doorway, it occurs to me just how long it's been since I last bothered to bathe. Funny how removing the threat of death can put these sorts of things into perspective.

"Rai told me earlier she set aside some clothes for you in the washroom, which is at the end of the hall through this door. I'll wait for you out here while you clean up. I know it's been a while, so take your time."

His nonchalant remark about my lack of cleanliness would be insulting if it wasn't so painfully true. Now that I'm free of the DSD, the awareness of the stench exuding from my skin makes me shudder. All I want in this moment is to wash it away, along with everything bad that's happened to me over these last few months.

My cheeks burn as I dash through the doorway, and I don't dare slow my pace until my feet carry me into the washroom, beyond the reach of Jenner's piercing gaze. Although his presence brings me much-needed comfort, it's also overwhelming at times. The way he looks at me… I don't think I'll ever get used to it.

My breaths are ragged as I step into the empty room, and although I'm thankful for the solitude, I feel like a trespasser, like I shouldn't be here. I whip around at the slightest noise, whether it be the low thunk of pipes or the slow dripping of water, afraid of who might be waiting around every corner or in the shadows.

*This isn't like the DSD,* I remind myself, letting out a breath. *These are good people. They aren't like Dr. Richter.*

I inhale through my nose, and once my pulse is steady again, I begin to undress. It's like peeling off a second layer of skin, the fabric stiff with sweat and stinking of odors built up over several months that have been collecting on my skin and could turn even the strongest stomach. It's remarkable Rai and Jenner could stand being near me. Come to think of it, the thick, musty stench in The Vega was probably the only thing masking my odor from Ezra.

Wincing at the smell, I kick the clothes off, leaving them in a heap on the white cement floor, before stepping into the nearest shower cubicle and turning the valve until the water is scalding. The heat feels good against my aching skin, and I sense a weight lift off my shoulders the longer I stand under the spray, as if the water is burning away my trauma.

As steam swarms my body, I glance down at my bandaged wrist for the first time since removing the chip. The thought of looking before frightened me, but now, I want to see what lies under the dressing. I *need* to see what I've done to myself. What price I paid to escape Dr. Richter.

My teeth bite along my lip as my fingers carefully unravel the linen covering and remove the gauze. Apart from some swelling and the uneven line of stitches holding my sliced skin together, the wound doesn't look too bad. It doesn't appear to be infected anymore, at least—thanks to Rai. I count myself lucky considering how differently things would've turned out if Ezra hadn't bothered to help me and Rai hadn't worked tirelessly to get me through those first few days when they weren't even sure I'd survive.

From the moment I stepped inside The Vega, Ezra held my life in his hands, even if he didn't know it. As far as he was concerned, I was the enemy. He could've let me die. He could've let me bleed out to ensure his own survival and safety. But he didn't.

He *chose* to save me.

That knowledge, along with several other small discoveries I've made since I woke up in this place, reiterate that PHOENIX isn't at all what I expected based on what I was told growing up. But I'm also still not sure if I should trust them, regardless of what they've done for me so far. As I keep telling myself, trust is dangerous. Trust gets you killed. Plus, I don't exactly feel safe here, and I definitely don't belong with these people, despite what Jenner and Rai keep saying. And yet, I know I *have* to be here—that this place will help me discover the truth, not only about my visions but about my disease.

Ezra is the key, but I'm struggling to reconcile that grief-stricken man in my head with the hardened rebel who wants to keep me locked up. Then again, he was holding a gun in my vision.

Maybe I've been wrong about everything, and my future ends with him using it on me.

An icy prickle trails across my naked flesh as my fingers grip the valve again, the pipes squealing in protest when I shut off the water. As I step out of the shower, my eyes land on the clothes Jenner mentioned. They sit neatly folded in a pile on the side of a wide metal basin—one of many positioned under a long row of mirrors. A toothbrush, a tube of toothpaste, and a towel lie just beside them on the edge of the sink, and boots and fresh socks sit nearby on the floor.

I leave the filthy garments from the DSD where I tossed them before, abandoned in a mound on the floor, happily trading them for the fresh clothes: a pair of tight-fighting brown cargo pants and a faded black long-sleeved shirt. I know I should pick up the physical reminders of my torment and discard them before someone else has to do it, but I can't bring myself to look at them, let alone touch them again. They hold too many bad memories.

Memories I never want to revisit.

My fingers comb through my tangled hair as my eyes lock on my reflection in one of the mirrors. I recoil when I meet the gaze of the gaunt-faced girl in the glass, unprepared for what I see. My skin is pale, almost sallow, and prominent bags hang under my eyes, darkening the skin like bruises. I've deteriorated since I last looked at myself.

Now, I look to be mere moments from death.

I push that thought away and hurry out of the washroom, running from the reality of my disease with the same determination with which I ran from the DSD. In the corridor outside, Jenner leans against the wall opposite the doorway, humming a soft, unfamiliar tune. With his eyes closed, he looks serene, beautiful even. At peace.

More than anything, I wish I could know what that feels like.

His eyes pop open at my approach, and he flashes that charming lopsided grin. "Look at you, all cleaned up. I mean, hey, you were cute before, but now…!"

A blush spreads from my neck to the tips of my ears. I suppose I should take it as a compliment he finds anything physically appealing about me, considering the horrifying effects this disease is having on my appearance. In reality, I suspect his reaction might have more to do with the obvious lack of age-appropriate females residing here. Other than Rai, I don't think I've seen any other females around our age in this place.

Sensing my embarrassment, he changes the subject. "Shall we continue?"

Over the next hour, Jenner leads me through the rest of the compound. There isn't much left to see that I haven't already, but then again, I don't know what more I was expecting. This facility seems to serve as a residence, rather than as a base of operations, and the majority of the rooms are either general living areas or individual sleeping quarters.

When we reach the end of the tour, Jenner guides me back into that warehouse-like room with the domed ceiling where we had our first conversation earlier this week. A crowd has gathered, but we loiter at the outskirts of the space, watching in silence as the two dozen people before us take turns patting a middle-aged man on the back.

They repeat the same phrase to him, over and over, some shouting the words while others sing them. Rai pushes her way into the center of the crowd, carrying a heavy-looking crate of glass bottles. When she sets it on the floor, everyone cheers before reaching for the bottles—which I assume must contain alcohol considering PHOENIX's affiliation with The Vega— like a pack of starving wolves.

"Amazing," I whisper, awe leaching into my tone. "With everything you have going against you, you still find time to celebrate birthdays."

Birthdays are just markers of time with a singular purpose: to denote how many years we have left until we become contributing members of society. In the State, the only birthday that matters is our eighteenth, which is when we go for our placement exam.

At least, that's how it normally is, and how it was in the years after Father died. Before then, he always made that day special and would even give me little gifts when Mother wasn't looking—always disposable, so no one would ever find out about them, like a poem or a piece of music. Nothing tangible. Even though the gift was fleeting, it meant the world to me as a child.

My birthday is when I feel his absence the most.

"Well, it's the little things that make life worth living," Jenner murmurs, his voice so low I barely hear it. "Besides, we have to enjoy this while we can since we could all be dead tomorrow. The birthdays we have now... They could be our last."

Jenner and I don't speak again as we watch the celebration unfold. My gaze moves from one end of the room to the other, observing this brief moment of bliss in the many smiling faces around me. My attention catches on one particular face in the crowd and on the hazel eyes cutting into me, hard and cold.

The second I process Ezra's expression, meeting his gaze, the world around me shifts, and pain explodes inside my head as a spiraling succession of images beats through my brain, each one another stab. Screams rip from my lungs as the vision overtakes me, dragging the room into total darkness.

As I fall to my knees, a new vision takes shape behind my eyelids, bringing me back to the shadowed alley at the border of Zone 7 where I cut out my chip. Before me, an entourage of Enforcers forms a barrier around a group of people all dressed in identical knee-length white coats. I recognize those coats at the same moment Dr. Richter steps into my limited range of vision. He turns toward me with his lips pressed together, glaring down at his hand where a bloodied glint of gold rests in the center of his palm.

The corners of his mouth pull into a sneer as his fingers clench into a fist around the chip.

"Clever girl," he purrs.

My body convulses against the cold concrete floor, my head repeatedly slamming into the hard surface as the vision melts away. I can't regain control of my movements or quell the tremors running over my limbs, and within seconds, the metallic stench of blood fills my nose.

Through the hazy black spots spreading in front of my eyes, I glimpse the vague outlines of figures huddling over me.

"Wynter!" Rai calls out. My name is a panicked cry on her lips.

I try to answer her, but I can't get my mouth to cooperate.

The echo of Jenner's voice reaches my ears. "What the hell's happening to her?" He's shouting, and there's a slight wobble behind every word.

*He's scared,* I realize. But whether he's scared *of* me or *for* me...I don't know.

The pain spreads, threatening to swallow my body whole. Jenner and Rai lean over me, and through the haze obscuring my vision, I can just make out the concern and fear twisting their faces. But they aren't what I'm focusing on. They aren't what I'm searching for—what I need to see—in this moment before my long overdue death descends, finally ready to claim me.

Ezra stares at me from between the blurred faces, his expression no longer cold and hard, not at all like it was the last time I met his gaze.

Now, as the darkness pulls me under, those sad hazel eyes say only one thing.

He's afraid.

# FOURTEEN

MY EYELIDS CRACK OPEN, AND a low moan escapes me when a throbbing pain beats against the walls of my skull, the ache behind my eyes made worse by the blinding light shuddering overhead. I lift my hand to block out the glare, and squinting, I can just make out my surroundings. The storage room is blistering—or maybe I'm feverish and it's my skin that's on fire—and the scent of dust and mold clouding the air is more potent than usual.

*That smell isn't coming from me, is it?*

My tongue darts out to lick my dried lips. I don't remember ever being so thirsty.

Once my vision adjusts, my arm drops back beside me and a frown tugs down the edges of my mouth. Ezra, Jenner, and Rai all stand by the door, keeping their distance from me. For good reason, too. They've witnessed what I can do—what I told them they'd have to see to believe—and shocker, here I am again…

Back in my little prison.

This can't mean anything good. I tell myself their fearful expressions suggest they're merely taking measures to be cautious—although, for my sake or theirs, I'm not sure—but that line of thought does little to comfort me. Can't say that I blame them.

I would be frightened of me, too.

Every part of my body hurts as I move to sit up, the forward motion triggering a jolting stabbing pain in my temple. I press the heel of my hand against my forehead, hoping the pressure will counterbalance the ache. When that doesn't work, I drag in a deep breath and try to ignore the dread twisting my stomach.

My visions are getting worse, my reactions more severe. This level of pain… It's not normal. Losing consciousness isn't normal. What will happen when the side effects of this disease become too much for me to bear?

What if, next time, I don't wake up?

The idea of death hovers at the front of my mind. Not that long ago, the escape of it would've been welcome, but now, I find myself clinging to life with every ounce of desperation my frail body can muster. Maybe it's my survival instincts kicking in, or maybe I'm just not ready to follow in my father's footsteps.

Either way, I don't want to die. Not yet.

"It's time you tell us what the hell is going on." Ezra steps toward me, crossing his arms. His leering gaze burns into my face, making me squirm.

My answer slips out between raspy breaths. "I told you it was something you had to see to believe."

His eyes narrow. "What happened to you back there? What was that?"

My tongue sweeps over my dry lower lip once again as I contemplate what to say. It's time to tell them the whole truth before my silence gets me killed, but what possible explanation will make them believe me?

*There isn't one*, I realize.

I'll just have to throw caution to the wind and hope for the best.

"The condition I have… It allows me to see things," I whisper.

"What kind of things?" Rai asks, staring at me, her almond-shaped eyes wide and pressing. Jenner and Ezra both wear the same expectant expression.

I waver, sucking in another deep breath, and as my lungs push the air out, the words expel along with it. "Things that haven't happened yet."

The hush that follows is agonizing. My attention settles on Ezra first, then on Rai, hoping one of them will say something to quell the strange tension sucking the oxygen out of the room. They make it a point to avoid my probing gaze.

Jenner suddenly unleashes a loud bark of a laugh, making me nearly jump out of my skin. The sound is harsh against the backdrop of silence. "That's impossible," he scoffs.

Rai casts an uncertain glance at Ezra, drawing my focus back to his face, which is pale, his expression pinched and unmoving, as if his features have been carved out of stone. A sinking feeling weighs in my gut as the seconds seem to tick by at a snail's pace. It's as if everyone in the small room is waiting for Ezra to say something.

Especially me.

A strangled breath climbs up my throat when he finally speaks. "What did you see?"

I blink a drop of sweat out of my eyes, my heart racing, as I carefully select my next words. "That doctor I told you about… Richter." I pause. "He was with a group of other researchers along with Enforcers in the alley where I left my chip. They found it. They know I cut it out."

I roll my lower lip between my teeth as a thought occurs to me. It's been nearly two weeks since I escaped from the DSD. Dr. Richter would've found the tracking chip long before now; he wouldn't have waited this long to come find me. Unless… maybe these visions aren't just of the future but of things I haven't seen with my own two eyes—future, past, or present. Which would mean Dr. Richter was wrong and my visions aren't only of what's destined to happen days, weeks, months, or even years from now, but of anything this disease or fate or whatever is triggering them decides it wants me to see.

Just what is all this leading me to?

My father's face surfaces from my memory, gripping my heart and lungs in a vise. Could I see him again if I learned to control this ability?

Would these visions let me see the dead?

"It's not possible!" Jenner repeats, his voice raised.

The mattress squeaks beneath my weight as I recoil, my body shrinking back against the cold wall at the abrupt change in volume. I don't like Jenner shouting. Like water and milk, the two don't go well together. I wish I understood why he's so angry. I wish I knew how to bring back his smile.

He turns on Ezra, his cheeks turning ruddy. "Come on, man, seeing into the future? I think our little captive here must've hit her head. There's no way you can actually believe what she's saying."

Rai reaches out and plants a tentative hand on his shoulder. "Jenner—"

"No!" He sneers, stepping out of her grasp. "It's just not possible!"

Everyone goes silent again, and one by one, they all look down at the floor. Except me. Me, who was taught to never make eye contact or draw attention to myself. My gaze hangs on Jenner. Despite the kindness he's shown me, what I've said has driven a wedge between us for some inexplicable reason. Eighteen years of my mother's lessons ring in my head, telling me to mind my own business, but…this *is* my business, isn't it? I want to know what I did to offend him. I wish I knew how to set it right.

In my peripheral vision, Ezra lifts his head, and his solemn expression coaxes goosebumps up along every single inch of my body. When he speaks, the words that break the silence knock all the air from my lungs.

"Yes, it is."

I stare at him, half in shock and half in confusion. Is he saying what I think he's saying?

Does this mean he believes me?

Jenner poses the questions I can't find the words to ask. "How do you know? How *could* you know?"

Ezra's eyes snap to mine, and for the briefest flicker of a moment, all I see is the stranger from my vision, the tears carving lines down his cheeks. "Because I've seen it before—"

"Ezra," Rai interrupts.

I glance at her, surprised by the warning edge to her tone. My gaze shifts back and forth between her and Ezra as it dawns on me that this revelation isn't news to her like it is to me and Jenner. Whatever information Ezra has that gives him knowledge about my condition, whatever he's been through, whatever he's seen, one thing is certain: Rai knows about it.

Jenner shakes his head. "It's not—"

Anger distorts Ezra's features, and he slams his fist back against the concrete wall behind him. "My mother had the same illness, all right?"

Dropping his gaze, he slumps to the floor and rubs a hand across his eyes. A million thoughts run through my head in this moment, and I can't ignore the monumental realization that there's something else connecting us beyond what I saw at the DSD. Something that proves I'm not his enemy.

Is this link why he was in my vision?

Is this link what drove us together?

"She kept muttering these strange things that didn't make any sense." Ezra's voice is low, as if he's speaking to himself, and I find myself leaning in, eager to take in every word. I focus on his moving lips with rapt attention. "Everyone thought she was crazy, even my father. That's why he had her institutionalized. I guess he figured she wouldn't get better. At least, not without professional help. I can't really remember how long she was in the asylum since we were never allowed to visit. All I know is she died alone in that place."

A gasp rises in my throat, but I swallow it. Like the Detention facilities, asylums are located in Zone 7, far away from respected society. Unlike Detention, where we're told rehabilitation is possible, those unlucky enough to be institutionalized will never see the light of day again. Institutionalization is a death sentence—they might as well be sent to Termination. After all, the State only cares about contributing citizens, and those institutionalized cannot contribute. Even old age is frowned upon, although the State rewards a lifetime of servitude with cushy pensions once we reach seventy to entice compliance. But those at asylums… The only reason I can think of as to why they aren't disposed of like criminals is because no laws were broken resulting in their sentence. The State probably fears the outrage that would ensue if it started executing people just because they're unwell.

I think back to my first real conversation with Dr. Richter. As we sat on opposite sides of that long metal table, he had asked so many questions and explained things I still have difficulty wrapping my head around. He also showed me the files of the other known individuals who suffered from this disease. From Ultraxenopia. Individuals who probably died in an asylum—or, in more recent years, as the result of Dr. Richter's experiments once he realized what they were and the DSD got hold of them. Looking back, I wish I had thought to memorize their names. Maybe then I would know if Ezra's mother had been in that pile.

"It was the unusual circumstances of what happened to my mother that contributed to the selection of my brother's career," Ezra continues. "I guess now I know he's finally gained some insight into her condition after all these years."

"What do you mean?" But as the words breach my lips, it dawns on me that I know the answer. It can't be a coincidence. Not after the way Ezra and Rai—who I now know were childhood friends, thanks to Jenner—both reacted when I mentioned him.

"That doctor from the DSD… His name is Austin."

A door seems to open in front of me, revealing an obvious physical resemblance between Ezra and Dr. Richter. I can't believe I didn't notice it sooner. Although their eyes are different colors, they share the same angular jaw and the same furrowed brow. Even their noses and hair color are similar, the latter only differing by a few shades. Whereas Ezra's is dirty blond, Richter's hair is tinged auburn, warmer in hue, which I find ironic, considering his cold personality. Not that Ezra is exactly a fuzzy ball of sunshine.

I don't want to be right about this, terrified of what it could mean if I am. Because, if Dr. Richter is a monster…what exactly does that make his brother?

"Are you sure?" The question barely makes it past my lips, my voice hitching.

As Ezra nods, Rai, who has been silent up to this point, extinguishes any remaining doubt I have. "We knew which sector he was projected to enter."

"Wait a minute. One of those DSD scumbags is your *brother*?"

I look over at Jenner, watching as tremors of rage pin his arms to his sides and his hands clench into tight fists, the knuckles draining of color until the skin is bleached bone white. Before Ezra can answer, Jenner lunges across the small room, closing the distance between them. He only manages to grab hold of Ezra's shirt before Rai steps between them, shoving him back.

"Jenner! That's enough!" she shouts.

His upper lip curls back, revealing his top row of teeth, but he releases his grip. Seething, he turns away from us, cursing.

I risk a glance at Ezra, and it only takes a few seconds for me to recognize the emotion warping his expression, having felt the very same conflicted feelings toward my own mother that he must be feeling right now. But is his resentment directed at Jenner or at the brother who's causing this rift between them?

Scowling, he runs a hand through his hair. "Listen, I haven't seen or spoken to my brother in years. We became estranged shortly after my mother's death, at which point, he got permission to go by her maiden name, probably as a middle finger to our father. When I left home to join PHOENIX, he cut off all contact. He wanted nothing to do with me, and I never bothered to find out what he was up to. Case closed."

As Ezra speaks, I'm distracted by the look on Rai's face and by the tears glistening in her eyes at his words. Once again, I'm left wondering about her connection to the man who tortured me. Since she and Ezra have known each other since they were children, that must mean she knew Richter, too.

"You should've said something," Jenner grumbles, clicking his tongue with a disapproving tut. "That's a messed up thing to keep from us. Do you even realize what kind of danger that connection can put us all in?" He lets out a humorless laugh. "Lies and omissions like that make you no better than the State."

I wrap my arms around my legs, pulling them close to my chest, keeping my back to the wall and trying to make myself as small as possible. This conversation might have started with me, but it sure as hell hasn't ended with me.

Now, I'm nothing but an unwanted intruder.

"Jenner, let's go for a walk," Rai pleads.

He casts a begrudging look at her before stomping into the corridor, slamming the door shut behind him. She moves to follow but hesitates long enough to brush a hand against Ezra's shoulder. They exchange a silent glance, but neither one of them utters a word.

My eyes dart between them as Rai pulls open the door. Ezra doesn't move from his spot on the floor, his posture stiff and gaze downcast, and as Rai steps out of the room, the door clicks shut behind her, leaving the two of us alone.

# FIFTEEN

"I THINK I KNEW THIS whole time," Ezra murmurs. It's the first time he's spoken since Rai and Jenner left the room several minutes ago. "From that moment in The Vega when you said that you saw me, the way you said it…" He laughs under his breath. "Even then, I think I knew you and her were the same. I could see it—the fear and pain behind your eyes that I always saw in my mother's."

I hesitate, unsure what to say. We've both been affected by Ultraxenopia and made victims of it but in far different ways. I don't know if I can understand what he's been through any more than he could possibly comprehend what I've suffered.

As I stare at him—his eyes, both familiar and yet those of a stranger's, swimming with a glimpse of tears born of grief—I ask myself who this condition is worse for. The person who has to bear the brunt of the disease? Or the ones left behind who have to watch them deteriorate?

This line of thought never occurred to me before now since my own mother gave me up without question. She was all I had in the world. There was no one else for me to leave behind. No one to watch me succumb to this illness.

No one who loved me to watch me die.

I bite back tears and look down at my hands where they fidget in my lap, pinching the hem of the shirt Rai lent me—now soaked through with sweat and blood—between my trembling fingertips. When Ezra appeared in my vision, I didn't give much thought to who he was as a person. On the surface, he was simply my ticket out of the DSD, a cardboard cutout representing my freedom. After months of torture, finding an escape from Dr. Richter was all I cared about. Sure, his presence piqued my interest, but who he was—his life, his pain—were of little consequence to me.

But now, instead of a potentially imaginary stranger in my head, he's a living, breathing person in front of me, and I can no longer ignore the who behind the hazel eyes boring holes in my skin or what horrors or trauma made him that way.

For the first time, I realize how selfish it was of me to seek him out. With what little I know about his family and past, I can't help wondering if my being here is a problem for him. I can imagine all too easily what he's been through between the death of his mother and the broken bond with his brother—my own life an eerie mirror image of his pain. But what if those similarities between us are stirring up memories he'd rather forget?

What if the very thing drawing us together is also the thing that pushes us farther apart?

"Austin..." The forlorn timbre of Ezra's voice drags my gaze upward, and when our eyes meet, he clears his throat, hesitating for a moment before finally asking, "What did he do to you in there?"

I cock an eyebrow. Can he not guess what I went through? Maybe he just doesn't want to envision the suffering his own brother is capable of inflicting.

The memory of those unfeeling gray eyes washes over me. "I'll spare you the gruesome details, but I *will* tell you Richter won't stop until he gets what he's after. He didn't have any issue with risking my life in pursuit of it, and I doubt he cares about anyone else's."

Ezra frowns, turning his eyes to the floor. "It's my fault."

I blink, taken aback by this confession. "What? How do you figure?"

Silence stretches between us for so long I begin to think he won't answer. Then, in a quiet voice, he says, "My brother and I have always had different stances when it comes to our political viewpoints. Between the two of us, I've always been the more liberal one, dedicated to justice and helping others, whereas he's always been all about the future and his personal contribution to society. The perfect citizen of the State. Despite that, we got on well enough, but our relationship took a turn after our mother passed and it only worsened when I told him I was leaving home to join PHOENIX. He spouted off the typical nonsense about it being a terrorist organization and that I was setting myself up for a hard life at best and a painful death at Termination at worst. But, I knew in my gut, it was the one place where I could really make a difference and do something more with my life. Where I could escape the confines of a tyrannical government that was dictating my every decision and that had snatched my free will away the second I was born." Passion blossoms behind every word as he rants, his eyes alight with fire and fury. He pauses to lick his lips and draw in a breath. "So, I ignored him and did what I wanted to do. It didn't help the situation that Rai chose to come with me."

There it is again—that connection between Dr. Richter and Rai. But what *is* the connection? What were they to each other back then?

What are they to each other now?

As if reading my mind, Ezra adds, "My brother and Rai have a complicated history. Let's just say, her joining the rebellion wasn't the future he had envisioned for them."

It takes me a moment to grasp what he means. Ezra's relationship with Dr. Richter is estranged—he admitted that much earlier when Jenner freaked out about them being related. But what about Rai's relationship with him? What happened between them before she left home to join PHOENIX?

I recall the way she asked me if I thought Dr. Richter was a good man and the devastation that had filled her gaze when I said no. As I remember that moment, I find myself wondering if her affection for him was mutual. If it was, how did she feel when she left him?

If it was...does that mean he wasn't always a monster?

"How old were you when this happened?" I ask.

Ezra scratches the back of his neck while his other hand picks at a thread on his pants. "Well, I left home right before Austin took his placement exam, so fifteen. Rai was seventeen. It's been almost eight years, and neither one of us have seen or heard from him since."

*Eight years...* Is nearly a decade long enough for someone to forget that kind of abandonment?

I think back to my time at the DSD, reliving the sequence of events that occurred the day Dr. Richter's tests were finally successful. The day he saw my vision. The day he saw Ezra, his younger brother, again. The hairs on the back of my neck stand on end at the memory of the crazed look that flared in his eyes when he realized who it was I had seen.

*No,* I realize. Eight years isn't enough.

Ezra peeks up at me, his expression almost gentle, not that unlike how it was in my vision. Silence once again swells between us, and as the seconds tick by, I try to work out why someone like him would ever shed tears over someone like me. Brusque demeanor aside, he's a far better person than I am… or have ever been. He left behind the comfort of society to help other people, while I'm just trying my best to survive.

I don't deserve his remorse.

*"I'm sorry, Wynter."*

*Why?* I wonder again. *What are you going to do?*

"Why did you really come looking for me?"

I suck in a breath, unprepared for this question. I don't know why—he's already pressed me about that day and why I came to The Vega. I suppose I'm flustered by it this time because I know I won't keep getting away with some half-assed answer about the truth being complicated. If we're ever going to move forward, if I'm ever going to understand what's happening to me and what part he plays in my vision, then I need to tell him what happened.

He needs to know what I saw.

"During one of your brother's daily experiments on me, I saw you in a vision. By that point, he had already run more tests than I had bothered to count, and that was without the added motivation of knowing he could use me to locate PHOENIX or anyone else the State might want him to find. If I had stayed, he would've used my visions to hunt every last one of you down. Or kill me in the process of trying."

"So, you left," he finishes, slightly breathless.

I nod, ignoring the sharp pain that shoots through my left wrist when my hands squeeze into fists. "My reasons for leaving were purely selfish. I was being tortured. It was escape or die. I wish I could pretend otherwise, but the truth is, I didn't fully understand Dr. Richter's motivations or who else would be in danger because of me. Because of what I'm capable of."

I avert my gaze, not wanting to see even a hint of the disappointment I'm certain I'll find if I look Ezra in the eye. With this admission hanging in the air between us, I must look so small and unworthy of his help.

Swallowing, I force myself to continue. "That last day, once I'd made up my mind, I saw a glimpse of The Vega just before I escaped. I didn't have anywhere else to go, and it felt like the vision was pointing me in a single direction, a beacon of light guiding my way through the darkness that had cast such a huge shadow over my life in such a short space of time. The opportunity fell into my lap, so I took it, and that path led me to you. I'm only here because I want to understand why. And because I didn't know where else I could go where *he* wouldn't be able to find me."

Ezra sits up straight and narrows his eyes. "What was your vision about? The one where you saw me."

I shift, uncomfortable beneath the touch of his gaze, as reluctance overwhelms me. Maybe because there was an intimacy to what I saw that I'm embarrassed to voice. Or maybe because I don't want to burden him with what that future means.

Ezra cocks his head to one side, and there's something subtle about his expression that reminds me of how he looked at me in my vision.

Of how he *will* look at me.

"I-It was just you and me," I stammer. "You were saying you're sorry."

"Oh?" A trace of amusement crosses his face. "What was I apologizing for?"

My throat constricts. "I don't know."

*And I'm not sure I want to.*

His eyes flutter closed, and he exhales, his sigh strained. For whatever reason, he doesn't press me on the matter. "I suppose I do have a lot to apologize for. Rai would happily tell you as much."

My pulse quickens. "Like what?"

"The way I've treated you, for one," he answers with a lazy shrug.

He opens one eye to look at me, and an unfamiliar heat rises on my face, which I quickly hide behind my uninjured hand. My words escape through the cracks between my fingers. "You weren't sure if I could be trusted, I get it. The precautions you took were necessary."

"But the way I treated you wasn't. I should've at least listened to you first, been open to offering you the same help I've extended to everyone else here. The truth is, I was blinded by hate. I was blinded…" He trails off.

I arch a brow. "Let me guess. By the white coat?"

A laugh more like a huff parts his lips. "Yeah. Once I saw that DSD insignia, my fear took over. I allowed it to cloud my judgment."

Except, that's not entirely true. If it was, he wouldn't have bothered to save my life when I was bleeding out at The Vega. Despite what happened between him and his brother, despite his fear of the DSD, he pushed all those feelings aside to help me, a stranger who would've died if he hadn't.

Ezra pushes up from the floor and crosses the room in a handful of steps, holding out his right arm in front of me. As he stands beside the cot, waiting for me to take his hand, there's a split second where I see the man from my vision. He looks at me with those bewildering tears in his eyes, whispering those same three words that now haunt my every waking thought. But why is he begging me for forgiveness?

What is he going to do?

I blink, and suddenly, the Ezra of the present is back and the future that seems so far but so impossibly close is gone. A ghost of a smile plays at the edges of his mouth, and as my eyes drop down to his hand, I will myself to jump across this chasm between us. To do the opposite of what Dr. Richter warned me about in the moments right before I fled the DSD. To do the one thing I've been too scared to attempt since the day my father was taken from me.

To trust someone.

To trust Ezra.

The instant my hand slides into his awaiting grasp, he steps back and yanks me off the mattress. The nerves in my stomach flip when he turns and tugs me along behind him toward the door.

Panic seeps into my voice when I ask, "Where are we going?"

Ezra flashes a sly grin at me over his shoulder, the warmth lighting up his face unexpected and bright, like a ray of sunshine breaking through storm clouds.

"Out of this room," he says, his tone buoyant. "You're not our prisoner anymore."

# SIXTEEN

**EZRA LEADS ME ON AN** unfamiliar path through the corridors, the air between us charged with a strange sensation that makes my skin prickle and itch. I'm not sure what it is I'm sensing. The silence permeating the air isn't exactly unpleasant, but there's a noticeable shift between how he was acting before my latest vision and how he's acting with me now. A slight smile teases at the corners of his lips, only adding to my confusion. Maybe I'm just picking up on the fact that the distrust he's been clinging to seems to have vanished.

I watch him out of my peripheral vision, wary of the unknown motivation behind his sudden change in attitude. As much as I want to trust him, the difference is far too great and came on too quickly to be convincing. For that reason, I don't buy it. There's something he's not telling me.

Something he doesn't want me to know.

"Here we are."

He pushes open an oval-shaped bulkhead door to my right, stepping over the metal lip into the small but cozy space beyond. Curious, I peek past him into the empty quarters, immediately taking note of the bed. I don't need to look at the plump mattress for more than a few seconds to know it's way more comfortable than anything else I've slept on for months.

"I think you'll find this much more to your liking. We aren't in the business of holding prisoners here, and that other room is actually more of a storage closet, so it wasn't really a long-term solution."

A breath sticks in my throat. Long-term? Does this mean he wants me to stay here with PHOENIX? Rai said something along those lines, but is staying here really even an option for me?

Hope swells in my chest, but its presence is fleeting, like a fire doused by a downpour of water. Too many bad things have happened to me in my life, and now, my brain is programmed to think nothing good ever can. Or will. Even the thought of a new life here with people who might actually care about me is marred by doubt and suspicion.

My movements are cautious as I step into the tiny square room, my gaze skirting along the gray walls. Although the aesthetic is reminiscent of my cell at the DSD, this space still feels like home in a way the terraced house I shared with my mother in Zone 2 never did. Maybe because I always sensed a distance between us—a deep river she wasn't willing to cross, further proven when she handed me over to Richter. But here, the people didn't turn me away the second my life was in danger and I needed their help. Here, every river they face has a bridge.

Upon coming full circle, I meet Ezra's gaze, a frown forming between my brows.

"I know what you're thinking, and don't worry," he says. "You aren't taking this bed away from anyone. This place is big enough that we actually have rooms to spare."

"That wasn't exactly what I was thinking."

"Oh." Uncertainty flashes across his face. "Okay, then what were you thinking?"

I hesitate, watching my foot as the bottom of my shoe scuffs against the concrete floor. "I was wondering if it's okay that you're offering me this. If you actually have the authority to decide who is and who isn't a prisoner here."

His expression hardens. "You let me worry about that. I'm on your side now. That's all that matters."

*But why are you?* I want to ask. Is he only doing this because of his mother? Because we're victims of the same disease? Or is it because of something else I'm not seeing?

What's changed?

I'm tempted to press the matter, but I hold back the words of protest building up in my throat. I don't want to test the limits of Ezra's graciousness when we finally seem to be making progress.

My teeth bite down on my lower lip as I sneak a longing glance back at the bed. There's no reason why I shouldn't accept this small comfort. If I reject it, I'd only be doing so to punish myself. Between months of torture at the DSD and my recent brush with death from blood loss and sepsis—according to Rai when I pressed her one day about the time I spent unconscious—I think I've been punished enough. Clearly, Ezra seems to think so, too.

The silence between us drags on for a few seconds too long to be natural. Clearing his throat, Ezra looks over at the door. "I'll get Rai to find some extra clothes for you. There are bound to be some lying around here somewhere. If not, we'll figure something out."

"Thank you," I whisper.

When I speak, that ghost of a smile returns and it's like I'm looking at a different person than the man I met in that dingy bar in Zone 7. In the brief time I've spent with Rai and Jenner, I've discovered how compassion can be a driving force, especially when distanced from the draining nature of the State, which discourages such sentiments. Sympathy—or in Ezra's case, empathy, considering he's seen what I'm going through before with his mother—can alter a person's mindset toward anything, regardless of the circumstances.

Or, in our case, because of the circumstances.

Since learning I suffer from the same disease his late mother had, Ezra's visibly softened toward me—his eyes now warm and curious rather than hard and glistening with distrust and suspicion. By now, he must know I'm not a spy for the State but a victim of it, just like everyone here. Just like his mother, who was abandoned in an asylum to die alone. Otherwise, why would he be doing all this? I have to believe he wouldn't show me such kindness unless he knew I wasn't a threat.

An awkward hush fills the room as I shuffle forward and plop down on the bed, the mattress welcoming my weight with a creaking sigh of the springs. A smile spreads across my face as I fall back against the blankets, forgetting Ezra's presence and pushing aside the unending stream of questions plaguing my mind.

I've only been here for a brief time, but I can sense something changing within me, as if all the emotions the State has encouraged me to repress my whole life are inching closer to the surface. Perhaps, like me, they're reaching for freedom. Freedom from a life of conformity. Freedom from fear.

Freedom to live life how I choose.

"I'll, uh…leave you to get settled, then," Ezra says.

Rubbing a hand across the back of his neck, he turns for the door, stepping over the raised threshold without uttering another word. I follow his rigid movements with narrowed eyes, wondering why he suddenly seems so out of sorts. But the answer never comes to me and I'm too exhausted to care.

Shrugging, I relax against the soft mattress, and as my body unwinds, a fog of sleep washes over me. My eyes drift closed, embracing the darkness, but I'm pulled back into full awareness by the sound of my name.

"Wynter."

My eyes peek open and lock on Ezra where he wavers in the doorway. As he stares at me, I realize this is the first time I've heard him say my name—well, the first time in person and not in my head—and hearing it reminds me of what I saw in my vision. Of that future where we stand together, just the two of us alone at the end of the world.

"I have to ask." He hesitates, averting his gaze. "Did my brother say what he wanted with you?"

I bristle at the mention of Dr. Richter. I understand why Ezra would want to know more about my time at the DSD and my connection to his villainous brother, but the memory of what I went through is distressing, and I'd really rather not talk about it if I don't have to. Still, knowing what I do about his mother and accepting that the story of my disease doesn't only belong to me, I decide he deserves to know.

Frowning, I shake my head and sit upright. "No. Just that I'd be doing a service to the State if I cooperated. I know he planned on using my visions to lead him to PHOENIX, but he never told me anything else. I assumed I was just some guinea pig for him to study and then dispose of once I'd exhausted my usefulness."

I consider this line of thought for a moment. Now that I know Dr. Richter and Ezra are brothers, I wonder what the former really wanted with me. Did he just want to locate PHOENIX so he could track down Ezra and get his revenge? Or was he hoping to find Rai and bring her home? Or was it a combination of both and also doing his duty to the State? Perhaps, it was something else altogether.

Ezra stares at the wall behind me, his eyes glazing over. Then, as if coming to some internal revelation, he crosses the room and crouches in front of me. "I think it might be best if we keep this to ourselves for now. Don't tell anyone else what the State wants with you, and whatever you do, don't mention your condition or my brother, okay?"

I gape at him, bewildered by his unexpected request. I get why he wouldn't want me to say anything about Dr. Richter—the news of their familial connection might not reflect well on him considering how long he's kept it a secret—but I don't understand why he wants me to hide the rest. What does he think will happen if I don't? Aren't all the people here also running from the State?

Don't they protect their own?

*But you're not really one of them, are you?* an annoying voice in the back of my head reminds me.

"I can't control what's happening to me," I snap. My tone is sharper than I intend, but I don't apologize for it. I lost much of my ingrained politeness thanks to the hell I went through at the DSD. "And a friendly reminder, I *just* had a seizure in front of everyone living here. Sure, maybe they won't think much of that now, but they will the second it happens again. And when that time comes, they'll start asking questions."

He knows I'm right—I can tell as much by the disgruntled expression spreading over his face. The effects of this disease will be impossible to hide. Sooner or later, the others will demand to know what's wrong with me and why I'm really here.

Sooner or later, the truth will come out.

"No one else has to know the details," he says. "Let them think what they want. The important thing is that we keep you safe."

*Why?* I want to ask. Why is what happens to me so damn important to him? Hopefully not because of anything having to do with his brother or the DSD. Then again, refugees or not, these people are part of a rebellion. It would be foolish of me not to acknowledge that a tool of the enemy is also a weapon against it.

A shiver runs across my skin at the thought.

As I silently question Ezra's reasoning and motives, something occurs to me. "Are you just saying this because of what happened with Jenner?"

Ezra lowers his gaze. "You know, I can count on one hand how many times I've seen Jenner mad. Like, *actually* mad. I must've really pissed him off."

"Will he forgive you?" My voice catches a little, and I take a deep breath to hide the unease racing through me. Forgiveness is as much a part of my world as empathy or understanding. The State doesn't care about your point of view or why you did anything. It only cares if you follow the rules and what punishment you deserve should you break them. Forgiveness is never even on the table.

"Of course." Ezra waves his right hand dismissively. "We've

been friends for years, and it'll take much more than one fight to jeopardize what we have. He'll calm down once he realizes I've done nothing wrong."

I can't even fathom that notion—one built around the concept of forgiveness. Forgiveness doesn't exist in the State. One mistake, and you're guilty. End of discussion. And guilt always leads to punishment of some kind, some worse than others. Some deadly. People don't even risk arguments with family or friends out of fear of what outcome it might lead to.

Ezra, Jenner, and Rai were all raised in the Heart, just like me. They would've experienced the line we all have to toe for the sake of avoiding the vengeful wrath of the State. And yet, it hasn't escaped my notice that, ever since my arrival, all they've done is argue, as if the submissive traits they had growing up have all worn away the longer they've lived outside normal society. It's fascinating to watch, except for the fact that the disagreements are almost always because of me. I might not know them well, but that doesn't mean I want to be the wedge that drives them apart. I came here to find Ezra, to find answers about my condition and the future we're all unknowingly barreling toward. Not to make his life or anyone else's harder than it already is.

"You know, I wasn't too receptive to the idea when Rai first ran it by me, but I've been thinking a lot and I agree with her now." Ezra laughs at the confused look on my face, the sound flooding my body with warmth while simultaneously spreading through me like a chill. A gentle smile curls up his lips. "You should stay," he clarifies. "You belong here as much as any of us. Maybe more so considering the bastards you've run from."

That feeling of hope returns to my chest, but it's fleeting, a weak flicker, like a faltering heartbeat.

"I'm not a rebel, so I don't know how much help I'd be," I admit. "I didn't come here to try to change the world."

*Only my own.*

He shrugs. "No one in PHOENIX is claiming to be a hero. We're all just trying to get by and do whatever we have to do to survive. Sound familiar?"

My eyes widen. That does sound familiar. My entire life has been built around the need to survive. Ever since my father was arrested and executed, I've been on constant alert, always in sight of the State's watchful eye. But here, the State can't reach me or see me. Here, I can do more than just survive and spend my days living in a bubble of fear.

Maybe, here in this place, I can live.

The memory of my vision floods my head as Ezra rises from the floor and shifts onto the bed beside me. The unspoken connection I sensed between us intensifies the closer he gets, like heat against my skin. I flush, wondering if he feels it, too.

We sit, side by side, neither one of us daring to penetrate the hush with empty words. As the silence thickens, what Ezra said about hiding my condition drifts back to the forefront of my mind. What will these people do when they find out why I'm here? What will they do when they find out what I am?

"I know we didn't exactly get off on the right foot, and it might seem odd given my recent behavior, but you can always talk to me if you need to get something off your chest. I'm not a bad listener."

I peek over at Ezra, and he smiles again, raising one tawny brow in encouragement. The words stick to the roof of my mouth, held back by eighteen years of forced emotional suppression. I gave in with Rai, but even then, I knew opening up on that level to someone could reveal a weakness they could then exploit. And that's exactly what it would be if I spilled my guts to someone who I would've sworn hated me only an hour ago. It would be weakness. It would expose the desperate desire for human connection I didn't even realize was present within me.

At least, that's what the State has trained me to think. But now, as my eyes fix on Ezra's, the alternative hangs before me. Perhaps divulging my concerns is the first step in bringing us closer together and will help me uncover the extent of our connection and how it leads to that desolate future.

Maybe this is the key to understanding my visions.

"You haven't seen how everyone here looks at me," I blurt out, unable to keep the agitated edge out of my voice. "I've lived in fear long enough to recognize the signs. They're terrified of me."

I almost miss the avoidance I encountered every single day in the Heart. I'm not used to so many eyes staring at me. I'm not used to being viewed as the enemy. In some ways, I almost feel like the evil creatures from the fairy tales my father told me when I was young—dark, haunting stories forbidden in our society. Stories he never told me around my mother. To the people here, my motives are unknown. To them, I could be dangerous.

To them, I might very well be a monster.

*You killed someone,* that infuriating voice chimes in. *They'd be right to think that.*

Luckily for me, they don't know what I did. I don't even allow myself to wonder how much would be different if they knew the truth.

Ezra places a hand on my shoulder, and to my surprise, I don't shy away from his touch.

"I'll talk to them," he promises.

"Is there really any point?" I press. "They're going to find out about me eventually. You can't hide the truth from them forever. Then, they'll realize they were right to be afraid."

Ezra holds my gaze for a moment, searching for answers I have no incentive to give, then says, almost to himself, "You're right. Maybe we shouldn't, then."

My stomach clenches. "What do you mean?"

"We tell them the State's after you without saying why. If they ask, we make something up. Something that won't give anyone reason to—" He clamps his mouth shut, cutting off the rest of whatever he was about to say. When his eyes shift to mine, I furrow my brow at him.

*Reason to what?* I nearly scream.

Ignoring my silent question, he says, "It's been a long time since we had anyone new join our sect, so they probably just want some assurances that you aren't going to get us all arrested. Or killed. Once that suspicion is gone, they'll accept you into the fold. They just need to believe you're one of us first." He jumps off the bed and extends his arm in front of me, his hand palm up in offering. "It's a bit of a long shot, but I have an idea. You in?"

I stare at Ezra's hand, leery of his scheming expression. As if to reassure me—or possibly warn me—a slideshow of images from my vision manifest in my mind, once again showing me those hazel eyes and the tears over whatever it is he's going to do that makes me wonder if I should trust him.

Warnings flash like neon lights behind my eyes, but I ignore them and slide my hand into his. I'm not sure what's running through his head, and that frightens me. But, at this moment, at least for right now, I want to believe he has my best interests at heart. I want to believe he's on my side, as he claimed. I want to believe I can trust him.

Now, it's time to find out if he's lying.

# SEVENTEEN

I WATCH EZRA, TRAILING A few feet behind him, my eyes trained on his back every step of the way. His stride is confident, which is almost reassuring, considering what he's planning on doing. Almost.

"Are you sure about this?" I ask, a slight tremble to my voice.

"As sure as I'll ever be." Despite these words, he doesn't meet my gaze.

I shadow him through the labyrinth of corridors as we retrace the path Jenner and Rai took me on just this morning, before I passed out from my vision. The fluorescent strip lighting seems to get brighter the longer we walk, sprouting black spots in front of my eyes and giving me flashbacks to Dr. Richter's experiments.

I swipe the back of my hand across my forehead, brushing away a sheen of sweat. I don't know why I'm so nervous. Regardless of what happens next, the path I'm on can only lead one way, meaning any worries I have about the situation are pointless. From what I've seen, the future—*that* future—is set in stone.

A shudder races over my skin at the thought. I'm not sure if it's comforting or terrifying knowing that nothing Ezra is about to do really matters.

He leads me back to that large central room, the space empty compared to how crowded it was the last time I was in here, before I collapsed. As we pause at the threshold, I spot Rai and Jenner huddled together on a bench in the distant left corner.

Jenner notices us almost at once, his eyes flickering from me to Ezra, where they hang for a moment, narrowing in lingering indignation. I'm tempted to smile or wave or whatever it is normal people do in greeting, but all I can think about is the way he reacted when I told him, Ezra, and Rai the truth about what's wrong with me. About what I can do. Of the three of them, I figured he would be the one to believe me.

Of the three of them, he was the one who didn't.

A hollow ache wraps around my heart and spreads outward, infecting the rest of my body, until I'm nothing more than agitated nerves in a shell that merely resembles a person. To distract myself from the gnawing sensation, I focus my attention on Rai. Her mouth shapes words, but I can't make them out.

Jenner says something back, waving his hands in an animated gesture as he casts a sidelong glance in our direction, but Rai just rolls her eyes and grabs at his arm, jumping to her feet and dragging him up along with her. He doesn't put up a fight; he just scowls, shoving his hands into his pockets like a sulking child. When Rai crosses the room, he follows behind her, keeping his gaze pinned down on the floor.

Once they're both within earshot, Ezra jerks his chin toward the exits. "Gather everyone for an emergency meeting. It's time we introduce Wynter properly."

Rai hesitates, examining Ezra's face for a moment, as if

hoping to glean more information from his silence. Or maybe she's wondering if he has permission to go through with this. From where I'm standing, his stony expression gives nothing away, but she must see something in his gaze that assures her because she nods and veers out of the room to complete the task given to her, no questions asked. Jenner, on the other hand, stops dead in his tracks, his eyes no longer on the floor but locked on my face. Unlike before when I was tempted to smile or wave, I only want to look away. He doesn't even spare a second glance at Ezra.

A gasp parts my lips when Ezra's hand grazes mine, my heart jumping into my throat as his fingers move up my arm and come to rest on my shoulder. Heat flushes my skin when he meets my gaze, but I'm not sure if it's the intense look on his face causing this reaction in me or the fact that Jenner is watching us.

"Wait here," he instructs in a quiet murmur, his breath tickling my ear.

Fire ignites in my blood at his touch, but the unexpected thrill rushing through me is nothing compared to the sinking sensation taking hold of my stomach. I can't explain it, just as I can't explain why, as he walks away, I feel exposed and alone. After all, I'm used to a life of isolation. That's all I've ever known. But life in this compound is nothing like life in the State, and without him beside me, I have nothing to shield me from the wary stares of the handful of people present in the room. The distrust blazing in their eyes as they stare at me is like an inferno burning over my skin.

I immediately lower my gaze, unable to face the suspicion assaulting me from all sides. Ezra's plan won't work. No one here will ever believe I'm not a threat. They won't trust me. They can't. They—

*Know what you are,* a crooning voice finishes in my head. It reminds me of Dr. Richter. Hell, maybe it is. Maybe all that torture has rooted his cruelty into my very subconscious and it's only now rearing its head to torment me. *They can sense the danger emanating from you,* the voice continues. *They suspect what you did…murderer.*

I shiver as goosebumps rise along every inch of my body. No, I refuse to believe that. They can't know. How would they? Not even Ezra knows. Then, a more disturbing thought strikes me, hard and fast, like a knife to the chest. If he did, would he still say he's on my side? Or would he turn against me?

I swallow as the dull thud of footsteps resounds in my ears, and the hairs on the back of my neck stand on end when black boots enter my line of vision. Dread sends my heart racing as my eyes leap upward, fixing onto the face of the person they belong to.

"Hey."

The left side of Jenner's mouth pinches into that kind, lopsided smile I've grown so fond of, but behind it, he seems nervous. Uncertain. The slight dimple in his cheek fades when he frowns and rocks back onto the heels of his feet.

"Listen, I'm sorry about earlier. I didn't mean to imply that you're a liar or anything. It's just…what you said… It put this nagging thought in my head. If *I* had this power you supposedly have, if I had known what was going to happen to my family, would things be different now? Would they be alive? Would I have still found myself in the position that forced me to choose between death at the hands of the DSD or joining PHOENIX?

I guess, on some nonsensical level, it didn't seem fair you had this advantage and I didn't."

*Advantage?*

I've never looked at it that way. To me, it's always been more like a curse. I suppose, from an outside perspective—from the viewpoint of someone not suffering through this disease—I can understand why he might see it like that.

Dr. Richter certainly did.

I open my mouth to attempt to say something consoling, but the words fail to form on my tongue. Jenner's experienced a devastating loss and bears the burden of that pain even now, so I can appreciate why he would think what I can do is unfair, even though he isn't alone in his grief. Even though others have also had their fair share of it in their lives. Including me.

"Then, hearing about Ezra's brother… Well, I guess that just kind of tipped me over the edge. Ez and Rai know everything there is to know about me, and today, I realized, I can't say the same about them. Which, of course, made me wonder what else they aren't telling me."

"I get it. They've become your family. If you can't trust them, who can you trust?" I ask. If only he knew how much that concern haunts me, too.

"Yeah." He grimaces. "Exactly."

An awkward hush spreads between us, wrapping the room in an almost tangible silence that presses down on my lungs, strangling my breaths. As I search for something to say, desperate to return to how things were before he knew the truth about me, I realize how much I miss the Jenner I've come to know over the course of the last week. The Jenner who made sure I felt comfortable and welcome when nearly everyone else avoided me out of fear. The Jenner who, despite being a stranger, disclosed things to me that were personal—things we're taught not to dwell on or share in our world because nothing and no one should matter more than our purpose within the societal structure of the State. The Jenner who showed me it's okay to feel. The Jenner who I could call my friend when I never knew what friendship was before coming here.

I search for him in the features of the man standing before me. To my relief, he stares back at me through those piercing blue eyes.

"So, this *gift* of yours..." He casts a quick look over his shoulder, dropping his voice to a conspiratorial whisper. "Is it always like that?"

I wish I could lie. I wish I could say what I know he wants to hear, but what good would that do either of us? It wouldn't make this disease any easier to bear. It wouldn't cure me or take away what I've been through or what still awaits. If I were to lie, I'd only be doing so to spare myself from his inevitable horror.

No, being dishonest at this point is useless. I can't lie to him about it any more than I can lie to myself.

"For the most part, yeah." I shrug, as if it's no big deal the disease ravaging my body keeps treating my brain like an over-boiled egg about to explode from the pressure constantly building up inside it.

"Wow." He balks, and it takes him a few seconds to recover as he comes to terms with my confession. Nostrils flaring, he drags in a breath and lets it out slowly, muttering, "That must *really* suck."

His bluntness pulls a laugh out of me, but the sound is strained as it springs from my throat. Jenner doesn't seem to notice. He laughs as well, and after, we just grin at each other, comfortable in our silence again.

The smile only slips from his face when his eyes drift from mine, glancing over my right shoulder and narrowing at something in the distance behind me. Swallowing, I follow his gaze to where Rai stands in the closest of the two doorways to the large central room, ushering a small group into the space. Ezra arrives through the other entryway a few minutes later, bringing what I assume must be the rest of their community.

Jenner and I say nothing as we watch Rai and Ezra herd everyone into the room. When he doesn't move from my side, I glance up at him, but the confusion and worry I expect to glimpse on his face are nowhere to be found. He doesn't know what Ezra's going to say or how much he's about to reveal about me—for all he knows, it could be everything—and yet, he doesn't seem concerned. If anything, he's unnervingly calm.

*That's because he trusts Ezra,* I realize. Jenner might be furious with him right now, but he knows Ezra wouldn't go out of his way to hurt me, even though I'm a stranger to them. Even though my being here puts them all in danger. Because, to Jenner, I don't deserve the hand I've been dealt and he views me as an innocent, even though I'm the furthest thing from it.

I can't help wondering if he would still think that if he knew I killed someone.

The residents of the compound shuffle into the middle of the room, sharing curious glances and voicing their suspicions about why they've all been called together. As a murmur of confusion carries through the space, buzzing through the air in an incoherent wave of jumbled words, Ezra weaves through the crowd, gripping the edge of an empty wooden crate in his hand. Pushing out a breath, he drops the crate to the floor, steps up onto it, and locks eyes with the perplexed sea of faces.

In one cohesive movement, the crowd shifts its attention from Ezra to me, and my body buckles beneath the weight of the speculative whispers, even with Jenner's comforting presence beside me. His fingers wrap around my shoulder and squeeze.

When Ezra lifts his arms, the drone of conversation dies away, replaced by an eager, expectant silence. I peek up at him out of the corner of my eye, noting the way his chest rises and falls with each breath, as if he, too, is anticipating what will come next.

As his arms drop back to his sides, he speaks, his voice an authoritative boom of thunder cracking through the room. "I know you're all wondering about our latest addition. About who she is and why she's here. Well, let me put the rumors to rest. The answer is simple. She's here because she needs our protection, the same as any of you."

"From what?" A man who appears to be a few years older than Ezra steps forward from the crowd, grasping the hand of a young girl, who stumbles after him, her face as white as a sheet. Her wide eyes dart to mine, shining with fear.

I glance over at Ezra as he clasps his hands behind his back and lifts his chin, standing just a little bit taller. Although his stance is strong and his expression commanding, I see this facade for what it is: a lie.

Just like the lies he's about to spew about me.

As the overhead lights reflect off the sweat beading just beneath his hairline, a realization hits me. I glimpsed it before when I collapsed in this room, and I see it again now, glowing in the amber-tinted depths of his gaze. The look I find there gives away his true feelings at this moment, just as it gave away his grief in my vision.

He's afraid.

"Re-education," he answers, not missing a beat. "Her nerves got the best of her during her placement exam, and she ran out before finishing it. You all know what the State is like. Punish first, ask questions later."

Ezra doesn't elaborate any more than that or clarify when my exam actually was. The way he says it would make anyone think my exam occurred the day we met at The Vega, as if I'd sought out PHOENIX right after. Considering what we're trying to hide, it's best if that's what everyone thinks.

A rumble passes through the crowd as some bob their heads in agreement while others look even more perplexed than before. I peek at Jenner, then over at Rai, but they're both masters of deception, their faces still and blank, as if this information isn't news to them, reaffirming the lie. I suppose it isn't, but they also know Re-education was never what Dr. Richter had planned for me.

*They trust Ezra*, I repeat to myself as my eyes crawl over the group. *They trust that he knows what he's doing.*

"Typical. The exam is a joke," one woman scoffs, offering me a pitying smile.

But the man beside her doesn't look as convinced.

"Is it true she confronted you in The Vega while wearing a DSD-issue coat?" he asks, his dark eyes fixing Ezra with a challenging stare that sends a chill over my skin.

When Ezra doesn't answer straightaway, my anxiety heightens, constricting my lungs. Jenner, sensing the tension coursing through me, once again squeezes my shoulder, his warm fingers an immediate comfort to my nerves. I melt into his touch, wishing this could be over.

Before I can look back over at Ezra to see what he's doing and try to work out how he'll skirt around the truth this time, he recovers, expelling his next lie with ease. "Yes, we met at The Vega. She had been running since morning, was tired, thirsty, and had stumbled into the bar looking for water. As for the coat, her mother works at the DSD as a lab technician in Engineering. She stole it from their house to disguise herself before making her way to Zone 7. Bumping into each other was nothing more than dumb luck."

It takes all the self-restraint I can muster not to raise an eyebrow at him in disbelief. My mother...an employee for the DSD? If it wouldn't reveal that we're lying, I'd laugh. My mother works for an insurance company—the closest she comes to torturing people is denying them cover when they make a claim.

Pushing the sheer absurdity of the notion aside, why would Ezra say my mother works for the DSD after he was so insistent no one find out about his brother? Won't the people here view me as an even bigger threat if they think my mother works for the most feared institution in the State? Then again, we needed a believable explanation to account for the coat—too many people at The Vega saw me that day—and without a plausible cover story, it would be easy enough to discover the truth if someone here wanted to dig deeply enough or poke at the holes in Ezra's lie. As for the rest of what he's said, about our meeting being nothing more than coincidence, no one else was part of our brief conversation that day. No one knew why I was really there or that I knew exactly who Ezra was the moment I saw him. But the coat...

Everyone at The Vega saw it.

An outcry of panic drowns out Ezra's voice, and as his gaze passes over the crowd, I realize why else he opted for this lie. He's feeling everyone out, seeing how they react upon learning that someone they know is related to an employee of the DSD. It's risky, but he wants to see if they'll turn on him if they find out about Dr. Richter.

"They'll come after her!" one woman screams, hysteria creeping into her tone.

"They'll kill us all!" cries another.

Countless outbursts flood the room with everyone trying to talk over each other, and the distrust I sensed from these people before is intensified now that they've swallowed Ezra's falsified version of the truth. But unlike before, when that suspicion was kept at a safe distance, the general feeling in the room is hostile.

Now, these people are out for my blood.

Ezra meets my gaze as the crowd inches forward, closing in on me, but he doesn't look worried or even surprised by this chain of events. Was this his plan all along? What is he hoping to achieve by stoking the flames of their fear?

Jenner pulls me back a few steps as Rai puts herself between me and those standing at the front of the group, her arms spread wide, forming a barrier. "They can't track her," she shouts over the uproar. "She cut out her ID chip—"

The crack of a gunshot brings an end to the chaos, silencing everyone in the room. All eyes turn to Ezra, whose hand is raised high above his head, tightly clutching his pistol.

"Let me finish," he says, his voice stern, like a parent

disciplining their children. "Even if the State was interested in locating Wynter, it would struggle to find her since her tracking chip is gone. She cut it out before we met at The Vega. As it stands, the only person at risk here is her mother, who will now be viewed as a traitor on the basis of helping her child escape. That's how the State will swing it to cover the scandal, and the missing coat will be all the proof it needs to convict."

His words fade to a soft murmur in the back of my mind as dread pools in the pit of my stomach, a poison slowly flooding my system. He's right. I remember thinking as much when Jenner told me the story about his family and how they were all executed at Termination when he disappeared from their lives. Mother and I got lucky when Father was arrested, but what about when I was taken into custody after my placement exam? She had seemed so calm that day with the Enforcers stood on either side of her, but what happened after that? Is my mother still alive, or did she succumb to the same fate as my father?

"So, she sacrificed her mother to save herself? Is that really the kind of person we want here?" a woman at the front of the group asks, her tone biting.

Her words are a slap to the face, and it takes all the self-restraint I can muster not to flinch. If it wouldn't jeopardize our cover, I'd set the record straight about exactly the kind of person my mother is.

Luckily, I don't have to.

"We've already spoken to Wynter about that, and she has assured us her mother is every bit the heartless savage the DSD is known for recruiting. If anything, she did us a favor by framing her. One less monster for us to deal with."

My heart seizes at that word. *Monster.* Doubt shivers through me. Despite everything she's done to earn the title, my mother still isn't as bad as me. Between the two of us, *I'm* the murderer.

Between us, I'm the real monster.

When no one speaks up again, Ezra continues. "I know you're afraid, but just try to remember how *you* felt when you first left life in the State to join PHOENIX. We didn't know you, and yet, we never treated you the way we're all treating Wynter now. She isn't the first of us to have ties to the DSD. If you'll recall, we even saved some of you from a one-way trip to Termination. This isn't anything new, so why are we treating her as if she's different?" He pauses a moment, letting what he's said sink in before adding, "I'm asking you to trust me the same way you did when you came here. I didn't lie to you then, and I'm not lying to you now. I promise, she isn't a threat."

*Sure,* I agree. *So long as I don't leave.*

Ezra's eyes meet mine, and, in that moment, I know we're thinking the same thing. If I were to wind up back in the hands of the DSD, it's almost guaranteed Dr. Richter would use me to hunt down PHOENIX. He would tear open my mind and rip out my thoughts until every last rebel was accounted for.

The only way that won't happen is if he never finds me again. The only way that won't happen is if I never leave this place.

"And if the DSD *is* looking for her? What then?"

A middle-aged man with pale blue eyes and ashy blond hair moves to the front of the crowd. I recognize him immediately. It was his birthday that everyone was celebrating earlier.

The birthday I interrupted with my seizure.

He looks up at Ezra, crossing his arms. Unlike the others, his expression is calm but pressing, as if demanding an answer. As if he's entitled to one.

A spark of curiosity festers within me, and as I study his face, I remember how Ezra dodged my question when I asked about his authority here and how Rai had insisted he isn't in charge. But what about this man? He's at least twenty years older than either of them, making him a more suitable age for leadership.

Could he be the one who's been making every decision about my presence here?

Ezra offers a nonchalant shrug. "Well, if the DSD *is* looking for her, it's probably in our best interest to ensure they don't find her. We're in a position of power if we have what they want."

Although his words hold no malice, my heart still beats against my ribcage as the doubts I told myself to ignore flare up again, overtaking my thoughts.

I knew before I went looking for Ezra that he and the others in PHOENIX might not accept me, just like I knew I was walking into the middle of a decades—if not centuries—long war. But after everything I've been told, after everything Rai and Jenner have done to make me feel welcome, is this what it's come to? Is this why Ezra's taking my side now and trying so hard to get me to trust him? After everything he said to me…am I only a pawn?

Or is this just another lie to protect me?

Once again, I'm reminded of the last thing Dr. Richter said, just before I escaped the DSD.

*"If you think you can trust him, you're wrong."*

I didn't want to believe him then. I still don't. But I can't deny that part of me wonders if he's right.

Can I really trust Ezra Laramie?

"So, she's a tool against the enemy?" someone asks, calling out from the back of the room.

This idea spreads through the space like a ravenous wildfire, moving over every face staring at me. Several members nod their approval while others look at me, confused—probably trying to figure out how I can possibly be used to their benefit.

The whole time, Jenner's hand stays on my shoulder. His grip tightens to console me, but I find little comfort in his touch as the discontented mob moves forward. If anything, his hand is a cage. It holds me in place, refusing to let go.

*Maybe I made a mistake coming here.*

This isn't the first time this thought has crossed my mind, but I brushed it off and told myself I was just being paranoid. But, now, as I stare out at the crowd, I realize my suspicions were right. I don't belong here.

And I never will.

Another gunshot cuts through the air, returning the room to a tense state of silence. Lowering his arm, Ezra jumps down from the crate.

He steps toward the group, which parts down the middle, making way for his approach. Once he's standing in the center of the room, he spins in a slow circle, looking at each face in turn.

"Why are any of you here? Perhaps you joined PHOENIX following the death of a loved one, or maybe you were fed up with the unjust nature of our society. Either way, you wanted an out and we gave you one. It's no different for her."

Every set of eyes in the crowd follows the direction of his outstretched finger, landing on me. The scrutiny of their combined gazes sends a rolling shudder over my skin.

"If we abandon her now just because we're afraid, then what the hell do we stand for?" he growls.

Another unsettled murmur casts a cloud over the room.

Some people voice their uncertainty, while others hang back, too afraid to speak. Really, who can blame any of them for reacting this way? They're worried their sole means of survival is threatened, and thanks to me, everything they've worked so hard for could change or collapse at any moment.

I never wanted to negatively affect anyone's life—I just wanted to save my own, and now, my selfishness has put these people in danger, more so than they even realize. Everyone here has sacrificed so much already. It isn't right that we're asking them to risk what little they have left to protect me, someone they don't even know. I haven't earned that loyalty.

I don't deserve it.

Ezra keeps talking—his voice building in volume and urgency, ringing in my ears—and I gape at him, hardly able to believe what I'm hearing. My heart picks up speed, beating in time with each syllable. "By accepting those who run, we make ourselves stronger. And that strength will, in turn, make the State weak! Wynter is one of us now. So, let's start acting like it."

Why is he doing this?

*Why is he fighting for me?*

An ominous hush blankets the crowd, but with the silence comes something that wasn't there before. I glimpse whatever it is in their faces, their expressions now shed of that familiar suspicion.

I risk a glance at Ezra, and although he meets my questioning gaze, he says nothing.

One by one, the people gathered in the room shuffle toward me, but their advance lacks the anger and hostility it held before. Regardless, fear bubbles under my skin, and I hold myself still, ready to face their judgment. Instead, they each take a turn welcoming me, with some even going so far as to also offer a kind word or smile. I struggle to think of anything to say in response, unnerved by this strange procession.

As the crowd thins—everyone departing the room now that the meeting is over—my eyes keep straying to Ezra's. Once everyone has gone, he crosses the empty space, closing the distance between us. Rai repositions herself in front of me and pats my hand, although her expression is cautious.

Beside me, Jenner crosses his arms. "Well, *that* was interesting. Quite the yarn you spun there, Ez. You don't really believe they're all okay with this or that anyone actually bought that lie, do you?"

"I'm not an idiot," Ezra scoffs. "Although, it would've been fine if Nolan hadn't opened his mouth. I just needed to buy some time so I can figure out what to do and how to guarantee Wynter's safety."

"*We*," Rai corrects him. "And you know, maybe we won't need to do anything. We don't even know if the DSD is still looking for her."

Ezra and I both stare at her, giving her the same dubious look. Rai glances between us, raising her eyebrows.

"Of course, they are." I shake my head. "Richter won't stop until he's found me. You don't—"

My mouth snaps shut, cutting off the rest of that sentence. I was about to say they don't know what he's like, but then I remembered that's not true at all. Ezra and Rai probably know Dr. Richter better than anyone. Even me.

Unless he really has changed since they knew him, in which case, my pointing that out will only serve to make them both feel worse. The situation is volatile enough already without me adding any fuel to the fire.

Ezra lets out a long, withering sigh. "I have a really bad feeling about all this. I just wish we could know what he's planning."

As he says this, Jenner and Rai both look at me, and the same unspoken question is written across each of their hopeful faces. I know what they're thinking without having to ask.

If we knew what Dr. Richter was planning, we could assess the risk and make our own plans accordingly. Plans to keep everyone here safe, even me. Plans that might actually give me a future.

And they want me to be the one to find that information. They want me to use my visions to help them. Trouble is, I can't control this power. Like I tried to tell Dr. Richter, I'm of no use to anyone.

Ezra flashes them both a steely glare, clenching his jaw. "No. That's not an option."

"Why?" Rai asks. "I mean, I know it's not ideal, but, if we want to be sure, what other choice do we have? It's not like we have anyone on the inside to help us, and it wouldn't take much for someone like Nolan to pick apart those lies you just told. Besides, don't you think it should be Wynter's choice? Let's ask her—"

"No," Ezra says again, his voice a threatening snarl. "We aren't using her like that. Case closed."

"Hey, earlier you were just as eager to toss her out of here as everyone else," Jenner says. "What's with the sudden change of heart? Why are you so against the idea of her helping us?"

Variations of this question have been nagging at me, clawing at my insides where they sit, heavy, in my chest. They've lived there since Ezra told me I was no longer their prisoner, and they reside there still now, questioning my wavering determination to trust him.

I want to believe his intentions are good. I want to believe his desire to keep me safe is out of remorse for what happened to his mother and not because of some diabolical scheme to use me. But I'm not so sure I do believe that. I'm not convinced he doesn't have other motives. After all, my time with Dr. Richter has made me aware of the deceits people are capable of.

The seconds tick by without anyone speaking, and in that silence, I suddenly hear it—what it is Ezra's refusing to say. The unspoken truth hits me with the force of a lightning strike.

Of course, I know. If I'm really honest with myself, I think I've known for a while. How could I not, given what happens every time I have one of my visions? The effects this condition have had on my body are proof enough of the fate waiting for me.

How else could this all possibly end?

"Because he thinks it'll kill me," I breathe.

Ezra recoils, and the look on his face cracks my heart into a thousand irreparable pieces, leaving behind a black hole in my chest. I glance away, unable to bear the pain I find in his gaze that seems to mimic my own so acutely. To my horror, the expressions on Jenner's and Rai's faces are worse.

Rai looks at Ezra, her gaze pitying. "Your mother died in an asylum, Ezra, and with her, died any answers about what she went through in there. We don't know it was her illness." Her somber tone implies the many other unspoken things that could have ended his mother's life.

"We don't *not* know it was her illness either," he retorts. "Austin was pretty damn convinced of it."

"Austin was in denial and was looking for anything to blame that would give him some sense of purpose." She sighs, and it's a heavy, weary sound that tells me they've had this conversation before.

"He's right," I mutter, the words escaping of their own volition, triggered by my acceptance of the facts.

And the fact is, this disease will kill me.

Rai's eyes dart to mine. "Wynter…" Her tone is gentle, as if she's talking me off a ledge.

As she takes a step toward me, I stumble backward, shying away from her hand, which reaches out to touch my shoulder. She freezes in place, and the wounded way she stares at me makes me want to bury myself under a rock and never resurface.

So, I do the next best thing.

Their voices chase after me as I turn and run from the room as fast as my legs can move. I ignore their calls, sprinting blindly through the corridors, racking my brain for the best place to go. Where the hell can I go?

As I run, I realize how frightened I am. At my weakest point, I would've welcomed death into my arms, but now, the idea of it is like a slow-moving drug trying to paralyze me. It creeps through my veins, crippling my every breath.

At first, I feared death at the hands of the DSD. Then I escaped and the new threat became PHOENIX. As the days passed and I grew closer to Jenner and Rai, that fear began to fade and I dared to imagine a new life for myself. But there is no life to be found in death, and death from this disease is unavoidable. I can't run from it. I can't fight it.

My only option is to succumb.

Tears obscure my vision, but when I wipe them away, new ones rise to take their place, blurring the path ahead. A growing heat attacks my body, the corridor increasingly hazy and warm until the growing inferno seems to burn through my flesh, consuming me.

A fever presses down on my head, hot and heavy and relentless in its fury, matched only by the brutal stabbing pain in my temples. I continue to run, but my legs weaken with every step.

I fling myself through the next open doorway and stagger forward until the details of the room take on some form of clarity, sliding into view. *The washroom. I'm back in the washroom.* Dizzy, I throw myself into the nearest shower cubicle, my fingers convulsing against the cold metal handle. A scream breaches my lips when the water emerges from the pipes and strikes against my fiery skin.

The vision explodes in my head at the very same moment the water devours me, the images sharp and eerily clear, as if what I'm seeing is actually happening. As if it's in front of me.

As if it's real.

The emptiness. The debris. The destruction. Every detail is the same, aside from one addition.

This time, I also see myself.

A steady trickle of blood streams from my ears and nose, mixing on my trembling lips with the tears spilling from my eyes, which are entirely black. A choked sob escapes me, warped by the harsh wind.

"I'm afraid!" I cry. "I don't want to kill anyone else. I don't want to do this. I don't want to die!"

A sharp breath catches in my chest, and as the image around me shifts into that terrible ending with the world swallowed by a blinding light, it occurs to me how wrong I've been about everything.

What I witnessed at the DSD might've led me to PHOENIX, but nothing I saw was ever about them at all. Or about Ezra... despite the central role he's seemed to play in those visions. From the beginning, this has always been about me. About this disease.

About what I am.

Rai. Jenner. Ezra. Everyone here... They're nothing but unwilling victims I'll drag down with me when this all finally comes to an end.

The walls crack beneath my touch. My fingers slip away, rushing upward to claw at my skull, as the pressure building inside me teeters on the brink of exploding. With a scream, it rushes out of me in a wave of release.

The pipes in the walls burst through the concrete, showering me with a surge of water and pounding into my aching bones, forcing my already weak body down to the floor. As the ongoing rush of water pummels my skin, I surrender to the pain and to impending unconsciousness, lacking the will to fight any longer.

Darkness casts a thick veil across my eyes, and I give in to its call. As I do, one tormenting thought rolls through my head.

The vision has always been about me.

*I am the one who will end the world.*

# EIGHTEEN



Someone calls my name, but I can't see who they are.

Everything is hazy.

All I'm aware of is pain.

I'm trapped somewhere between unconsciousness and waking with the fog in my head muffling the voices around me. I can't tell them apart. I can't even remember who they belong to.

"Is she breathing?"

"I don't know—"

I try to wrap my head around the words in my ears, but the pictures overtaking my thoughts make it difficult to concentrate. They come together, forming a vision, and the world ends in front of me just as it did that first time. There's nothing I can do to stop the destruction. Nothing I can do to protect anyone from the person I now know will cause that future.

From me.

"Why is there so much blood?"

Static distorts my surroundings, warping the image. When it

settles, forming a clear picture again, Ezra steps into my line of vision—his eyes locked on mine and a gun in his hand. Tears leave streak marks on his cheeks, cutting through the ash and dirt on his skin.

"*I'm sorry, Wynter.*"

*Why?* I want to ask, but my lips refuse to move. *Why do you keep saying you're sorry?*

Static again. This time, when it passes, I only see myself—or rather, the monster this disease is turning me into. Black soulless eyes. Blood covering my skin, symbolizing the evil power rotting within me. It's like a parasite weaving itself through my body. There can be no running from it. No escaping it. This frightened but deadly creature…

"Help her. Do whatever you have to."

This is what I will become.

Warm arms swaddle my legs and torso, lifting me up as if I weigh nothing. As the ground falls away, a soft voice speaks into my ear. "Wynter…"

Tears burn my eyes as recognition tugs at my brain, guiding me toward a place I have no hope of reaching in my current state. A place I'm not sure I'll ever reach again. Darkness washes over everything, pulling me into the long-awaited embrace of what I'm sure can only be death.

*I don't want to die.*

"Please, wake up…"

A strangled breath expands in my throat as my eyes flutter open, the lids heavy, weighted with exhaustion, but the fatigue quickly ebbs. As I force them wide, the room around me comes into sharp focus, and I glimpse the plain walls of my new living quarters—the one part of this compound that's mine.

I blink. No one else is here. Despite the echo of voices still speaking to me, I'm alone.

This must be a dream. I turn in place. *Of course, it's a dream,* I chide myself. Why else would I be standing when only seconds ago I was sleeping? No other explanation makes sense.

Unless, of course, this is something else altogether.

"Wynter."

A shiver shoots up my spine as the familiar timbre of Ezra's voice seeps into my ears. I know it so well now. It's always in my head, always speaking to me. Haunting me. Interlaced in my every waking thought.

A dizzy spell leaves me unsteady on my feet as I glance at where he stands in the doorway, glaring at me with an incensed expression that rips the air right out of my lungs.

"Ezra—"

"You can't do this," he growls, interrupting me. Anger pushes out every word and burns behind his eyes, unnerving me. I've never seen him so irate before, and that's saying something considering how many times he's held a gun to my head.

I gape at him, swallowing, and hesitation creeps into my tone as I dare to ask, "Do what?"

A wary breath spills from my lungs when he doesn't respond. Bracing myself, I repeat the question, my racing pulse throbbing across every inch of my body until I can feel my beating heart everywhere.

Again, he doesn't answer me, and when I repeat myself for a second time, someone else talks over me, overpowering my voice with their own.

"I have to."

Confusion throws me even further off balance as it suddenly

Bewilderment sinks into the depths of her eyes as she takes a shaking step away, forcing some space between them again.

I try to speak, even though they won't hear me, because I don't understand what the hell's going on and I can tell the other me doesn't either. How could she? Ezra and I are from different worlds. Maybe it didn't start that way, but he escaped our warped society far sooner than I did. He's had time to adjust to our inbuilt emotions whereas I still struggle to know what I'm feeling. The desperate look in his gaze…

I don't know what to do with it.

"I don't want you to go," he whispers.

I sense his warm breath against my cheeks when he speaks, as if the two of us are connected across time. I suppose, from that very first vision, we have been. Despite the suspicion, despite the distrust, I always sensed something between us, anchoring our fates together in a way I couldn't understand or explain. And from that very first moment I saw him, something in me began to change.

From that moment, I knew I would never be the same.

And I haven't been. Since I met Ezra, Jenner, and Rai, everything I've always been told to suppress has been steadily surfacing, exposing emotions I've never been permitted to feel without me even realizing what was happening. Ever since I found Ezra, the rules I followed to survive my day-to-day life in the State have ceased to exist, not because I've forgotten them but because they don't need to. Here, I can allow myself to be who I really am, whoever that person is.

Here, I think I finally understand freedom.

"Stay here," he murmurs. "Stay with me."

*Stay?* I blink, unsure what he means. Where else would I go?

Where else *could* I go?

A veil of darkness whisks me away, and as it fades, my eyes open, thrusting me back into reality. As my hazy vision adjusts to waking, I consider the possibility that what I saw just now was only a dream. That seems far more plausible than the notion of Ezra and I ever being together that way. But, if what I just witnessed *was* a dream and not a vision, why would I see that?

What could've triggered those thoughts about Ezra?

A sudden vertigo swirls through my throbbing head, my scalp burning as the pain in my temples urges bile up into my mouth. I swallow it, pushing down the nausea until I'm confident I won't vomit or choke.

Exhaling, I take stock of my surroundings. I'm in my new quarters, just as I was in my dream, but this time, I'm actually lying in bed, my head sinking deep into the pillow.

*See?* I say to myself. *It was a dream. Just a dream.*

My body aches in protest as I push myself up, my muscles and bones screaming in pain as if every inch of me has been broken and reset, healed, then broken again in a cycle of torture. Unlike in the storage room, when I battled infection and I— according to Rai—was lucid enough at times for her to feed me small doses of soup, this time, an IV stand is positioned next to the bed on my right, the thin feeding tube trailing from the bag connected to my upper arm.

What's happened to me? Based on the way my head is pounding, I think I can assume the worst. Gradually, the memories resurface, confirming my fears, and I remember the cracking tiles in the shower, the burst of water knocking me down, the blood…

The vision where I end the world.

I bite back a sob as the memory of my terror spreads under my skin like a rash with no cure. A whimper parts my lips, and as a deep breath responds in the darkness beside me, I freeze, nearly collapsing back into my pillow in fear. Holding my breath, I squint at the shadowed person sitting in the solitary chair pushed up against the left side of the bed, my tired gaze locking on the dozing figure's face.

"Ezra...?"

How long has he been here? Has he stayed by my side the whole time I've been unconscious?

He starts when I mumble his name, bolting upright, his eyes blown wide, searching the shadows for danger where there is none. Unless, of course, you count me, which he should, especially after this most recent vision. When his gaze locks on mine, he visibly settles, letting out a breath of relief.

"You're awake," he says, the words weighted. Then, rubbing the sleep from his eyes, he asks, "How are you feeling?"

I cough to clear the dryness from my throat and force a one-shouldered shrug. "Honestly, I've felt better."

He lowers his gaze, his expression distraught. "I'm so sorry," he breathes, his voice barely audible.

*Why?* I want to ask, just like I've wanted to ask him a thousand times before. But the question is eclipsed by the recollection of those three fateful words that led me here. To him.

*"I'm sorry, Wynter."*

"Still not it." When he blinks at me, confusion creasing his brow, I manage a smile. "You're not off the hook yet."

Comprehension spreads across Ezra's face, and I can tell he's remembering the same moment I am, when he first gave me this room and I finally told him about my vision and the words he'll eventually say to me.

Despite the fleeting grin he offers back, his eyes swim with guilt. He stares at me with such remorse in his gaze, as if what's happening to me is somehow his fault, even though we both know it isn't. I can't even blame Dr. Richter for my condition, despite all the horrible things he did to encourage its progression.

No, if anyone is to blame, it's my mother for abandoning me to die as a result of these visions. Because that's what this disease will do.

It will kill me and take everyone I care about with it.

This realization crushes my chest, affecting me far more than I expect it to. I barely know these people. How have they buried themselves underneath my skin and in the depths of my heart so quickly? How, after being subjected to the harsh world I was raised in, did I not even notice I was letting them in?

Driven by a need for comfort, which I was always denied growing up in the State—even by my own mother—I reach out, squeezing Ezra's hand where it rests on his knee, touching him for the first and possibly only time, with what little strength I have left.

To my relief, he squeezes back.

"Where is everyone?" I ask, turning my face away slightly to hide the tears welling in my eyes.

"Sleeping." Ezra tugs his hand from mine and lifts his arms above his head, stretching, then sinks back into his seat with a sigh. "It's nearly dawn."

"How..." I hesitate, taking a moment to build up the courage to ask the only question that truly matters right now. "How long have I been out?"

Ezra seems reluctant to meet my gaze, his own rife with unease and something else... Something almost like fear. He only answers when I arch a questioning eyebrow at him. "Six days," he whispers.

A rush of panic ripples through me.

*Nearly a week?* It's been that long?

My teeth bite down hard on my lower lip until the metallic taste of blood fills my mouth. The longest my unconsciousness has lasted as a result of these visions has only been a half-day at most. To jump from that to an entire week...

Trepidation rips through me. I already knew my condition was worsening, but if things continue to progress the way they are now, then I don't have much time left.

My hands tremble in my lap as I consider what this drastic change could mean, not only for me but for everyone here. For Ezra, Jenner, and Rai. Is the abrupt escalation of my symptoms a sign that my apocalyptic vision is creeping closer?

How long before we're all out of time?

"There's something else." Ezra stares down at his fingers as if purposely avoiding my gaze, fidgeting with the hem of his shirt. "The other day, we received a transmission from someone who claims they want to work undercover for PHOENIX. He's a high-ranking member of the State. You've probably heard of him."

I blink, my brow furrowing, as I try to wrap my brain around such an impossible concept. Why would anyone installed in a position of power within the State's hierarchy want to switch sides?

"Who is it?" I ask in a breathless voice.

A long moment passes before Ezra looks up at me. "His

name is Wren Bilken. He's a senior advisor for the State, who works in direct correspondence with the city magistrates. He's also the CEO of W. P. Headquarters."

My hands clench into fists, sending spasm-like jolts of pain up both of my arms, especially through my left wrist, which still aches from the incision where I cut out my chip. Right now, though, I barely notice the pain.

Wren Bilken. I met him once briefly when I was sixteen, and that one time was more than enough. He conducted my work placement interview and ultimately decided which sector I was projected to enter. He personally oversees all education leading up to the exam from the moment we're first old enough to enter school.

I only saw him two other times in my life—in the elevator at W. P. Headquarters and again on the screen, wishing us luck at the beginning of my exam.

Unease settles deep in my bones. Something isn't adding up. Why would Wren Bilken, of all people, have any desire to help PHOENIX? How could someone in his position benefit from the State losing power?

Plus, doesn't anyone find it suspicious that he sent this transmission only *after* I came here? The timing can't be coincidental, and if it is, why didn't Bilken reach out sooner? PHOENIX has been around for years, so why now? And how did he even figure out how to contact them?

What isn't Ezra telling me?

"It's a trap." The words breach my lips in a rush.

Ezra gives a stilted nod. "Probably. But even so, we'll take the bait. We don't really have any other choice in the matter."

I gape at him, startled by his cavalier attitude. What could the transmission have possibly said that warrants putting himself in harm's way? What did it say that could justify his death? Because that's what will happen if he goes. He'll die, and the answers I came here for will die along with him.

"Listen to me," I hiss, reaching for his hand again. Maybe if I touch him, he'll actually listen. "Wren Bilken isn't someone who will turn against the State. Whatever he's asking you to do, *don't*. This has the DSD written all over it."

The frustration running through me is like an itch I can't scratch. If my body wasn't still weak, I would jump out of this bed and shake some sense into him.

Scowling, Ezra rips his hand out of my grasp and jumps up from the chair with a huff. "By all means, give me another option," he begs. "You're new here, so you don't know what it's like. Living in isolation. Relying on generous benefactors for food and other necessary supplies. Rarely ever seeing the sun. We're basically a glorified homeless shelter, and honestly, I don't know how much longer we can survive this way." Groaning, he runs a hand through his hair. He looks exhausted, as if he hasn't slept in days. A pang of guilt strikes my chest. Considering how long I've been asleep, maybe he hasn't. "We've been waiting for an opportunity like this for a really, *really* long time. What Wren Bilken is offering could change everything for us."

"How?" I ask, the volume of my weak voice building strength. "What information is he willing to give you? What is he asking for in return?"

"Nothing." He answers a little too quickly, and I narrow my eyes, certain he's omitting something important. "He just wants us to meet him in person first to hammer out any details before we agree to anything permanent."

I glare at Ezra, amazed by how foolish he's being, especially since I know he isn't stupid. Something weird is going on. This is obviously a trap. He must know that as well as I do.

So, why is he going along with this plan?

"You could die." These words are like sawdust in my mouth.

His eyes latch back on mine, and he smiles. A small, sad expression that's all too reminiscent of how he looked at me in my vision.

"I know," he says, his tone resigned. "But I don't have a choice. It isn't my decision to make."

*Whose is it, then?* I'm tempted to press, but I've lost the will to argue about this. Nothing I say will change his mind. He's going, with or without my blessing.

Instead, in a half-hearted breath, I ask, "When are you leaving?"

He holds my gaze, his voice filling the space between us, which seems to span the width of an ocean in this somber moment. The air is heavy with something that feels strangely like mourning. "Tomorrow night."

*So soon?*

I think of all the days I've been asleep in this bed—how many hours I've wasted unconscious, which I could've spent getting to know Ezra better. Hours I could've spent learning who he really is and getting answers to the questions that have been piling up ever since that first vision of him. Hours I could've used to finally decide if I trust him, although, in my gut, I know that I can...and that I already do. Someone doesn't sit by your bed for six days while you're sick if they plan to stab you in the back.

So much wasted time...

What if these are our last moments together?

What if he doesn't come back from this mission?

I clamp down hard on the inside of my cheek. Although I'm silent on the outside, on the inside, I'm screaming.

"How will you get to wherever it is you're going?"

I don't really know why I ask. It doesn't matter, and the answer won't make any difference. Maybe I'm just trying to stall the inevitable. The more questions I ask, the longer he has to stay here with me where it's safe.

*Safe…*

A fluttering sensation stirs in my chest, like the wings of a butterfly beating against the bone cage surrounding my heart.

I wonder, when did his safety start mattering to me? Before this latest vision, before I slipped into a coma, I was still trying to figure out if I could trust him and dealing with the realization that this disease will eventually kill me. So, why does that seem so unimportant right now?

Why does my heart ache at the thought of him leaving?

*It's the dream's fault,* I tell myself. That dream of us kissing that's making me imagine something between us that isn't really there. Or maybe that's just an excuse I keep telling myself to avoid how much this whole situation reminds me of how I lost my father.

And I really don't want to lose anyone else.

"The compound is linked to a web of underground tunnels that have exit points throughout the city," Ezra explains, his tone steady. Distant. As if he's trying to push me away. "It's the safest method for us to travel without being seen since the State's scanners can't detect our heat signatures through all the metal underlay in the ground."

As he speaks, an idea strikes me as suddenly as those

lightning-like bolts Dr. Richter drilled into my head so many times during each of his experiments. It's insane, but it's also the only way to keep us together.

Despite the unexpected friendships I've found in Jenner and Rai that have made me want to stay, I'm only here because of Ezra. He's not going anywhere without me until I figure out what part he plays in the future awaiting us, however small it may be. Every day, that vision is inching closer, and the time I have left to understand it and how it comes to happen is running out. We can't waste any of it apart.

"I want to go with you."

It's a futile request. I'd be putting myself in danger, which is the opposite of what Ezra has said he wants, and by leaving this place, I'd only be making it easier for the State to find me. For Dr. Richter to find me. Not to mention, I doubt anyone here would actually *let* me leave considering the threat to their safety if I were to tell anyone the location of the compound.

Regardless, I can't bear the idea of Ezra leaving me behind, of going where I can't follow. Not if there's a chance he might not come back, despite what my vision keeps showing me. As I already told him, I'm not a rebel. I'm not here for PHOENIX.

I'm here for him.

Besides, he saved my life at The Vega when he had no logical reason to, and I guess a part of me feels like I owe him. Maybe, by going on this mission, I'll find a way to repay him…even if all the future holds for me is pain. Pain he might be responsible for.

Pain that'll spur him to say those three words.

Ezra sits back down in the chair, fixing his bloodshot eyes on the floor, staring at nothing in particular.

"What?" I goad. "Aren't you going to say no or try to tell me that's a bad idea—"

"No," he murmurs, cutting me off. "If there's one thing I've learned in the short time we've known each other, it's that you're nearly as stubborn as I am. Besides, Rai and Jenner will be glad for the company."

I let out a stunned breath. "Seriously?"

I was so prepared to fight him on the matter that him relenting so easily takes me aback. I don't know what to think of it. What happened to keeping me safe? What happened to someone else making the calls about what I'm allowed to do here and where I'm allowed to go, even with supervision? I had expected at least some kickback from him, not this weird capitulation that doesn't make any sense.

Another thought occurs to me. Is he breaking some rule by saying yes to my request? Or is this just a ruse to get me to do exactly what the person in charge here wants me to do? Maybe he always knew I'd ask.

The sadness in his gaze makes me fear the latter.

"Sure." He shrugs. "You can be our lookout. You'll see the enemy coming long before any of us do."

A smile splits his face, and he lets out a forced laugh that makes me wince. I fail to find anything funny about this. Ezra is a walking contradiction—one minute, I'm a prisoner, the next, he's determined to keep me safe, and now this...whatever the hell this is. I can barely keep up with how often he changes his mind.

Then there was his vehement opposition when Rai and Jenner asked about using my power. How is what they wanted me to do any different than what he's suggesting now?

If anything, his reaction back then exposes the truth behind his choice at this moment. After what happened to his mother, he wouldn't want me to use my power this way—not unless someone else is forcing his hand. Not unless there's something he doesn't want me to know. Something he's determined to hide.

And I'd be willing to bet that something is why he's agreed to let me tag along.

Dread claws at my skin, but I bury it down deep and urge myself to think only of the task ahead. Regardless of what's coming, we'll face it together.

I will follow him, wherever this transmission leads.

# NINETEEN

I PRESS MY BACK AGAINST the cold wall, trying my best to stay out of everyone's way. I want to help, but I don't know where to begin or even how to prepare myself for the task ahead. This mission will go against everything the State has instilled in me over the last eighteen years. Every rule I followed, every ideal it taught me to aim for…

What we do tonight will unravel them all.

I can't help wondering who I'll become without the State always whispering in my ear, telling me who I'm meant to be. Once we make contact with Bilken, I'll be just the same as everyone else in PHOENIX—an outcast who's turned her back on society. There will be no returning to the life I once knew.

Not that I ever planned on going back anyway or that it's even an option given what I am, not to mention my impending death and the potential destruction of the world if I can't figure out how to change that future. Even if I hadn't met Jenner and Rai and learned the truth about PHOENIX and the attacks on the State, the DSD ensured going back to a normal life would never be an option for me. I'm stuck on this path.

Now, I need to embrace it.

My chest rises and falls with a sigh as my eyes scan over the shelves laden with supplies. So far, I've only filled my pack with water and food, although I should really be looking at the weapons. I've been avoiding those particular shelves out of cowardice and sheer inexperience. I don't know anything about guns. Even if I held one, I wouldn't know how to use it.

Ezra loads ammunition into his pistol, and I wince at the sharp click of metal on metal as the slide locks back into place. My eyes follow the deft movements of his long fingers until his hand suddenly freezes around the black grip. He looks up at me, his hazel gaze hard and unreadable. The hairs on the back of my neck stand on end, and I shift my weight from foot to foot, uncomfortable beneath the heat of his stare.

What could he be thinking right now? Perhaps, he's second-guessing his earlier decision and has changed his mind about letting me come. I wouldn't be surprised. If anything, I'm stunned he hasn't backtracked on it sooner. I still can't figure out why he so readily agreed to let me join them after making such a fuss about keeping me safe and especially after insisting he wouldn't use my power because of the risk to my life.

As he crosses the room toward me, I can already imagine it—his stern voice stating I'm staying behind and my own pitiful attempts to protest that decision. What would I even say? What *could* I say that wouldn't end up sounding like the ramblings of a mad woman?

My lips part to speak, but my lungs release only air.

Ezra's eyes are probing as he comes to a standstill in front of me. I gulp down a breath, anticipating his order. But it never comes.

Instead, he extends his hand, his fingers spread out in offering.

The gun he was prepping before lies flat against his palm.

"You'll need it."

I blink, stammering, "A-Are you sure?"

Because I'm sure as hell not.

A grin pulls at his lips as he nods. "I trust you. Besides, we should all go armed, just in case."

*"I trust you."* A weird sensation floods my chest at these words, and yet, they still don't make me feel any better about the situation. Regardless, I wrap my fingers around the metal— the surface warm from Ezra's touch—taking a firm hold of the handle to appease him. It's heavier than I thought it would be, which only serves to heighten my unease.

Although I've killed before, it wasn't intentional—I didn't realize what was happening, couldn't control what I was doing. But this... Using this gun would be my choice. If I'm going to carry this weapon, I need to be prepared for the very real likelihood it may be used to take someone's life. If I pull that trigger, I won't be able to blame my condition for my actions or pretend the resulting death was a terrible accident. It would be entirely my fault, and I would have to carry that guilt.

Could I do it?

Could I use this weapon to kill if I had to?

As the others prepare their supplies, I consider whether it's necessary for me to have a gun of my own. I don't have a clue what I'm doing with it, and everyone else is already armed. What if I shoot the wrong person by mistake? What if I accidentally hurt Jenner or Rai?

*Or Ezra.* Nausea grips my stomach at the thought, although I struggle to understand why. We barely know each other—he's a stranger to me, even more so than the others—and yet...the notion of his death hurts the most.

But am I really afraid of losing *him*, or am I afraid of what will happen if I never get the answers I came for? Without those answers, without understanding his part in my vision and the why behind those three words, will I be helpless to change that future?

Will I be helpless to stop myself from becoming a monster?

Jenner brushes up next to me, making me jump, and slings an arm across my shoulders. "Don't worry," he says, his breath hot on my ear. "I'll take care of you. But, if it would make you feel better, I can give you some one-on-one shooting lessons."

My brow hitches upward as he takes a step back, pulling his arm away from my neck. Turning, he lifts his gun and smiles.

"All you have to do is find your target, and once you have him in your sights, release the safety and just squeeze the trigger."

Time seems to slow as I follow his gaze, and my heart almost stops when I see where he's aiming.

"Bang!"

My hand flies to my mouth as I gasp, but Ezra only seems annoyed by the outburst. Reaching forward, he closes his fist around the end of Jenner's gun and pushes the barrel away from his chest.

"Stop messing around," he snaps.

Jenner snorts and hits Ezra in the left bicep, who then punches him back, suppressing a grin. I glance between them, unnerved by this faux display of violence considering the situation we're about to find ourselves in. At least Ezra and Jenner seem to be getting along again.

As I watch them laugh and joke with each other, it really hits me what we might be walking into. How many of us will make it out of this, if any? Perhaps that's why Jenner feels the need to hide behind a shield of light-hearted behavior. If that's the case, I don't blame him.

I don't want to think about what awaits us either.

"Is everyone nearly ready?" Rai asks. Her fingers adjust the thick strap across her chest, which is attached to a flat bag on her back.

"As ready as we can be," Ezra says. His eyes fix on mine. "Are you ready?"

Panic constricts my lungs, suffocating my breaths, but I nod, although my terror is slowly eating away at me from the inside. I'm frightened, not only for myself or for the others who have agreed to go on this mission, but for all those who we're leaving behind.

What will become of them if we don't come back? How will they know what's happening or if any of us have been captured?

How will they know if it's safe to stay here?

These worries beat around in my skull as I shadow the determined steps of our party through the compound, hanging at the back of the group. The corridors we traverse seem to go on for miles until we enter an area I wasn't shown during my tour.

The passages here are dark and narrow—a maze most likely built with the intention of disorienting any intruders. I find myself noting the directions we turn. Left. Right. Right. Left again. We carry on for at least twenty minutes, but the pattern changes every time I think I'm getting the hang of the route, putting a dent in the mental path I've been drawing.

I can understand the precaution. If an enemy were to overrun this place, the maze would have them turning in circles, giving those living here time to escape. Assuming they have another way out.

Eventually, we wind up in a cramped, tapered room that appears, at first glance, to be a dead end. Squinting through the shadows, I note the outline of a hatch door embedded in the opposite wall.

*This is it,* I realize when Ezra steps forward.

The first leg of our journey starts here.

I stand back while everyone else congregates around the circular door, once again doing my best to stay out of their way. Accompanying us are three older men who haven't said a single combined word since we set off from the compound's supply room. The man with the bulky frame, whose bulging muscles threaten to explode through his shirt, is named Duke, but I never caught what the other two are called. Frankly, I don't care enough to ask.

A deafening metallic squeal cuts through the silence as Duke grips the large wheel attached to the hatch and turns it three times, his large arms straining. At the end of the third turn, he yanks the door open, letting in a rush of stale air and heat.

One by one, we step into the blackness of the tunnel beyond the opening. A thin layer of water covers the ground, soaking the outside of our shoes, but my feet stay dry thanks to the thick socks and rubber inserts Rai gave me just this morning. Now, I get why she was so insistent I wear them.

Beams of light illuminate the rounded walls as the others all click on their flashlights. I reach into my pack in a hurry to do the same, always keeping one eye on Ezra, watching him at all times out of my peripheral vision. He huddles with Rai, shining his light over the black disk-like device in her hands, which looks vaguely familiar. As a hologram materializes in the air just above the gadget, it hits me where I recognize it from. It's identical to the one Dr. Richter used to show me the surveillance footage of my exam.

Ezra moves the beam of his light in a circle, signaling for us to gather around the glowing map of what I now realize is the tunnel system. The layout is so intricate and complex it would take me weeks to work out the tangled web of passages or understand where each one leads. Rai, on the other hand, seems to read the map with ease.

After examining the hovering image for barely more than ten seconds, she stores the device back inside her pack and retrieves her flashlight. Turning, she directs the blinding beam down the left side of the tunnel where the route branches off in a fork and leads in two separate directions.

"It's this way," she says.

The others each make a note of the route, and then we all follow Rai through the waterlogged passage, walking for ages without speaking a word. The only sound is the repetitive splash of our footsteps, the echo of which trails our group like a stranger stalking our every move in the shadows.

I cast a wary glance behind me—not because I'm afraid someone's following us but because every step brings us farther away from the compound and from relative safety. Despite the community's cold reception toward me, the compound still felt a thousand times safer than where we are now and especially more so than where we're heading.

So, why did I leave? Did I really opt to come just to stay close to Ezra—a guy I don't even know all that well, who may or may not play a vital part in the future where I destroy the world? Sometimes, I question my judgment, especially since I'm risking a one-way trip back to the DSD if we get caught. Is my need for answers about my condition—about Ezra—the only reason I'm going on this mission? Or is something else guiding me down this path?

Something like friendship.

I sense a camaraderie with Jenner and Rai that I never knew growing up in the State. Before them, I didn't have friends—such a concept was incompatible with how I was raised. But what about Ezra? Is he my friend?

What exactly are my feelings toward him?

My pulse quickens, my hitched breaths deafening in the dank hush of the encompassing tunnels as images from my dream fill my head once again. A shiver rolls over my skin, but I force my thoughts elsewhere.

To distract myself from the mental picture of Ezra's lips against mine, I reflect on what I've been told about the transmission from Bilken and, for the first time, urge my brain to show me what's going to happen once we get through this tunnel. I've never tried to call to my power before, mainly out of repulsion toward the pain that comes with it, but the fear lurking under my skin is worse than any possible side effects.

Although I insisted on joining this mission, I can't shake the suspicion that my greatest nightmare awaits us at the end of this path. If I'm right and the DSD is behind this…

We're all as good as dead.

Slowing my steps, I focus my thoughts…but nothing happens. No vision, no static, or flickers of people or places. Nothing. Not a single glimpse of the future, past, or anything remotely helpful at all.

I push out a disgruntled breath and press on, picking up the pace to catch up to the others. I'm so consumed by my apprehension of the unknown, I fail to notice Ezra walking beside me.

"Are you nervous?" he asks in a quiet breath.

I flinch at the sound of his voice, and he frowns, his eyes hooded and dark with what seems like concern.

When I don't say anything, he lowers his voice even more. "Whatever happens, I'll look out for you. I promise I won't let anyone hurt you."

"Why?" I counter, rounding on him. "Not that long ago, you were ready to kill me yourself. Now, what? You're suddenly my protector?"

A swell of guilt bubbles up in my chest. I don't know why I'm so angry, but I do know my frustration is misplaced. Even if Ezra is hiding something from me, I also know he's trying to make amends for how I've been treated, and, I imagine, attempting to fix some of the damage his demented brother inflicted on me. Why should I begrudge him that? If anything, I should encourage that forgiveness since it'll only bring us closer and perhaps clarify this mystifying connection between us.

There's also the possibility he feels responsible for me because of my condition. He couldn't save his mother from this disease, but maybe, somewhere in the back of his mind, he believes he can still save me. Or, at the very least, just be there when everyone else has abandoned me to suffer through it alone.

As my thoughts come full circle, a scream of vexation builds in my throat, poking at the brink of my lips. If he really does want to keep me safe, then why did he say I could come on this mission? What does he think he's protecting me from?

Or, maybe, the better question is, who?

An apology hangs on the tip of my tongue, but I swallow the words, torn over what to say and whether or not I'd actually mean it. I glance at Ezra, but he doesn't say anything either.

We continue our trek through the long, winding tunnels, the minutes passing with a silent monotony that would make even the strongest person question their sanity. The unchanging rhythm of our forward progression only falters when we reach yet another crossroads.

Rai digs through her pack for the handheld device and clicks it on with a tap of her finger. The hologram flares to life, throwing a soft blue light across the walls around us.

"Where do we go next?" Ezra stops beside her and peers down at the map.

"Well, based on the information in the transmission, we're roughly three miles away from our target." Rai pauses to trace a finger along the glowing blue lines, then raises her flashlight and shines it down the path to our right. "That's the way we need to go."

As she stores the device back inside her bag, Ezra turns to face the rest of us. "We'll stop now for a quick ten-minute rest. Check that all your guns are loaded, and make sure you stay hydrated."

From the murmurings around me, I gather we'll reach our destination an hour or so before midnight. Taking advantage of our last chance at peace before facing the very real possibility of death—or, in my case, a return to torture at the DSD—I drop my pack to the ground and lean back against the damp wall with a sigh, making sure to sit on the sloped edges of the floor to avoid the thin layer of water.

I choose to rest on the opposite side of the tunnel as everyone else in the group, needing some time and space to think. Aside from the lingering concern that there's something Ezra isn't telling me, and realizing that I know absolutely nothing about our mission, it's dawning on me that I'll only get in everyone's way once we get there…wherever there is. In my weakened state, and with no control over my visions, I struggle to see how I can make myself useful.

Why did I think it would be smart for me to join them? And why the hell did Ezra agree?

The shuffle of approaching footsteps draws my gaze upward, dragging me out of my spiraling thoughts. Jenner hesitates a few feet away from me, holding out a canteen of water.

"May I?" He jerks his chin toward the ground.

Accepting the offered water, I take a tentative sip as Jenner plops down beside me, filling the empty space with his comforting warmth and calm demeanor, both of which I need to assuage me right now.

Several moments pass without either of us speaking, and as the seconds stretch on, the quiet turns threatening, like a hand reaching out in the darkness to choke us. I'm overcome by the urge to say something—*anything* to break the silence—when mutterings reach me from the other side of the tunnel.

My eyes drift to the man sitting across from me on the opposite slope, the toes of his boots touching the gully of water separating us. Beads of sweat glisten along his upper lip, his mouth twitching as he chants the same handful of sentences over and over again.

"We will not die. We will be reborn among the ashes and

overcome any adversary who stands against us. We will endure. We will survive. We will not die…"

My heart rate quickens with every word he recites until I find myself repeating them back in my head.

*We will not die…*

Jenner nudges my arm to get my attention. "Are you okay?" he asks.

Glancing up, I look from him to the man and then back again. "What does it mean?"

Frowning, he fixes his gaze on the mumbling man, his expression pensive. Forlorn. "I guess you could say it's our motto. A sort of promise we all make to keep the rebellion going, even after one of us dies. We'll never give up. We'll keep on fighting until there's nothing left to fight for. We'll rise past the deaths of those who paved our way, like a phoenix rising from the ashes."

While I admire the notion behind such a sentiment, it fills me with the worst kind of dread. I don't want to think about anyone dying, least of all Ezra, Jenner, or Rai. If I could have it my way, we'd all turn around right now and race back to the compound. To safety.

"You know," Jenner says, his voice dropping to a rumbling whisper, "Despite everything, I'm surprised Ezra let you come with us." His eyes turn back to mine, holding me to him, and my stomach clenches as the weight of my returning uncertainty bears down on my shoulders.

From the moment Ezra relented to my request, I've wondered about his unspoken motives. Why am I here? What help can I be to these people? Why did he let me come? Surely, he didn't only agree just because he knew I'd fight him on the matter.

"Why?" I ask past the sudden tightness in my throat.

Jenner shrugs. "Well, if the transmission really is a trap set by the DSD, we stand to lose the one thing that could give us the advantage against them."

*"So, she's a tool against the enemy?"* That's what someone had asked when Ezra rallied everyone before my illness put me into a coma. Clearly, he wasn't the only one thinking it.

I don't like the implication behind Jenner's words—the idea that I'm a pawn to be used, thrown back and forth between two opposing sides. Of course, no one in PHOENIX aside from him, Ezra, and Rai know what I can do.

Do they?

When I don't say anything, Jenner hastily adds, "I asked him about it, but he just said you'd be safer with us than alone at the compound without anyone who knows what's really going on. I couldn't exactly argue with that, not after seeing how riled up everyone was. Suspicion brings out the worst in people, not to mention, I'm not sure anyone else would know what to do if, you know…*you had one of your visions."* He silently mouths the end of that sentence, his eyes flicking left and right, as if he's worried someone might be listening in on our conversation.

I merely blink at him, confused. *Riled up?* Does he mean before Ezra's speech…or after? Everyone at the compound accepted me because of what Ezra said, didn't they?

Jenner's expression goes slack at the look on my face. "Shit. You don't know, do you?"

"Know what?" The words barely penetrate my lips.

An eternity seems to pass in the time it takes for him to answer. "You have to understand, in small communities, rumors spread. It's inevitable."

"What sort of rumors?"

His eyes drop to his hands, which fidget nervously with his canteen. "Like ones connecting you to the transmission from Bilken."

I open my mouth to ask why anyone would link me to Bilken, even though I already know why they would. I knew I couldn't be the only one who thought the timing of the message was coincidental.

Jenner clears his throat. "Only Ezra and Nolan know what was on that transmission, but that doesn't stop the rest of us from having our own theories."

"Nolan?" I recognize the name, but I can't place the face. Too many details from the day Ezra made his inspiring speech about me are fuzzy thanks to the crippling side effects of my vision.

"He's the Head of our sect. The transmission from Bilken was addressed directly to him."

This revelation only further compounds the nagging feeling that's been eating away at me. "Where does Ezra fit into that? And how did Bilken even manage to contact PHOENIX?"

Jenner waves a flippant hand. "Ezra's sort of his second-in-command in our merry band of misfits, so anything requiring us to go out on missions or considered need-to-know, he knows. Nolan's more of a behind-the-scenes kind of guy." His expression darkens. "As for the transmission, I heard it was encrypted in this week's Enforcer rotation schedule. We monitor that stuff to time our movements topside, and Rai picked up on the abnormality in the code."

"How did he know you'd be checking the schedule?"

Jenner shrugs again. "Smart guy, I guess? I mean, it's common sense that we would."

I nod, but foreboding claws at the back of my brain. Exhaling, I murmur, "If I ask you a question, will you answer me honestly?"

He pulls back just enough to give me a curious look, his eyebrows dragging down into a vee. "Sure," he says, although he seems anything but.

"Do you think…" I trail off, my resolve paper-thin. Steeling myself, I force out the words. "Do you think PHOENIX would hand me over if someone in the State gave you an offer that was too good to refuse?"

*Someone like Wren Bilken.*

He freezes with the canteen an inch from his mouth, the water dribbling down over his chin. Lowering his arm, he asks, "Like what?"

"I-I don't know. Something that would ensure your safety, maybe? Something that would allow you to lead normal lives…"

Jenner snorts. "The last thing anyone in PHOENIX would want is to go back to the State's twisted version of *normal*." He spits that last word like it's left a foul taste in his mouth.

"What about Ezra?"

He arches an eyebrow. "What *about* Ezra?"

I roll the words around on my tongue for a few seconds before finally pushing them out.

"Would he hand me over?" I breathe.

Jenner's eyes nearly bulge out of their sockets. "No way!" he retorts, his tone accusatory, his expression livid. "Why the hell would you even think that?"

My cheeks flush, burning red-hot with shame.

*Because I want to trust him but I'm afraid, and everyone else I ever trusted has either betrayed me or died.*

Instead, I say, "Because there's something he's not telling me, and I don't understand why else I would be here." It's not a lie, but it's not the whole truth.

Gradually, the shocked look on Jenner's face softens.

"Listen to me." His voice is both soft and hard, like a warning wrapped in a consolation. "Every person in our sect has Ezra to thank for saving their lives. Every single one, even me. *Especially* me," he adds with a humorless laugh. "He found us all and guided us to a new life, to safety, and yet, I've never seen him fight or stand up for anyone the way he has for you. I don't know what's changed, but he's risked his good standing with everyone we know just to keep you safe, which has to say something, right? Plus, he's too stubborn to back down on anything, so trust me, he's not about to give you up or send you packing to the DSD. You don't deserve what they did to you, and you sure as hell don't deserve to go back to those assholes."

"But you don't know what they did to me…"

And really, Ezra doesn't either.

"You're right," Jenner admits, his gaze slipping away. "I can't even begin to imagine what you went through. That's how I know it was bad."

Before I can comment, Ezra waves a beckoning arm from farther on down the tunnel. "On your feet. We're moving out."

Jenner stands, offering me his hand, and I take it, dodging his eyes as he pulls me up, helping me back onto my feet.

"Thanks," I mumble. Bending forward, I grab my pack and hoist the thick strap over my shoulder.

Jenner opens his mouth to say something, but the splashing of footsteps nearby cuts him off. We both turn toward the sound to find Ezra beside us, face pinched, lips pulled tight, and eyes narrowed.

"Head up the group with Rai," he barks at Jenner, who seems to be the source of his annoyance.

So much for them playing nice again.

Jenner either takes no notice of Ezra's hostility or just doesn't care. He runs a hand through the messy charcoal strands of his hair. "Sure thing." He then winks at me and walks off, leaving the two of us alone.

Every beat of my heart is erratic as Ezra inches closer, demolishing the distance between us with only two steps. I glance away before I can see his expression and focus on adjusting the straps of my pack, unsure what to say. Unsure what to think. To my dismay, the belt attachment doesn't want to cooperate.

"Here, let me help you."

Ezra takes the bag from my fumbling fingers, and, as he reaches around my torso, his hands graze my back, sending an involuntary shiver racing through me. I hold my breath. Even through my shirt, the skin he brushed against tingles as if his touch remains, branded into my flesh. In a strange way, the sensation reminds me of those lightning-like bolts used to spur on my visions at the DSD. Except, now, the electricity is far from painful.

Now, it almost brings me pleasure.

I swallow and lift my gaze to the ceiling, searching for something to distract myself from Ezra's unexpected proximity as he adjusts the tightness of the straps. The wet stone offers little in the way of diversions.

Ezra shifts, and the heat of his body against mine tempts the memory of my dream to the surface again. Despite how hard I fight to shove it back down, the mental picture of that imagined kiss floods my head. I've barely thought of anything else.

I tell myself it's because such affection isn't commonplace in my world. Most people are too afraid to let anyone that close because they fear betrayal or because they don't want to risk losing them and living with that pain once they're gone. Affection barely even exists within families—I certainly never saw it between my parents, assuming it ever existed at all. And, as such, I never expected it for myself. After all, as my mother always drilled into me, affection is weakness. Love is weakness.

And weakness can be used against you.

I figured, when the time came, I'd be partnered through one of the State's partnership agencies and I'd fulfill my required contribution to population growth, just like everyone else. I never allowed myself to think I could ever have anything more.

And that's exactly what that dream of Ezra has stirred in me—this idea that I could find something real and meet someone who actually cares for me. It's given me hope that I could, one day, have love.

Assuming I don't destroy the world first.

"There." Ezra's voice shakes me free of my thoughts. "Now, the pack won't come loose if we need to make a quick getaway."

Our faces are unbearably close when he says this, and I can't stop myself from looking at him, my eyes drawn to his lips, as if pulled there by a magnetic force. The memory of their touch overwhelms me.

I glance away, hoping the darkness of the tunnel will hide the heat flaring up in my cheeks. If Ezra notices my embarrassment, he doesn't say anything, but I'm not sure if I'm relieved by his silence or disappointed. I suppose a combination of both.

Clearing his throat, Ezra takes a step back and falls into line behind the others. As he walks away, a shaking breath expels from my lungs, and my pulse throbs across every inch of my skin, leaving me flustered and disoriented. I'm completely incapable of understanding what I'm feeling, and right now isn't the time to get lost in thoughts of anything but our impending mission.

*Priorities, Wynter,* I chide myself.

Drawing in a steadying breath, I push whatever this is taking hold of me to the back of my mind to revisit later and follow Ezra's lead down the tunnel, trailing a few steps behind him.

Our trek continues in the same eerie quiet as before but with an added level of tension. As we trudge along, my eyelids grow heavy, the humdrum sound of our repetitive footsteps making me drowsy, lulling me until I'm practically sleepwalking.

I snap out of my daze when a hand grabs my arm.

"Wait," Ezra hisses, holding me back.

He's stopped walking, and my eyes, now wide and alert, dart between the drawn features of his face and the retreating figures of our friends. My heart pounds like a hammer against my ribcage as Rai, Jenner, and the rest of our party disappear into the shadows.

Once the others are out of earshot, Ezra releases his hold on me. I glare at him, bewildered by his behavior, but he doesn't meet my gaze.

"I get it, you know," he says after a moment. "After everything you've been through, why the hell should you trust me? But I'm not like my brother. I'm on *your* side. I don't know how else I can make you believe me."

The frustration in his tone ties my stomach in knots, but the pleading in his eyes is what breaks me. Sweat drenches the palms of my hands as I whisper, "Trust has nothing to do with this."

"Then what?" he presses. "Help me understand."

His eyes jump to mine, and I wince as their scrutiny cuts through the protective wall I've built up around myself over the last eighteen years. Every day was just another brick in the barrier separating me from anything outside myself that could hurt me.

The pained edge to his voice sends that wall toppling over. "Please, Wynter."

I cross my arms over my chest, shrinking into myself. "I'm just struggling to understand why you're so determined to help me, to *lie* for me, when you were all too quick to hold a gun to my head, not once but twice since we met. Is it because Richter's your brother? Because of your mother?"

I don't voice the last option—the fear bubbling up in my chest that he might be planning to use me to PHOENIX's advantage. Or his own. Not only because I don't want to believe it, but because I can't bear to hear if it's true.

*It isn't*, I tell myself. *It can't be.* Because, despite my constant wavering on the matter, I trust him. I do. What I don't trust is the effect desperation can have on people when they run out of options. And Ezra… His entire life is a series of difficult choices and limited recourse. The reality is, he's not in a position to put me first. To choose me, a girl he just met—someone who has only brought the reminder of pain and chaos back into his life.

Ezra scratches the tip of his finger against his chin, considering me. "Would it be ironic if I said it's complicated?" An unexpected smile tweaks the edges of his lips as I bite back a laugh at his words. Not that long ago, I enraged him with this very same explanation, and now, here we are, the roles reversed.

However, our humor is short-lived, and his smile fades as he rubs a hand across the back of his neck.

"What I told you about my mother…" He hesitates, as if choosing his next words carefully. "A lot of my anger about the situation stems from the fact that there was a time when I thought she was crazy, too. She would say the same thing to me every day, over and over. Always the same thing. *'One green, one blue. Look for winter.'* I had no idea what she was talking about. Her words seemed like a warning, but after a while, I tried to ignore them because nothing happened and my father constantly insisted it was just random gibberish. After she was locked away, I forgot all about it…until you came along."

I suck in a sharp breath as he takes another step toward me.

"At first, I didn't trust you for obvious reasons, like your link to the DSD and how easily you found us. I thought for sure you were lying. But then you told us your name, and something clicked in my head. One green." He points at my left eye. "One blue." He then points at my right. "That's when I realized what she had actually been saying."

He stands so close to me now, I can feel his every word on my lips when he speaks.

"Wynter, she had said. Look for *Wynter*."

"She saw me?" A million questions fly through my head, but I don't know which one to give voice to first. My indecision chokes me, making me mute.

"From the moment I heard your name, I recalled that gut feeling I had when I was younger, the one that once made me so sure what my mother said was a warning. And, for a while, that's what I thought it was. I thought you had been sent by some higher power to tear our world apart," Ezra says.

Apprehension ripples through my body as I wonder where this conversation is heading. He isn't entirely wrong. I am going to tear their world apart. Just probably not in the way he's thinking.

Still, I can't tell him that. Not yet.

"And now, you don't think that?" I hedge.

"I can't really explain it. Another gut feeling, I guess. But when you collapsed…and then when you told us about that vision, I knew."

Staring at me, he brushes a hand across my cheek, tucking an errant strand of hair behind my left ear. The bewildering thrill of his skin against mine rips a gasp from my lungs and makes my knees tremble.

His next words are a weighted whisper in the silence of the tunnel.

"She wanted me to protect you."

# TWENTY

"ARE YOU SURE THIS IS it?" Ezra squints at the ceiling.

Rai nods. "It's as close as we're going to get."

We all stare at the rusted hatch door overhead. Danger lurks on the other side of the metal, its call a hypnotizing temptress, urging us to climb up into its mouth where it can then devour us whole. Shadowy fingers slink out of the darkness and wrap around my ankles, grabbing at me, keeping me from taking another step forward, even though I have to.

My nerves send a hair-raising chill up my spine.

This is the end of the line.

"Give me a boost." Ezra smacks Jenner's arm without looking at him, and the latter turns, knitting his hands together with Duke's, forming a step with their joined fingers and flattened palms. I stand back with Rai, watching, as Ezra places one foot in their grasp and they hoist him to the door, their shoulders providing the needed support for him to keep his balance.

As Ezra straightens, one of the other two men who accompanied us here hands him a long black bar curved at one end, which he wedges between the spokes of the wheel attached to the hatch for leverage. Grunting, he pushes against the thin bar, his weight shifting as he throws his body forward—Jenner and Duke adjusting their stance to keep him steady and upright. The wheel creaks in protest as flakes of decaying iron flutter to the floor.

Inch by inch, the rust loosens and the wheel turns, the squeal of each rotation like an alarm screeching through the stone passage around us. With one final turn, Ezra pushes the door, and it crashes open, slamming against the ground overhead.

A shudder spreads over my skin. What if someone heard that bang? What if we're caught before we even exit this tunnel?

Unease grips my chest as Ezra hauls himself up through the hole, his legs disappearing into the blackness beyond as if he's been swallowed. I wait with bated breath for him to reappear and inform us the coast is clear, trying my best to ignore the niggling thought that something has gone terribly wrong. Maybe the Enforcers are already here. Maybe they've captured him, and any moment now, they'll descend on the rest of us, too.

A moment later, Ezra leans over the opening, the glow of our flashlights reflecting off his face, washing out his features. He holds up a hand to shield his eyes from the glare, and my lips part with a gasp, relief barreling through me, as the beams of light fall away. Clenching his teeth, he bends down to help the next person up through the hole.

Jenner goes first, followed by the two older men whose names I still don't know and then Rai. When it's my turn, I click off my flashlight and, with a boost from Duke, extend my arm to grab Ezra's awaiting hand, which hangs through the opening, ready to pull me out of one darkness and into another. His fingers glide across my skin, sending a shock of electricity racing through my body, which starts at my wrist and travels all the way down to my toes. Holding my gaze, he pulls me up through the hole and, for the briefest moment, into his arms.

Heat swells under my cheeks as I push away and quickly clamber to my feet, scurrying aside to stand with Rai. I don't look back at Ezra to see his reaction.

Duke is the last one out. Once we're all gathered on the surface, he ties a rope around the wheel, then helps Ezra close the hatch, sealing off our escape. For now. We'll come back this way once we're finished.

Assuming we make it out alive.

A biting wind nips at my clothes, and a shiver rips through me as the winter air skims over the hot sweat coating the back of my neck. The damp warmth of the tunnels seems miles away as I peer into the shapeless gloom of the courtyard.

"Where are we?" I whisper to Rai, leaning in to keep my voice as low as possible. I can't recognize our surroundings in the thick darkness.

"Zone 1," she murmurs back under her breath. "Outside the city magistrates building."

My gaze skirts across the expansive plaza, flitting through the shadows and moving up toward the sky to trace the shape of the structure before us. Even without street lights to guide my vision, I can sense the building's familiar enormity.

As my eyes adjust to the night, allowing me to take in the finer details of our surroundings, I'm overwhelmed by the chilling feeling that someone is watching us. All around me, the shadows shift and change as if waiting for us to make our next move.

"Is this really where Bilken wants us to meet him?" Suspicion rings behind my tone.

Rai glances at me, her eyes black in the darkness. "It makes sense. All city officials have offices here, even if they hold their main jobs somewhere else. Perhaps, he figured the more conspicuous the better. Sometimes, plain sight is the best place to hide."

"Unless, it's a trap," I grumble.

Maybe Rai has a point. This building is massive, typically well-guarded—since it's off limits to even normal rule-abiding citizens—and is surrounded by an open plaza, meaning we're sitting ducks out here if anyone does decide to attack. Surely, the State wouldn't expect us to do something so reckless? Then again, desperation makes fools of us all, and it might suspect we'd take the risk if we had a reason to.

A reason like the promise of a potential influential ally.

My thoughts go in a maddening circle as I muse over the likelihood that this mission will turn out the way everyone hopes. Maybe I'm just a pessimist. Or maybe PHOENIX has been exiled for so long they've forgotten what the State is capable of.

Another option occurs to me—one I'm not eager to entertain. Still, I can't ignore the possibility that, maybe, we've been sent here under the guise of meeting Bilken when, in reality, we're here for an entirely different reason altogether. One none of us is even aware of, aside from Ezra, if he's really clued in on the details as much as Jenner seems to think.

I remember what Jenner said about someone named Nolan being the Head of their sect, the one who, presumably, makes the decisions. I don't know who this person is, but—thanks to what I've been through—I see dubious morals and suspect the motivation behind everything now. After dealing with someone like Dr. Richter, I wouldn't be surprised if there was some nefarious reason for this mission. Just as I wouldn't be surprised if all of us were deemed expendable if our deaths meant achieving whatever the aim of it is.

Someone in the group clears their throat, and in the darkness, I find Ezra's face. A sense of urgency hardens his gaze. "In the transmission, Bilken said a door on the northwest side of the building will open at exactly 11:15. The locking mechanism will only allow entry for sixty seconds, so we have to be precise and get there before then. Otherwise, we'll miss our window."

Rai looks down at the device in her hand. The hologram illuminates the courtyard for only a few seconds before she shuts it back off.

"Well, we better get a move on," she says. "We only have eleven minutes."

We move in a tight herd through the densely packed shadows, my legs mimicking the others' hurried pace as much as my fatigued muscles allow. In our haste, we pass at least a dozen entrances to the magistrates building, although none are the one we're looking for. Regardless, I note that not a single door is guarded, which is highly unusual given the classified intel stored inside the building. Where are the Enforcers who would normally be posted here?

Once again, doubt scratches at the back of my brain, but Ezra and the others don't seem to share my concerns, which makes me wonder if I'm overreacting or seeing red flags where they don't actually exist. Is it possible the time I spent at the DSD has infected my mind with paranoia? Because of Dr. Richter—and my mother's abandonment—I find myself questioning everything and everyone, suspecting the worst of their actions. Maybe I shouldn't. Maybe I should just take a step back and believe Ezra when he says he won't let anything bad happen to me.

Rai periodically checks the device, which now serves as our compass, keeping it clutched in her hand as we run. The glow of the hologram diminishes after a moment, shrouding us again under the cover of darkness.

"Five minutes down," she hisses. "Six remaining."

We make it to the correct entrance with only thirty seconds to spare. Panting breaths form steaming clouds in the freezing air as we huddle around the locked door, waiting.

The seconds seem to stretch into hours. I glance first at Ezra, then at Jenner and Rai, tempted to ask them to abandon this mission—to turn back now while we still have our lives. I open and close my mouth several times, but no matter how much I wish to utter those words, I can't find the bravery needed to say them.

At 11:15, the door in question clicks open, just as Bilken promised it would. Gripping his gun in one hand, Ezra uses the other to reach for the door, his fingers twitching as they jiggle the handle. The locking mechanism doesn't fight his advance.

He hesitates, throwing a nervous glance back at Rai, but she just purses her lips and nods, saying nothing. My pulse stutters as it occurs to me what that look between them must mean. They're preparing themselves for what I've been saying from the first moment Ezra told me about the transmission.

*This is a trap.* That thought beats against the inside of my lips, but I stop it from passing, well aware voicing it won't help anyone or deter us from stepping through this door.

I'm not sure what frightens me more—walking into the unknown or knowing there will be nothing I can do to help the others if we run into trouble. My fingertips brush against the gun at my belt, but touching the metal only makes my restlessness worse.

"Hey." Jenner clamps a hand on my shoulder, his mouth pulling into that crooked smile I always find so reassuring. "Don't worry. Everything will be fine."

For a moment, I almost allow myself to believe him.

Ezra pushes the door open the rest of the way and slinks forward, pressing ahead into the unlit corridor. The rest of us follow behind him with our guns at the ready, our eyes peeled for danger.

I imitate the others, watching them closely. When they press their backs to a wall, I do the same, flattening my body against the nearest object in sight. When they freeze, I go as still as a statue, not daring to move a muscle until Ezra gives the all-clear.

My chest expands and contracts with each breath as my heartbeat throbs inside my ears, a deafening cacophony of terror that spreads, swelling in my throat and then building behind my eyes, making my vision fuzzy and squeezing my windpipe until I can hardly breathe. Everyone else is calm and focused, but their composure only exacerbates my fear.

My gaze cuts through the gloom, searching for Rai. She sits cross-legged by the entrance we came in through—the door propped open by the bar Ezra used on the hatch in the tunnels, its interference keeping the locking mechanism from activating in case it attempts to close and lock us all in. She stares down at a compact computer propped open in her lap, and the illuminated screen radiates a soft green-tinted glow across her face.

As her fingers dance across the keyboard, I slink along the wall, inching back toward the door until I'm squatting beside her in the corner. Curiosity draws my gaze over her shoulder.

Red dots blink across the screen, separated by thin green lines, which form an interior schematic of the building. I only comprehend what I'm looking at this time since the layout closely resembles the diagram from W. P. Headquarters the day of my placement exam—the one I saw prior to entering the exam room that showed me which desk I was allocated.

Rai peeks back at me and winks, then taps a button on the keyboard with a flick of her finger. One by one, the red dots on the screen fade to black.

"Cameras are out," she says with a smirk.

The others all relax at her words and step away from where they stood with their backs pressed flat to the walls, their relief ringing out in a chorus of sighs. Despite easing their rigid stances, everyone keeps their guns firmly at hand.

As Rai stores the computer back inside her pack, I stare at her in awe, wondering how she managed to do that. The answer comes to me quickly.

*Hacker.*

I remember hearing about the dangers of hackers in news alerts, but I never really understood what they were capable of. Until now. What she just did—shutting off the building's cameras with the same ease as drawing a breath—explains how PHOENIX has remained undetected for so long, how they always manage to elude the State's clutches. If the State can't see them, it would never even know they were there.

The technique is brilliant in its simplicity, and yet, it still doesn't answer one crucial question.

"How have you managed to stay under the radar for so long? Can't the State still track you?" I ask.

When Rai meets my gaze, I glance down at her wrist then at my own where the thick bandage hides the jagged self-inflicted incision. PHOENIX might know how to turn off some cameras, but the State has other methods to track us.

Her hands freeze on her half-packed bag.

"When PHOENIX first started, they used to cut the chips out like you did, but a lot of people died from blood loss or infection. Weapons are one thing, but it isn't that easy to get our hands on medicine because of how tightly regulated it is. Yet another of the State's many methods to keep us all under control. So, there wasn't much anyone could do in the early days except clean them up and just hope for the best. You were lucky we happened to have antibiotics on hand."

As she says this, my thoughts travel back to my school years when we were taught how terrible life was before the State and learned of the previous regime's policy on drug use, medicinal and otherwise. Recreational freedom led to a massive downward spiral of productivity, resulting in a population that had become dependent and lazy. When the State came to power, it chose to keep our health under lock and key for what it claimed was our benefit. Even something as simple as a headache can now only be treated by going to a health center.

No exceptions.

"In those early days, PHOENIX was always on the move. The sects were constantly changing their location to keep the Enforcers from discovering where they were organizing and to protect their suppliers," Rai continues, her voice a low thrum in the silence. "They fluctuated between hiding above ground and below, so the State wouldn't piece together where the real hideouts were.

"During that time, the founding members worked on different ways of disabling the tracking mechanism in the identification chips, going through failure after failure and countless unnecessary deaths in the process. Eventually, they realized that, by using a localized electromagnetic pulse, they could just fry the chips without having to resort to dangerous invasive procedures to remove them.

"The chips are in that place for a reason, to stop us from tampering with them. We just had to find a way around it. The scanner we use now has gone through various updates over the years, but it still does the trick." Grinning, she flaunts her wrist in front of my face. "The chip is just a harmless piece of metal now. The State couldn't track me, or any of us, even if it wanted to."

I gape at her, impressed but also slightly unnerved. The State has always been vocal about the far-reaching extent of its power and knowledge. So much so that, up until this very moment, I didn't think it had any points of vulnerability.

But if what Rai is saying is true, then PHOENIX has discovered a chink in the State's armor, an imperfection—a weakness— that could potentially be used against it. Knowing that, it's terrifying to think what these people might've accomplished if they hadn't abandoned society. Perhaps, if they hadn't been driven away, the world would've been a much better place with their contribution.

*Or a worse one,* a small voice in my head counters.

Before I can question Rai any further, she jumps to her feet and trots down the hallway, slinging her bag back over her shoulder and securing the strap in front of her chest. I follow in her footsteps, counting every last one as I walk in a futile attempt to distract myself from the deafening beat of my pulse in my ears. By the time I make it to where the others all stand gathered together, I can barely hear what Ezra is saying.

"You three take the first two floors." He gestures to Duke and to the other two men who came with us. "Rai, Jenner, and Wynter will go up with me to the third and forth. Make sure your communicators are active, and call me if you find anything, no matter how insignificant it might seem."

I stand off to one side of the corridor as our group splits in half. Duke leads the other two men down the hallway, while Rai and Jenner hunch over the hologram map of the building, now displayed on the handheld device, mumbling to each other about which nearby staircase would be best to take.

As I push a shaking breath from my lungs, warm fingers brush down the length of my arm. They then grip my hand, forcing me to meet Ezra's gaze.

"Stay close to me," he whispers, "and stay behind me. Remember, no matter what happens, I won't let anyone hurt you, okay?"

With a careful smile, he lets go of my hand and proceeds down the hallway, only looking back once to make sure that I'm following him.

We shadow Rai and Jenner up to the third floor where we find a more extensive corridor stretching before us, long and winding with several different additional hallways branching off from the main path. The construction of the interior is vastly different to the handful of government centers I've been in before. Whereas most other buildings are composed of metal, marble, and glass, the furnishings here consist almost solely of wood. It's a material not often used anymore—I imagine because the others have been proven to last longer. It's all about longevity, just like Jenner said. Or, maybe, that's just the excuse the State uses to get away with eradicating any reminders of the old world.

The world which existed before we did.

After five or so minutes of walking, Jenner waves his hand, signaling for us to stop. I pause behind Ezra while Rai leans against the nearest wall, consulting her blueprint of the building.

"Yo, Ez," Jenner mutters. "Did this Bilken guy say where he wanted to meet?"

"No, but he has an office here, so he probably figured the answer was obvious."

A skeptical look flashes across Jenner's face. "Yeah…maybe. Man, this place gives me the creeps. The sooner we find Bilken and get the hell out of here, the better."

I cast a sidelong glance at him, frowning. If I'm not the only one who has a bad feeling about all this, why are we still here?

Why don't we leave now before it's too late?

This mission doesn't make any sense. Even Ezra couldn't give me a clear, logical answer as to why it was so vital we take such a risk. PHOENIX has been around longer than I've been alive and has managed all this time without someone on the inside to leak them information. So, why change that now? And why Wren Bilken?

Why is he so important to them?

My eyes drift back to Ezra as he lets out a sigh and peers down both lengths of the corridor we're currently searching.

"Tell you what, we'll cover more ground if we break off into pairs. Jenner, you and Rai take the east side. Wynter and I will take the west side. Call us if you find anything."

I want to ask if he thinks splitting up is a good idea, considering our group has done so once already, but neither Rai nor Jenner question his judgment, which makes me think I shouldn't either. They each give a curt nod before heading one way as Ezra urges me to follow him in the other.

A prickle of fear raises the hairs on my arms as I hesitate, watching Jenner and Rai walk away. My doubts from before come surging back, and in a quiet breath, I beg the world, or fate, or whatever might have a hand in deciding our futures that this won't be the last time I see them.

"Ready?" Ezra breathes into my ear, his sudden proximity making me jump.

Swallowing, I take a step back and bob my head once in answer.

We continue through the empty corridors, searching the passing rooms, but find nothing. No people. No clues. Just empty offices. I mirror Ezra's steps, keeping pace as we walk, my eyes and ears on high alert for anything out of the ordinary.

As we near the end of yet another long hallway, Ezra stops in his tracks, and I stumble, nearly colliding face-first with his back. Shuffling to stand at his side, I peek up at him.

"What's wrong?"

He silences me with a finger to his lips and jerks his chin toward an upcoming office door just ahead on our right. I follow his unblinking gaze to the name engraved on a gold plate fixed to the wood.

## W. BILKEN

My heart sinks as I gape at the plate, and a strange sense of understanding settles in, seeping into the very marrow of my bones. Two possible futures await us from here. Either we'll meet Bilken and he'll turn out to be exactly what he promised...

Or we'll find something else altogether.

Ezra unhooks the communicator from his belt and murmurs into the mouthpiece, "We found something. We're going to check it out."

The nerves writhing in my stomach lash out, making me feel like I'm going to vomit. I draw in a steadying breath and grip my gun tighter.

Despite how frightened I am by the prospect of what lies on the other side of this door, I find solace in knowing I won't face it alone. Ezra and I will confront it together.

And yet, that comfort also fills me with fear. Not that long ago, he was just some unknown man I saw in a vision. I didn't really care who he was beyond the lingering question of why I was seeing him and how he was connected to that future, and I wasn't concerned with his wellbeing or fate.

But now—

Rai's muffled voice diverts my focus away from that thought. Her words are intermingled with static. *"Ezra, don't do anything stupid—"*

Her voice cuts off as he disconnects the call and places the communicator back on his belt, returning both hands to his gun. As he cocks the slide, he catches my eye.

"Remember, stay behind me," he breathes.

I nod again as he pushes open the door.

# TWENTY-ONE

THE DOOR CREAKS OPEN ACROSS the wood floor, brushing onto a thick layer of carpet. Ezra steps over the threshold with his gun raised, his eyes intently scanning the darkness, while I follow behind, staying close just like he instructed.

Shadows permeate the office like smog. My pulse pounds just under my skin, and my breaths are ragged as my shaking hand guides my flashlight across our dim surroundings. The beam reflects off a large glass desk positioned in the middle of the room, but in terms of inhabitants, the office is empty.

I creep along behind Ezra, our footsteps muffled by the pristine white carpet spanning the wide stretch of unoccupied floor. The office branches off into two smaller side rooms, separated from the main space by rounded archways decorated with swirling patterns carved into wood the same color as blood.

Swallowing, I take in the details around me, noting how this place seems almost like some sort of parallel universe to the one we reside in. The wood features we saw throughout the rest of the building continue in the foundations here, except, they're accented with the familiar, clean-cut addition of metal, marble, and glass. It's like a strange combination of two worlds. The world I grew up in…

And the old world, which no longer exists.

I inch along the wall closest to me, my gaze drawn to the rounded glass shelves slotted into the built-in wooden casing stretching from floor to ceiling. Along them, hundreds of volumes of browning, tattered books are organized in clean rows, the spines lined up according to size and color. At even intervals, the pattern is interrupted by curious trinkets, some made of metal, others of stone—objects I've never seen before and lack the names for. Objects which serve no practical purpose that I'm aware of, which can only mean one thing.

They're contraband.

Each year, the State makes it a point to perform a thorough search of every residence in the country to ensure no one possesses illegal goods. What were once considered normal everyday items to own are now…

"Forbidden," I whisper.

I stumble back a few steps, knocked off balance by the anger bubbling up within me. There's so much contradiction, so much hypocrisy in this room, it makes me sick to my stomach. Why are State officials allowed these items when ownership by normal citizens isn't permitted? Why are *they* allowed them without consequence when such possession by anyone else is seen as the worst sort of crime?

A crime punishable by death.

Nausea blinds my senses, and my knees buckle beneath me, nearly dragging me down to the floor. Despite everything I've been through between the execution of my father and the horrors of the last few months, I wasn't aware how much I truly despise the State until this very moment. And that hatred festering in me like a cancerous tumor all boils down to the maddening injustice staring me in the face.

What happened when I was a child… At the time, I never even considered the possibility that it was immoral or evil. It was just the way things were. A wrong that needed to be corrected. To a child who didn't know any better, the State was always right. It was everyone else who was wrong.

But now, seeing this—

"I don't think anyone's here."

A gasp more like a squeak breaks through my lips when Ezra lays a hand on my shoulder. Blinking away the tears budding in the corners of my eyes, I nod, averting my gaze, and help him do another sweep of the office. The second search confirms our suspicions.

We're alone.

I don't understand. If the offer contained within the transmission was genuine, then where's our contact? Where's Wren Bilken? On the other hand, if this is a trap, like I suspect, then where are the Enforcers? The State wouldn't leave such an important establishment unguarded, which means it's probably only a matter of time before someone arrives to either kill or detain us. But, if that's the case…what are they waiting for?

What are they hoping to accomplish by waiting?

Ezra crosses the room to the imposing glass desk and presses a hand to the crystalline surface. The hidden screen flickers to life with a shuddering glow, the light slicing clean through the night.

*Tap, tap, tap.* His fingers skip across the touchscreen, marching in time with my racing heart. Each beat drums in my ears, in my throat, in my stomach, pulsing everywhere at once until my apprehension is all I'm aware of. It grows until it's a physical lump in my chest, blocking the air from reaching my lungs. As I wheeze, my eyes fix on the cause of my panic.

A ball the size of a pregnant belly hangs motionless in the air above the top left corner of the glass desktop, suspended over a brass base by an attached curved bar that runs along one full side of the sphere. Uneven shapes protrude in a bumpy texture across the exterior of the ball with elegant script written in the middle of each. I only recognize one of the names. The rest are unfamiliar to me.

Sweat forms along my brow as I try to recall the name for this miniature model of our planet. The answer rises in the back of my head, digging its way out from the recesses of my memory. It taunts me in my father's voice.

*"Globe."*

Hysteria crushes me as the memories attack from all sides. My hand shoots out, clutching at the edge of the desk to hold myself upright through their brutal assault. How have I never thought to question this before now, especially considering everything my father once taught me? How am I only just now seeing what the State has been doing to me and to everyone else trapped in its grasp?

We've allowed the government to limit our education, reducing what we're taught down to information those in power deem appropriate for us to know. The State determines what we learn and what we don't, shaping us into mindless followers who are blind to anything other than the controlled system put into place to imprison us. Beyond what I've been told in school and by news reports, I realize now I know nothing.

I know nothing of the world outside this country.

I know nothing of the world outside this city.

I, along with everyone else, only know what the State tells us and wants us to know. Whatever twisted variation of the truth that may be.

Holstering my gun, I trail my fingers across the knobbly surface of the globe and give it a push, my eyes following the rotations, one after another, until my head is spinning. As the sphere turns, Ezra's fingers continue their hypnotic dance across the desktop.

"What's this?"

His voice snaps me out of my trance. A shudder rips through me, but I shake it off and wander to the other side of the desk where I gaze over Ezra's shoulder at the illuminated screen below. I'm not sure what we're looking at but sprawled across the top are two words printed in large red letters.

"Project W. A. R.," Ezra murmurs.

I follow the movement of his hand across the screen, taking in a few disjointed sentences as he scrolls down through the rest of the file. From what I can understand, we seem to be looking at notes recorded by a doctor.

Some lines stand out to me more than others.

## DAY 22

**Subject refuses to eat.**
**Have undertaken measures to avoid malnutrition.**

My pulse quickens, and my mouth goes dry as the vivid memory of that tube down my throat comes rushing back. Terror settles under my skin, but I force myself to keep reading.

# DAY 48

**Subject is weak but is withstanding tests.
Appears to be more resilient than past subjects.**

A scream claws up my throat, but no sound manages to pass through my lips.

# DAY 116

**Test has succeeded. Pursuing extracted information.
Will continue testing.**

At the end of each entry are the initials AR. If I had any doubt as to who these notes were referring to, seeing Dr. Richter's name would've wiped them away. But I don't have any doubts.

I'm well aware these are all about me.

I want to beg Ezra to stop reading, but I can't seem to remember how to speak. I'm frozen from head to toe, unable to do anything except relive the most traumatic part of my life from the perspective of the very person who dragged me through that hell.

Ezra's eyes dart back and forth, scanning through Dr. Richter's recorded entries. With another tap of his finger, the screen changes.

Then his hand goes still.

Now, instead of documents, we're exposed to the visual evidence of what the DSD did to me. The first image to pop up is a mugshot from just before the experiments started—back when I still looked healthy, before the DSD sunk its claws into me and the torture began. Further images appear, showing the daily disintegration of my health. Video footage is available as well, enticing us with a blinking icon in the bottom right corner of the screen.

Thankfully, Ezra doesn't click it.

A tremor of terror rocks my body, urging my legs to turn and run from this room. I can't bear this. I don't want to see any more. I don't want to relive it.

"My god…" Ezra breathes.

I can feel his eyes on my face, his gaze burning hot, but I can't bring myself to meet it. How can I look at him the same way now that he's witnessed the one thing I wish I could forget more than anything?

My lungs draw in a strangled breath as a realization suddenly strikes without warning. "It's initials," I gasp. "Project W. A. R." I pause, working the monogram out in my head. "W…A…R… Wynter Arabelle Reeves."

I risk a glance at Ezra, and his horrified expression twists my already aching heart to near breaking point. My lips part, but all that escapes is a whimper.

Ezra's eyes soften with understanding, and reaching out, he takes hold of my hand, his fingers settling over mine, slowly easing my distress as I fight back the need to cry and scream and rage over everything that's happened to me. Over and over again, he caresses the back of my hand with his thumb until I'm no longer trembling.

"Why is this here?" he asks once I've calmed down.

My thoughts have been circling around this same question. Why would Bilken have this information on me? He doesn't have any ties to the DSD that I know of, but that doesn't mean Richter hasn't been forced to share information with those above him in the State hierarchy. Even so, I'm failing to see the connection. What interest could the CEO of W. P. Headquarters possibly have in *me*? It doesn't make sense, and considering how easy it was to crack Bilken's computer and access these files, I'm left to conclude that this information was planted here for a specific purpose.

Like for us to find.

But that can't be the case, surely. Bilken had no way of knowing I'd be here. As far as he or the State are concerned, the only people on this mission would've been members of PHOENIX. Assuming they knew that and this file *was* planted here, why would they want PHOENIX to see it?

What does any of this mean?

A sinking feeling burrows in the pit of my stomach, and I can't shake the gnawing thought that we're missing something vital—a piece of the puzzle that would help me see the bigger picture. Doing my best to shrug off the sensation, I lean forward and swipe my free hand across the touchscreen.

My jaw clenches as I scroll through the notes and images, but I don't stop to look at any of them longer than a few seconds each. Ezra stands beside me, still holding my hand, watching my frantic search without saying a word.

A sharp breath catches in my chest when a military order pops up on the computer, positioned at the end of the file. My heart rate increases with every word, and the more I read, the more confused I become. The order requests the use of Project W. A. R. in any future assaults on neighboring countries, but I don't understand why. How would that even work?

When the realization finally hits me, I'm tempted to slap myself for not seeing it sooner. Aside from my ability to witness events at any given point in time, my visions have also revealed what I'm capable of…or will be soon enough. Although I haven't wanted to admit it, what I did to Dr. Richter's attendant was only a small taste of the sort of power I will eventually possess. Even now, I can sense that power humming under my skin, expanding, growing. When it finally matures—assuming I don't kill us all first—Dr. Richter and the State will have the ultimate weapon.

My hands clench into fists as anger swells inside me like a ravenous hunger. They knew all along. *He* knew. Dr. Richter understood what I would become, which not only means he lied to me when I was his prisoner but that he's known this entire time what I was intended for.

Biting back my rage, I comb through the rest of the order, devouring every word. It goes on to request my use for the premeditated protection of the State from any outside attacks. I assume that means it plans to use my visions for more than just tracking down members of PHOENIX, like Dr. Richter claimed.

"Good luck with that," I hiss, seething.

*I* can't even control this power, so what on earth makes the State think that it can?

Ezra squeezes my hand, and my eyes shift to his, the warm depths of his gaze loaded with so many silent questions. The way he looks at me compels me to speak.

"The State's planning to wage war against…" *Everyone,* I think to myself, but my voice trails off before I can finish the sentence out loud. Shaking my head, I ask, "Why would it do that?"

Ezra scowls at the screen. "Complete control and domination. The State clearly thinks it has the tool to achieve that end, and it seems like it's more than willing to use it."

Letting go of my hand, he leans over the desk and taps the

screen once more, flipping through the pages of the file again. I'm not sure what he's looking for, and I don't bother to ask. Instead, I back away, crossing the room, putting some much-needed distance between myself and the documented evidence of what I am.

And of what I might yet still become.

I return to the bookcase I was admiring before and skirt along the wall until I pass one of the two side rooms veering off from the office. Something large and black catches my eye, enticing me through the archway. Ezra calls my name, but I ignore him.

Unlike the main part of the office, this space is comprised almost entirely of glass. Tiny mirrors no bigger than my palm line the sole circular wall right up to the highest point of the domed ceiling where a crystal chandelier dangles from the center of the tiled pattern, exploding downward into a long, pointed sculpture resembling a cluster of icicles. My face fills each of the glass fragments surrounding me.

In the middle of the room stands the imposing object which drew my gaze: a grand piano, its shining ebony surface as smooth and reflective as still water. The sight of such an item here startles me. Whereas the contraband articles in the office were small and could be easily tucked away during a search, something like this isn't owned with the intention of being hidden.

No, this is a display. And a proud one at that.

Goosebumps rise on my arms, and I shiver. Seeing this piano standing here so openly, in plain sight for anyone passing to see, is an affront to all the people who were put to death over the years just for owning instruments like this one. People who just wanted to cling to what little beauty still remained in the world.

People like my father.

This display…

This *exhibition*…

It's a mockery of the individuality and creativity they all suffered for.

Exhaling, I trail my fingers along the ivory keys, just as I did to a similar piano all those years ago when I was first exposed to the greatest secret I would ever know. I was young then, so I didn't understand the consequences.

Not like I do now.

My father wasn't a bad person, and he definitely didn't deserve what happened to him. He was merely a lover of history and appreciated anything that commemorated the old world. He didn't want us to forget where we came from, like the State encouraged us to. Instead, he felt it was his duty to preserve that past. To cherish those little pieces of our history. So, he would restore and collect banned items and stow them in a hidden place no one else knew about, all for the sake of safekeeping that knowledge.

It was for that reason he was executed.

As far as I know, I was the only person he ever shared the full extent of his secret with, and in exchange for my silence, he would teach me about the books and other objects he had collected—some of which were instruments. That secret stood at the center of our relationship and strengthened our bond in a society that discouraged such closeness, familial or otherwise. After all, our loyalty was meant for the State, not for the people around us, regardless of shared blood.

My mother never understood our camaraderie and tried to sway us toward the more commonplace reservation and distance we observed among other families. Over time, her suspicion grew, and eventually, she uncovered what we were up to. When that happened, she didn't hesitate. She did her duty to the State, as was expected, and reported my father.

Looking back, I'm surprised she didn't turn me in as well, regardless of the fact I was only a child, just shy of seven, at the time. If she was willing to hand over her own husband, why not her child?

I suppose she must've felt the blame lay with my father and that I was merely a victim of his influence. Or maybe he begged her to protect me and she honored his dying wish. It was the least she could do.

Still, I can't help wondering…if she hadn't found out my father's secret, if we hadn't been caught, would she have so readily given me up to the DSD like she did? Maybe if our family hadn't already succumbed to such tragedy, she would've protected me the way a mother is supposed to. The way any child deserves.

My eyes brim with tears as my fingers stroke a handful of keys, pressing down just enough to call up each note. As the ping of the strings bounces off the tiled walls, echoing throughout the small space, I recall the melody my father once taught me. I wish I had thought to ask how he knew it.

His face springs to the forefront of my thoughts, and in my memory, I hear the gentle lilt of his voice instructing me to follow his hands. I strike each note at the same moment he does, playing side by side—my father in the past and me in the present—as if we're finally together again. As the music grows, the memory in my head changes.

Behind my closed eyelids, all I see is his face, bloodied and beaten rather than smiling—the way I wish I remembered him.

The happy memories were tarnished the moment the State stepped into our lives, and now, instead of his warm voice guiding me, all I hear are the words that have tormented me for years.

*"I'm sorry, Wynter."*

Tears stream down my cheeks, but I keep hitting the notes, the thrum of the vibrating strings reverberating into my fingertips.

"Wynter."

The coppery stench of blood fills my nose, and the wetness tickles my lips before splashing onto the keys and across my fingers. The sound of each drop *ping, ping, pings* in my ears.

"Wynter—"

A hand reaches out and touches my shoulder, grabbing me just like the Enforcer's hands did that day. I remember the feel of those fingers, strong and firm, as they pulled me away from my father.

Pressure balloons in my head as my lungs fill with air, bursting with a scream that rises up, pushing at the inside of my lips. I won't let them do this to us.

Not again.

A stabbing pain hammers into my temples, and with a shriek, my building power rips out of my body like the lash of several dozen whips. As the pressure pushes outward, the mirrored wall shatters.

Aside from the deafening crack of glass, the only sound that registers in my brain is a strange muffled grunt. Above me, the crystal chandelier swings from side to side as the tiles shower to the carpet like rain.

I spin on my heel, lured by the abrupt surge of energy tearing through my body like a drug, and glare down at the cowering man on the floor, his back pressed against what remains of the mirrored wall. When I take a step toward him to finish what I started, his frightened expression stays my hand.

As he stares up at me, familiar hazel eyes wide with fear, the memory of who he is takes shape in my head, bringing me back to myself and releasing me from my temporary insanity. Horrified, I glance from the bleeding gash on Ezra's right cheek to the glass shards scattered around us.

A single thought breaks through the fog dulling my senses. *What have I done?*

I blink as the pressure regains control, pushing all sense of who I am back down under the surface, like a parasite finally taking over its host. My head snaps to the side, my attention focused, as heavy footfalls plod against the carpeted floor. As I turn, glancing back into the main part of the office, at least a dozen Enforcers file through the doorway.

When they raise their guns, I feel it—this disease, this *power*, taking hold of me. Its sole focus is self-preservation, and it succeeds in its task by ripping the weapons from the Enforcers' hands and turning them back on their owners.

I'm barely aware of what I'm doing as bullet casings launch into the air. The ammunition perforates the beautiful shelves behind the soldiers, breaking the glass and destroying most of the rare objects and books they held. If I wasn't so wholly consumed by this power, I might mourn the loss of such priceless treasures.

Crimson spatters the carpet, and, for the briefest of moments, I have the most bewildering thought that I am like the white fibers under my feet—once pure and untainted but now, thanks to this disease, irreversibly tarnished, slowly rotting as the evil within me spreads. Like this carpet, I am forever stained by the blood I have spilled.

Once the last Enforcer goes still, I release my mental hold on the guns, and when they fall, I welcome the glorious relief of pressure as a weight seems to lift off my skull. Without that pressure to burden me, I drop to my knees, more exhausted than I've ever been in my life.

A familiar warmth catches me before my head hits the floor.

"Wynter," Ezra breathes in my ear. His tone is drenched with worry.

My movements are sluggish as I search for his gaze, my body rigid with shock and fatigue as the last of my energy fades, leaching out of my body like a tide drifting back out to sea. Blood still oozes from the wound on Ezra's cheek, but when I try to lift a hand to wipe it away, he flinches, afraid of my touch.

*He's scared of me,* I realize.

And he should be.

I glimpse the movement of his throat as he swallows, his eyes flickering away from mine, drifting back toward the open area of the main office space. I follow his line of sight to the mutilated bodies piled in a heap before us, their corpses surrounded by weapons, empty casings, and fragments of the inhumane world I allowed myself to get lost in.

In my head, I'm screaming, *Not again!* But when my lips finally move, they only manage to say, "What have I done?"

Ezra doesn't answer me.

Hot tears stream down my face as I gape at the massacre before us. *I did this. I killed those people.*

*Me...*

I killed them.

*See?* that taunting voice says in my head. *You can't change what you are…and what you are is a killer.*

My fingers weave through my sweat-matted hair, gripping my head as a glint of light reflects off the glass on the floor, catching my eye. Hand shaking, I curl my grasp around the nearest shard, but when I raise the broken mirror, I don't recognize the person looking back at me. No, not a person.

*A monster.*

My eyes are black, a far-stretching abyss with only a sliver of white on each side. My usually alabaster skin is gray and sickly, the color contrasted by the streaks of blood seeping from my nose and the corners of my eyes, making me look possessed.

I choke back a sob. Ezra places a hand on my back, and when I try to hide my face, not wanting to see his reaction to this terrible, monstrous thing I've become, his fingers graze my chin, forcing me to look at him.

When our eyes lock, fresh tears burn across my vision and broken cries rack my lungs. Ezra pulls me into his chest, hugging me as tightly as either of us can physically bear. Despite his horror, he holds me close when anyone else would run away.

I slump against his chest and press my eyes shut, desperate for consolation from my guilt, but reality seems intent on dragging me away from even the smallest comfort. My eyes spring open again as slow footsteps pad across the blood-soaked carpet, bringing my worst fear into view.

I glance up, meeting that familiar cold gaze that haunts my every waking thought.

"Hello again, Wynter," Richter says with a smile.

# TWENTY-TWO

 it takes to push me to the edge. The deranged hand of fear rushes out from the darkness in the back of my head where I've been trying to keep it and clutches my throat, crushing my wind pipe until I can't breathe. My screams are silent as I fight for air.

I try to clamp my eyes shut again, begging myself to wake up from this nightmare. But I can't find the strength to look away from the monster in front of me, and even if I could, doing so wouldn't change a damn thing. Because I know this isn't a dream.

This is real, and my torturer has finally found me.

Dr. Richter meets my gaze with his trademark sinister grin, his expression soulless and devoid of feeling—much like the vacant faces worn by the slew of bodies littering the floor. He doesn't seem surprised by the corpses. If anything, he seems pleased by them.

"Austin," Ezra gasps beside me.

I peek up at Ezra, pulling out of his arms just enough to get a good hard look at his face. The shock and pain I find there remind me that I'm not the only one this reunion is hard for.

Steeling myself, I turn my gaze back to Richter. The smile has vanished from his lips, and the gray depths of his eyes have shifted their focus, turning from me and locking instead on his brother. As they glare at each other, it sinks in, more than ever before, that I was right about this mission.

We never should have come to this place.

"Ezra," Richter snarls through clenched teeth.

Dread and anxiety both prickle my flesh as the weight of reality pins me down to the floor. Only one coherent thought manages to form in the swirling vortex filling my head.

*I was right. The DSD planned all this.*

Ezra unfolds his arms from around me, and I'm cold without his reassuring warmth to keep me sane. As he rises to his feet, the jaws of madness open up from the ground beneath me. Before they can close and trap me in a cage from which I might never escape, Ezra reaches down and snakes a hand around my waist again—a lifeline saving me from my own self-destruction. With a gentle tug, he pulls me upright, away from the darkness and back into the light.

My surroundings are a muddled blur as the room begins to spin, slowly at first, then building…faster…faster…faster… Vertigo distorts my senses, and my knees buckle, sending my body tumbling sideways into Ezra's chest, my fingers gripping his shirt as if it's the only way to keep me here on this plane of existence. He catches me, holding me close to his side.

As my vision clears, bringing the room back into sharp clarity, I focus on Dr. Richter, trying to make sense of this riddle and work out how he's managed all this. Trap or not, there's no way he could've known I would be part of this mission. So, does that mean he's actually here to see his brother and the transmission from Bilken was merely a ploy to reunite them? To finally carry out whatever twisted revenge he's been planning since Ezra and Rai left all those years ago?

I wouldn't put it past him.

Then again, back in the tunnels, Jenner said that the transmission was addressed to Nolan, not Ezra. Does that mean Nolan had a hand in orchestrating this set-up? If so, why? Why would someone in PHOENIX want to work with the State— their enemy? What would he and Bilken get out of this ruse?

Dr. Richter lowers his gaze to the broken bodies sprawled across the floor. As he nods his approval, his fingers graze his chin. "You made short work of those Enforcers. You're progressing much more quickly than I had anticipated."

I bite down on my tongue to keep my anger at bay. After eighteen years living in the State, it should be as easy as breathing to suppress my emotions, and yet, Dr. Richter gets under my skin and affects me in a way no one else ever has. Every word, every breath, out of his vile mouth stirs up a homicidal rage I never knew existed within me.

"What do you mean?" Panic warps Ezra's tone, and a thousand unspoken questions swim in his eyes when he looks at me.

From the moment I read the first words of the military order we found on Bilken's computer, I understood what I am and what the State plans for me to become. Now, Ezra will finally understand, too. He'll see what I've gotten PHOENIX involved with.

He'll grasp how dangerous I really am.

My voice breaches the silence in a venomous hiss as I hurl an accusatory glare at Dr. Richter, my eyes like knives penetrating their target. "You knew this power was more than just visions. You knew what it would turn into, what I would become."

Flashes of vivid memories fill my head, showing me the faces of everyone I've killed—first, the attendant at the DSD and now, the Enforcers sent ahead to confront us. Even with all I've learned about the impossible nature of this disease, I still can't wrap my head around how I did it. I didn't even have to lift a finger. Every movement, every action was done with my mind, and what's more frightening is I had absolutely no power to stop it. It was like I was a slave to my whims. I wanted to kill them, so I did.

It was as simple as that.

Smirking, Dr. Richter gestures toward the glass desktop and the light emitting from the glowing computer screen. "I'm assuming you've seen your file? You should know by now you're not the only one we've tested on. So, yes. Of course, we knew. Did I not tell you that you were evolving and I had my suspicions as to what you were? How else would I have known that, I wonder, if I didn't have extensive insight about your condition?"

His words swarm my thoughts, and a buzzing sound floods my ears as I recall that initial interrogation at the DSD. All those other files he showed me, all those people... I knew the truth ever since Ezra told me about his mother, but still, I didn't want to believe it. I didn't want to believe so many others like me have existed and that they all died at the hands of such evil.

If Dr. Richter is capable of remorse, he doesn't show it.

"Your visions aren't the only reason the State wishes to use you. It's what you are becoming that's of far more interest to us." He steps over an unmoving arm, his shining black shoes squelching against the crimson-stained carpet. "It's fate, really. Even your initials agree. W...A...R..." He purrs each letter. "It's like you were destined to become the weapon that would allow us to conquer the world."

"I don't understand," I breathe, my voice ragged. "Why would you choose to start another war when one is already happening within our own walls?"

Dr. Richter cocks a bemused eyebrow at me. "You mean PHOENIX?" He scoffs—a cruel, mocking bark of a laugh—and pushes his glasses farther up his nose. "They aren't a problem. They never really were."

Ezra tenses beside me, and the confusion on his face mirrors the jumbled tangle of thoughts in my head. Dr. Richter chuckles as he continues to skirt around the mangled bodies between us.

"PHOENIX was more of a menace to begin with, but over the years, you've made yourselves quite useful. What better way to subjugate the public than to frighten them with the constant threat of terrorism? It was the perfect starting point for the State to strengthen its hold. We could've easily disposed of you at any time. Keeping you around just happened to align with our interests."

As much as I wish this was just another deceit, what Richter is claiming lines up with what Jenner said about the attacks blamed on PHOENIX. How they were all devised and carried out by the State. That PHOENIX was merely a scapegoat to mask the real instigator behind those horrors.

Still, if what he's saying is true, that doesn't answer why he constructed this trap. Or what he's hoping to gain in the long run. Why is he here?

Why are *we* here?

"Why go through the trouble to bait them to come here if the plan wasn't to trap PHOENIX?" I ask.

"I'm not after PHOENIX," Dr. Richter says, a slight cryptic

laugh in his voice. "Well, not all of them."

"Rai…" Ezra whispers, his skin chalky.

I should've seen this coming. From the moment I suspected the DSD was behind the transmission, I should've known this wasn't only about me. I've learned enough about their past relationship—and of Richter's personality—to know he would never forget Rai's betrayal. Or forgive it.

As I once said to Ezra, Dr. Richter won't stop until he gets what he wants and anyone who gets in his way is an acceptable casualty.

Dr. Richter slides closer to me until the heap of corpses no longer stands between us. Nothing does. He could reach out and touch me if he felt so inclined.

"While I have my personal reasons for being here, I actually came to retrieve you, Wynter."

Ezra shoves me behind him with a sweep of his arm, baring his teeth. An animalistic growl rumbles deep in his throat. "She's not going anywhere with you."

"Are you sure about that?" Dr. Richter flashes his signature smile, and that one look says so many things I don't want to acknowledge. It screams of victory. "Surely, you knew the potential consequences involved with bringing her here. You knew the risk, and you took it anyway. Or perhaps, you couldn't resist the temptation and wanted to see her power for yourself, the same way I always wondered about Mother's. After all, we do come from the same stock, Brother, despite how greatly we might both wish to deny it."

Ezra winces as if Dr. Richter has struck him, then risks a glance over his shoulder at me. I shake my head, hoping to convey what I'm unable to find the words to say. I want to tell him that I know Dr. Richter is lying, and that I know he only brought me here to protect me from something, even if he's too afraid to say what. That he's not the same insatiable monster his brother is. I want to tell him that I don't blame him for whatever comes next, even if it means I end up back at the DSD. Even if all this ends with me dead.

If I was honest with him—and with myself—I would admit that outcome is what's best for everyone.

Tears prick at the corners of my eyes as I swallow, pushing down the lump in my throat. "What now?" My voice is barely audible despite the hush.

"Well, unfortunately, you killed all the Enforcers I enlisted to detain you, not that I'm entirely surprised," Dr. Richter says, without sounding the least bit contrite. "No matter, I've called for more, and they should be here any moment now. Then you'll go back to where you belong."

My fingers grab at the back of Ezra's shirt, my nails like pincers, holding me to him. "You're crazy if you think I'll go with you willingly."

A bored expression crosses Dr. Richter's face, and he shrugs, indifferent to my protests. "If you wish to leave with your new friends, that's your choice. But just know that it's inevitable you will return to my care. Although, if I were you, I'd do so sooner rather than later. That power of yours won't monitor itself."

Ezra whips around, bringing his mouth to my ear. Between us, he holds his communicator clenched in his hand. My eyes flick down to the message flashing across the small screen.

### 10 E SPOTTED. T2G.

*E? T2G?*

"We have to get out of here," he whispers in a rush. "The others have sighted more Enforcers, and if we don't leave now, we won't be leaving at all."

Then it clicks. The E must stand for Enforcers and T2G...

*Time to go.*

I nod. He doesn't need to tell me twice. I don't plan on sticking around here any longer than necessary, not if the end result means I'll wind up back on that cold metal table at the DSD.

Ezra wraps his arm around my waist and helps me toward the door, my body drained from my confrontation with the Enforcers. Dr. Richter stands by, watching us with those unfeeling gray eyes and an amused grin taking form on his lips. He does nothing to stop us or prevent our escape.

Just as I allow myself to believe he's letting us go, his voice plunges into my back, stabbing me.

"There's a cure."

Every inch of my body freezes. Ezra tugs against me with a quiet plea to keep moving, but Dr. Richter's words hold me in place. Against my better instincts, I peer over my shoulder.

"Your condition is progressing far too quickly," he warns. "Without proper treatment, your symptoms will worsen, and we all know where that will leave you, don't we, Brother?"

*Where will this condition leave me?* I wonder.

Ezra and Richter have only ever seen this disease end with death. But I'm not concerned with *my* death. I'm concerned with the deaths of those I care about. The fatalities I will cause if my condition does continue to worsen. I've already murdered at least a dozen Enforcers, and I'll never forget what I did to Dr. Richter's attendant. I don't want to carry the burden of taking any more lives.

I don't want to hurt anyone else.

Like so many times before, the recollection of that vision of the future manifests in my head. The end of the world takes shape, flaunting the approaching destruction and death I, alone, will cause.

How many people will I kill when that future clashes with the present? How many lives will I take because of this disease? Because of what I am?

*A cure...*

A cure would take all that away.

"He's lying, Wynter." Ezra's hand tightens around my waist. "We have to go *now*," he urges.

I walk forward a few steps, but my eyes linger on Richter's smug face, searching for the lie I know must be concealed there beneath his conniving guise. I know he'd say anything to get me to go with him, but what if, this time, he's actually telling the truth?

What if there really is a cure?

Can I risk walking away without being sure?

"If you come back to the DSD willingly, I will ensure you get the cure before it's too late."

Too late? When will it be too late? And how long would he allow my condition to progress before administering this so-called cure? How long would he continue to use me before my body would be so ravaged that a cure wouldn't even help me?

I'm hesitant to believe him, given what I've already been through and the fact that he's neglected to mention anything about a cure until now. But I also can't ignore the possibility he's presenting.

That future…

The end of the world…

What if this is how I prevent it? What if the cure is real, and with it, no one else has to die because of me? Because of this horrible *thing* I'm becoming?

The options before me beat against the walls of my skull, but I'm too exhausted to know what to do. If I were to go with Dr. Richter, I'd be giving myself up with no guarantee the cure even exists. Torture and death would mark the rest of my days.

But if I don't go with him, I'd be dooming everyone in the world to die. I wouldn't be the only victim of this disease anymore, and I would be responsible for every life lost because of my cowardice. If I don't go with him, it would only be because I don't want to leave the people who have since entered my life.

Rai.

Jenner.

Ezra…

We've barely had the chance to really get to know each other, but the thought of leaving them now, of never seeing them again, is a physical weight on my chest crushing me. No…if I don't go with Richter, it would only be because I'm selfish.

Because I'm afraid.

Ezra hauls me from the room before I can make a decision, his fingers digging into my side, steering my movements forward when I can barely find the focus to guide my own steps. Side by side, we fumble over the threshold.

Dr. Richter's raised voice echoes down the corridor, chasing us as we limp away from the office. Every word he shouts tempts me back.

"Think about it, Wynter. You know where to find me."

# TWENTY-THREE

**MY BREATHS ESCAPE IN RAPID** succession, ravaging my lungs and leaving my mouth and throat parched. I try to swallow, but every attempt feels like hot gravel grinding against sandpaper, making me shudder with the effort. I'm desperate for water, but there's no time to stop or rest.

Right now, our only focus is getting out of this place.

Ezra's arm tightens around my waist, his breathing strained as he supports my weight while trying to keep a decent pace. I try to ease his burden, but I'm tired and weak, and every step is a tremendous effort. The after-effects of what I did in Bilken's office are wreaking havoc on my body, crippling my muscles and limbs until they stop functioning altogether. At that point, Ezra has no choice but to drag me.

Despite everything I know about his character, I half-expect him to abandon me and save himself, but he doesn't even seem to consider doing that. He simply grits his teeth and carries on as if it's the only thing he can do.

As if it's the only option he has.

The hallways seem to go on forever. Was this building always so big? Darkness creeps in at the corners of my eyes, and I'm not sure if what I'm seeing past the haze impairing my vision is real or imagined. I can't think straight, and the exhaustion consuming me is only making my symptoms worse.

Distant voices enter my ears, jerking me back from the pull of unconsciousness. Ezra quickens his pace, and when we round the next corner, I glimpse the distorted silhouettes of Jenner and Rai at the opposite end of the corridor. Their concerned faces sharpen as we barrel toward them.

"Where the *hell* have you been?" Jenner asks through clenched teeth.

Relief rushes through me as my eyes lock with Rai's. Her golden-tinged brown skin is pink with exertion, and she's breathing hard, her chest heaving, but she appears unharmed as far as I can tell.

Breaking away from Ezra, I throw the full weight of my body at Rai, choking back a sob. Moisture springs into my eyes as my arms wrap around her back, hugging her to me as tightly as I can—as if my brain won't really believe she's here with us otherwise. My useless legs fail to hold me upright, and as I sink to the floor, she kneels alongside me.

"What's going on?" she hisses over my head.

Warmth spreads through my chest as she brushes a careful finger over my cheek, wiping away the blood and tears. I can feel the sticky streaks on my skin, but I lack the strength to care about how frightening I must look to her. All I can think about is her safety and how much I want to get out of here before Dr. Richter finds us again.

Ezra speaks in a hurried voice, filling the others in on what happened while we were separated. "Bilken was a dead end. It was a set-up by Austin. He's here for Wynter."

"He's here?" Rai asks, her tone fraught. A tremor rolls over her hands, and she quickly flattens her palms to my back to still them.

"We have to go right now," Jenner snaps, casting a panicked glance over his shoulder. "The others are already out and waiting back in the tunnels. But they won't wait forever."

Rai unhooks my arms from her body as Ezra steps forward and lifts me up off the ground. My eyes drift from her face to his.

"Right," he grunts, adjusting his hold on me. His fingers brush against my waist. "Let's get out of here."

We continue through the far-stretching corridors in tense silence. Ezra and I trail Jenner's lead, our movements awkward as he holds up the bulk of my weight and we try to keep our steps synchronized. Rai follows behind us, bringing up the rear of the group, to keep an eye out for Enforcers.

We head back the same way we came, since finding an alternate exit would also mean finding a new route back to the tunnels, and we don't have time for that. Taking our original path isn't without its own share of danger, but, luckily, we don't run into any resistance or trouble of any kind along the way.

Like before, the building is eerily empty.

*What happened to the Enforcers the others spotted before?* I wonder through the residual pain in my head. Has Dr. Richter called them off, or are they lying in wait, preparing to attack us when we least expect it?

Sweat beads along my brow and hairline as we push ahead through the soundless hallways, and a fever flares along my skin, burning hotter with every laborious step. The heat spreads into my nose and travels down into my lungs where it chokes me like a thick layer of smoke.

Despite my suffocation, a scream explodes up my throat as the stabs in my head appear out of nowhere, hitting me in that same familiar pattern. I trip, falling…falling…falling…but through the growing fog darkening my surroundings, I think I hear Ezra call my name. I can just make out the blurred features of his face, his unblinking eyes staring down into mine as he pulls me against his chest.

His voice slips away, swallowed by the sudden onslaught of convulsions that happen every time I go through this. I try to go back to him—to escape the future intent on pulling us apart—but I can't seem to figure out how.

I'm too weak to fight what's coming.

A long moment passes where all I'm aware of is pain. Then, as if waking from a dream, I open my eyes to find myself back in Bilken's office. The broken bodies still litter the floor, their blood soaking into the once pristine white carpet. Nothing is any different than it was when we were here less than twenty minutes ago.

My gaze crawls from one end of the office to the other, starting at the shards of broken mirror on the floor and ending at the window behind Bilken's desk. Dr. Richter stands in front of the panes, his hands knitted behind his back, staring out into the unending darkness of night on the other side of the glass.

"Austin."

A rush of fear sweeps through me at the sound of his name, and sucking in a sharp breath, I whip around to find Rai standing in the doorway. She hesitates before inching into the room, her eyes drawn to the carnage forming a small mountain between them.

"Raina..." Dr. Richter whispers.

As if lured by his voice, she gasps, crying out, "I had to see if it was true for myself. I had to see if it was really you behind all this."

A grimace warps his lips. "And now that you know? How does that make you feel?"

"I just want to know why!" She raises a clenched hand up in front of her chest, as if doing so will hold her aching heart in one piece. "None of this is doing your mother's memory any justice—"

"My mother?" He scoffs, letting out a soft laugh. "My work has nothing to do with honoring my mother."

I glance between them, noting the doubt on Rai's face. The same uncertainty overwhelms me. From the moment I learned about Ezra's and Richter's mother, I assumed her death was the latter's motivation for pursuing others afflicted with the same condition. Perhaps because of lack of closure, or maybe he really has been working toward a cure this whole time as a way of honoring her memory—not that his personality exactly oozes with sentimentality. Either way, I assumed her demise was the reason for why he is the way he is.

"My mother's illness might've initially been why I showed an interest in this line of science, but after a while, my tragic origin tale no longer held any bearing. All that mattered was progress. And what incredible progress I've made."

His words send a tingle of unease up my spine, even though, in the physical sense, I'm not really here.

Tears well in Rai's eyes. "Then why?"

"Can you think of no other reason?" he asks her. "Can you honestly not figure out why I might desire the power to locate whoever I want?"

"All this…because of me?"

"You gave me no other choice," he growls. "You left me. You *chose* Ezra."

"I didn't choose Ezra!" Denial erupts from her lungs as a single tear spills down her cheek. "I chose freedom over slavery. I chose a new life. A life with meaning and purpose—"

"Slavery?" He sneers. "Is that how you saw it?"

She flinches. "It's how I still see it. Everyone in this corrupt country is a slave, even you."

Nodding, he paces in front of the window. "And what sort of life would you say you have now? Always in hiding. Always running. Where is the meaning and purpose you yearned for in such a sorry existence? What kind of life is that?"

"One I chose." Her voice wavers, breaking a little. "One where my free will wasn't stolen from me."

He stills at these words and glares at Rai with eyes as cold and lifeless as the corpses between them. "It pains me to hear that's how you pictured a life with me. And here I would've given you the world."

Rai shakes her head. "That world you say you wanted to give me is broken. What you were offering me was merely poison wrapped up in a pretty package. It would've killed me if I'd stayed. Would that have made you happy?"

Dr. Richter lowers his gaze but doesn't utter a word, and as the seconds tick by without either of them speaking, I realize any feelings they may have once shared have been pushed aside and overridden by anger. Anger born from the opposing paths they chose to take all those years ago.

Paths that led to very different futures.

What was the defining moment that broke them apart? Was it Ezra's decision to join PHOENIX, or did it go back even further to an event before that? Perhaps back to the moment when Dr. Richter's career path was decided? Or when his mother started showing peculiar symptoms that first drew his interest?

If he had been projected for another sector, would things have turned out differently for them? Would he still have become this obsessive, heartless sadist, or would he have maintained whatever decent qualities once made her care for him?

"I never stopped thinking about you."

Dr. Richter and I both glance at Rai, equally stunned by her confession. My eyes jump back and forth between them, and for a flicker of an instant, I glimpse something in his expression that almost makes him seem human.

That flicker disappears just as soon as it surfaced.

"There's nothing I can do now, Raina. You must know that."

A tight, bitter smile tugs at the edges of her trembling lips. "Once an enemy, always an enemy, right? Isn't that Termination's mantra?" With a trembling breath, she clamps her eyes shut. Tears slip from between her closed lids. "I've known from the moment I left you what would happen if we ever saw each other again. If it's any consolation, I'm sorry. About everything. My choice was selfish, but I never wanted to hurt you."

"I wish an apology was enough, but you've left me no choice now that I see your mind won't be changed. You've brought this upon yourself." Every word is a stone he flings at her, all cast with a single intent.

To maim.

Time seems to slow as he reaches into his pocket, and when

he raises his arm, a scream tears from my lungs. Although I race forward, determined to put myself in his path, I know there's nothing I can do. I'm a mere apparition with no substance to intervene or change anything about this moment.

I'm completely helpless.

Still, I reach out a hand, and as my fingertips brush where the barrel of his gun meets the air, a murky cloud descends upon the room, abruptly ending the vision. My surroundings darken, pushing me back into consciousness, as Dr. Richter's voice fills my ears.

"The irony is almost poetic, don't you think? You ran, and yet, the poison still got you."

My eyes snap open.

"Wynter!" Ezra leans into my line of vision, relief washing over his face like a rush of color flooding into pale cheeks.

I inhale through my nose, but my breaths hit a wall. My airway is blocked. I let out a whimper. If I can't breathe, I can't tell Ezra about what I just saw, and I need to tell him right away.

I need to warn him about what's going to happen.

Sensing my distress, he holds a canteen up to my mouth, and the water is a welcome respite, easing the burning pain inside me. The liquid loosens the blood sticking my lips together, helping me to speak.

"Ra—" I wheeze.

Nausea grips my stomach. Gagging, I twist away from Ezra, hurling onto my side, and spew across the wooden floorboards. Icy shivers travel up my spine with each heave.

Ezra's hands are like hot coals on my skin, but I never ask him to move them away as he holds me with one and rubs my back with the other. He keeps me steady until the sickness passes.

Once my stomach is purged, I give a shuddering sigh and allow my body to go fully limp, resting my head in Ezra's lap. For a few moments, I lie still, simply getting my bearings. His voice in my ear brings the world into focus.

"Wynter…what did you see?"

The memory of Rai's face in my head rockets through me. "Rai…" I try to explain what I saw, but my mouth struggles to shape the words.

"What about Rai?" he presses. "She's right—"

He turns, gesturing with his thumb over his shoulder. I follow his gaze, but, like I foresaw, the only person we find standing behind us is Jenner.

Ezra's head snaps side to side, his eyes searching. "Where is she?" he practically shouts. The muscles in his arms strain against my sore body.

Jenner's face goes ashen as he fumbles for his communicator, calling Rai on the encrypted frequency band they're using for this mission. When she doesn't answer, he shakes his head in disbelief. "She was right behind us! Where the hell did she go?"

Ezra grabs my shoulders, his fingers gripping tight enough to leave bruises. "Where is she, Wynter? Where's Rai?"

My head is spinning, and quick, panting breaths part my lips. Pain echoes in my brain like a rumble of thunder after a lightning strike, obscuring everything around me. I can see Ezra. I can hear him.

But it's so hard to reach him.

"Rai…" I breathe, fighting to speak. "Ri…Richter…"

Ezra's mouth flattens into a thin line, the acceptance and fuming rage in his gaze both telling me he's realized what she's done without me needing to say anything more. I suppose he must've known it was always a possibility she would hunt down his brother once she found out he was here. Hell, maybe that's the only reason she came on this mission in the first place. Maybe she suspected Richter had something to do with the transmission and wanted to end things between them once and for all.

"I have to find her," Ezra says.

It occurs to me, past the haze in my head, that he's asking me—*begging* me—for guidance.

My throat is tight, like a hand around my neck, as I manage to push out the words, "Bilken's office."

With a faltering breath, Ezra leans in close to me until our faces are only a few inches apart. The growing distance in his eyes unnerves me.

"I need you to go with Jenner. He's going to get you out of here and help you to safety—"

Dread and panic both smother my chest, and my stomach seems to drop, falling into my feet. I don't know why, but I have a terrible feeling that surges further at his words. It scratches at the back of my brain, saying the same thing over and over again, like a warning. It tells me that, if Ezra leaves me now, I'll never see him again—regardless of the many visions and dreams that have suggested a different future awaits us. After all, how can I be certain those visions are showing me the truth of what will come to pass and not just one possible path?

How can I be sure the future won't change when I least expect it to?

All I do know is that our fates are intertwined, and my gut keeps telling me that if I survive tonight, he will as well. But I can only be sure of that if we stick together. Besides, I only came on this mission because of him. No way in hell is he abandoning me now after everything we've been through. If he leaves, if he *dies*, I'll never get the answers I sought PHOENIX out for. And if I never get those answers, then I exposed them all to my cursed existence for nothing.

No, if he wants to help Rai, he's taking me with him. Otherwise, I fear the worst. Otherwise, I'm certain I'll lose them both. As much as I want to save Rai, I can't let that happen.

As much as I want her to live, I can't watch him die.

"Wait—" My voice cracks as my fingers clutch his coat, holding him to me. Any other words I attempt to utter fail to form. My body isn't cooperating, and it's costing us all valuable time.

"Uh, I hate to spoil a perfectly good plan," Jenner interrupts, "but we have company."

Heavy footfalls trigger tremors in the floorboards, the sound of the enemy reverberating in the distance like the faint beating of drums. My eyes dart to the far end of the hallway as the first Enforcers round the corner, cutting off our intended exit. They raise their guns, preparing to fire.

Ezra jumps to his feet, cursing under his breath, and hoisting me up, he runs back the way we came, dragging my limp body beside him. If he wants to save Rai, he has no choice now except to take me and Jenner with him or risk sacrificing us to the Enforcers, which we both know he won't do. He'll find a way to save us all because that's just who Ezra is.

Clenching his jaw, he tightens his hold on me.

I try my best to keep up with him as he sprints through corridor after corridor back in the direction of Bilken's office. Each step is more draining than the last, sapping me of what little strength I still retain after my vision. Before long, I'm too weak to continue.

Ezra charges ahead, and I can sense his increasing frustration at my slowness. My feet fumble against the floor despite my silent pleas for them to move.

*We'll never make it at this rate*, I realize.

Ezra must be thinking the same thing because he bends down mid-stride and scoops me up off the floor. He carries me in his arms, building momentum, even with the added burden of my dead weight. As we run, the Enforcers' footsteps fade.

After several minutes, we find ourselves back in the dead end hallway where Bilken's office is located. Ezra's ragged breaths beat against my cheek, matching the frantic tempo of my erratic pulse. Our destination is so close now and moving closer with every second.

Rai's face appears in my head, and I pull at Ezra's shirt, urging him to move faster—ignoring the guilt blossoming in my chest that tells me he would've reached her already if he hadn't been forced to bring me along. Ignoring the realization that says, if she dies, it will be my fault.

*No,* I tell myself. *We're so close. We're almost there.*

Just a few more steps.

An ember of hope sparks to life in my stomach, igniting my nerves, but it's snuffed out before the flame can form, extinguished by the ringing echo of a gunshot. We don't see Rai. We don't have to. The splash of blood sprayed across the floor mere steps ahead of us is all the indicator we need to tell us what just happened.

At the sight of the blood, Ezra's grip on my body slackens, and he drops me, his arms going limp at his sides. I try to find my footing, but my legs are like twigs supporting a building of bricks. As they give out beneath me, strong arms take my weight.

"I got you," Jenner murmurs in my ear.

I crumple against him, my eyes drifting from Ezra's blank face to the bloodstained wooden floorboards.

This can't be happening. We were here.

We had made it.

"We…we're too late," I breathe.

"No!" The anguish in Ezra's voice breaks my heart. He stalks forward, reaching for his gun, his heated gaze focused on the open office door before us.

I know what he's going to do—or, at least, what he intends to do. He has a new mission, and its focus is one thing and one thing only.

To kill Dr. Richter.

I thrust out a shaking hand, wishing he'd stop and walk away from this vendetta while there's still time for us to escape. One death is enough.

*Don't let it become two!* I shout in my head, but exhaustion prevents the words from forming.

As if reading my mind, Jenner places me down on the floor, then dives after Ezra, snatching him by the neck of his coat and yanking him back.

"There's nothing we can do! We have to go!"

Ezra turns, his expression livid, and shoves Jenner away from him, who raises his arm. I wince at the sound of Jenner's fist making contact.

Ezra falters, stumbling to the side a few steps. His hand flies up to touch his red cheek.

"Listen to me!" Jenner barks before grabbing Ezra roughly by the shoulders. "Are you ready to die for revenge? Are you ready to let *her* die in the crossfire?" He points at me, his other hand tightening its grip, the skin of his knuckles turning white from the pressure. "I need you," he pleads, lowering his voice. "I can't save her alone."

Ezra balks at these words, the anger in his eyes overshadowed by the most peculiar fear. He stares at me as if he isn't quite sure what he's seeing.

The corridor quakes with the approaching sound of our doom. The Enforcers have almost caught up to us.

If we're going to escape, we have to go now.

Jenner releases Ezra's shoulder and returns to my side, easing me up off the hard floor and cradling me in his arms, holding me firm to his chest. With one last ominous glance in the direction of Bilken's office, he sets off down the hallway back the way we came, then turns right, following the only path left to us even though the route is blind.

My voice is raspy as I bellow for Ezra to follow us, my plea an incoherent rambling as my tongue trips over my words. Ezra hesitates for only a moment, then stalks Jenner's steps, pushing into a sprint to catch up with us. Relief squeezes my heart as I close my eyes, exhausted by this whole ordeal. When I open them again, Ezra's head is bowed, his gaze pinned on the floor, avoiding my gaze. He doesn't look at me again for the rest of our journey. And why should he?

Because of me, Rai is dead.

It takes longer than I'm sure any of us would've liked, but we finally make it back to the courtyard. Thanks to Jenner, we arrive at the tunnels in one piece. He places me on the ground— this time, on my feet—as he braces himself to lift the hatch door. The metal hinges screech, piercing the night air, when he pulls.

A bright light shines up to greet us from the depths of the

hole. "What the shittin' hell took so long?" Duke yells, the glow of the beam reflecting off his face.

"I'll explain later!" Jenner positions my body in front of his, supporting my weight. "Catch her, will ya?"

He helps me sit down at the lip of the hole then lowers me into the darkness by my arms. As I drop, my stomach flips, even though the fall isn't far. Duke catches me almost at once, his muscles like rocks as my back smashes into his chest, forcing a groan from my lips.

For a long moment, he doesn't relinquish his hold on me, his eyes taking in the dried blood smeared across my face, his broad mouth slightly ajar in abject horror. His reaction doesn't surprise me, but I still look away.

Ezra follows next, probably forced by Jenner who likely doesn't believe he would follow us otherwise. Once he's back underground, he stands to one side of the group, waiting in silence.

When it's Jenner's turn, he tests the rope attached to the wheel, checking to make sure it's still secure, then jumps, splashing into the thin layer of water.

"Close it up," he orders as he trots back to my side.

Duke cocks a confused eyebrow at the hatch door before lobbing suspicious glances at Ezra, Jenner, and me. "What about Rai?" he asks, his tone wary.

My lips press together. Beside me, Jenner's body goes rigid. We both peer at Ezra, who stares blankly into the darkness around us.

"She's gone," is all he says, his voice lifeless.

Everyone gapes at Ezra's retreating figure as he turns and proceeds down the tunnel. He doesn't spare me a glance as he passes. He doesn't even look at Jenner. He simply walks by, his unfocused gaze set straight ahead as his body sinks into the shadows.

# TWENTY-FOUR

**THE JOURNEY BACK TO THE** compound is long and quiet. No one speaks out of fear of upsetting Ezra, or maybe we just can't find the words to describe our grief. It follows us in the darkness like a stray dog begging for scraps—constantly nipping at our heels no matter how many times we try to shoo it away.

The sadness writhing in my own heart is an unwanted but familiar companion, and with each sodden step through the tunnels, my thoughts naturally drift to my father, recalling the day he was taken from me with unsettling clarity. The pain I felt then... It was exactly like this.

With Rai gone, it's like I've lost him all over again. She had become that person in my life—the parental figure I had begun to rely on since I can no longer rely on my mother and my father is gone, his spirit torn from this world. And, just like my father, her death is my fault. If he had never included me in his illegal activities, if I hadn't been so hell-bent on staying with Ezra, both my father and Rai might still be alive. But, because of me, they aren't, and now, instead of the agony of only a single loss creating a hole in my heart, I'm assaulted with the pain of two.

Now, my grief threatens to break me completely.

It's strange how someone can be there one minute and gone the next, their existence stamped out with the same ease and speed as drawing in or releasing a breath. It shouldn't be that easy.

Her life was worth more.

My eyes flit to Ezra, locking onto his back. He lumbers ahead of us, barely keeping within sight of the reach of our flashlights, the beams like fingers constantly trying and failing to grab hold of him and keep him from drifting farther away. It disturbs me to think how close he came to becoming just a memory, like my father and Rai. If Jenner hadn't intervened, if he hadn't stopped him from going after Richter—

Tears drip down my cheeks at the thought of losing him, this stranger who has somehow grown to mean so much to me despite our initial apprehension and distrust of each other. I scream Ezra's name in my head, but the silence swallows it whole. I scream, and I scream, but he doesn't look back. He just keeps walking, his pace steady and unchanging—the echo of his movements like a metronome counting the steps taking us farther away from what we've lost and will never get back again.

Steps that widen the distance between us.

I struggle to keep up with the others, even with Jenner's help. He holds me close, one arm propped around my waist with the other holding my hand where it lay slung over his shoulder. Every so often, I sense him looking down at me, but I never meet his gaze. Part of me doesn't want him to see the guilt in my eyes while another part doesn't dare turn away from Ezra, too afraid of what might happen if I were to glance away for even a second.

As I stare at the distant shape of Ezra's retreating figure, I imagine his face, expression drawn, the skin of his cheeks slick with tears. Silent, endless tears just like the ones from my vision.

*"I'm sorry, Wynter."*

I wave the recollection of his doleful voice away because he has nothing to apologize for. If anything, I'm the one who's sorry. No matter which way I look at it, we were in a lose-lose situation. Even if I hadn't stalled him and he had gone after Rai without me, those extra few seconds wouldn't have made any difference. Rai's fate was sealed the moment she went after Richter.

But knowing that doesn't ease my guilt, and I can't help thinking that if I had some control of this power, if I had seen what was going to happen sooner, then maybe I could've done something about it.

Stop it.

Change it…

Can the future even be changed? If it can't, then what's the point of these visions? Why show me such things if they can't be prevented? It's cruel, and I'd rather live in ignorance than be tormented by the inevitable.

Rai's smiling face fills every void in my head. In the short time I knew her, she made me feel loved and accepted, but more than that, she gave me a sense of protection—the only thing I ever really wanted from my mother. She made me feel welcome in a world where I had never experienced that feeling. Or expected to. She was full of hope, gentle, and kind.

And because of me…she's dead.

Time passes in a daze until we arrive back at the compound. Together, Jenner and I hobble toward the round hole in the wall marking the end of the tunnel, and as he lifts me over the threshold, my eyes instinctively search for Ezra. He disappears into the darkness of the maze before I'm even fully through the hatch door.

"Maybe I should go after him," I mutter, gasping, leaning against the nearest wall to catch my breath.

"No." Jenner jerks his head. "What Ezra needs right now is space. We should all just leave him alone."

I open my mouth to protest but immediately snap it shut again at the warning look on Jenner's face. He's right. It's not my place to go after Ezra. Besides, I'm reluctant to chase after him anyway, worried he'll blame me for what happened to Rai. And he should. Why else would he have brought me along if he didn't intend for me to use my power to warn them? To keep a vigilant look out for danger? But if that's what he wanted, why couldn't he have just told me as much? I would've happily gone through the pain of these visions if it meant I could keep them all safe.

Tears prick at the corners of my eyes as a warm hand wraps around my shoulder and squeezes. Sniffing, I peek up, meeting Jenner's gaze. The tenderness I find there alleviates the pain in my heart just a little.

"Hey. You're already starting to look like yourself again," he says, a crooked smile touching his lips.

A flush crawls over my clammy skin, and I swallow, relieved he doesn't elaborate and even more thankful no mirrors are readily available for me to see the damage for myself. Back in Zone 1, Duke had looked at me as if I wasn't a human but a thing to be feared. Not that I blame him. The first time I witnessed the side effects of this disease, I thought I was staring into the eyes of a monster.

*You're a murderer,* that small voice says in my head, as if I had somehow forgotten. *Of course, you're a monster.*

Jenner returns his arm to my waist and carefully helps me away from the wall before leading me back through the maze without speaking a word. Once again, I find myself memorizing our steps, imprinting the turns we take on my memory. He only breaks the silence about thirty minutes later when we're standing awkwardly outside my quarters.

"You should get some sleep. It's been…" He trails off, looking flummoxed, then shakes his head in dismay. "Well, it's been a long night."

I nod, placing my fingertips on the door handle. "What about you?"

He lets out a sigh, raking a hand through his hair. The sooty strands stick up in several directions. "I don't think Ezra's in the right headspace to report on what happened, so I'll have to do it for him. They're going to want an explanation about what went down out there, not only with Bilken but with Richter and Rai. I don't think we can hide the truth about Ezra's relation to him anymore."

The worry lines creasing his brow set me on edge.

"Who will?" I ask in a breathless whisper. "Nolan?"

Jenner nods. "Among others."

He averts his gaze, and I wonder if he's being intentionally vague—if he isn't allowed to disclose that information or if he just doesn't trust me enough to tell me the details. I hope it's the former. After what happened tonight, I don't want to lose anything else, not even something as intangible as Jenner's trust.

Assuming I ever had it in the first place.

Suddenly, I recall something Ezra said when he first told me about the transmission from Bilken. I had pleaded with him not to go, and he had said it wasn't his decision to make. Like I first suspected then, someone else is calling the shots behind the scenes. Someone else made us go on that mission.

And that someone probably knew it was a trap.

"You mean whoever sent us to meet Bilken," I growl, not bothering to mask my anger.

He nods again but doesn't say anything more. As much as I'm involved in the events that transpired tonight, I'm still very much a stranger to PHOENIX. No matter which way I look at it, regardless of whether or not Jenner trusts me, I'm an outsider.

And outsiders are kept on the outside for a reason.

"I wish there was something I could do."

Rough fingers graze my cheek, applying pressure just under my chin, tilting my head back until I'm forced to look up. Jenner stares down at me, his dark brows furrowed.

"There is," he says, his tone slightly scolding. "You can rest. You've been through a lot tonight."

Maybe he's right. I mean, what else can I do?

Shoulders sagging with exhaustion, I sigh and turn the handle, plodding into my quarters. Jenner catches the door before it clicks shut behind me.

"Wynter." I glance back, meeting his gaze through the crack. "What happened wasn't your fault. It was no one's fault, you understand? I don't want you thinking otherwise."

Although he's wrong, I lack the energy to argue about it. It doesn't matter what he or anyone else might think. What happened to Rai was my fault for the simple reason that I could've prevented it. The pain everyone is feeling right now over her death...

It's all because of me.

I swallow and quickly slam the door shut, needing to escape those piercing blue eyes, which have this way of seeing straight into my soul. Pressing my ear to the metal, I don't move a muscle until his footsteps retreat down the corridor.

Once I'm certain Jenner's gone, I nudge open the door. As tired as I am, my body is filthy and I'm desperate to wash the stain of the past several hours off my skin. With a longing glance back at my bed, I quietly slink into the hallway.

The compound is empty as I head for the washroom. I shouldn't be surprised, considering the late hour, but still, the silence is unnerving. It's as if this place has been abandoned, stripped of all life in the hours we've been gone.

When I finally reach the showers, the fluorescent lights overhead flicker on automatically. I wince, unaccustomed to the glare after so many hours shrouded in darkness.

My fingers tremble as I unstrap my pack and peel off my clothes one piece at a time. The fabric, stained with sweat and copious amounts of blood, drops to the floor with a thud.

Shivering, I reach into an empty shower cubicle and turn the valve until a drizzle of hot mist warms the cool air. The heat is inviting, and I'm about to step under the water when I make the mistake of looking back at the mirrors. A scream catches in my throat when I see the ghoulish girl reflected there.

Blood and sweat are caked on her face and tangled in her wild, unkempt hair, the whites of her eyes streaky and red, as if she hasn't slept in days. Or weeks. Her irises—one green, one blue—have been swallowed by sinister inky black pools.

I stare at my reflection in horror, lifting a shaking hand to my face as if hoping the girl in the mirror won't copy the action. As if this isn't really me that I'm seeing. This girl with her terrifying black eyes…she's nearly identical to how I saw myself in my vision of the end of the world. So, does this mean that moment is creeping closer? Does this mean there's truly nothing I can do to avoid that future?

Hysteria claws at my chest, and in a fit of panic, I hurl myself under the cascading water. My fingers scratch at my aching skin, my nails biting into the flesh, scraping away the dried blood and sweat with fury. The residue rushes in streaks down my naked body, filling the base of the shower with red.

Tears spill down my cheeks, one after another, until my legs give out beneath the weight of my guilt and fear. Collapsing to the floor, I sob into my hands.

I'm not sure how long I sit here, weeping in a pool of crimson water. Seconds turn into minutes, which turn into hours, and yet, the shower is never able to cleanse the horrific images from my mind.

The attendant seizing on the cold tile.

The Enforcers, now a mountain of mangled bodies.

Rai, her blood splashing onto the floorboards.

The world and all life crumbling into ash.

When I finally step out of the shower, my eyes are red and raw from crying. In a sluggish daze, I peer down at my garments where they sit in a heap across the wet tiles. Like the last time I stripped off bloody clothes here, I don't bother to pick them up. They're dirty and I'm clean, so I fail to see the point.

What's the point of anything anymore?

My thoughts are foggy and distant as I trudge back to my quarters, the underground air nipping at my naked skin, although I barely notice the chill. Once back inside the isolation of my room, I collapse onto the bed and cocoon myself in the sheets, burrowing into the mattress as if I don't intend to ever resurface. Why would I?

It would be best for everyone if I don't.

I press my eyes shut. The emotions I've been working to bury are trying to force their way out of the box I've shoved them all into, but I know I won't survive them this time if they do manage to throw back that lid. I plead with my body to let me escape them, but sleep—sweet, blissful sleep—evades me.

When those emotions emerge and the pain strikes all over again, tears well in my eyes, burning like fire and carving scorching lines down my cheeks, leaving a salty residue on my skin. I cry, over and over, until I lack the energy to stay awake any longer and the darkness finally takes me.

I don't even notice my descent into sleep since the world beyond waking is just as grim. Like all the other times, I'm greeted by the familiar scene of destruction as the vision takes me back to the place where all this began and where everything will ultimately end. As I gaze upon the desolate wasteland, it's as if I'm standing at the edge of the world. Everything that ever mattered is gone, and I'm alone, just like I've always been. Just like I should be.

If I'm alone, no one else has to die.

I close my eyes. When they drift open again, nothing around me has changed. Ezra isn't here, although he usually is by this point in the vision.

For some reason, I'm still alone.

Is this the same vision I've grown so used to seeing? Or has something happened to change that future?

A faint moaning draws my gaze over my shoulder, and I

whip around, expecting to find Ezra behind me. I blink against the haze of dust and debris, peering through the blinding fog toward several dark shapes rising up from the ground in the distance. As they shuffle closer, their faces sharpen.

My hand lifts to my mouth, stifling a scream, as I scramble backward, my eyes unable to look away from the figures moving toward me. As their feet drag through the dirt and the distance between us shrinks, I realize I recognize their faces. The PHOENIX members living in the compound are all here, looking at me, their hooded gazes vacant.

No, not just vacant. *Lifeless.*

I search the scattered mob in desperation until I spot Jenner's recognizable blue eyes staring at me from the farthest depths of the crowd. His name is barely a breath on my lips as my feet dart forward, cutting a path through their bodies. Heart racing, I push them aside until I'm standing face to face with my friend.

His eyes share the same empty look as the others. Unsure what to do to snap him out of his daze, I press my fingertips to his cheek.

If my touch is the trigger, the screams erupting around me are bullets. They cut through the air in a merciless hail, each shriek another perforation in my sanity, as the people I've only just met…start to die.

One by one, they drop to the ground. Only a few pass quickly. The others aren't as fortunate, writhing and twitching and screaming in the dirt. Their agony echoes around me in each unending shrill note.

My hands slam against my ears to drown out their screams, but, through the chaos, I somehow hear Jenner's voice. When he says my name, it's like a gunshot slicing through the cries engulfing the world.

"Wynter..."A spurt of blood spews from his lips as his eyes slip down to his chest, widening in surprise. I follow his gaze, cupping my hands around my mouth and nose to muffle my sobs.

A red stain spreads from the middle of his torso, expanding outward across the pale fabric of his shirt. I shake my head, but the pressure spreading through my body is building, and as my own scream breaks free of the cage of my lungs, my power lashes out, striking one of the only people I ever wanted to protect.

I can feel it. I can *feel* myself doing this to him, but no matter how hard I try, I can't stop it.

Control is always just out of my reach.

As his blood spatters my face, I collapse to my knees, and clamping my eyes shut, I scream again at full volume. I don't want to see any more. This isn't real. This isn't happening.

*Please, let this never happen. Please, make this end.*

As if hearing my prayers, the world around me goes silent. Swallowing, I peek open my eyes and pin my arms to my sides to quell the vibrations of fear spreading through me. Jenner is gone. The people from PHOENIX are gone. No one is dying.

I'm alone once again.

I abruptly regret my previous desire to sleep, now wanting nothing more than to wake from this nightmare. I beg my brain to return me to reality, but, instead, my surroundings blur and I realize the nightmare is far from over. The horror...

It's only just beginning.

Ezra steps into my line of vision, materializing in the dusty wind like a mirage. A single tear trails down his cheek when he speaks. "I'm sorry, Wynter."

This is where the vision always ends—just after he says these words. But this time, the vision is different.

This time, the nightmare doesn't end.

As the vision concludes, revealing a harsh truth I've been too afraid to fully acknowledge, I rush forward, yelling out his name. But, no matter how hard my legs push, I can't reach him.

Just like with Jenner, I'm helpless to stop this.

"No, no, no!" I cry.

Ezra doesn't move or scream like the others did. He simply sheds those silent tears as death takes him, starting at his feet and slowly devouring the rest of his body, disintegrating him piece by piece. His smile is the last thing I see, and then he's just gone, mere dust in the wind.

I wake to the deafening sound of my own despair. As my wails reverberate through the room, I bolt upright, my body fighting to breathe through the build-up of thick tears lining my throat. The cool air nips at my exposed chest as the bed sheets crumple around my waist.

Leaning forward, I rub a hand over my face and brush the sweat-matted hair from my eyes. Was what I saw just now only a dream?

Or was it a vision?

If it was the latter like I fear, then that means I will be responsible for far more than just the end of the world.

PHOENIX.

Jenner.

Ezra...

They won't die because of some apocalypse my powers inflict on this planet, alive and then gone in the blink of an eye, their deaths painless and quick. Nothing about what I just witnessed was quick, and although I always knew their deaths would stain my hands, it's only now I grasp the full extent of what my vision has been saying.

It's always been me…

I will be the one who kills them.

# TWENTY-FIVE

**I SWING MY LEGS OVER the side of the bed. The air is cool against my naked skin, but I** don't move or try to cover myself, my body paralyzed by the haunting images branded into my thoughts, plaguing me.

Pushing out a trembling breath, I wipe a hand over my face and tuck my sweat-matted hair behind my ears.

*What I saw could've just been a dream,* I tell myself. After all, there were no side effects, no bloody noses or seizures, like there usually are after one of my visions. Like the dream I had of Ezra, it was just that—a dream with no proof of any physical consequence.

Still, I can't help wondering…what if it wasn't?

The end of the world is unavoidable. Try as I might to ignore that fact, the end *will* come and *I* will cause it. And with the end of the world comes the end of all life. The ruin of our planet will go hand in hand with the deaths of everyone, including those I care about. On some level, I always understood that.

But seeing them die like that… Seeing their faces… Hearing their screams… Seeing *his* face… That was the point when this nightmare felt too close to reality. That was the point when I finally came to terms with exactly what my vision has been showing me.

My fingers comb through my still damp hair, the strands messy and tangled with sleep. Sniffing, I draw my legs toward my chest as my thoughts buzz around my skull in a dizzying circle.

Is there no way to circumvent what I saw?

Is there nothing I can do to prevent that future?

Ezra's face fills every available space in my head, and all the times I've seen him—both in person and otherwise—play through my mind on a loop. I see every moment…

Even the ones I don't want to.

I watch him die all over again. Pain stabs my chest like a knife plunging into my heart, the blade pushing deeper until I don't know where this agony ends and I begin. As the grief consumes me, I understand what has to be done. Acceptance sinks into my bones, even as I mourn everything I'll be giving up.

Dream or not, Ezra will die if I do nothing.

Before our mission to Zone 1, I would've been helpless to change that, but I have options now that Dr. Richter has revealed there's a cure. He could be lying, but I can't just assume he is. Not when a cure would solve everything.

Not when I'm already dying and that terrible destruction I saw is racing closer.

A cure would mean we avoid that future. It would stop the world from ending. It would stop me from committing any more massacres like what happened with those Enforcers at the magistrates building. Above all, it would save the few people I care about.

The few people I have left who I want to protect.

A breath puffs out my cheeks as my gaze turns to the spare

clothes piled up in the corner. Although my body is still sore from last night, I drag myself out of bed and throw on a pair of pants and a long-sleeved shirt in a hurry. There's no time to waste. Every vision takes me one step closer to that vile future. If I'm going to do this, I have to go now.

I shove my feet into the extra pair of boots Rai gave me and rush through the doorway without looking back. My mind is made up. Nothing and no one will deter me from my decision, but I do need to see to one last thing before I walk away from this place for good.

I make my way through the network of hallways, searching the rooms without any clue where to find Ezra. The compound is immense, and there are countless places where he could be hiding, wallowing in his sorrow. With no other option, I explore every corner. Time might not be on my side, but I refuse to leave until I've seen him and Jenner again, just one more time to say goodbye.

I'll keep looking, no matter how long it takes me.

As I scour the compound, the quiet hum of night gives way to the chaotic din of morning. I'm eager to avoid the watchful leers of my waking neighbors, but I don't have to try very hard to ignore them. They seem just as content to pretend I don't exist.

*Maybe they blame me for what happened to Rai.*

I shake my head with fervor, discarding that thought. Considering how late it was when we got back, I doubt anyone is even aware of her death yet. Even if they did know about it, that wouldn't give them any logical reason to blame me. No one else here knows about my condition. No one else knows I had the power to save her or that, because of my lack of control, I let her life slip through my fingers. Therefore, if they do end up blaming me, it's only because they never trusted me in the first place.

Tucking my head down, I continue my search. There are more important things to worry about than what the people here might think of me. It's not as if any of them have bothered to get to know me except for Ezra and Jenner. No one else has risked life and limb to look out for me, especially given the short time I've known them.

Maybe the rest of the world can sense what I am and Ezra and Jenner are blind to that danger. After all, look what happened to my father and Rai. They each got close to me, and now, they're both dead.

Tears flood my eyes as it dawns on me that Ezra was right to keep his distance when we first met. I almost wish he had kept it that way.

Leaving would be so much easier if he had.

I swallow. As much as I don't want to tell them, it's only right Ezra and Jenner should know what I'm planning. They have to know. I need them to understand so they won't try to come after me.

It takes over an hour for me to find Ezra. He sits hunched in the corner of the small unlit room where the generators are stored, his head propped on his knees, his body engulfed by shadow. He doesn't look up when I step into the room. Maybe he doesn't hear me, or maybe he lacks the energy to care about anything now that Rai's gone.

I take care not to startle him, sliding to the floor, making sure to leave plenty of space between us to ensure we aren't touching. Despite the distance, I can feel the heat radiating from his body, and as it reaches for me, I fall into the memory of the dream in which he kissed me. How I long to feel his arms around me for real.

I suck in a breath, fighting the desire to shift closer to him. The cramped space isn't helping the temptation—if anything, it's only making me far more aware of his presence. Of his fingers, only inches from mine.

Of his lips, which I can't stop staring at.

I swallow again, biting back my alien urges. He lifts his head just a bit, and my eyes leap to his, taking in his impassive expression. I have no idea what to say. I've never consoled anyone before. In the State, we are raised to accept death without question or remorse. Like with all our other emotions, we're encouraged to suppress our grief. Mine has long since found its way to the surface, but that doesn't mean I know how to alleviate his.

Ezra's eyes flick to the concrete floor, and I follow his absent gaze to a picture lying next to his left foot. He makes no protest when I pick it up, my fingers skirting along the edges of the thick, shiny paper with care. The photograph is crinkled and has faded with age, but the image is clear and I immediately recognize the three smiling faces. They're much younger—only children at the time this was taken—but I'm certain it's them. After everything we've been through together, I would know those faces anywhere.

In the image, Ezra appears to be around seven or eight years old. He's missing his two front teeth and grinning at an older boy beside him. His brother's smile is far more reserved, but there's kindness behind the expression, unlike the way he looks now that he's older and hardened. Richter has one arm slung across Ezra's shoulders and the other draped around a pretty girl's waist, pulling her into his side.

Rai.

She's smiling broadly, her bronze cheeks rosy, her eyes fixed on the tall boy beside her with an admiration that spills from the picture. The affection between them is palpable, even at such a young age.

If only those cheerful faces were aware of the heartache awaiting them.

Choking back tears, I place the picture back down on the floor. I can't stand to look at it any longer knowing I'm responsible for their pain. Even Dr. Richter, who I loathe with every fiber of my being, manages to earn a shred of pity from me.

I cast a sidelong glance at Ezra. On top of the agony of losing Rai, I imagine he's tormented by his reunion with Richter. It must've been awful for him to see his brother again and have to accept that he's no longer the smiling young boy in that photograph. These were two people who once meant the world to him, and now, they're both gone from his life.

"Did you love her?" I whisper.

I've asked myself this question countless times since that heated argument I witnessed between him and Rai when I first arrived here and they were on opposite sides of the can-we-trust-Wynter debate. I'm aware of Rai's history with Dr. Richter, but her past with Ezra has never been as clear to me.

His movements are lethargic as he props his head back against the hard wall. The minimal light flooding in from the hallway reflects off his cheek, highlighting the black and purple bruise forming from when Jenner punched him earlier in the magistrates building. As awful as their brief fight was to watch, that moment likely saved his life. I'll never have the words to thank Jenner for that.

I peek down at my fidgeting hands, clasping them together in my lap to still them. A long while passes before Ezra speaks.

"Rai was like a sister to me. She's been in my life for as long as I can remember." His voice breaks, and out of the corner of my eye, I glimpse the way his body shakes with cries he's trying so hard to hold in. "I took it for granted," he whispers, dejected. "Like an idiot, I assumed she'd always be there."

The tears budding in his eyes finally break through, and as they fall in an effortless and unending stream, I watch him, stunned and lost for words. I've glimpsed his tears in my head so many times, and yet, seeing him cry in person is somehow so much harder and more painful to witness. Each silent droplet breaks my heart a bit more.

"How do you do it?" He turns to observe me, those hazel eyes pleading. His desperation for an answer is written all over his face. "How do you kill someone you love? How could he do that? How—"

He breaks down, weeping, before he can finish that sentence. I gape at him, wishing there was something I could say, but any words I might come up with are trampled by the memory of that all-important vision. I've seen this face so many times. Not quite as it is in this moment, but the sadness...

The sadness is what's familiar.

The recollection of that image strikes again without mercy. I see his face. I see his tears.

*"I'm sorry, Wynter."*

I blink, and the memory changes. Now, instead of destruction, I see my room here in the compound. Now, instead of tears, I see his lips muttering words I still don't understand.

*"Stay here. Stay with me."*

The look on his face when he whispered this plea is seared into my brain and into the backs of my eyelids, so it's all I see every time I close my eyes. Even now, those words vibrate through my soul and settle in the crevices in my heart, almost making me feel whole again. They have a bewildering power over me, even though I know they aren't real.

Even though they never will be.

Although Ezra's sobs are like thunder in my ears, that imagined moment between us is all I can think about right now. The kiss, which will never happen because I'm leaving after this.

The kiss I find myself wishing for.

An unfamiliar heat tears across my chilled skin. I know this isn't the time or the place, but something inside me is fighting to get out. Something new. Something different from the monster I'm growing so used to unleashing.

The monster that I'll soon become.

Part of me tries to fight this strange desire while another part wants to set it free—to see what this feeling is and embrace it, especially after so many years of keeping everything bottled up in a cage I never wanted or asked to be in. A cage I never even realized I could have a life outside of.

A life that, thanks to this disease, I'll never get the chance to explore.

With that realization rushing through my head, I abandon all sense of self-control. Wanting just a taste of the life this disease and the State have both stolen from me, I lean in close to Ezra, pressing my hands to his cheeks, and turn his face toward mine, interweaving the tips of my fingers through the disheveled strands of his hair. His cries cease at my touch, and we stare at each other for a moment before I allow whatever this is raging in my chest to take hold of me. Before I allow it to consume me. To *change* me.

The emotions Ezra has been gradually pulling out of me since we met all wash over my senses. The sensation is intoxicating, like a much-needed breath of fresh air, and I can't stop myself from reaching for more, from wanting to explore their depths at least once in my life before it's over for good. Soon, I won't have another chance.

This moment is all I have.

I pull him toward me, finding his mouth, and as our lips meet, every erratic beat of my heart is a ticking time bomb, threatening to explode. My stomach is turning in circles, making me nauseous, and yet, every second of this discomfort is glorious.

This feeling… Is this what love feels like? Am I even capable of such an emotion?

*Yes*, I realize as I deepen the kiss. What else could this pressure squeezing my heart be?

I think part of me loved Ezra from that very first vision. Maybe these feelings developed as an unintended consequence of fate pushing us toward our set roles in that dire future—of which, his still remains a mystery to me. Or, maybe, the visions were a path of breadcrumbs, guiding me to him because that was what fate intended all along and that future is just the way our tragic story was always meant to come to an end.

Regardless of which came first or caused the other, regardless of the fact we barely know one another, the affection in my heart is real. And knowing that only makes what I have to do worse.

My eyes press shut, and I see us together at the end of the

world, facing our future.

*"I'm sorry…"*

My heart tears open, spilling its contents onto the cold floor, and all too quickly, I remember what will happen if I stay.

With a reluctant breath, I drop my hands to his shoulders and push away, breaking the kiss. His eyes follow mine, but he doesn't say anything. Silence spreads through the room like fog.

Fear creeps through me at his shocked expression, followed by horror, and finally, disgust. What have I done? How could I inflict my complicated array of emotions on him so soon after what we just went through? How could I pursue this knowing what he must be feeling right now over Rai? How could I allow myself to reach for such comfort without taking his own trauma into account?

I scramble to my feet, mortified, and backing away, blurt out, "I'm sorry."

Before he can speak, I'm sprinting through the open doorway, running as fast as my legs can carry me. I don't look back, even though my heart is begging me to stop. How could I be so thoughtless? Ezra was grieving for Rai, for our *friend*, and I was selfish enough to act on my impulses when, instead, I should've been grieving with him. I was only thinking of myself.

I was only thinking of what *I* was feeling.

Once I'm certain Ezra isn't following me, I dart to the nearest wall and plop down to the floor, fighting to breathe through a barrage of tears. As I drag in a breath, my forefinger trails over my lips where the skin still tingles from our kiss.

Regardless of everything that's happened between us, I care for Ezra, possibly more than I've ever cared about anyone. But loving him—if that's what this is—isn't enough to change what's coming for us all, and staying here certainly isn't an option.

Dr. Richter could very well be lying about the cure, but if trusting him is the only way to stop me from killing the people I care about…then I'll do it.

I'll do whatever is necessary to avoid that future.

After a few calming breaths, I scooch my back up the wall until I'm on my feet again. My wobbling legs are unsteady beneath me, but I'm composed enough to move forward. I proceed through the hallways, never once looking back.

This is it.

This is what I have to do for all our sakes.

# TWENTY-SIX

**I HESITATE OUTSIDE THE OPEN** doorway, making sure to keep just out of sight. I had thought this was the right thing to do, but, now, I'm not so sure I can do it. I've been psyching myself up for hours, but after my miserable failure with Ezra this morning, this feels more like a betrayal than the well-intended farewell I was aiming for.

Still, shouldn't at least one person know where I'm going so they don't attempt to come after me later? Or should I just cut my losses and run with no one the wiser about my plan? That's what I'm going to do anyway, so wouldn't it be better for everyone if I just disappear now and save them from further heartache? Besides, goodbyes are unnecessarily painful. I would be sparing them that pain.

I would be sparing myself that pain.

I peek around the corner into the supply room, watching Jenner from my hiding place. He's alone, sitting on top of an upturned crate, his head down, as his fingers nimbly reload the ammunition in various weapons. One after another, he slides a fresh magazine into the grip of each gun.

The frown on his face suggests he isn't doing this monotonous task because he enjoys it. If anything, this is likely his way of getting his mind off troubling thoughts and feelings, such as those stirred up by the loss of a friend. Perhaps he's trying to distract himself from the pain so it won't overwhelm him the way it's already overwhelmed me.

Pins and needles spread over my thigh as the leg I've been leaning on begins to go numb. It seems as good a sign as any. I've stood around long enough.

Now, it's time to do what I came here to do.

Reaching inside and grabbing hold of my courage, I rap my knuckles against the door frame. Jenner raises his head at the sound, and a smile brightens his face the instant he sees me.

"Come in," he urges with a wave of his hand.

My cheeks twitch as my nerves rampage through my stomach, the depths of my belly twisting in such a way I fear its churning contents won't remain there much longer.

Jenner pulls a crate from the corner of the room and flips it over, placing it beside his own makeshift seat. I plop onto the creaking wood, avoiding his gaze.

I must've rehearsed what I plan on saying to him at least a hundred times. Yet, now that we're in the same room, those words are lost to me. As soon as I open my mouth, they disappear into thin air.

"You look a lot better now," he says after a moment, breaking the torturous silence.

I don't have to look at him to know what he's referring to. The blood. The pale skin. The inhuman black eyes. The monster I'm becoming versus the dying girl I am.

A shy smile upturns my lips, but I still can't find the strength to speak. Why is this so difficult? I've known him for, what...

the better part of a month? A large chunk of which I've spent unconscious?

It shouldn't be this hard to say goodbye.

I consider turning and leaving at once, releasing us both from the torment of this awkward encounter, but I don't move, my body held in place by the very emotions encouraging me to escape this. Emotions I have to face if I'm going to leave this all behind.

"How are you holding up?" Jenner asks, seemingly oblivious to my internal struggle.

I shrug. "As good as can be expected, I guess. How about you? Did you go see whoever you needed to speak with?"

He lets out a strained breath and rocks back on the crate. I scrutinize his face, noting the dark smudges of exhaustion staining the skin under his eyes.

"Things are…" He hesitates, frowning again. "Well, they're a mess. Truthfully, they have been for a while, we've just been turning a blind eye to it all. After last night, it's only a matter of time until the news of Rai's death begins to spread and everyone learns of Ezra's connection to Richter. Then, everything will be a thousand times worse." With a disheartened huff, he leans his head back against the wall. "Everything around us is falling apart."

His words anchor onto my heart and pull downward, as if determined to tear my body in half. Maybe now isn't the right time to leave, after all. Jenner and Ezra could use me here. I could do some good in getting this place back on track.

But, even as I tell myself this, I know the only way I can truly help is to go. If Ezra is under question after last night, I can't imagine how much worse it will be for me once everyone connects the dots and finds out why I'm really here. Besides, I'm running out of time.

By staying, I would only be making things worse.

"Damn it. Where do we go from here?" Jenner asks, his voice a rumbling growl. "What the hell can we even do? Those assholes are always one step ahead of us. No matter what, we always seem to lose."

He throws his arm backward, slamming the side of his fist into the wall behind us. The room seems to vibrate from the contact, or maybe it's the tremors rocking his body I notice. Either way, I can't put this off any longer.

I have to tell him, and I have to do it now.

"Jenner, there's something you should know."

He blinks, the rage in his eyes dissipating, their depths now alight with worry. "What is it?"

I sink my teeth into my lower lip. "That doctor—Richter. The one who—" But I can't bring myself to finish that sentence. I can't even finish that thought. I swallow, trying to push away the lingering images of Rai and Richter in Bilken's office. "He said there's a cure for my condition," I whisper.

Jenner stares at me, eyes wide and mouth agape. "What? You don't believe him, do you?"

"I'm not sure. I know he probably just said it to lure me back, but…" My voice trails off as I lean forward and brush my fingertips across Jenner's arm. "What if it isn't a lie? What if there really is a cure?"

His eyebrows knit together, and slowly, realization spreads across his face like the first light of day soaking up the horizon. "You're leaving…"

When he recoils from my touch, I pull back my hand and lower my gaze to the floor, flinching. The way he looks at me brings back the memory of the nightmare I had and I can't face it again. I can't allow myself to remember how it felt to watch him die.

"There's something I haven't told any of you—" I falter, uncertain if I should continue. Does he really need to know what I've seen since there might be a way to prevent that future, if Richter's claims about a cure are true? Even if Richter's lying and that future is unavoidable, shouldn't I just let Jenner live the rest of his short life in blissful ignorance? In peace?

*No*, I decide. *He deserves to know.*

After everything he and Ezra have done for me, *risked* for me, I can't leave without one of them knowing the truth. I need them to know what I'm hoping to change so they can understand why I'm leaving. Otherwise, they might try to come after me.

If that happens, there will be nothing I or anyone else can do to save them from the State.

"The very first vision I had, right before I was taken to the DSD..." I clench my hands into fists and force my eyes upward until they lock on his face. As hard as it is to face him right now, I need to look at him when I say this. I need to welcome this pain because, once I leave this place, that's it.

I'll have no one, and Jenner will be only a memory.

"It was of the end of the world. I saw it all as if I was actually there, as if it was really happening." I speak in a rush, pushing out each word until they fall out of me willingly. But, instead of lifting the weight from my shoulders, they only seem to add to my burden, dragging me down, crushing me. My voice hitches. "As my condition grew worse, I saw more of the vision. And then I saw Ezra. We were the only ones left as everything around us crumbled into ash."

Jenner shakes his head. "I don't understand—"

"It's me. What I am," I interrupt, biting back tears. "It will happen because of me."

His mouth opens, as if he's about to say something, then closes again, snapping shut with a click. In the silence that follows, I glimpse the realization building behind his gaze. He doesn't need me to tell him that he'll die in that future. He doesn't need me to say that I'm the one who will kill him. He knows.

I can see in his eyes that he knows.

Of all the emotions he must be battling with at this moment, I presume fear would land at the top of the list. And he does seem afraid. Yet, there's something in his expression that doesn't suggest fear for himself…but for me. Here I am, telling him we're all going to die because of this rare disease I have, and *I'm* the one he's thinking of. *I'm* the one he's feeling sorry for. It's not right.

I don't deserve it.

"My life ended when I had that first vision, but you…you're all still alive. I can't let anyone else die because of me."

The moment I utter these words, he lunges forward and grabs my shoulders, almost knocking me off the crate in the process.

"I told you what happened with Rai wasn't your fault!" His eyes shine with tears as his hands grip me tighter.

I fight to breathe past the ache in my chest. "You say that, but what if I'd seen it sooner? If I had, then maybe we could've saved her. We both know that, so why don't you blame me?"

Jenner reels back as if I've slapped him, his eyes wide, his hands slipping off my shoulders. I scramble, trying to find the words to explain what I'm feeling.

"That's the dilemma I'm faced with now. Even if what Richter said is a lie, how can I turn my back on the possibility of a cure when I know where that other path will lead?"

"M-Maybe the vision was wrong," he stammers, combing a trembling hand through his mop of black hair. "Maybe—"

"It's not wrong," I snap, my tone forceful. That line of thought will lead us nowhere; it's better to nip it in the bud before it can form roots. False hope won't help anybody right now, me least of all. "The visions never are. Besides, I've seen what my power can do. If you had been in Bilken's office when the Enforcers first arrived, you would've seen it, too."

That moment is hazy to me, even now. But through the fog of confusion, I'm all too aware of what I did to those soldiers. Those *people*. It was the same thing I did to Dr. Richter's attendant. The same thing I almost did to Ezra before I snapped out of my daze.

*Murder,* that small voice in my head says again.

This power… I can't control it, and I don't think I will ever be able to. I won't live long enough to try. This disease will spread through my failing body until there's nothing of me left in this shell. Until I'm a mindless killing machine intent on destruction.

I jerk my head to escape that image. "I won't be able to live with myself if anyone else dies because of what I am. A cure is the only hope I have to stop this and to keep you all alive."

"But I don't want you to leave." Jenner's gaze is pleading, his voice the barest breath of a whisper.

My lips wobble with the increasing threat of tears, but I push them back and force a smile. "I'm so glad I got to know you… even if it was only for a short time." Rising from the crate, I place my hands on his shoulders, bend down, and plant a kiss on his cheek. "Be safe," I mutter in his ear.

Gulping down the lump in my throat, I turn to face the open doorway, prepared to move on with my goal in sight. Prepared to move on and never look back. But, as I take a step, something stops me.

Something keeps me here in this room.

Jenner's hold on my uninjured wrist is firm, and as he spins me around, I lose my footing, stumbling into the safe embrace of his arms. When he crushes my body to his, I hear everything this moment is trying to tell me. I hear everything *he's* been trying to tell me.

I sense his affection for me in the gentle way his lips brush over mine, but, as he kisses me, I can only think of one person.

And that person isn't Jenner.

After what seems like a lifetime, his hands relax, and he pulls away, releasing his hold on me. His watery eyes peer down into mine with urgency.

"Stay," he begs. "Please."

Stay.

Stay...

*"Stay here. Stay with me."*

This moment is so reminiscent of my dream, but the details are wrong, like puzzle pieces that don't quite fit together, even though it looks like they should. But Jenner isn't the one I should be embracing right now.

Jenner isn't the one I want to ask me to stay.

The pain cutting through me when I glimpse his expression is worse than anything I endured at the DSD. All at once, I understand why the State is so unfeeling. Why our society is so unfeeling.

This misery… Why would anyone ever *want* to feel this? From what I've seen, even the good things—like love—end in pain, so maybe the State was right to try to spare us from that.

"I'm sorry." The words barely make it past my lips.

Jenner lets out a tiny choked-off laugh, and I can hear the sadness behind it. "If I can't get you to stay, what will?"

I don't answer him. The truth is, nothing will make me stay. Nothing can anymore. Not when there's so much dependent on me leaving.

"Goodbye, Jenner."

The tears finally spill over, running in rivers down my cheeks, as my feet pull me into the hallway. It takes every last ounce of willpower I have to stop myself from looking back.

My movements are listless on my way through the compound. On more than one occasion, I consider running back to the supply room and trying to fix what I've broken. That wasn't how I wanted to leave things between us or how I wanted—or expected—our farewell to go. But I also know if I turn back now, I'll never find the strength to leave.

I plot out my plan of action to distract myself from my sorrow and guilt. The pattern of turns I need to take through the maze to get to the hatch are seared into my memory now. Assuming I make it that far, finding my way through the tunnels beyond should be easy enough. The journey will take a while, but I'll get to my destination in the end.

All that's left is to prepare myself, and then I'll go. I'll do it quick. Just get what I need and make for the door. No more detours.

No more goodbyes.

Ezra's face flashes through my thoughts like a lightning

strike. I already tried to say goodbye once, and it didn't go the way I had planned. Still, I can't bear another attempt after everything we've been through, especially considering how I feel about him.

Wiping away the tears obscuring my vision, I fix my gaze on the path ahead, resolved.

*No more goodbyes,* I promise myself.

# TWENTY-SEVEN

I REACH DOWN AND PLUCK my pack off the washroom floor, brushing excess water from the sodden straps. The droplets rejoin the shallow puddle at my feet.

Lips quivering, I glance at my filthy clothes where they lie undisturbed in a heap where I left them. While I know I should clear the mess away instead of leaving it for someone else to clean up, I can't bring myself to disturb it. The bloodstained fabric holds too many bad memories.

Memories I only want to forget.

I tear my gaze away from the clothes and open my pack, checking over the minimal contents inside. Everything looks to be in order, although the flashlight and a canteen of water are really all I'll need to see me through my trip back to Zone 1. My journey there will be one-way. Beyond that, anything I need will be provided for me by the DSD.

I shudder at the thought of being a prisoner again, held captive in that tiny, drab room. A lifetime seems to have passed since I first escaped Dr. Richter's insidious clutches, yet the memory of my time there is still painfully fresh—like a scar from a wound that will never fully heal.

It haunts me, even more so than the guilt that stabs at my heart every time I think about Rai. The trauma I've managed to push back these last few weeks is rearing its ugly head, feeding an anxiety I'm no longer sure I have the strength to suppress. It spreads, creeping through every last inch of me, just like this disease taking over my body.

Bile rushes up into my mouth as a wave of vertigo disorients my senses, making the bright room spin around me. Dizzy, I reach for the nearest wall for support while ragged breaths crush my lungs, scorching my throat.

As I heave, I throw myself over a sink, gripping the edges of the basin so tightly my fingers ache, but nothing comes up. My stomach is empty of everything except the fear of what I'm about to walk into.

For the first time since settling on my decision, it really hits me that I'm going back.

I draw in a few quick breaths through my nose, my inhalations deep and slow, and think about what I want to protect. I picture Ezra and Jenner, and I see all too clearly what will happen to them if I stay. Their deaths are burned into my brain. There's no other way to prevent that future from happening.

This is my only option.

I blink once, then drag my eyes upward and force myself to look in the mirror. It's strange, but the girl reflected there is someone I no longer recognize. Maybe what I'm seeing is the last of my innocence, the ignorant version of me the State created—the version I have to abandon if I have any hope of moving forward. All the pain blackening my heart, all the feelings I wish I had time to explore... They'll remain here at this compound with her.

With the me I need to leave behind.

Turning, I slog out of the washroom and traipse through the corridors as if in a trance. Every step is a struggle, and by the time I make it back to my quarters, I'm worn down by exhaustion.

My legs give out beneath me as I slump down on the bed, and a sigh parts my lips as my hands grip the blanket. I could've had a new life in this place, a life free from the State's control. If things had been different, I would've embraced it. I would've fought to protect this freedom, just like everyone else here.

But things aren't different, and life is far from fair. The fresh start I was offered… It was nothing more than a pipe dream.

I should've known it could never be mine.

Tears prick at the corners of my eyes as I take in every detail of the room one last time. Everything and everyone I've come to care about here…

I silently say goodbye to it all.

An uncomfortable dull pain shoots through my wrist as I draw my legs into my chest and wrap my hands around my knees. Rotating my arm, I peel back the bandage—still damp from my breakdown in the shower—and peer down at the raised incision protruding from the still tender skin.

It's terrifying to think what would've happened if Rai hadn't been around to help me that day. How we all would be walking a different path if she hadn't worked tirelessly to heal me. If Ezra hadn't spared my life and had chosen instead to let me die. Maybe, if they hadn't intervened, Rai would be alive now. If I had bled out in The Vega, we wouldn't be faced with the monumental problem of our impending doom.

Because I'd be dead, and that's the way it should be.

If I had died then, everyone here wouldn't be at risk now. Rai would still be alive, Jenner and Ezra would *stay* alive…

And I wouldn't have to go back to the DSD.

Fat tears roll down my cheeks as I pull my pack onto my lap and lower my legs, letting out a shaky breath. There's a roll of bandaging in the side pocket, which I use to rewrap my wrist, although my efforts are clumsy. Not that it matters. I'm only doing this to delay my departure. Once I'm back at the DSD, the doctors there will tend to my injuries properly, with the added bonus of probably shoving a tracking chip back into my wrist to replace the one I cut out. Dr. Richter might even pretend to care about my health and well-being if it means I give him and the State what they're after.

I smother a humorless laugh and circle the gauze around my arm four times. Once the incision is covered, I have nothing left to do. I'm out of excuses to stay. Besides, I've wasted enough time here already.

Pinching my eyes shut, I suck in a breath. The seconds tick by as I yell at myself to get up—to rise from this bed and march out the door, like I should've done hours ago. I hear my own words shouted back in my head until the voice in my ears sounds nothing like me at all but like someone else.

Like Ezra.

"So, that's it?" he asks.

My eyes spring open and dart toward the doorway where Ezra stands at the threshold, a mere silhouette against the light pouring in from the hallway. His gaze exudes rage as he steps into the room.

"You were just going to leave?"

My tongue trips over itself as I try and fail to find an answer. What can I say? What *is* there to say? I didn't expect to ever see him again, and I still have to leave, regardless of any feelings I think I have for him or any argument he might make to tempt me to stay.

My departure is non-negotiable.

"I take it you spoke with Jenner," I mutter.

My name falls from his lips like a plea as he takes a panicked step forward. "Wynter... You can't do this."

The anger in his tone is like a chisel chipping away at my heart. If only he could see what I've seen.

If only he understood what will happen to everyone here if I stay.

"I have to," I whisper, looking away.

My fingers fidget with the bandage around my wrist, unwinding it, rewrapping it, then unwinding it once more to distract myself from his lingering gaze. His eyes follow my movements, and I can feel them burning into my face, but I don't dare look up.

"Look at me." Crossing the room, he tears the roll of dressing from my hands and tosses it to floor. "You have no idea what you're getting yourself into."

My hands clench into fists. "And you do?"

My eyes snap upward, locking on Ezra, as I'm struck with the sudden urge to slap him. Does he really think I want to leave—that I *want* to go back to the DSD and be tortured for who knows how long before death finally takes me in its eternal embrace?

I'm only doing this so he can survive.

The temperature in the room seems to rise as indignation

and frustration swell between us like heat. We glare at each other for what seems like hours until I can't bear the hurt glistening in his eyes a single second longer. It cuts away at my wavering resolve.

Shaking my head, I push to my feet, once more avoiding Ezra's gaze. I hoist my pack off the bed and sling it onto my shoulder, a jittery breath escaping my lungs as I take one step and then another toward the open door. As I brush past Ezra, I stop for a moment and reach for his hand, hesitating. My fingers freeze just short of touching his.

This is why I didn't want to say goodbye. The pain cracking my heart into pieces…

I didn't want to feel it.

Grimacing, I retract my hand and force myself to continue walking. The distance to the hallway seems never-ending, but I fight through the growing heartache in my chest, even as it tears me in two.

Half of my heart stays behind, an anchor holding me to this room, to this compound, determined to keep me here. The logical part of my brain presses onward, but then my legs lurch to a standstill, and I realize something else is also holding me back. It isn't just my heart that wants to stop me from leaving.

Warmth snakes across my waist from behind, and my eyes follow its spread to where Ezra's arms circle around me. They pull me back, hugging me tight to his chest, draining my body of any instinct to fight and instantly erasing my desire to leave.

He turns me around so we're standing face to face, our noses almost touching. I flush at his sudden proximity, my breath hitching at the realization his lips are so close to mine I could kiss him again if I wanted to. Which I do. So badly.

Ezra smiles, as if he knows what I'm thinking, and flattens a hand against the small of my back, pulling me even closer. Then, as if gravity itself is pulling us together, he bends down at the same moment I rise onto my toes, meeting each other halfway.

Just like in my dream, Ezra's lips press to mine, and as the heat from my body melts into his, I stare at his closed eyes, trying to make sense of what's happening. My heart is pounding so furiously I struggle to inhale as it repeatedly slams into my ribs, and my frenzied nerves are pulling my senses in a thousand different directions at once. Pleasure and pain course through my veins, hand in hand.

When we break apart, the raging hurricane of my inexperienced emotions threatens to suffocate me. I gape at Ezra, afraid to blink or speak.

"I don't want you to go," he says, his voice soft. His words are warm against my face as he says them, each one a separate kiss of their own. The touch of them sends a shiver over my skin. "Stay here. Stay with me."

My eyes spring wide. *The dream was real.*

My heart swells with affection and longing until a different thought strikes, cutting through both. It casts a shadow over this bittersweet moment.

I never saw what came after these words. My vision ended with his plea, depriving me of knowing what awaited us next. Because of everything we've been through, I'm not sure if I believe what he's saying…or if I even can. Ezra isn't in his right mind—he's consumed by the pain of losing Rai, and his actions are probably being guided by panic more than logic or sense. How can I be certain he isn't just saying these things because he's afraid of being alone? How do I know he isn't just looking for comfort in the one place he knows he can find it? If I hadn't so brazenly kissed him before, maybe he wouldn't be saying these words now at all.

I recall our conversation back in the tunnels and the confusion I felt when he promised to protect me. I can't help mimicking what I said to him then.

"Why...?"

I anticipate his response with bated breath, even though what he says won't change anything. I'll still leave this place to protect him and Jenner. Leaving is the only way to avoid their deaths. Putting distance between us is the only way I know to save them. The closer they get to me, the more likely they are to die.

His hand trails across my cheek as he frowns. "I don't think I can handle losing anyone else."

My heart sinks, and disappointment settles under my skin. After what happened to Rai, I understand why he would feel this way. He brought these people together, so each death or loss must weigh on him. His own personal burden. But if his grief is why he's asking me to stay, that means I'm nothing more than another number. Another notch in the PHOENIX belt.

Which also means he's using my feelings for him as a weapon to coerce me.

But why? Because he feels responsible for me?

Or because whoever's in charge here doesn't want me to leave?

If Nolan or someone else high up in PHOENIX is working with the DSD like I fear, then ensuring I don't run away is probably their top priority now, especially after Richter failed to retrieve me during our disastrous mission—no thanks to Ezra, which makes me think he isn't involved with whatever shady deal is going on behind the scenes. I still can't figure out what

PHOENIX would possibly get out of such an arrangement, but something in my gut tells me I'm right.

Alternatively, if PHOENIX *isn't* involved with the DSD and has no idea what I'm capable of, it's still only a matter of time until they find out the truth. Then, like Ezra even said in his speech last week, these people will grasp how they're in an advantageous position if they possess what the State covets.

It won't matter that I will be the death of us all. The only thing anyone will see is my power and how it can be used as a weapon.

I bite my lip, suppressing a frustrated groan. I wish I could see the full picture and gain a better understanding of all the players on the board. I don't know anyone's motivations, which scares me, although, right now, I only care about Ezra's.

I peek up at him, tormented by doubt.

"Why did you take me with you?" I ask. His eyes narrow as I step out of his grasp. He tries to pull me back, but I push him away as a terrible fear comes alive in my stomach. "Why?" I press through rising tears. They stick in my throat, choking me.

His eyes soften at the look on my face. "Because I was afraid if I left you behind, I would never see you again, even if we did somehow make it out alive. I know it was stupid and risky to take you, but I wasn't ready to say goodbye to you yet. And I'm sure as hell not ready now."

My heart aches with hope, but I shove it away. Because, through the disbelief keeping me silent, I notice the lie behind his words.

What he's saying, no matter how hard he's trying to sell it to me, isn't the truth. Or, at least, it's not the whole truth. There's another reason he brought me that night. A reason he's adamant not to admit.

His touch ignites a shiver over my skin as he tucks a stray lock of hair behind my ear. "When Jenner told me you were leaving, it dawned on me just how badly I want you to stay. And trust me, it has nothing to do with my brother or mother."

A sly grin appears at the corners of his lips, sending my pulse into overdrive. He's deflecting, using my feelings against me again, but I struggle to care anymore because these words, the ones he says now…they're the truth. I can sense that as plainly as I sense the depth of my own growing affection for him.

Any doubts I have about his motivations for keeping me here drift away and dissolve in this moment. I no longer hear or care about what he isn't telling me.

I only welcome in what he is.

From the day I was born, I've been taught to repress my emotions, brainwashed to integrate into a society it's taken me eighteen years to realize is poisonous. Humans aren't meant to shut out their feelings, and what I never grasped before is you can't. One way or another, they'll climb to the surface. One way or another, they'll find a way to break through.

Stifling my emotions for the better part of two decades leaves me wholly unprepared for this moment. Each emotion tears through me, burning everything that made me who I am until I'm nothing but a pile of ashes. From those ashes, what rises up is the new me.

The me, who, for once, is permitted to feel.

Another shudder rolls over my body as Ezra skims his fingers across my lower lip, wiping away the tears pooling there.

"Please, don't cry," he whispers.

His breath caresses my lips and cheeks as he combs his fingers through my hair, making me light-headed. Bending down again, he slants his mouth over mine, and all the emotions I've been bottling up since that very first vision of him pour out in this kiss.

It's strange to think that I never would've known this kind of connection if my placement exam had gone off without a hitch and everything in my life had continued as normal. From that point of view, looking at what's transpired since then, it's hard not to find the good in my condition. Despite all the bad, it's brought me to Ezra, even if our time together is temporary.

Even if it can never last.

Another tear spills down my cheek, but I ignore the cruel burn of it and focus on my shaking hands as they slide across Ezra's chest and up under his shirt, trembling with uncertainty. Although I don't have the slightest clue what I'm doing, I give in to my confusing urges. I don't want to have any regrets. If this is the only time in my life when I can experience this sort of closeness—a bond of meaning the State has robbed us all of—then I want to do it with someone I care about. With all the pain and grief I've experienced, I just want to feel something good for once.

For a moment, I just want to forget everything else.

Ezra reciprocates my touch, and as we fall onto the bed, I kiss him with fervor, losing myself to my erratic emotions and surrendering myself to this fleeting bliss. Thanks to Dr. Richter and this fatal disease, I don't have much time left in this world, regardless of any possible cure. Even if I don't die after this, I know we'll never see each other again. This world where feelings and love are possible for me will be nothing more than a memory. So, if this moment is all we'll have…then to hell with it.

I plan on making it count.

# TWENTY-EIGHT

I LIE STILL, LISTENING TO the gentle hum of Ezra breathing softly beside me. His bare chest rises and falls in slow repetition, his lips parted slightly, releasing hot breaths. A sweaty lock of blond hair lies flat across his forehead, and I'm tempted to reach out and brush the strands away—to touch my hand to his skin one final time. I resist the urge. He looks so peaceful in sleep, and after everything he's suffered through, I don't want to disturb him.

Besides, it's better for both of us this way.

Sitting up, I scoot toward the edge of the bed. The shift of the squeaking mattress doesn't wake him, which disappoints me a little. Although I know this path I'm on can only end one way, part of me wants him to stop me. I want him to pull me back into his arms and take away any desire I have to leave this place.

To leave him.

My feet graze the cold floor as the air nips at my skin, the weight of our handful of precious hours together pressing down on my chest. Every inch of my body aches with the urge to sink back into his embrace and find comfort in his touch as many times as it takes to heal me of this disease and this pain.

Instead, I sit still on the bed, hesitating.

How can I leave him so soon after losing Rai? How can I abandon him and Jenner to suffer through the consequences of our mission alone?

*Because you have to,* I remind myself. *It's the only way to keep them both safe.*

My eyes dance across Ezra's exposed torso, carving the vivid recollection of his body into my brain. Every whispered word we shared, every touch…

At least I'll have the memory of these moments together to see me through what must come next. No matter what happens from here on out, at least I'll always have that brief comfort.

Hours seem to pass in the minutes I spend watching him sleep. It's as if the blood coursing through my veins is hardening into stone, freezing me and holding me in place. It takes all the self-control I can muster to convince myself to go. I've already stayed too long, allowing the night to slip by in his arms. If I don't leave now, he'll wake up, which is the last thing I need. If that happens, he'll just try to stop me—not that doing so will require much effort on his part. If we get to that point, any will I have to leave him will be non-existent.

But, if I go now, while he's asleep, it'll be a clean break for us both.

If I go now, it'll be easier for everyone.

Leaning over his sleeping form, I take in the details of his face—his closed eyes, his long lashes—and plant a barely-there kiss on his lips. I don't apply enough pressure to wake him, just enough to leave my mark. His cheek flinches where my breath tickles his skin.

Biting the inside of my cheek to hold back the tears, I stand

and pull on my clothes, careful not to make any noise. My fingers fumble with the strap of my pack, hooking it around my chest, as my feet reluctantly drag me toward the door. My heart sinks a little more with every step. Why does this feel so wrong when I know it's the right decision? The only decision? Why does this hurt so much when I know that my leaving is the only way to keep him alive?

Not for the first time, I wonder if maybe the State has the right idea encouraging distance in its citizens' lives. Affection is dangerous because it's painful, because it leaves you open to get hurt. By pushing us all apart, we're spared that pain and can live our lives ignorant of that heartache. There's sense in that logic, even if it's lonely.

Still, I want to believe it's been worth it—that everything I've been through up to this very moment has been worth the sadness I'll now carry with me. If I can change what's going to happen, if I can save Ezra and Jenner from that terrible future that, even now, haunts my every thought, then it will be.

I would embrace any amount of pain necessary if it meant my sacrifice would save their lives.

I pull open the door but pause at the threshold and cast a worried glance over my shoulder. Will Ezra understand my reasons for leaving, or will he see it as an act of betrayal? Will what we shared be destroyed as a result, just like what happened with Dr. Richter and Rai?

Will Ezra turn against me just as Richter turned against her?

*It doesn't matter,* I realize. If his hatred is the cost for saving his life, then it's a price I'll happily pay.

The tears spill over now, carving lines down both my cheeks. My teeth bury into my lower lip as I turn and finally step through the doorway.

This time, I don't allow myself to look back.

The compound is silent as I stalk through the unlit corridors, retracing my steps to the maze after a quick stop at the now empty supply room. After a series of memorized turns, the room housing the tunnel entrance slides into view. Since night has fallen once again and everyone in the compound is asleep, there isn't a single soul in sight to intervene or try to stop me. For a moment, I half-expect Jenner to show up until I remember what he said to me yesterday.

*"If I can't get you to stay, what will?"*

He must've genuinely believed Ezra would be able to change my mind about returning to the DSD. Why else would he have told him what I was planning to do unless he suspected how I felt?

Thinking about Jenner only causes my guilt to resurface, especially after what happened with Ezra. I try my best to push these feelings aside, reminding myself that what I'm about to do is what's best for everyone. Not only for him and Ezra... but me.

Abandoning these thoughts, I flip open my bag and pull out a curved black bar like the one Ezra used when we were last in the tunnels. Positioning myself in front of the hatch door, I wedge the bar between the spokes of the wheel and throw the full weight of my body against it. Sweat beads on my brow as the metal creaks in protest and flaking bits of rust fall to the floor.

Even with the bar, turning the wheel is a struggle, especially with my aching wrist. Still, I keep pushing, determined to see this through, and after a few attempts, the door gives way. It swings open before me as if in support of my mission.

Panting, I stow the bar back inside my pack and clamber through the hole into the blackness of the tunnel beyond. My fingers fumble with my flashlight and quickly click it on. The beam of light breaks through the thick gloom with ease.

I follow the same route Rai led us on to Zone 1, the splashing of my feet in the shallow covering of water providing a much-needed break from the silence. The journey feels longer this time, being on my own. My eyes shift in and out of focus, my body once again lulled by the hum of my steps. To keep myself awake, I rehearse why I'm doing this, chanting the reasons over and over again in my head. If I say them enough times, maybe I'll believe them.

*I'm doing the right thing.*

*This is my only option.*

*This is the only way to stop the world from ending and to keep me from killing the people I care about.*

*This is the only way to save Ezra and Jenner.*

I continue repeating these thoughts until I arrive in what I think is the general area of Zone 1, based on the timing of my journey. Pausing for a drink to rouse myself from my fatigue, I glance down both lengths of the tunnel, peeling my tired eyes in search of an exit. After another ten minutes of walking, I spot a platform of steps veering off on the left side of the tunnel. Upon further inspection, the platform cuts into the rounded wall and leads up to an obscured rust-covered entrance. I race up the steps with the bar in one hand and throw myself against the wheel.

The door opens after a few attempts, protesting my entry with a piercing shriek. Beyond the exit, another tunnel stretches out before me, but this one is tilted slightly uphill. My breaths are heavy and my feet slip against the grime on the floor as I hurry up the slope.

Flecks of dirt and water spray across my face as I push against the barred gate at the top of the incline. It creaks open into a shallow stream lying under a low-hanging bridge in a park, and as I step into the fresh air, my eyes take in the dim morning light marking the beginning of the sun's ascent over the horizon.

My stomach twists as I shrink back into the cover of darkness. I don't want to be seen in daylight. I don't want to attract unnecessary attention. I don't want outside influences pressuring me to go back to the DSD. I want to do this on my own.

I want it to be my choice.

With a faltering breath, I inch out from under the bridge, scanning the frosty greenery around me for movement. I see nothing except for the slight rustle of leaves and the whipping of branches in the cold morning breeze. Based on the upkeep of my surroundings and the looming buildings positioned along the edge of the park, I know without a doubt I'm back in Zone 1.

Somehow, knowing that makes this all easier. My journey has almost reached its end.

Using the landmarks as my guide, I make my way to the DSD, comparing where I am in retrospect to what I saw when I escaped a few weeks ago. To my surprise, I locate it far quicker than I expected I would. Maybe the fear had imprinted the details of the night I fled onto my brain. Either that, or a part of me always knew I'd eventually have to come back here.

I hesitate on the opposite side of the street, staring up at the domineering building in front of me. I don't think it ever occurred to me before how something so ominous stands in plain view of our society, as if the State is proud of what they do here.

Proud of what they'll soon be doing to me.

My heart jumps up into my throat, blocking my breaths. I try to come up with a reason to run—an excuse to abandon my mission and get the hell out of here before it's too late to turn back. But I can't.

Too much depends on me.

"For Ezra and Jenner," I whisper, steeling myself.

As my feet usher me across the quiet street toward my doom, I think of what my life was like before my birthday. How different I was then. How scared. How the only thing that ever mattered was survival. How nothing else even existed to me.

*Don't stand out. Blend in. Remain invisible.* Those are the rules I lived by—the rules I thought would keep me alive. I was wrong. But, maybe, with my sacrifice, Ezra and Jenner can survive. I have to believe that. I have to believe doing this can make a difference.

I have to believe I *can* change the future.

Lifting my chin, I storm through the revolving glass doors. As if expecting my arrival—I was probably spotted by one of the many surveillance cameras littered throughout this zone— Dr. Richter is already in the lobby, surrounded by his usual flock of attendants. They all stand in a line facing me.

I stop in front of him, and he meets my gaze, gracing me with that eerie smile of his. If I didn't already know what to expect, I might think he's sincerely happy to see me.

"You made the right choice." He rests a hand on my shoulder—a gesture any normal person might mistake for kindness.

But I, Wynter Arabelle Reeves, am not normal.

Narrowing my eyes, I spit through clenched teeth, "You win. I'll do whatever you want. But you will never go anywhere near Ezra again. Deal?"

Dr. Richter appraises me for a long moment before stepping to the side, his hand sliding from my shoulder as his arm sweeps through the air, gesturing me back into the DSD.

I meet his eyes one final time, the malicious intent in them burning like fire.

His smile deepens. "Welcome home, Wynter."

## END OF BOOK ONE

## FOR A BONUS CHAPTER FROM EZRA'S POV,
### SCAN THE QR CODE BELOW

M.A. PHIPPS
TYPE X
A PROJECT W. A. R. NOVEL

# DEAR READER,

Thank you for reading *Ultraxenopia*! I hope you enjoyed the first part of Wynter's story and that you'll continue this journey with me in the second installment, *Type X*.

To keep up with the latest news about my work, sign up for my newsletter at www.bookishden.com.

For more information about the *Project W.A.R.* series and for an interactive version of the map found at the beginning of this book, please visit www.maphipps.com/projectwar.

I love to chat with readers, so feel free to get in touch! You can contact me through my websites or through any of my social media accounts. Or you can join my fan group on Facebook—just search for The Bookish Den. We'd love to have you!

Lastly, if you enjoyed this book, please consider leaving a review on your retailer of choice, BookBub, and / or Goodreads. Reviews help authors, like myself, gain exposure, so we can keep sharing our stories with the world.

Thanks again for reading *Ultraxenopia*. I hope you'll continue to enjoy my work!

# ACKNOWLEDGMENTS

First and foremost, I would like to thank Martina McAtee for being my rock in the publishing world. I don't think I'd stay sane without you.

I would also like to thank my phenomenal cover designer, Nathalia Suellen, for creating the perfect cover for my story and for bringing my vision to life.

To the friends and fellow authors who gave me the confidence to pursue a career as a writer, I will never be able to thank you enough for your guidance and incredible support. In particular, I want to say a huge thank you to one of my favorite people in the world, Alisha Wood. If anyone deserves Jenner's unconditional love, it's you.

I would also like to extend my gratitude to Taylor Ramsay Barger, without whom I wouldn't have a title for this book. Thank you so much for your help!

Finally, I would like to thank my husband, Daniel, and my father, Michael. Thank you both for always encouraging me to chase after my dreams. I don't know where I would be without your support.

# ABOUT M.A. PHIPPS

**M.A. PHIPPS** is an American-born British author, who resides near the ocean in picturesque Cornwall with her husband, daughter, and their Jack Russell, Milo. A lover of the written word, it has always been her dream to become a published author, and it is her hope to expand into multiple genres of fiction.

*Ultraxenopia* is her debut novel.

Visit her online at **www.maphipps.com** or **www.bookishden.com**.